*L*EAVE ME ALONE!" SHE S(... AS too tight. "Leave me alor ... purse, but he had her arms ju ...

He spun her around, pinning her in front of him so that they both faced me. "Don't think I didn't recognize you," he said to Eve as he kissed her neck. "I know who you are." One hand traveled down the length of her torso, stopping near her hips. "And I know what you like."

"Leave her alone!"

He smiled. "Make me."

Anger rose up inside me as I remembered a similar incident in a bar parking lot. Two men had thrown me into their car, then tried to assault me as I begged them to stop.

Shane had come then, ripping them off me.

But I didn't need Shane now. I didn't need anyone.

I charged at the man, full force.

I felt an electricity course through me, an energy gathered from the air and the ground around me: the magick of Dark Root. A blue spark shot from my hands as I slammed into his beefy arm. He fell backwards, his eyes half-closed as he hit the brick wall. He slid down the wall, blood trickling from his mouth. When he landed on the ground, his entire body fell over.

"Maggie!" Eve gasped, running to him and holding up his limp wrist. "What have you done?"

I opened my hands, stretching out my fingers. Blue currents buzzed around my fingertips.

"I think he's dead," she said, looking helplessly up at me.

"No," I said, joining her on the ground. We listened for his heartbeat, his breathing, his pulse, any indication that he was still alive. None came.

Yer father had the deathtouch.

Eve's face was drained of color. "Maggie! I think we killed him!"

The Magick of Dark Root

Book 2 in The Daughters of Dark Root Series

BY

APRIL M. AASHEIM

THE MAGICK OF DARK ROOT
(Daughters of Dark Root Book 2)

Copyright 2014 by April M. Aasheim

Published by Dark Root Press

Second Edition
ISBN-13: 978-1499611953
ISBN-10: 1499611951

Cover Art & Design by Jennifer Mnswami at
J.M. Rising Horse Creations
www.facebook.com/RisingHorseCreations
2015

Printed in the United States of America
2013

To my dad, who told me about the garden.

Acknowledgments

I could never have written this book without the help of many people.

Here are a few of them:

My husband, who read every word of my book and helped me to make it better.

My editor, for being such a great friend and constantly pushing me to improve.

My writing group, for being the best support system a person could ask for.

Michael and Nick, for being you.

Maddie, for reminding me about magic every single day.

Marilyn, for inspiring me with her courage.

My fans, for reading the first book and letting others know about it.

My mother, the real reason I write anything.

My brothers: Kris and Phil. For all those hours of role-playing games.

My three real life sisters: Dawn, Niki, and Jami. You were my childhood friends and my adult confidants.

Thank you.

FEED THE TREE

The Forest of Dark Root, Oregon
Winter Solstice
The Distant Past

S ASHA BENBRIDGE RAN THROUGH THE FOREST, HER CHESTNUT HAIR streaming behind her, its tips alight in the near-silver sun, like fairy dust trailing a shooting star.

Light on her toes and nimble with youth, Sasha rushed towards the spot where she'd seen the sterling cord of lightning strike the earth minutes before. Excitement threatened to swallow her whole as she raced towards her destiny. Her mother had predicted that she would find her tree today, and Sasha never knew her mother to be wrong, at least in the matters of witchcraft.

"Hurry!" she encouraged herself, though her voice was lost to the wind that whipped through the endless woods around her. She quickened her pace, leaping over the fallen branches and dense brush that impeded her path. She couldn't risk losing her tree. At twenty years old, she had waited too long already. But today was the day she would take her wand and come into her full power as a witch. She just knew it.

Sasha heard the rush of water ahead of her and she ran full speed towards the sound. At last, she found herself out of the shadowy woods, standing within a still-green field divided by a gushing turquoise river.

Good.

Though she was a daughter of the forest, she wanted a clear view of her surroundings before performing the ritual.

To her right, she glimpsed a man-sized shape crouching among a clump of bushes. She could only hope it was a bear. Her mother had taught her that there were more frightening things in the world than wild animals, and until Sasha had her wand, she doubted that she could match the worst of them. She touched the amulet that hung around her neck and said a brief spell of protection. Without sound, the shape slunk back into shadow.

Sasha inhaled the crisp morning air as she surveyed her surroundings.

In the center of the meadow, at the top of a gentle slope, just feet from the river, rose up a solitary tree: a thirty-foot willow with moonbeam-colored limbs that bowed towards the earth in smooth, clean arcs. The ground around the tree was slushy with ice, evidence that winter was on the horizon. Sasha approached it carefully. One misstep and she would certainly slide down the steep embankment and into the treacherous river that roared at her like a hungry lion.

The willow's branches undulated in the wind like long, sinuous fingers, beckoning her forward.

Sasha lifted several of the lower boughs and ducked into the tree's canopy as near darkness enfolded her in the secret chamber. She crept beneath the limbs, towards the tree's center, one hand gripping her amulet as she reached forward with the other.

When she reached the trunk, she ran her hands along its circumference, feeling the bark beneath her palms. Her hand touched a very warm patch of wood and she pulled away instinctively. Even in the darkness she could tell that the trunk had been scorched.

A smile crossed her face. This was the tree that had been struck by lightning. Her mother's prophesy had been correct. *The Lightning Willow.*

She would have her wand.

Satisfied, Sasha crept back out and stood before the tree. Being the only willow she had seen in the area, Sasha knew it had absorbed all the magic-rich nutrients of Dark Root reserved for trees of its kind.

Her fingers twitched and tingled as she pondered the possibilities.

"Blessed tree," she began, kneeling with arms outstretched. "My name is Sasha Benbridge and I have come to ask permission to take one of your limbs in order to create my wand. I am pure of heart and I will not use its magick to inflict harm upon others."

Sasha waited, watching for a response.

The boughs dipped, as if in acquiescence.

She stood and retrieved the small knife from the garter concealed beneath her cotton dress. She displayed the knife, giving the tree a moment to reconsider. When it did not move, she stepped forward.

"I'm sorry if this hurts," she whispered as she carefully sawed off a thin branch the length of her forearm. The tree flinched and she stroked it until it calmed.

"Thank you," she said, encircling her palm around its severed limb.

Within seconds the Lightning Willow had healed.

To her right, Sasha noticed a figure emerge from the woods: a tall, lank woman in a scarlet cloak.

"Larinda, were you following me? I suppose you will run to Mother and tell on me? Well, she knows I'm here and..."

"Dear cousin," Larinda interrupted. "You misjudge my intentions. I'm only here because I worry about you. I saw you disappear into the forest. What possessed you to run off so far into the woods without telling anyone?"

Sasha held out the branch. "After all these years, I have found my wand!"

Larinda threw back her hood, revealing hair as black as the night and skin as pale blue as the moon. Her thin red lips curled somewhere between a snarl and a smile. "You have waited so long already, dear cousin. What makes this branch so special?"

"It is from a special willow. The only of its kind in Dark Root. And,"

Sasha said with flashing eyes, "it's been kissed by lightning. Doubly blessed!"

"A willow? Will you devote your life to the healing arts then?" The right side of Larinda's lips rose up, no longer able to hide her contempt. "Perhaps you will become a nurse, walking the battlefields like Clara Barton?"

"Perhaps," Sasha answered, her eyes watching the black birds that had amassed in the trees at the edge of the clearing. "But there's so much more. Don't you see Larinda, with this wood, and the magic that runs through our blood, I can live forever if I choose!" She raised her face to her cousin, waiting for Larinda to grasp the implications.

"You mean..." Larinda turned her attention on the willow tree.

"Yes, I will hardly age! I can stay healthy and young and free forever!"

Larinda charged at the tree, yanking at one of its limbs. "I want that power. I didn't know about it. It isn't fair!"

But the branches pulled back and Larinda could not touch a one.

"You have your wand," Sasha said, stepping towards her cousin. "And it is a good wand. Illusion is a powerful magick. Besides, you know that a tree only gives up one wand."

"Nothing is as powerful as eternal life," Larinda said. "You get everything and I get nothing."

Sasha placed her hand on Larinda's shoulder to comfort her. "You are my blood. I will use the wand on you as well. We will be young forever, together."

"You promise to always take care of me?"

"Yes, my darling. Now we must hurry back. Tonight is the solstice and Mother and I are performing a shielding ritual to keep those out of Dark Root who wish to use its magic against us. When we are done, she will pass the Circle onto me."

The two women turned back towards the forest.

Larinda gave the Lightning Willow a final, longing glance. "Sasha, what will we do with eternal life?"

Sasha blinked, lifting her chin towards the sun before entering the darkness of the woods.

"I shall travel, become an actress, have a million lovers, and grow famous. Maybe I'll change my name to something more theatrical. What do you think of Sasha Shantay, Mistress of Magick?"

PART I

ONE

MEET VIRGINIA

Harvest, Home: Dark Root, Oregon
November, 2013

I LIFTED THE CORNER OF THE HEAVY DRAPES OF MY BEDROOM WINDOW, TO GET a better view of the backyard. Ravens had gathered near the edge of the lawn, arranging themselves into a straight line, like an army of pawns on a chessboard. They appeared restless––clawing at the wet earth and cocking their heads as they listened to the sounds of the forest around them.

Their agitation abated as another bird joined them, twice as large as the others, with wings as sleek and black as oil and eyes that glimmered red like dragon fruit. The others cawed at her arrival, making room for their queen at the center of the formation.

Suddenly, thirteen heads turned to stare at Harvest Home.

With unblinking eyes they surveyed the structure, turning towards my window. I caught my breath and closed the drapes except for a small slit, so they wouldn't see me watching them in return.

It was not uncommon to see birds in Dark Root at this time of year, especially ravens and crows, who did not fly south when the land grew cold.

But this flock unsettled me. There was a strange intelligence in their

9

eyes as their heads tilted this way and that, scanning the house, locking in every detail of the rambling Victorian home with its wraparound porch and two chimneys.

Maybe they had just come for the wreath: a circlet of pine cones, twigs, dried leaves, and berries that Eve had hung on the back door that very morning. As autumn wore on, food grew scarce. Perhaps the only malice they intended was procuring a few of the wreath's deep-red berries for themselves.

The queen raven turned her attention away from the house and the others followed suit. They now faced the garden where pumpkins had grown only a few weeks earlier. It laid empty now, long rows of red dirt waiting to be brought to life again in the springtime.

A gust of wind rushed through the trees that delineated our property.

All around our home grew a vast forest––deep, ancient, beckoning––still not fully mapped. The wind continued to push into the clearing, scattering most of the birds. They flapped their wings as they rode the currents into the sky––all except the queen, whose talons gripped stubbornly at the soft dirt beneath her, fighting the wind as she hopped her way into the garden. Her keen eyes caught sight of a mound of dirt where the field met the trees.

Aided by the wind, she scratched and pecked at the mound.

My heart nearly stopped as I realized what she was doing.

She was going for Gahabrien, the demon my sisters and I had sealed in a glass jar and buried at the far edge of the garden.

"Shoo!" I yelled, as I threw back the curtains and pulled open the window.

She glanced at me but continued her digging.

"Shoo!" I called again more forcefully, wondering how deeply my secret was buried?

"Caw!"

The raven lifted her beak and spread her wings as she locked eyes with me in a challenge. I stared back, just as forcefully. A mighty gale caught her in the chest and sent her sailing backwards, smashing her into a tree. I stared, open-mouthed.

Though I did not want her digging up my secrets, I didn't wish her dead either.

She lifted her head and warbled onto her chest. Giving me one last look, she limped into the forest, her wing useless.

"Poor thing," I said, shutting the window. "She was probably just hungry. I should have taken some berries out to them."

"To whom?" my sister Eve asked.

I had sent her to the kitchen to get me cookies. I frowned when I saw that she returned with nothing but a tray of plain crackers and soda water.

"The birds."

"Never feed the birds, Maggie" she said, placing the tray on a chair and pointing to my bed. I complied and flopped down, lying on my back as she lifted my t-shirt and placed five icy fingers on my abdomen. "Once you feed something, it never goes away."

"Ah, that explains why you're always here."

"Funny," she said, setting her ear to my belly as she continued her examination.

"What do you think?" I asked.

"Seems normal enough. Didn't feel any protruding horns or pointy tails."

"So, you're saying I won't be giving birth to a devil-child then? How boring. And I already registered at Demons-R-Us."

"Whoa. I didn't say that. It's still half your kid so there's always the possibility. And..." she paused. "Are you even sure it's Michael's?"

Eve removed her hand from my belly and stepped deftly to the side just as the light bulb over her head burst, shattering across the floor.

"Now see what you've done," I said, sitting up while Eve retrieved a broom from the hall closet. Since finding out I was *with child* a week ago, I had popped a half-dozen light bulbs.

Eve hardly flinched anymore.

"I wasn't trying to get you angry, Mags," Eve said, sweeping up the glass from the worn hardwood floor. She put the broom away and returned with a pack of sixty-watt bulbs. "Paul can put one of these in later," she said, referring to her boyfriend who currently resided in our attic.

"Maybe I should buy a lamp instead," I sighed, pressing my hands to my temples.

"Or maybe we just make do with glow sticks," Eve teased. When I didn't respond she added, "You know, you really should learn to control that temper of yours? Especially now that you're going to be a mother."

She raked her fingers through her long, dark hair and returned to her earlier task of rummaging through my closet, staring disapprovingly at a wardrobe collected mostly from lost and found bins.

"I'm working on it," I said, testing the chill of the floor with my bare toes.

I pulled back my foot at the cold and decided I should probably invest in a pair of slippers if I were going to survive the upcoming winter with my toes intact. Back in Northern California––where I had spent the last several years with Michael––the climate was temperate, nothing like the down-in-your-bones cold of mountainous Central Oregon.

"...And to answer your question," I said, still irritated. "Of course, its Michael's. Who else's could it be?"

Eve shrugged, sliding an ankle-length khaki skirt across the rod with the tip of her finger. "I don't know what goes on in those religious communes, Maggie. Could be a free-love baby."

"You watch too much television. Just because we bought a compound, kept ourselves distanced from society, and waited for the aliens to come and teach us about enlightenment, doesn't mean we practiced free love."

I crept towards my dresser, planting my feet on the lone sunbeam that pushed through the crack in the curtains. Shivering, I decided I needed new pajamas too. How I would get them, with less than four hundred dollars to my name and not a job in sight, I didn't know.

Too bad Eve wouldn't let me raid her closet. She had several pairs of pajamas but preferred sleeping in the nude.

"Sorry I've been in such a foul mood lately," I apologized as I opened a drawer. Eve had been one of the few people who had visited me since I went into seclusion a week ago and I didn't want to run her off. "It's been hard since discovering..." I pressed my hand to my belly, feeling the slight swell beneath my palms.

Eve waved her hands in the air dismissively. "You're just upset because you're knocked up and man-less. I get it. But don't take it out on me. I'm here to help, remember?"

"Some help," I muttered.

As much as I loved her company, I could probably do without a lot of Eve's so-called help. She had spent the last hour sitting on my bed, flipping through swimsuit magazines while giving me a rundown of all of the horrible things I could expect in the next few months.

"Your nipples are going to leak at the weirdest times, so keep tissue in your bra. You'll get stretch marks the size of Band-Aids in the strangest places. And you may never regain your pre-baby figure, or any figure for that matter. I knew this actress in New York whose boobs were two different sizes after nursing. The only gig she could get after that was as the before girl in plastic surgery commercials. Good thing you aren't in show biz."

"I do thank you for the help," I said, trying to hide the sarcasm as I removed a pair of denim overalls from my bureau. Perfect. They were roomy in the hips and waist and if my nipples happened to leak I could cover them up with the straps.

Eve snatched them away from me and tossed them into the wastebasket.

"All I know," Eve said, still scrutinizing my wardrobe. "Is that I'm glad it's you and not me. No way would I want to be saddled down with a kiddo right now. You can't do anything when you have a kid." Eve looked at me, catching my worried expression.

13

"Don't worry, Maggie. You don't do much now anyways."

I pulled out a dress, a sage, rectangular piece I had sewn myself at Woodhaven during one of the required home economics classes, a class I failed twice.

Once again Eve grabbed it away. "You're not wearing that pillow case either."

"Well, I don't know what to wear," I said.

We were going to our mother's house today––*summoned*, as Eve put it––to resume our training in *the craft*. It had been so long since I had practiced that I wasn't sure what the proper dress code was anymore. In our youth, we had worn sunbonnets and floral dresses for daytime spells and velvet gowns with lace-up boots for nighttime rituals. Mother and her Council usually donned robes that covered their entire bodies and most of their faces.

I didn't have any of those items. Nor would I be purchasing any. If Mother wanted me to take over as Council Elder she was going to have to accept that a few things would need to change, starting with the freaky '70s wardrobe.

At last I found a dark gray dress with a drawstring waist and held it up for Eve's approval.

"If you're going for the sad nun look, you've nailed it" she said, puckering up her pink-glossed lips. "But I guess that's as good as we're going to get until we take you maternity clothes shopping. At least it looks like it will fit."

She left the room while I put on the dress, and returned with a pair of ribbed tights and a strand of mulberry colored beads.

"These will keep you from looking like you're in mourning," she said. "Put on those new brown boots of yours, too."

I dressed as instructed, trying not to think about the fact that the last time I had worn my *new brown boots* was a week ago. Shane Doler had driven me home after The Haunted Dark Root Festival and we had spent the night curled up in the back of his pickup truck, talking and holding hands until the sun came up. There was a moment when we

14

almost kissed, when our lips were so close I could almost taste him, but neither of us made the move.

Still, it had been one of the most romantic nights of my life.

Of course, the next day I found out I was carrying Michael's baby and everything changed.

I couldn't face Shane and hid myself away in the house, ignoring his calls and his frequent visits. Dark Root's a small town and I knew I would have to tell him eventually, but for now, avoiding him was easier. I wanted to keep the fantasy of that night alive as long as I could before reality shattered it like one of my light bulbs.

"You look better already," Eve said, stepping back to view me. After a quick once-over she removed her hoop earrings and handed them over with a look that said, *you need these more than I do.*

"Remember when you pierced our ears?" I asked, flinching at the memory. "Mother had a fit."

Eve raised and lowered her shoulders. "I had watched her shove enough needles into dolls and doves. It didn't seem that hard."

"Merry's poor ears were infected for a week."

"How was I supposed to know you were supposed to use clean needles? I was only nine."

"I'm not sure how I feel wearing jewelry. Michael didn't let us wear these things in Woodhaven. He said it made us vain."

"Michael's not here, is he?" Eve gave me a coy look. "Don't worry, Maggie. You're not going to hell for wearing jewelry. If that were true, there'd be no women in Heaven, and what fun would that be for the men there?" She turned me towards the mirror that hung over the bedroom door. "You look great."

I grimaced, not so sure. "What happened to the beautiful glow of pregnancy I'd heard about?" My already-pale skin had turned a tombstone white, my once-red hair now looked a lackluster brown, and I had developed a second chin, with a third in queue.

"If you think it's bad now, just wait," Eve said, flopping onto the bed and crossing her right leg over her left as she straightened her back.

Her round, surgically-enhanced bosom pulled against her sweater. "I've had friends whose boobs swing like jungle vines after breastfeeding. It ain't pretty."

I clutched my small breasts, ready to save them if they started to plunge. "Why do you keep telling me these things? You're supposed to be supportive."

"Hey, if my boobs were going to fall like broken elevators, I'd want to know. That's why I had preemptive surgery." She thrust out her chest, once again revealing the small snow globes beneath the fabric. "You can always get a lift afterwards, but you'll never be the same."

I left the mirror and slumped down next to her.

She wrapped an arm around me, resting her head on my shoulder. Her normal earthy smell was replaced by the scents of cinnamon and vanilla, evidence that she'd been baking.

"I'm sorry," she said, her voice taking on an unexpected note of sincerity. "This whole *being supportive* thing is new to me. But I'll learn." She planted a soft kiss on my cheek and squeezed me tighter.

We sat there, sister-to-sister, comfortable in the silence. We'd made great strides in our relationship over the last two months, growing from rivals into friends. She was doing her best and I loved her for it, horror stories and all.

"Are you scared?" she finally asked, placing her hand back on my abdomen.

"Terrified," I answered, setting my hand over hers.

Our hands rose and fell with each breath I took.

"Whatever happens, I'm here for you," she said.

"I know."

We were startled by a knock on the door. Paul's dark blond pompadour peeked inside. "Sorry to interrupt you ladies," he said. "Eve, the Explorer's loaded up and ready to go. And I've got a huge surprise for you!" He disappeared as suddenly as he had arrived, the chains around his tight dark jeans jingling down the hallway.

"I'm coming," she called after him, rising. Then to me she added,

"Cheer up. Merry makes motherhood look easy. You will too."

"Thanks. Evie. I appreciate it. Give me five minutes to go to the bathroom and then I'm ready, too." The last week I had spent a considerable amount of time in the bathroom, either peeing or puking or a crazy combination of both.

"Oh, didn't I tell you?" Eve grinned from behind her black bangs. "I've arranged alternate transportation for you."

"What?"

"Yes. Sir Shane Doler shall come for his lady fair at around ten this fine morning."

"You didn't!"

"Oh, yes I did." She tossed her hair, shutting it before I could catch her.

Great.

I rubbed the sides of my temples as I caught sight of a book sitting on an upholstered chair in the corner of the bedroom. With all the new developments in my life, I had almost forgotten Mother's spell book. I opened it to a page entitled *How to Call the Rain*.

If there was a spell to change the weather, I reasoned, perhaps there was one that could change time.

I tucked the book into my tote bag and headed downstairs to question Aunt Dora.

The shutters rattled and knocked, rapping against Harvest Home like a new convert selling door-to-door religion.

I grabbed my alpaca sweater and hurried down the winding staircase that creaked and moaned with every step. It was cold in the old house, the only source of heat emanating from the parlor fireplace on the lower floor. Aunt Dora would fire up the furnace on the first day of December, and not one day sooner.

I passed the formal dining room where Mother and The Council had once gathered around the massive oak table as they discussed coven business. I stopped in the formal living room with its stiff, Victorian furniture and wall-to-wall bookshelves to check the weather on Aunt Dora's massive, flat screen TV.

The weatherman said it would rain all day. I grimaced. I hadn't expected much else in Dark Root in November, but I had *hoped* for a nice day, after my week-long hibernation. I thought of all the sunny days in my life that I had squandered sitting in dark rooms watching television or taking a nap. I wished I could take them all back.

The smell of nutmeg lured me into the heart of Harvest Home: the kitchen.

"Good mornin', lass!" Aunt Dora's lilty voice called to me. She smiled over her shoulder as she pulled a tray of muffins out of the oven. "It's good ta see ya up an' about." Her ample bottom fluttered beneath her blue-checkered house dress, cut from the same cloth as the kitchen curtains. She set the tin on the stove, then poked a toothpick into the center muffin.

"Perfect," she declared, wiping her hands on her bleached white apron.

"Morning," I said, suddenly embarrassed.

Preferring to wallow alone in my misery, I hadn't made an appearance in the kitchen for several days. Luckily, Aunt Dora and Eve had taken turns delivering trays to my room so that I wouldn't *waste away*.

"Mmm," I said, sniffing the air. "Blueberry?"

"Aye. Good nose. Still peein' on Popsicle sticks?" she asked, her eyes twinkling as she slathered a muffin in butter. She set the muffin on a white China plate and handed it to me.

"No. I gave up," I sighed.

I had taken so many pregnancy tests I could be a shareholder in the company by now. With each test I took, I closed my eyes and focused my energy, trying to change the outcome.

But witchery was no match for the little pink cross.

I opened the relic that served as a refrigerator, one of those iceboxes that kids used to crawl into and never come out of. When Aunt Dora turned away, I took a long swill of orange juice straight from the container, then quickly put it back.

Thirst quenched, I plopped myself onto one of the wooden chairs around the small kitchen table.

"We really need to get these things fixed," I said, rocking back and forth on the unsteady seat. The chair was probably older than Aunt Dora.

"If it can stand my weight, it can stand yers!" Aunt Dora patted her hips and laughed. "Besides, we don't get rid of things just because they get old. Understand?"

I nodded obediently.

"Goin' ta see yer mother?"

"I have to," I said, taking a tentative bite of my muffin. When my stomach didn't object I took a larger bite. "When Sasha Shantay summons you by name, you'd best answer the call."

Aunt Dora hooted, slapping her thigh so hard I could see the flesh ripple beneath her nightgown. "Maggie. Since when do ya answer anyone's call? I remember a girl who liked ta stay out way past dark just ta give her mother fits." She smiled at the memory and gave me a wink.

"Yeah, well, things change," I said, setting the muffin down.

She nodded in understanding. Mother had been very sick and until a week ago, we had all thought she was going to die. An event like that tends to put things in perspective.

My stomach spun. "Aunt Dora, do you have anything for nausea?"

"Aye, an' I'm surprised ya didn't ask me before. The craft isn't all about spells. It's also about takin' advantage of what's around ya." She removed the lid from a teakettle on the stove and then placed the kettle on the table. Next she measured in a teaspoon of one ingredient and added a sprig of another.

I sniffed the air, trying to recall what they were. "Mint and ginger?"

"Yer coming along." She clapped her hands, sending bits of ginger into the air. She poured two cups and handed one to me. "Let it steep fer a moment then drink up. An' eat! I won't have any skinny babies in my house!"

It was futile to argue with Aunt Dora, so I obliged, taking small bites and sipping on my tea. I had to admit that it felt nice to be taken care of, even if it was under duress.

"Aunt Dora," I said, while she rinsed off a spoon in the sink. "Do you think I'll make a good mother?"

She quit her task and turned in my direction, her eyes narrowed and sharp.

Leaning back against the counter she said, "Maggie, I love ya with all my heart. Ya know that, right?" She reached behind her, pulling a dish towel from the bar on the oven door.

"Yes. I know," I said, immediately regretting my question. "And you don't have to answer."

She lifted a hand to halt me, the towel dangling from her fingers. "Remember when ya were kids? Ya and yer sisters had been given homework by yer Uncle Joe ta grow plants."

I pressed my lips together, nodding.

I was seven and Uncle Joe had given us each a flower and a week to nurture them. Seven days later we returned with our assignments. Merry's flower had doubled in size, each petal soft and perfect. Eve's flower had transformed from a dullish gray to a vibrant pink with a scent so heavy you could smell it across the room. Even Ruth Anne's flower seemed to be thriving, and she didn't even believe in magick.

In stark contrast, my own flower had actually shrunk, receding into itself like it was trying to hide from me in its pot.

I'd handed it to Uncle Joe as Eve shot me a smug look.

"I tried," I explained to him, looking down at my feet. "I used all my powers."

"Not everything boils down to magick," he said, examining the plant. "Some things just require love and common sense."

He then handed the plant to Merry who cupped it in her dainty hands, closed her eyes, and blew on it like a birthday candle. She set the pot in a windowsill and within hours the flower perked up. Under Merry's care, it survived and outlived them all.

"Ya have come a long way since then," Aunt Dora said, her eyes still slits. "But we're still not sure what yer powers are, only that they are strong. Some say yer father had the *deathtouch*. Maybe ya do, too."

My eyes widened and my hands shot to my abdomen. "The *deathtouch*? What's the *deathtouch* and why hasn't anyone told me about it before?"

She tossed the cloth in the sink and shrugged. "It is as it sounds. Point is, use that noggin of yers girl. Got it?"

I looked down, afraid to meet her eyes as I asked the next question. "Is there anything we can do...about my situation? I wasn't prepared for being a mother, and now, thinking I might do something horrible to the kid..."

Aunt Dora's eyes flashed, her jaw firm as she spoke. "Maggie, ya made yer bed, so ta speak. Now it's time ta lie in it." She straightened her back, and though hardly five-feet-tall, she stood like a giant.

"I just meant..." I started to explain.

"I know what ya meant! Ya see a doctor if ya want that. Ya don't ask me!"

"No, no." I tried again. "I could never do...*that*. But isn't there a spell that can make things just...I don't know, go away?"

"What yer talking about, Maggie, is banishment. One o' the dark arts like demonology, summoning, and necromancy. Ya don' want ta start down that road. One bad apple in the family is all we can take."

The bad apple was my father, Armand, who had left The Council because he wanted to use the group's collective powers to summon and control demons.

"I'm not like my father. You know that."

She studied me quietly.

"What about turning back time, then?" I continued. "Can we do that?"

Aunt Dora cocked her head, placing a finger in the small dent of her chin. "Even the strongest witch is no match fer time." Her eyes softened and her shoulders followed. "An' if ya could, ya'd undo all that's been done. Would ya really want that?"

I shook my head and Aunt Dora exhaled, relieved.

"Well, good then." She took a plate and joined me at the table. "Now, ya do what every woman does in this situation."

"What's that?"

"Ya grow some balls." She threw her head back in a laugh then took a sip of her tea.

"Your wisdom never ceases to amaze me." I said, lifting my cup to her.

Aunt Dora reached across the table and took my hands. Mine were cold; hers were warm. "No more pity parties, okay? Not on my watch."

I agreed, then took the last swig of my drink. The roiling in my stomach had been quelled by her concoction. Checking the clock above the sink, I noticed that it was almost time for Shane to pick me up. But I had one more question for my aunt.

"You said that banishment is dark magick. So that means it can be done, right? That this kind of magick does exist?" When I saw the look of alarm on her face, I quickly added, "Not that I would do it. I just want to know what's out there, now that I'm going to be taking over as Council Leader. Know what I'm up against, so to speak."

Aunt Dora wiped her forehead with the back of her hand. "Aye, but yer mother locked those spells up. Didn't want just anyone reading them. Even if it wasn't locked, ta cast those spells ya'd need a wand, which ya don't have, an' a powerful amulet..."

Which I did have.

Our eyes fell to the bank of pink crystal on my wrist.

The Circle. It had once belonged to my mother but had now claimed me. I still wasn't sure what it did, but I was beginning to get an idea.

Aunt Dora regarded me with pursed lips. She mumbled something up to the heavens, and then reached for her walking cane. The table creaked as she pressed her weight into it, using it for leverage to stand.

"I won't do anything stupid," I said.

"Maggie. Ya can' help doing something stupid. Coming back to Dark Root, having a baby...its increasing yer powers. An' like I said, we still don't know all that ya can do." She leaned on her cane, scrutinizing me with her keen hawk eyes. "An' with great power comes..."

"Great responsibility?" I finished, knowing the adage.

"No. A great big pain in the ass."

Aunt Dora looked past me, into the living room as the music from her favorite television show announced that it was about to begin.

"And Maggie," she said after a moment's consideration. "There are eyes everywhere in this town, both helpful and not so helpful. Ya can't do anything without someone findin' out." Her eyes fell to the tote bag where I had stashed Mother's spell book. "That answers all yer questions?"

"Yes," I said, tucking my hair behind my ear and feeling like I'd just been released from the principal's office.

We said our goodbyes and Aunt Dora trundled into the living room. As I left the house I couldn't help but wonder who, or what, it was that watched me?

Two
UNTIL I FALL AWAY

T HE WIND WHIPPED ACROSS THE PORCH, PICKING UP AN ASSORTMENT OF sticks, bugs, and leaves, generating mini-cyclones around my feet as I sat huddled on the front steps waiting for Shane Doler to arrive. Raindrops the size of marbles plunked against the top of my head, threatening to put me out like a match.

I pulled the collar of the alpaca sweater up over my head, but it wasn't enough to keep me dry.

The land around the house was barren now, except for a few splotches of oatmeal-colored grass, the last remnants of summer. The small animals who'd been hunting for food only a few weeks earlier had all disappeared into their hidey-holes to ride out the coming winter. Even the sturdy maple trees that aligned the property had succumbed to seasons, their branches bare and exposed as they shivered in the wind.

The only signs of life were the miles of fir and pine trees that dotted the landscape in every direction, those green, steadfast soldiers who stood vigil over Dark Root all year long.

It will all return, I reminded myself, as I looked at my bracelet once again.

The circle continues.

My hands fell to my belly, cradling the small bump that had only now begun to show. Spring would bring life again; there was no stopping time.

I heard a rumbling in the distance and I craned my neck down the long dirt road, searching for Shane's white pickup truck. It must have been thunder. I considered walking the mile and a half to my mother's house, but I didn't want to risk getting caught in one of Dark Root's famous storms. I stood and paced beneath the balcony to pass the minutes.

Through the bay window, I spotted Aunt Dora lounging in her recliner, knitting what I hoped was a doily and not another baby hat. She hummed as she worked her yarn, glancing up now and then to watch the monolithic TV, the only luxury she had allowed herself in thirty years.

I felt a wave of love for the woman who had forfeited a family of her own to help raise me and my sisters. I wished that she was coming with me today, but the arthritis in her hip made even short travels difficult. Perhaps I could bring Mother here to visit, instead, when she had fully recovered.

I was a nervous wreck, I knew.

Nervous about seeing my mother, nervous about seeing Shane, nervous about being a mother. My chest tightened, making it difficult to breath, and I reached for the crystal pendant that hung around my neck. A gift from Michael. He claimed it would help calm and center me. It was one of the few things I kept from my days with him.

I laughed at the irony as I looked down at my belly.

"Michael, what have we done?"

I sat again, out of the rain, and closed my eyes, allowing myself to focus on what the baby might look like. Would it have my red hair, green eyes, and pointed chin? Or would it look like Michael, with brown hair, gray eyes, and a serious set to his jaw? Would it have my temper or Michael's pragmatism? Or some strange combination of both?

I settled deeper into my meditation, concentrating on the baby's face.

The veil around the child's image lifted and I could ...a boy.

I was going to have a boy. Large hazel eyes, a thatch of auburn hair, and fingers so small they didn't seem real. The nurse handed him to me, his tiny hands balled up into fists and his lips smacking as he searched for food. I tucked him into the crook of my arm, supporting his wobbly head. His eyes met mine and we stared at one another in awe and recognition.

"Baby," I whispered. "My beautiful baby." I stroked his cheek and kissed the tips of his fingers. "Mommy's here."

And then he screamed.

A heart-stopping shriek that pierced the halls. In an instant, his skin color changed from rose to ash and he fell silent. Deathly, deathly silent.

Yer father had the deathtouch.

My eyes flew open, my heart pounding in my ears.

I jumped up, clawing my way up one of the white pillars that supported the porch roof. It wasn't real, I told myself. This was not a prophecy. My sister Merry had given birth to June Bug and nothing bad had happened.

If our father did have the *deathtouch,* it wasn't genetic.

I placed my hands on my midsection, protectively. I had seen his face. He was mine now. I wouldn't let anything bad happen to him.

A raven fluttered down from the rafters, landing at my feet and regarding me with black, unblinking eyes.

A chill trickled up my spine, catching in my throat.

"Get!" I yelled, stomping my foot. "Get!" It hopped backwards, cocked its head, and then launched itself into the steel-gray sky.

My sweater constricted around me, soaked in perspiration. I tore if off and wadded it into my tote bag. When Shane's truck finally came into view I was overcome with relief. As much as I dreaded seeing him in my current condition, it was far preferable to being alone.

He didn't notice me as he rolled into the lot.

Lost in the lyrics of one of his country or classic rock songs, he tapped his thumb against the steering wheel and bobbed his head, managing to keep his cowboy hat on in the process. His lips drawn taught and his eyes half-closed, he pulled to a stop, leaving the truck running while the song played out.

When it ended, his head remained bowed, as if he was trying to digest every last bit of meaning from the lyrics before letting them go. At last, he lifted his slate eyes and spotted me, his terse expression morphing into a broad, welcoming smile. His teeth were perfectly white, made even brighter by the contrast of his tanned skin and lightly-stubbled jawline. He set his hat on the passenger seat and a lock of sepia-toned hair fell across his forehead.

My heart forgot to beat as I took him in.

It had only been a week, but it felt like an eternity. I noticed him appraising me too, and I pushed my hands in front of my stomach, wishing I had kept the sweater on.

I forced a quick smile and a wave as he hopped out of the truck.

"My lady," he said, sweeping towards me with twinkling eyes. He knelt before me, taking my hand to kiss it, like a knight returning to his queen after a long battle.

"Don't be a dork," I said, smiling as I pulled my hand away.

"Good. You're insulting me. That means everything's back to normal."

I clicked my tongue. "There's no normal in Dark Root."

"Perfect." He examined the area as if he hadn't seen the house in years. "I've had my share of normal. Now I want Maggie Maddock, the abnormal."

"If that's how you Montana boys sweet talk your women, I think you need more practice."

Shane rubbed his jaw, considering. "Works on cattle. Guess something gets lost when you try and transfer it from heifer to woman. I'll work on it."

"Please do."

"I've missed you," he said, draping an arm around my shoulders as he led me towards the truck. He stopped just shy of the door and sniffed me. "You smell like a farm, my dear. You've been wearing that alpaca sweater again, haven't you? We really need to take you shopping."

"If it's good enough for the alpacas, it's good enough for me."

I climbed inside and turned on the radio, hoping the music would distract him before he could ply me with questions about my recent hermitage.

He immediately turned it down.

"How about this weather?" he said, maneuvering the pickup into a neat U-turn in the dirt driveway. "Another month of rain and then we'll probably start getting snow. Maybe even ice. I sure hope Dora's done something about the heating in there. I'd hate to think of you ladies turning into snow people once winter hits. "

"I know what the weather's like around here," I said. "In case you haven't forgotten, I grew up here. Unlike you."

A bitch move, I knew.

Though Shane had not been born here, he loved Dark Root more than anyone I knew. I could tell I hurt him by his sudden silence, but I couldn't take any more of him talking about snow and ice and the winter to come. I had enough to worry about without him reminding me that things were going to get worse. I stared out the window, watching the trees pass by as we bumped our way along the beat-up dirt road towards Sister House.

Shane finally broke the silence by slapping the palm of his hand against the steering wheel.

"Damn it, Maggie," he said, his voice heavy with frustration. "We spend a night together, a great night, I thought, and then I don't hear from you for a week. Not a phone call, an email, a smoke signal, nothing. And now you're sitting here, looking great I might add, and I guess I was hoping that you'd been avoiding me because you were sick or something. Maybe that would explain things..."

He reached for his hat and pushed it back onto his head, his eyes staring accusingly at me.

"But now I know it's because you didn't want to see me. I'm a big boy, Maggie. You could have told me."

I glanced at him, unspeaking.

"Did I do something wrong?" he continued. "I've been racking my brain trying to figure it out, but I keep coming up empty. I'm a guy, Maggie. Sometimes we don't know we've done something stupid until a woman tells us."

I shook my head, willing my face to remain stoic. "No, you haven't done anything. It's me. I'm going through something."

I reached for Michael's pendant, finding comfort in the smooth lines of the crystal.

Shane caught me fingering it and tightened his jaw.

He blinked as we hit a pot hole. A few large splats of rain pummeled the windshield and he wiped them away.

"Okay," he said, shaking his head. "Whatever you say."

We traveled through a thicket of small pines and I rolled down my window, breathing in their pungent scent.

"I've missed the smell of pine so much," I said. "Michael never let us have Christmas trees at Woodhaven. Said that holidays were an excuse for consumerism. So I'd sneak off to tree farms and the Home Depot every December just to smell the trees. They reminded me of..."

"...home," Shane finished my sentence and rolled down his own window, letting the scent of the forest circulate through the cab of the truck. "It's cheaper than getting one of those car fresheners that hang from your rearview mirror. Only suckers spend two dollars on luxuries like that." He tapped the side of his temple with his index finger and grinned.

I smiled back, glad the mood had lightened.

He turned to me, his eyes alight. "Hey, since we're out here, let me show you something, okay? It will only take a few more minutes"

He had a wide, dopey smirk on his face and I conceded. My mother had waited seven years to see me. Surely she could wait ten more minutes.

30

Shane spun the wheel, changing directions, and we thumped down a road so narrow the trees scraped the sides of the truck, forcing us to roll our windows back up. We were deep in the woods now, where trees grew twice tall as light posts. We stopped in front of a cluster of evergreens, the ground beneath them covered in a blanket of red berries and needles.

"Get out," Shane said, opening his door and jogging around to mine. "C'mon," he insisted, pulling me out before I could object.

Though we were shielded from the rain by the forest, there was dankness to the air, and a soft mist sprinkled my face. The ground was spongy and red and I could make out the prints of raccoons and squirrels.

"So, you brought me here to see trees?" I teased. "Because I don't see enough of them already."

"Not just any tree," he said. "This way."

Shane pulled me along, leading me over mounds of needles, twigs, and worms.

"Here," he said, pointing to a yew tree tucked in amongst the pines.

"And?" I asked, surveying the tree. "Is he a friend of yours or something?"

Shane crouched down, running his fingers over a spot where a patch of bark had been chipped away. I stooped behind him.

"See?" he said, pointing to a crude, angled heart the size of my palm that had been chiseled into the side of the tree. Within the heart were the letters S.D. + M. M. I looked from the tree to Shane's eager puppy face. "I carved this when I was eleven," he said, almost blushing.

"And it's still here?"

Shane was in his mid-twenties, meaning the carving would be about fifteen years old.

"Amazing, huh?" He ran his fingers along the angles of the heart.

"How do I know you didn't come carve it this morning?" I asked, crossing my arms. "Or that the M.M. doesn't stand for Merry Maddock?"

He continued to stare at the engraving, not taking the bait.

31

"What were you doing out here in the middle of the woods anyway?" I asked, pushing my fingers into the grooves of the heart.

"Trying to follow my inner Thoreau, I suppose. Living deliberately and sucking the marrow out of life." He glanced at me over his shoulder, as if expecting a reaction. When it became clear that I had no idea what he was talking about he shrugged. "Sorry. I forgot you're not much of a reader."

As I pondered whether or not I should be insulted, he added, "Truth is, I'd come out here to think about mom and dad. Uncle Joe said it was okay to talk to him about them, but..." He dropped his hands, thrusting them into his pockets as he stood. "Uncle Joe had enough on his plate with the diner and your ma. No offense to your ma, of course."

"None taken. I know she's a handful."

"Besides," he continued as he reached out to help me stand. "I liked having my alone-time with my parents. Talking to them. Asking how they were doing. Telling them about school. Sounds selfish now but I didn't want to share those moments with anyone, even Uncle Joe." He looked at me, brushing my cheek with his thumb. "Except for you, Maggie."

I had spent most of my life complaining about my over-bearing mother and absent father, but Shane had lost both of his parents to his dad's drunk driving when he was a kid. How did anyone get past something like that? Yet he had.

"Why me?" I asked as his thumb found its way to my chin. I didn't understand why he liked me now, and I certainly couldn't understand why he had liked me then, when I was all legs and temper.

"Dunno. But from the first moment Uncle Joe brought me to your house and I saw you sitting in the kitchen all alone, stewing because your ma had just reprimanded you for setting the curtains on fire, I knew you were the one for me. Maybe it was because you seemed as lost and alone as I me."

"I never set the curtains on fire!"

"You did too!" He leaned back against the tree, crossing his arms.

"Your ma wanted you to light a candle with your mind and you kept telling her that it was impossible. Finally, after an hour of this you got so angry that you lit the curtains on fire instead. When I got there she told us the story and showed me the damage. You had her in quite a tizzy that day."

Shane howled and I shot him a cross look as the memory came back to me. Mother had placed me in lockdown that week, insisting I spend my evenings reading up on punishments inflicted on poor witches who hadn't been able to control their powers. Hangings, burnings, stonings, drownings. And my personal favorite: pressings.

Was it any wonder that I was such a neurotic mess today?

Shane and I stood facing one another, silently reminiscing about our shared history as we listened to the sounds of small animals scurrying in the forest around us.

"How did you find it again, after all these years?" I asked, stealing one more glance at the tree.

"That, my dear, is a silly question." He winked.

"Oh," I said, feeling dumb.

I had recently discovered that Shane could locate things that were lost, as long as he had seen them. Even things that everyone else had given up on.

Without warning, he pulled me into his chest, wrapping his sleight, muscular arms around me. I could feel his warm breath on the side of my neck, the tips of his fingers pressing into the small of my back, his hips locking onto mine.

My breath caught his, syncing up, our chests rising and falling as one.

The sound of his heartbeat through his thin, cotton t-shirt was almost deafening. I wanted to crawl inside him, fuse with him in a way I'd never wanted to with Michael.

I reached around, thrusting my hands into the back pockets of his jeans, and pulled him even closer. He moaned softly, growing hard against my leg.

33

"Shane," I whispered, lifting my chin with eyes closed and parted lips.

If he wanted to take me here in the forest, I wouldn't object. I'd been objecting to too many things for too long. I wanted to lose myself in his touch.

"Oh, God, Shane," I moaned.

"I love you, Maggie," he said, putting his hands on either side of my face and kissing the top of my head. "I love you so Goddamned much."

"What?"

I opened my eyes.

His jaw was hard, his eyes soft.

"What do you mean, you love me?" I asked, pulling away.

"I've waited so long for you, Maggie. Longer than you know. I realize I shouldn't be laying this on you, not like this. You deserve better." He reached for my hands, clasping my fingers in between his.

I shook my head, trying to make sense of it all. *Waited so long?* I'd only returned to Dark Root two months ago.

"What do you mean?" I asked.

He dropped his head. "I'm sorry. I forget sometimes."

"Forget?"

"Forget that we don't have the same memories."

I tried to process this.

I had almost given myself physically to this man, but he had said he loved me. In the blink of an eye everything had changed. Even if I did have similar feelings for him, my life was too complicated for love right now.

"Shane," I said, "I can't..."

"I know you've been keeping something from me, Maggie. Whatever it is, I'm here for you, okay? You just got out of one relationship and the last thing you probably want is to jump into another. But I've waited all these years," he said, glancing towards the tree. "I don't mind waiting a little longer."

"It might be a while," I said, laughing even as I wanted to cry.

"I hope it's not too long," he said, his handsome face softening. "I'd like to be able to kiss you while I still have all of my teeth."

"I'd like that too. I need to figure some things out first, okay?"

"I'm not going anywhere." He brushed a lock of my hair from my face and tucked it behind my ear, studying me. "You're so beautiful. Your hair. Your eyes. Your nose. Your freckles."

"I'm not beautiful."

"Yes, you are. And you don't even know it. It's one of your endearing qualities. With your looks and my culinary skills we'd make some pretty awesome children."

I laughed at the irony as a large raindrop fought its way through the trees, plunking on my head.

"Geez. And I wasn't even trying. Now let's get you to your ma's before you're soaked." He took my hand and led me back to his pickup.

Once we were buckled in, he said, "And whenever you're ready to talk, remember I'm here."

"Thank you. I'll remember."

He squeezed my hand and drove us out of the woods.

As we pulled into the large dirt driveway of Sister House, I gave Shane a kiss on the cheek. In an alternate universe––one where I didn't carry another man's baby––I would have invited him inside and introduced him as my boyfriend. We'd spend the holidays together, making plans for Christmas and New Year's Eve. Maybe making plans for the rest of our lives.

But this wasn't that universe.

Instead of inviting him in I said, "Hope you have a great day, Shane Doler."

He tipped his hat to me, a glimmer of sadness in his smoky gray eyes. "Ah, it's the plight of the cowboy to wander the world alone."

"Don't be a dork," I said again, climbing out of the truck and smiling as though nothing serious had transpired between us. "And for the millionth time, you're not a cowboy!"

"Hey, it's all I've got." He forced a smile. "See you around, Miss

Maggie Mae. And for the love of all that's good and holy in this world, get rid of that thing." He pointed to the alpaca sweater that peeked from the top of my tote bag.

Shane cranked up the radio, blasting Alanis Morisette's *Ironic* as he sped away.

I watched him go, then turned my attention towards my childhood home.

Sister House. Though only half the size of Harvest Home, it appeared massive as I stood before it: a sprawling, white Victorian, with a century's worth of secrets. My sisters and I had vanquished one demon here, but there were others, tucked into every nook and cranny of the manor. These were the ghosts of our pasts, and of things to come. Sister House had been waiting for us, and now that the daughters of Dark Root were all home, it could make its plans.

The trees that surrounded Sister House rustled as wind caught their branches, conjuring up sounds like whisperings. I stood on tiptoe trying to make out the words.

"Maggie. Maggie. We see you."

I scanned the forest, peering into the grayness through the rain. My skin crawled as I realized that someone watched me. Or something.

I charged towards the house, sloshing through mud that grabbed onto me like quick sand.

"Maggie. Maggie."

At last, I stood trembling before the door.

A covenant would be made within these walls today that would bind me to Dark Root forever. I turned the knob and walked inside.

THREE

WELCOME ALL AGAIN

November, 2013
Sister House
Dark Root, Oregon

K NOCK, KNOCK," I SAID, PULLING A SMILE ONTO MY FACE AS I STEPPED inside, nearly tripping over the orange tabby lounging in the entryway who merely yawned at my arrival.

"Aunt Maggie!" My five-year-old niece leapt over the cat and barreled into me, wrapping her arms around my legs. "You made it!"

"I couldn't stay away from you, Mae," I said, calling her by her birth name. She wrinkled her nose and I corrected myself. "I mean June Bug."

I bent down to give her a hug, as always astounded by how much she looked like her mother with her cream-colored hair and robin's egg blue eyes.

"Hey, lookie there. You lost another tooth!"

She opened her mouth, revealing a large gap in the top front row.

"At this rate the tooth fairy will be broke by springtime," I said.

June Bug grinned, brushing a wisp of fine hair from her face. "Grandma says we should put her dentures under the pillow and see how much money she gets for them. Gross!"

A week ago, we'd all wondered whether her grandma would ever

37

leave the hospital and here she was cracking jokes about her fake teeth. I couldn't help but laugh.

June Bug scooped up the cat, which my mother had also named Maggie. "Do you want the kitty cat? Aunt Ruth Anne's allergic."

I shook my head. The last thing I needed was something else relying on me. "No, honey. I'm sorry. Auntie can't take a cat right now."

"I guess we have to take him to a shelter then." Her bottom lip pushed.

She released the cat. He bounded up the staircase, as if understanding its impending fate. June Bug took my hand as Merry strolled into the living room carrying a steaming mug. Dressed in red velvet and brown corduroy, with her blond hair tied back in a bow, she looked like she belonged on the holiday cover of an East Coast magazine.

"How's it going, sis?" she asked, joining us and planting a kiss on my cheek.

"Aunt Maggie is afraid she'll kill the cat, mommy." June Bug answered, looking between myself and Merry. "Isn't that right, Aunt Maggie?"

I quickly withdrew my hand from June Bug's.

I had forgotten that she could read people when she touched them, able to feel and even take on their emotions. It was a gift she shared with her mother. I should have cleansed my energy before coming into the house.

"I think she's scared she's going to hurt her baby, too," June Bug continued. "But we won't let anything happen to them. Right?"

I raised an alarmed eyebrow to Merry. Though June Bug was an empath, she seemed to know more than she should, even with that gift.

Merry knelt down so that she was eye level with her daughter. "Well, that's understandable honey. Having a baby is a scary thing. But we are all going to be here to help Aunt Maggie, right? And let her know that everything is okay."

June Bug nodded and Merry resumed her standing position. "Now, honey, go tell everyone that Aunt Maggie's here, okay?"

June Bug darted off, a blur of blond hair and red satin, calling out "Aunt Maggie's Here! Aunt Maggie's here!"

"Are you sure she's only five?" I asked. "I don't remember being that wise when I was her age."

"That's because you weren't," Merry teased, nudging me in the ribs.

"She's like a little old woman. Maybe we shouldn't let her hang out with her grandmother so much."

"The two have been almost inseparable since Mama woke up. But I think it's good for both of them." Merry's eyes ventured to the staircase, mentally moving towards Mother's room on the second floor.

"Anyways," Merry continued. "Sorry about June Bug reading you like that. She's supposed to ask permission first." Merry turned her head in both directions, checking to see that we were still alone. Turning to me, she whispered, "I think her talents are growing. Evolving. She knows things. Everything."

"Like reading minds?" I whispered back, surprised. There were few witches who could read minds. It was one of the highest gifts given.

"No. I don't think so. It's more like reading motives and intentions, I guess. She told me the other day that she was going to ask her daddy to send more money so that I would stop wanting to *kill* him. I'd never spoken those words but that's what I was feeling."

Merry's ex-husband Frank had run off with a barely-legal barista the year before and sent child support payments only when he felt like it.

"You're a saint for not killing him already," I said, sliding my arm around her waist.

It worried me how thin she'd gotten. Merry was naturally curvy, claiming she put on five pounds every time she smelled a cinnamon roll. Now I could feel her ribs. She was under more stress than she admitted. I cleared my mind before she could read my panic.

"I bet Mother's got a few Voodoo dolls lying around here. We could make a Frank doll," Merry teased.

"She's probably used them up on her own men," I said.

"That would explain why they've all mysteriously disappeared."
Merry blew on her cup then took a sip from her mug. "Want some coffee? I can put a shot of brandy in it." As soon as she spoke the word brandy, her face went white. "Oh, Maggie. I'm so sorry. My mind's all over the place lately and I keep forgetting."

Our eyes fell to her mug as we both remembered a night last month when we'd stayed up late at Dip Stix Café, guzzling countless bottles of Shane's best wine.

Of course, I didn't know I was pregnant then, but what if...?

"I'm sure everything's fine," Merry said. "It was only one night. God only knows what Mother put in her body when she was pregnant with us."

"Not a good comparison," I snickered. "But you're right. It was only one night."

Yer father had the deathtouch.

I resisted the urge to touch my belly as Aunt Dora's words came back to me. Merry had enough on her plate with Frank, June Bug, and Mother. I wasn't going to let her take on one more worry.

"Besides," Merry continued. "I'm sure you ate very healthy at Hallelujah-Ville, right? That's gotta count for something."

"You mean Woodhaven?" I laughed. "Well..."

Michael had done his best to get me to eat healthy, insisting on organic and free-range everything, but my private diet consisted of Oreos and Diet Coke, and not much else.

This poor child didn't stand a chance.

June Bug returned to us, skipping, her hair divided into two fishtail braids that fell to the small of her back. Eve's handiwork.

"Aunt Maggie, come see what we're doing." She took my hand and dragged me towards the dining area as Merry threw me an apologetic shrug.

In the corner, behind the round oak table where I used to eat breakfast, stood an aluminum tree at least seven feet tall. It was a sad, shriveled-up old thing: a thin, metallic pole that spewed out silver branches with so much space between them you could see to the wall behind it. On each branch hung four, red, glass balls as large as melons. Chunky strands of tinsel separated each ball, giving the illusion that each ornament had its own stall.

Paul was crouched behind the tree, wrestling with a string of lights.

June Bug ran to the tree and added more tinsel.

"Hey there, rock star." Paul grinned at me through the branches as his fingers searched for a light socket. His dark blond pompadour had flattened, laying back against his head. His cobalt eyes twinkled for a moment, before returning to the task.

"Christmas, already?" I asked. "We're not even halfway through November."

"Isn't it beautiful?" he answered, undaunted by my lack of enthusiasm.

"If this were 1953, then yes."

"If only we could be so lucky. Things were much simpler in the past. Someone really needs to invent a time machine."

"You're preaching to the choir," I said, adjusting an ornament that looked ready suicide.

"You're just in time for the lighting ceremony. And cookies." Eve swept in carrying a silver tray filled with star shaped cookies. They'd been decorated with white frosting and red and green sprinkles. "Look at me," she said, lowering the tray for my inspection. "I've become a regular Betty Crocker."

"If the Hooters gals could see you now," I said as I reached for a cookie.

She swatted my hand and handed my cookie to June Bug instead. "For that comment, you get nothing."

"I'm telling Mother."

"Go ahead. Then I'll tell her how you used to fall asleep during Uncle Joe's lessons on sacred geometry."

"You wouldn't."

"Try me." She set the tray on the table, and then turned her attention to Paul. "Aren't you done yet? You've been working on those lights for almost an hour."

"In case you haven't figured it out, these things are archaic. They don't even make lights like this anymore." Paul lifted the strand to show us bulbs as big as our fists.

"We could get new ones," Eve said, putting her hand on her hip. "A new tree, too, maybe. This thing is so old."

"Blasphemy," Paul said, tightening a bulb. "They don't make things like this anymore."

"Because they suck." Eve sighed. "When you buy my ring I want a new one. Not an old hand me down? Got it?"

"*If* I buy you a ring, you'll get what you get. Understood?"

Eve was used to walking over men, so I think she relished her inability to conquer Paul. "Fine," she said, crossing her arms even as her eyes twinkled. "But no cookies for you, either."

Merry joined us at the tree. "Neither of you should be eating that stuff. It's bad for you."

She took the half-eaten cookie from June Bug and put it back on the tray. June Bug moaned but acquiesced. Merry was the kindest of all of us, but she could also be the most stubborn, especially in matters of nutrition. Merry sniffed the air and turned to the aluminum tree.

"With all the real pine around here why are we using this old thing?"

"Paul found this one in Aunt Dora's attic," Eve answered. "Said it reminded him of the trees they put up in those old Christmas movies. We can set up a real tree at Harvest Home or mom's shop."

Eve's eyes flashed mischievously.

"And I'm sure Shane could be persuaded to put one up at Dip Stix too. If Maggie works her, cough, magic."

"Watch it, scrawny. I outweigh you by a good ten pounds now," I said.

"Ten?" Eve blinked. "Try fifteen."

"Unless you want me to put a pin in those balloon bags of yours, you'd better be nice."

42

Eve folded her arms across her chest. "Stay away from them. If the magick shop doesn't work out, I'll need these babies to make us some money."

"Great idea. We can tie a rope to you and rent you out for parades."

"Funny."

"I thought so."

Paul cleared his throat and rustled the tree to get our attention. "As much as I like seeing two chicks fight, I could really use some help here. I can't see anything back here." He held up the end of a light strand that didn't quite reach the outlet.

"Fine." Eve pulled the tree away from the wall and directed Paul to move the plug *there* and then *there*. I leaned against the breakfast table, bemusedly watching the scene while Merry took June Bug into the powder room to brush *the sugar bugs* off of her teeth.

"If Eve cooks half as good as she gives orders, those cookies will be delicious."

My eldest sister Ruth Anne lumbered down the stairs in a pair of cut-off sweatpants and a stretched-out, Scooby Doo T-shirt. Her short brown hair shot up in corkscrews around her face and her glasses looked ready to topple off her button nose. I was seized by guilt as I realized I'd hardly seen her since she'd returned to Dark Root a week earlier. She sauntered to the table and picked up June Bug's half-eaten cookie, shrugged, then bit into it.

"There's no such thing as a bad cookie," she said, draping her free arm across my shoulders. "So?" she asked, taking another bite, "What's shakin' bacon?"

Her laid back greeting caught me off guard. "I'm sorry for not coming by," I mumbled, feeling my face redden as I searched for an excuse. "I've been a bit, uh, occupied."

"No need to be." Ruth Anne wiped the crumbs from her mouth with her hands. "If I can disappear for fifteen years, you're entitled to a week."

Her eyes scanned the massive, built-in bookshelves that lined

43

the north side of the family room. While Mother's library had never rivaled Uncle Joe's, it was still an impressive collection, especially to a bookworm like Ruth Anne.

"Besides, it's given me a chance to catch up on my reading. Did you know there are books here over a hundred years old? Many of them first editions." Her eyes gleamed beneath her square-framed glasses as she took in the wall of books. "They're a bit musty, but hell, so are most of the men I dated."

She stomped one foot on the hardwood floor, snorting at her own joke.

"I see age hasn't changed your sense of humor," I said, studying her.

In some ways she was exactly as I remembered. The same glasses, the same tom-boy attire, and the same short hair——a haircut she'd given herself when she denounced witchcraft.

In other ways she was completely alien to me. Her easiness. Her confidence. She'd been outspoken as a child, fueled by a sense of righteous indignation as she asserted her independence. Now, she possessed a go-with-the-flow attitude that was difficult to assimilate into my old notion of Ruth Anne.

I wanted to get to know her better, to find out who she had become in the years we'd been apart.

"Life is funny, Maggie. That's the most important thing I've learned. If we can't laugh at it, well...we're all screwed." Ruth Anne flung out her hands, dropping the cookie.

At once, the Maggie cat was on it, gobbling it up before anyone else lay claim to it.

"I suppose," I said, sensing there was a lot to her story. "It's good to have you back. Are you home for good?"

"Maybe. I can probably get a little work done while I'm here. Dark Root might be good for the muse."

"Your work?" I had no idea what she did for a living. "Let me guess. You're a librarian? No, a teacher! Wait, a philosopher!"

Ruth Anne stretched, grabbed two more cookies when Eve wasn't looking, and passed one to me. "Close. I write paranormal romances."

I waited for her to say "gotcha." The Ruth Anne I remembered hated all things paranormal. Not to mention romance.

"You're kidding, right?" I finally asked.

"Nope."

"Oh."

I tried to wedge this new version of my sister into my brain, making it somehow meld with the old version. It was like trying to squeeze into a pair of jeans two sizes too small. You could do it, but it hurt.

"So, what is a paranormal romance exactly?"

Ruth Anne finished her cookie and reached for yet another one, licking off the frosting. "The age-old story of boy meets ghoul. They have amazing ghost sex. Then they live, or die, happily ever after. Easy peasy."

"But why?" I asked, still confused. "I mean, why do you write it?"

"The hours are good, the pay is fair, and it's fun doing the research. With my background, I have a bit of a leg up on the competition." She leaned in and whispered, "Did you know that Dark Root isn't the only place in the world where people believe in witches and ghosts and things that go bump in the night? Everyone wants to believe that there is more to this world than meets the eye."

"I suppose you're right," I said, remembering the way Michael wished for the end of the world to come, so that his prophecies could be vindicated. "Do you make a lot of money?"

Ruth Anne scratched her head. "My first book did really well. Climbed some best-seller charts and kept me in macaroni and cheese for several years. But after that, well, I couldn't write anymore. Couldn't think of anything that would live up to the first, and so I stopped trying." She shrugged, her eyes finding the window behind me. "Anyways, I'm hoping some time here in Dark Root with family, will open up the mental floodgates."

I gave Ruth Anne a tight-lipped smile.

"I hope so, too. If not, there's always helping Eve down at the shop."

"Oh, God," she moaned, smacking her forehead. "I better write a best seller."

We laughed, reminiscing about all the hours we'd put in at the store when we were kids. Ruth Anne had vowed then never to return to the store, and that was a vow she intended to keep.

Our conversation was interrupted by Paul, who crawled out from behind the tree, a dark green cord in each hand. "We're almost ready," he said. "I think we replaced all the bad bulbs."

"It's cute to see him so excited. He's like a little kid," Merry said, returning with a clean-faced June Bug.

"His family didn't celebrate Christmas," Eve whispered. "Now, he's a junkie. Starts watching holiday movies in September."

"Everyone here?" Paul asked, counting heads. "How's the tree look?"

"Like it threw up tinsel," Eve said.

"Don't listen to her, Paul," Merry said. "It's beautiful."

"Thanks, Merry. Okay then. Here goes nothing."

We stood before the tree, admiring a relic that hadn't seen the light of day in half a century. I placed both hands on my belly, allowing myself to feel the small swell beneath my dress. By this time next year there'd be one more person gathered around the tree. Could I take care of it? I wasn't sure, but standing here, amongst my family, I knew I wasn't alone.

Paul went to fit the two ends of the cords together when June Bug stopped him. "Wait. Where's Grandma?"

Merry's fingers massaged June Bug's shoulders. Her face tense, she said, "I'm sorry honey. I think Grandma is having a hard morning. She won't be down for this."

I shot Merry a questioning look. She bit her bottom lip and shook her head, letting me know that something was very wrong.

"Go ahead, Paul," Merry encouraged him softly, and after a short hesitation he merged the two cords together.

46

"Ooh!" June Bug exclaimed as the tree came alive. Hundreds of multi-colored lights reflected off the glass ornaments, sending colorful prisms about the dining room.

The tree didn't' look sad anymore; in fact, it looked hopeful.

"Thank you, Uncle Paul," June Bug said, catching her reflection in an ornament. "It's lovely."

"See, ladies?" Eve said, tilting her head and placing a finger to her chin. "A little color and the right accessories does wonders."

We stood for a several minutes, each lost in our own thoughts as the lights twinkled across the silver Christmas tree.

Finally, Merry spoke up. "I hate to be a party-pooper, but we should turn it off. The electric bill is going to kill us." When June Bug frowned she added, "We can light it again this evening before bed. I promise."

Paul reluctantly pulled the plugs and we all converged on what was left of Eve's cookies, except for Merry and June Bug who munched on carrot sticks.

"Hey, Aunt Maggie," June Bug said in between bites. "Want to go download songs with me? The internet is working!"

"It is?" We hadn't been able to get online anywhere in Dark Root except for Shane's café on Main Street. And that was only sporadically.

"Yes!" June Bug said. "Auntie Ruth Anne introduced me to '90s music."

"Yeah, and thank you for that, by the way," Merry said. "She's been listening to nothing but *Black Hole Sun* and *Oops, I Did It Again* for the last three days." Merry rubbed the sides of her temples with both hands.

"You're welcome." Ruth Anne grinned. "Consider it payback for the Macarena torture you inflicted on us when we were kids."

"Yeah," Eve said, lowering her brows. "Thanks to you, Mom threw out the CD player and all my cds. It's called karma."

Ruth Anne raised a cookie. "Be thankful I haven't played *Achy Breaky Heart* for her yet."

"You wouldn't!" Merry's eyes widened and I had to laugh.

Merry had spent long days learning the dance in order to impress an older boy at school. He found the whole thing laughable and told his friends about it, sending Merry to her room for three days. A week later, he developed a case of mono, and we were never sure if it was his own bad luck or Mother's work. We didn't ask.

"You used to be such a romantic," Ruth Anne said.

"We all used to be something," Merry answered. "But yes, please keep that song, and story, to yourself."

June Bug tugged on my dress. "Come on, Aunt Maggie. There's this band called Spice Girls that I think you'll like."

"I'd love to," I said, taking my niece's hand as I mouthed the word "help" to my grinning sisters.

"I'm afraid she can't right now," came a raspy voice. Leaning against the banister at the bottom of the stairs, holding a cane as gnarled as her hands, stood my mother.

"Mama?" Merry ran to her and we followed. "How did you get downstairs? Are you alright?"

Mother waved her away with a shaky hand and tapped the end of the cane to the floor three times. "Ladies," she said, her effulgent blue eyes taking us in. "I've waited too long for this day. Let's make some magic."

Four

Santeria

Dark Root, Oregon
Sister House
October, 1993

N ow girls," Miss Sasha said, adjusting her wire-framed glasses over her round nose as she surveyed her daughters who sat quietly around the dining room table. All except for Ruth Anne, who watched the proceedings from the bottom of the staircase. "One doesn't enter into the craft lightly. You must take your vows with a glad heart, for once you take the oath, you are bound to the sisterhood, and remain a witch for life."

"But aren't we already witches?"

It was Merry who asked, her hands neatly folded in her lap. Eve cocked an ear and Ruth Anne inched forward, though still feigning disinterest.

Maggie stared out the window, wishing she could run and play on a day like this, when the leaves were crisp and the rain had silenced.

A finger snapped beside her face, bringing her back.

"Maggie, pay attention! How will you run The Council one day if you keep ignoring all your lessons?"

"I still don't know why Maggie gets to take over," Eve said,

49

chewing on the ends of her long, ebony braid. "She's not the oldest and she's not the best."

Miss Sasha leaned across the table, her eyes meeting Eve's. "No. She is not the oldest, but it's not for you to decide such things."

"But Merry's better," Eve insisted. "She can grow things and heal people and..."

"Quiet, Evie. Listen to Mama," Merry said. "I don't want that job anyway."

"Well," Eve argued. "Neither does Maggie."

This was true, of course.

Witchcraft bored Maggie. Casting spells was about as exciting as watching water boil and less predictable. Merry could have the job. Or Ruth Anne, for that matter.

"That is neither here nor there for now," Mother said. "You girls can't take the oath until you are fourteen. I am only trying to prepare you for what is to come."

Miss Sasha straightened her back and patted down her brown, frizzy hair.

Maggie noticed a coil of gray hair wound between the curls, but held her tongue. The last comment she'd made on Mother's gray hair had resulted in Miss Sasha locking herself in the bathroom with three boxes of hair dye for the entire day.

"Now, back to Merry's question," their mother continued. "Where do witches get their powers? Any ideas?"

Ruth Anne took another step forward and raised her hand.

"Yes?" Miss Sasha asked her eldest daughter.

"Magic isn't real so they don't get it from anywhere."

"That's enough, Ruth Anne," Mother warned. "If you aren't going to participate, go back to your books."

Ruth Anne clamped her mouth shut but didn't move from her spot.

Miss Sasha turned to the three girls at the table. "You all were born with magic. It's in your blood. But..." She raised a warning finger. "That alone doesn't make you a witch. You must take the oath.

It's an important day for any young women, something we all dream about and look forward to."

"Even better than a wedding?" Merry asked dreamily. Not quite ten, she had already begun putting together a hope chest filled with treasures and trinkets collected from around the house.

Miss Sasha sighed as she took a long sip from her teacup. Catching her reflection in the china cabinet, she put down her cup and ran her finger along a deep line that ran from her nose to her mouth.

"Dora," she called into the kitchen. "Do we have any aloe? My skin is feeling a bit dry."

"Aunt Dora's gone to help at Harvest Home," Ruth Anne explained. "Miss Rosa fell and hurt her hip."

"Is Miss Rosa okay?" Merry asked.

Miss Rosa was old, maybe the oldest person in Dark Root. She owned Harvest Home, the house where The Council conducted most of their business. She had taken on a grandmotherly role for the Maddock sisters, greeting them with warm cinnamon rolls and lectures on washing behind their ears whenever they visited.

"I think so," Ruth Anne said, chewing on the end of a pencil. "But Aunt Dora said she was going to stay and look after her."

Miss Sasha frowned again, the lines on her face deepening. "It's all changing," she said, her voice trembling. "The world is moving too fast and there's nothing we can do about it."

She looked at her daughters and her frown turned into a thin-lipped smile. "But there's always tomorrow. And as long as we have tomorrows, things will be okay. Isn't that right, girls?"

Merry nodded, Ruth Anne shrugged, and Eve tugged on the end of her braid. Maggie stared out the window. In the world of tomorrow she had plans for her life. And none of them included taking her mother's place at the head of The Council.

I took Mother's right arm while Paul flanked her from the left.

The others followed us up the winding, sconce-lit staircase, down the narrow corridor lined with portraits of people I couldn't remember, and past the nursery where we'd spent our early years until we were old enough to move into the attic bedroom.

At last, we came to the unremarkable door that led to Mother's bedroom.

Paul turned the knob and Mother's hand shot out, grabbing hold of his wrist.

"No men!" she hissed, her sharp blue eyes unblinking. Merry and Eve protested on his behalf, but she held her position. "I said no men! They can't be trusted."

Paul's phone rang and he pulled it from his pocket. Looking at the screen, he frowned.

"It's okay," he said, backing anyway. "I have to take this anyway."

"Who's calling?" Eve demanded, but Paul had already bounded down the stairs. "He's been acting really weird lately," she said, her eyes on him as Merry opened the bedroom door.

Stepping inside Mother's room was like falling down a genie's bottle: Rose and honey toned trinkets and bobbles winked at us from every direction. A burgundy canopy floated above the antique four-post bed, and thick billows of jasmine incense rose up from all four corners of the room.

"I feel like someone's going to sell us a magic lamp," Ruth Anne said, rubbing her hands expectantly.

Mother coughed loudly then clutched a bedpost for support. "Eve, roll that up please," she said, pointing to an emerald and ruby-colored Persian rug that covered the large expanse of floor between her bed and the east window.

Eve complied and we all gasped as a white shape was revealed beneath the carpet: a five-pronged star within a circle.

"A pentagram!" June Bug called out.

"That's right, honey," Merry said, taking her daughter's hand and leading her to a spoke. Without having to be told the rest of us seated ourselves on the remaining points as Mother entered the star's center.

"Now girls," Mother began in a raspy voice. "I've waited many years to see you all here. Time is short and I would have waited until I was in better health, but I'm afraid that day may not come."

"Mama, of course..." Merry began, but Miss Sasha stopped her with a stern look.

"I'm an old woman, Merry, and nothing can change that." She looked at us each in turn then cleared her throat. "Today, you take your oaths."

With the aid of her cane she hobbled to an unremarkable oil painting on the wall behind me, a portrait of a young man and woman riding horses in the forest. She removed the painting from the wall and set it gingerly on a chest beneath it. Next, she moved her hands across the wall until she discovered a knot in the plaster, a small white nodule completely invisible unless you happened to be looking for it.

In a wink she pressed her palm into the knot, and a panel slid open, revealing a small alcove.

"I'll be damned," Ruth Anne said, removing her glasses and peering at the wall.

"Not on my watch," Mother said.

"Is that a secret passage?" June Bug asked, rising to get a better view before being pulled back to her seat by Merry.

"No, dear, it's much too small to be a secret passage, but there are many secrets in this house, and in Dark Root. Some I will show you. Some you will find out on your own."

She reached inside and withdrew a brown leather pouch with a drawstring tie.

She studied it a moment, as if to re-familiarize herself with it, and with slow and precise steps returned to the pentagram. Merry went to assist her, but Mother shook her head, then gradually lowered herself to a seated position. She thrust her legs out before her and rested the cane across her lap.

"Maggie," she called, sliding the pouch to me. "Will you remove the items inside, please?"

The pouch was brittle and cracked. I reached inside and removed the first item: a scroll made of parchment.

"Should I open it?" I asked, my fingers tracing the wax stamp in the shape of a tree that sealed it shut.

Mother shook her head.

I set the scroll aside and removed a sleek, black vial filled with liquid.

Finally, I pulled out the final item, a silver needle as long as my palm. I lifted it carefully, avoiding its sharp end. Eve, who knew my fear of needles, shot me a look as I handed everything back to my mother.

"We will make a blood pact," Mother said.

A blood pact involved pricking your finger and then pressing your open wound to another's. It was an ancient practice, a ceremony performed to bind people together as family.

"But we are already family," I objected as I stared into the eye of the needle.

Mother gave me a wan smile. "This is the way it's always been done. We do not trifle with tradition."

She pricked her index finger and a drop of blood appeared on its tip.

She motioned for June Bug and my niece showed no fear as Mother lanced her skin. June Bug then took the needle to Merry and the two joined their wounds together. Merry did the same to Ruth Anne, then Ruth Anne to Eve.

At last, Eve knelt before me.

My hands trembled. I hated needles. I could hardly be in the same room with one. Needles symbolized all that was wrong in the world: pain, illness, endings, death. I reached for it, but couldn't bring myself to take it.

"I can do it for you," Eve whispered, taking my hand and turning it palm up. "It won't hurt. I promise."

"No."

I lifted my chin. They had all done it, even June Bug. Before I could talk myself out of it, I pierced my right index finger. Blood rose to the tip and it throbbed in pain.

Eve quickly grabbed my hand and pressed our fingers together.

"I'd love you even if you weren't my sister," I whispered to her.

"I doubt that."

"It is done," Mother said.

Mother unrolled the scroll, holding it up to show us that it was blank. "Eve, can you run a candle across this, please? A red one?"

Eve retrieved a candle and we watched as she ran it across the scroll. Wherever the flame touched the parchment, elaborate letters in black ink appeared.

"What does it say, Grandma?" June Bug asked, trying to sound out the words.

"That once we sign this document, the pact is sealed."

"I'll get a pen," Eve said.

"No." Mother pressed her pricked finger to the bottom of the scroll and motioned for us to do the same.

One by one we each added our bloody mark.

Once done, she rolled up the scroll and uncapped the vial. The sweet smell of frankincense wafted out.

Mother dotted our foreheads with the oil saying, "You are all now part of a sisterhood that has been around since the very beginning. Do not take your duties lightly, for much is as stake." She smeared a final drop of oil across the scroll, once again calling for Eve's assistance. "A white candle. Lit please."

Eve presented her with the item and Mother raised the scroll overhead, then lowered it into the candle's blue flame. In seconds it burned to ash.

When there was nothing left of it, she closed her eyes.

"You okay, Mama?" Merry asked.

Mother nodded and opened her eyes.

She was no longer the formidable Miss Sasha Shantay, but an old woman who could hardly lift her head.

With heavy lids she said, "I'm fine. Now, if you'll excuse me, I need to rest."

"I'll stay with you," I said, helping her to the bed.

"No." Her voice was firm but weak. "I need to be alone. Go be with your sisters now."

It was only a few steps to her bed, but every step was painful to watch. My heart was heavy as I left the room.

Time was not only short, I thought. It was also unfair. Time gave us things then took them away. A cruel thief. And there was absolutely nothing we could do about it.

FIVE

MYSTERIOUS WAYS

Miss Sasha's Magick Shoppe
Dark Root, Oregon
November 2013

"So what did you think of Mother's show yesterday?" Eve asked, as she carefully removed an hourglass wrapped in tissue paper from a cardboard box, placing it on a display shelf next to a dozen others.

I shrugged in response, returning to my own work.

Eve and I sat on stools sorting inventory in the early morning before the shop opened, sliding our chairs across the floor in small increments to keep pace with the sun shining through the large window. It was rare to have sunshine at this time of year and we relished every moment of it.

"Mother does like to put on a show," I finally answered as I emptied a box and broke it down for recycling.

"It's a good sign, I guess," Eve said, polishing a crystal figurine. "Kind of like the old days."

"Better than her lying there, hooked to tubes," I agreed, remembering how she looked just weeks before.

"Agreed." Eve stood, surveying her finished display. "Not bad, if I do say so, myself."

I had to admit that Miss Sasha's Magick Shoppe––my mother's old store and the cornerstone of downtown Dark Root––looked better than ever under my sister's fashionable eye. A discriminating witch would find everything she needed here, from lava lamps to do-it-yourself potion kits. Eve had stocked and modernized the place, bringing in an eclectic mix of customers from old-school practitioners of the craft to curious hipsters.

I grabbed the stack of cardboard and made my way to the back room.

"Wow," I called out as I ducked beneath the gauzy fabric that separated the two spaces. "You've been busy."

In the old days, we had used this room for storage, coffee breaks, and an occasional tarot card reading. But now it was another aspect of the store, a secret room for those with large pocketbooks or an advanced knowledge of the craft. Every shelf was piled with real parchment, old books, dove's blood, crystal balls and even Ouija boards.

"I need to put up an 'Employees Only' sign," Eve said, as I returned to the main room with full box of inventory. "To keep the wannabees out of there."

"Please do. I don't want to think about what would happen if a Ouija Board got into the wrong hands."

Eve raked her fingers through her hair. "I just don't want them messing up my displays. Some of that crap in there is pretty expensive."

I looked at the clock above the door. "We'd better hurry."

Outside the window, a small crowd of women were gathering. Though most of our sales were made around Halloween, we still drew some customers up through the Christmas season. In January, tourism would come to a grinding halt until summertime.

"They can wait. It's not like there are any other places to buy this kind of stuff around here." Eve pressed her lips together and turned to me. "She wants us to come back soon, you know? Maybe today."

"Who wants us to come back and where?" I peeked out the window again, noting that the line had doubled.

A few women saw me and waved as I ducked out of sight.

"Mom. Who else?"

"Oh. Well, we are officially in training. Who knows how long it will take? I feel like I'm in school again. I hope she doesn't give us homework."

"The whole blood-magic, soul-sisters thing seemed pretty juvenile to me," Eve continued as she dusted a shelf where a collection of glass pyramids stood. Like Eve, her store was beautiful and pristine, with nothing out of place. "Something we'd do when we were ten."

"I guess so," I agreed, unsure if she was miffed or musing. "But the way those words magically appeared on the parchment when you used the candle was pretty cool."

"Yeah, I was pretty great. I wish Paul had been there."

At Paul's name, I glanced instinctively out the window to Dip Stix Café across the street, where he and Shane were already serving up breakfast. Paul was most likely in the kitchen, stirring gravy and flipping pancakes, while Shane greeted customers, took orders, and cleaned the tables. I turned my head slightly, hoping to catch site of Shane without Eve noticing.

But she had an eagle eye when it came to things that interested her, and love always interested her.

"As I see it," she said, flipping the store sign to open and joining me at the window. "We can either summon Shane over here with a spell, or you can march your big butt over to Dip Stix and tell him you've been an idiot."

"Third option. You can stay out of it."

A small army of women pushed through the door.

Eve looked longingly at her dwindling supply bins. Most of the old merchandise had been sold, and Eve hoped the new inventory would last through the holiday season. Taxes for the shop were coming due, and even with our sales, we probably wouldn't turn a profit for at least another year.

But on this morning, the herd of women charged straight for me.

"What's going on?" I asked.

Eve grinned mischievously. "I told them that Maggie Magic was making an appearance today. Apparently you're a bit of a celebrity around here. Who knew?"

A dozen women surrounded me, thrusting notebooks and pens in my direction, drilling me with questions like, "How did you get all those flashlights to turn on?" and, "Do you teach classes?"

I tucked my hair behind my ears, embarrassed by the newfound attention. The fact that I'd been AWOL since the event at Haunted Dark Root only added to my mystique.

I signed everyone's notebooks, all the while insisting that the ladies support Miss Sasha's Magick Shoppe by buying things and telling their friends. As quickly as they had descended upon me, they receded back into the store.

"Albert, it's my money. I can spend it if I want it." A plump, middle-aged woman spoke as she rifled through a bin of red candles to my right. "You don't have any say in the matter anymore."

I did a quick glance around the shop, checking for "Albert."

As far as I could tell, she was alone.

"The poor dear," a woman with an armful of books on reincarnation said, as I rang her up. "She lost her husband Albert three years ago and has been a little off her rocker ever since. Claims he follows her. Sad, if you ask me. But I guess losing a loved one can make you go a bit mad, don't you think?"

I watched as invisible Albert and his very visible wife argued about what to eat for breakfast, before leaving the shop and heading across the street to Dip Stix.

Eve returned from the back room, placing a large glass bowl on the counter. Next, she pulled the corks from three glass vials and poured the contents into the bowl.

I raised a curious eyebrow.

"A new perfume I'm working on," she explained, sprinkling rose petals and vanilla into the mixture and stirring the concoction with a silver spoon. "I'm hoping to have it perfected by Valentine's Day. That should get us over the low-sales hump of the first quarter. If I get it right, it will drive men mad with lust. My own version of Obsession. I call it *Man Attack.*"

"Charming," I said, then added, "Sounds dangerous. Don't you ever watch daytime TV?"

"Some women like to be adored, Maggie." Eve pulled a tube of liquid glitter from a drawer beneath the counter and added a squirt to the mixture.

Several shoppers gathered around, asking questions about her potion. Eve obliged them—a little—assuring them that the finished product would be ready in February, when they could receive complimentary samples.

When the morning rush had subsided, Eve carried the mixture to the back room and I followed. She set the bowl on a small table and then pointed to a set of long, slender vials on a silver tray. I fetched them, bewitched as always by her handiwork.

Eve and I took different approaches to magick. She used spells and charms to work the craft, always measuring, adding, subtracting, and perfecting her skills.

I was deemed a *wilder*, a witch born with strong powers but who lacked the discipline to wield them properly. In one way I envied her.

In another way, it seemed like too much work.

Eve filled the bottles then lifted one to the light. Not quite satisfied, she added a drop of something that smelled like Myrrh.

"Your problem is that you're afraid Shane will reject you," she said, holding the vial once again to the light for inspection. "But one drop of this behind your ear and he won't abandon you no matter whose kiddo you're carrying."

"I thought we weren't supposed to use the craft for selfish purposes?" I said.

We'd had this lesson drilled into us since we were old enough to cast a candy spell.

"What's selfish about love? Besides," Eve said, her face taking on a gauzy look. "We were raised to be witches. Why not use our powers as we like, especially if we aren't hurting anyone? The old Council is gone, Maggie. We are the next generation. We get to decide how things are done now."

It was not the first time I'd wondered about this.

Why were we given powers if we were always taught to keep them locked up? It was the mystical equivalent of keeping your virginity: don't go giving it away to just anyone.

"I'm not afraid Shane will reject me," I said, as I corked her bottles.

Eve and I worked well together, I realized, able to anticipate what one needed before the other asked. Before corking the final bottle, I sniffed the perfume. It smelled like roses, dreams, and sex.

"I think you are afraid." Eve took the tray and placed it on a high shelf, where customers wouldn't see it.

"Maybe a little," I admitted as we moved back into the main area of the shop.

"I knew it."

What I didn't tell her was that the fear of Shane's rejection was only part of the reason I kept my distance from him. What I feared even more was that I would tell him my news, and then he would court me, date me, maybe even ask me to marry him...but not because he loved me, because it was the *right thing to do*. And Shane lived by the cowboy code of always doing the right thing.

That was something I couldn't live with.

I caught sight of him in the Dip Stix window. He smiled at a pretty woman as he took her order.

"One dab of Man Attack and you'll never have to worry about *that* again," Eve said, narrowing her eyes. "And believe me, honey, there are lots of *those* in the world, all waiting to snatch up someone like Shane Doler, without a second thought to you."

As Eve predicted, we were called once again to Mother's house that afternoon.

"Mama insists," Merry explained on the phone, her voice a pitch higher than usual. "I told her we could do it this weekend, but she won't hear anything of it. I guess we better humor her."

Eve and I closed the shop down early, ushering out several customers who'd been loitering for hours but hadn't purchased a thing.

At precisely four o'clock we gathered with Merry, June Bug, and Ruth Anne in front of Mother's bedroom and waited. At 4:01, she opened the door wearing a dress four sizes too big, earrings that hung to her shoulders, blue house shoes, and a black-feathered boa. She puffed on an unlit cigar and croaked out the words "my girls!" as if speaking burnt her lungs.

"These are for you," she said, handing us each a slender white candle.

She lit her own then passed the flame along to each of us in turn.

Eve rolled up the carpet on the floor, uncovering the Pentagram. We seated ourselves in the same positions, except for Mother, who stood holding the post of her bed with one hand and her candle with the other. She was even paler than yesterday and looked so frail a gust of wind could blow her away. She stood with shaking hands and labored breath while we waited.

After several hard breaths, she set her candle on her antique dresser, then reached into the top drawer, her fingers searching for something near the back.

A smile crossed her face as she pulled out a small, dried-out tree branch that looked as brittle as she was.

Holding the limb up for us to inspect she said, "Ruth Anne, do you remember this?" Ruth Anne's face displayed not a hint of remembrance and Mother let out an exasperated sigh. "Did you learn nothing?"

Mother tapped the stick on the dresser and a few meager sparks flickered at its tip.

"Every witch needs a wand," she said. "But for reasons I won't mention now, only Ruth Anne has selected hers already."

Ruth Anne had left home when she was a teenager. After that, Mother had given up on most everything, including our continued training. One by one we'd all followed in Ruth Anne's footsteps, leaving Dark Root, leaving Mother.

"It's okay, Mama," Merry said, her voice soft as a butterfly's wings. "We're all here now."

"Yes." Mother ran her tongue over her thin, cracked lips.

She had never apologized for our childhoods: her relentless insistence that we study and follow in her footsteps, her desire to have everything and everyone around her be perfect, and her unwillingness to admit that she was ever wrong about anything.

But in her eyes, I could see the guilt and the regret. I felt a surge of love for her now, and an even stronger need to protect her.

"Ruth Anne," she said, holding out the stick. "This wand is yours. I kept it safe for you."

Ruth Anne took the branch and turned it over in her hands.

"Abracadabra!" she said, rapping the stick against her crossed leg. "What? No rabbit?"

I shot my sister a warning look that took her aback. We had always been allies in mocking magic, and my lack of support caught her off guard.

"There is certainly a time for humor," Mother said. "But it is not now."

"Sorry," Ruth Anne apologized, saying nothing more.

"As you can see," Mother continued, "Ruth Anne's wand is not yet finished. Though she picked it herself *and* asked permission from the tree, she never completed the process."

"The process?" June Bug asked.

"Yes. Before a wand and its witch become one, the wood must

be stripped of its bark, anointed in a magick oil, and imbued with a gem. The wand must then spend a fortnight beneath its owner's pillow, absorbing its witch's character, and bestowing its power upon its owner. Every witch must pick her own wand, and every witch gets only one wand, so choose carefully."

"But a witch still has powers without the wand, right?" June Bug asked, raising her hand.

"Yes. That's right. A wand simply heightens her magic and refines her powers. They complement each other. And a wand picked from a tree grown in Dark Root, will be especially powerful.

"It's important that you think carefully about the type of witch you wish to become. Ruth Anne's wand is made of maple. This will increase her powers in the realm of knowledge. There are trees that will aid you in glamour..." She looked at Eve. "...And healing." She looked at Merry. "And, well, maybe temperance." She looked at me. "But I leave that to your discretion. Choose wisely, ladies. The Solstice approaches and we must rebuild the dome over Dark Root. The dome will be stronger if you each have your wand during the ceremony."

"I thought we already cast that spell," I said. "During Haunted Dark Root."

"That was to keep out the spirits and demons during Samhain, when the veil between worlds is thinnest. The Solstice ritual is meant to prevent practitioners from using the powerful magick residing *within* the sphere of Dark Root for evil purposes. Both spells work in conjunction with one another."

"By practitioners, do you mean other witches?" Eve asked.

"Yes. Those who wish to wield the magick of Dark Root for the wrong reasons." Mother put her hand to her chest and cleared her throat. "I'd like to see you all get your wands before I'm gone. Especially you, Magdalene."

"Where are you going?"

"Just focus on the time we have together now."

Anxiety welled up inside me. *Time together now?*

"One more thing," Mother said. "A witch always protects her wand. Though it will never be as powerful in the hands of another witch, it can still be used––or destroyed––by others."

"Where is your wand, Grandma?" June Bug asked.

I cocked my head. For all Mother's talk, I had never seen her use one.

She sighed dreamily, her blue eyes clouding over. "I had a very special wand, my dear. With the power to heal, and some say, grant eternal life."

"Whoa!" Ruth Anne burst out, then snapped her mouth shut.

"Was it destroyed, Grandma?"

"No dear. It just got...lost. Besides, living forever would be boring, don't you think?" She smiled, but there was wistfulness in her eyes.

Her lips trembled and she announced that our lesson was over. We shuffled out of the bedroom like zombies, our minds full of Mother's words.

"You don't really think Mama had a wand like that, do you?" Merry asked as we shut the door behind us.

"If she did, I'd think she'd of already used it on herself," I said. "Besides, you know Mother and her stories. Magic like that doesn't exist, even here."

"I suppose," Merry agreed thoughtfully. When the others passed us in the hall, she said, "I didn't want to bring this up, as it seemed irrelevant until today, but do you remember when we were kids? How vibrant and healthy she was?"

"Yes," I said, recalling the image of my mother, fifty pounds heavier and several decades younger. Her hair was wild and long, still thick as a skein of yarn. Now it was so thin you could practically see through the strands. "She got old, Merry. People get old."

"She looks decades older than she should. Most of my friend's parents don't seem that old."

"She may have started having children later than most people do," I said. "We still don't know how old she really is."

"Yes. I guess you're right." Merry looked at the floor then up again, her eyes twinkling. "But what if she really has a wand like that? Maybe we could..." She stopped herself and her eyes regained their somber expression. "I'm being silly. It's just that she is so frail. I give her energy every day, but it's like trying to charge a bad battery. One day she may not charge at all."

I touched Merry's pale cheek.

She always had a subtle light around her that illuminated her face. But that light was faded lately.

"Don't wear yourself out, okay? It will all be fine. I promise."

Merry nodded as we joined the others in the living room.

"You girls have fun stick-hunting in the woods," Ruth Anne said. "I think I'm going to watch Jeopardy reruns on my laptop."

"You have your knowledge wand. Maybe you should be a contestant?" I teased.

"Heck, I don't need a wand for that. Just the old noggin." She tapped her head. "Besides, I'm not sure this is a maple wand. I went out, asked the first tree I saw for a branch, and gave it a cookie in return." She grinned at the memory. "...And then I went back for my cookie."

"It's a maple wand, alright," Merry said, passing us on the way to the kitchen. "And if your smarty-pants wand really worked, you'd know that."

June Bug tugged on my shirt. "Grandma wants you again."

Sure enough, Mother called out from the staircase. "Magdalene, please come back up."

"Told ya," June Bug said.

"I'll save you a spot on the couch," Ruth Anne said.

I entered my mother's bedroom and sat on the edge of the bed, watching as she brushed her long, whisper-white hair in the vanity. I caught her reflection in the mirror, her pale blue eyes, a strip of red splashed across her lips, and small dots of rose blusher on her cheeks, not quite blended in.

"Magdalene," she said, swiveling her chair in my direction. "Do you know why I've always been so hard on you?"

"Because I'm not living up to my potential?" I guessed.

"No!" Her eyes blazed, the blueness swallowed up by the black pupils. She rolled her chair towards me, using her slippered feet to paddle across the room. She spoke, her breath smelling like gumdrops and coffee. "Because you're a fence sitter, just like your father!"

She pushed herself back a space, crossing her rail-thin arms as she studied my reaction.

"I don't know what that means," I confessed. "And why does everyone keep comparing me to my father? Merry and Eve are his daughters, too. Are they nothing like him? And what is so awful about Armand, anyway, that we keep using him as an example of what *not* to be like?"

It was a lot to ask at once, but the comparison to a man I didn't know was starting to weigh on me.

Mother took her cane and rapped me on the knee.

"Ouch!" I exclaimed. "What was that for?"

"Armand was a powerful warlock, but he was always...crossing the line." Her eyes settled on the oil painting of the man, the woman, and the horse. "When I first met him, he showed a lot of promise. You could see the energy around him sparkle, the way that water crackles on a river on a sunny day. He was practically blinding."

She half-closed her eyes, lost in her memories.

I understood what she meant. Michael had that same sort of energy; I noticed it the first time I saw him. I leaned forward to hear more.

"And charm. Boy, that man had charm. Could get any woman to do anything he wanted. Well," she added wryly. "Almost any woman.

"I came across him during one of my travels. He was younger than me, and a wilder, like you. Unable to control his powers. He was quick to anger and when he did, things happened. Machinery stopped or started. Floors rumbled. People clutched their chests, feeling like they'd had heart attacks..."

"*The deathtouch,*" I thought, my eyes widening.

"...He was dangerous out on his own, so I brought him to Dark Root where he could develop his abilities, to work on refining his powers, so to speak. He was one of the first to join The Council, and the only man."

Mother tapped her heels to the floor, the cushioning of her slippers thudding softly against the hardwood. "Dora warned me that having a warlock with such power around was dangerous. But if I didn't train him up, someone else would. We couldn't risk someone darker using his powers for their own gain. There was no other choice."

Her heels stopped tapping as she looked at me. "With training, he saw what he was capable of. Healing, growing, helping...in some ways he was the best in The Council. I've seen him bring back people that were beyond my realm of help. And he didn't even have a wand."

She pecked her head an inch forward.

"Magdalene, remember this: warlocks do not need wands. They need a witch to syphon power from. And he had a handful of them at his disposal.

"But it wasn't enough for him. His ego was strong and he grew restless, wanting something more. Something beyond Dark Root."

I felt empathy for my father as I recalled how desperately I, too, had wanted to leave Dark Root, but I kept my face expressionless.

"During that time," she continued. "We began to hear the prophecies: Nostradamus, Cayce, and your Aunt Dora. All powerful prophets predicting a cataclysmic end to things. There was a range of years, of course. Over a century, maybe longer if we were lucky. But a century, during the course of history, is but a moment. We abandoned our old lives and worked together to fight back the dark as best we could. If we could delay it, we reasoned, maybe we could change it."

Mother shook her head and slumped her shoulders.

"But Armand had other plans. He had grown in power, siphoning magic off the women, and wanted to embrace the darkness to come.

There was no stopping it, he'd argued, so why not ally with it? And when he insisted that we use our collective powers to..."

She stopped talking, her voice choking up.

"Summon demons," I said. I'd heard that story before. "He wanted to summon demons so that when the time came, they would be on his side, and not against him."

Mother inhaled deeply, her thin ribs expanding and collapsing. "Luckily he wasn't able to, at least while he was with us. But we *had* to make him leave, Magdalene. Him and all his followers, before they poisoned everyone. We cast a spells to keep them out, and others like them who wanted to abuse the magick of Dark Root."

"Couldn't he just practice elsewhere?"

"It's no secret that Juliana purposely chose Dark Root to practice her craft. The earth here is alive with electricity, and a witch's natural powers are increased here. Surely, you've felt it?"

I had. It was something I didn't notice in my childhood, as it had always been a part of me, but when I left, I felt my abilities depreciating, and I began to wonder if I had imagined them all along. But now that I was back, I felt the energy move throughout my body.

"Is this the only place?" I asked.

"No. There are spots all over the earth––if one knows where to look. And the ancients did, marking them with pillars and pyramids and stone. These regions form a grid across the globe. But Dark Root remained unmarked and only a local legend brought Juliana here. And the longer you are in one of these spots, the stronger you get. Armand spent a lot of time here. If he ever had a chance at summoning, it would be on this land." She drew in a long breath, her lungs whistling as she exhaled. "I never meant to keep him from you, but we couldn't take that risk. There is a rule in the craft, and that is: never summon that which you cannot be rid of. And a demon is pretty hard thing to be rid of."

I swallowed, thinking of Gahabrien buried in the back yard of Harvest Home.

True, I hadn't summoned him and he was a lesser demon.

Even so, he could cause trouble and he had never been successfully banished.

With the aid of her cane, Mother stood, her knees popping as she rose.

"That's why I've been so hard on you," she said. "You're so much like your father, always walking the line. And someone who walks the line, I'm sorry to say, is a liability. The one thing you have going for you, however, is that you are not a man."

"But I don't walk the line anymore," I said, standing to meet her. As a teenager we stood eye to eye, but now I towered over her by nearly a foot. "I'm on your side. Dark Root's side. Nothing's going to change that."

"Magdalene, you are going to be the target of many people who will want to use your abilities, like their own personal magic wand. And you're growing in strength, moving from the maiden stage into the mother stage of your cycle." Her eyes narrowed as they rested on my abdomen. "Only a crone is more powerful than the mother. And there are an abundance of crones who will be threatened by you. Take that as a warning."

"I won't cross any lines. You raised me. I'm not like my...I mean, Armand."

"I hope not. But sometimes we do terrible things for the best of reasons."

Six

Enter Sandman

T WASN'T THE SCRITCH-SCRATCHING SOUND OF THE BRANCHES OF THE GREAT oak tree that clawed their way back and forth across my bedroom window that woke me from my sleep on that cold November morning. Nor was it the steady drizzle of the rain as it pounded on the tightly-packed shingles of our Victorian home. It wasn't even the suffocating dream I'd been embroiled in, a half-mad montage of dark and light––my father's face merging with my own, twisting and turning, flipping and whirring, without rhyme nor reason.

Any of these things could have roused me from my sleep.

But the real reason I shot up, just before the break of dawn, when not even Aunt Dora prowled the house, was because I had the strangest feeling that I was being watched.

Pulling the sheet up to my chin, I gazed about my bedroom, scanning its corners and looking for shadows. The spaces where wall met wall were as dark as they needed to be, and not a shade more. I checked under the bed, lifting the bed skirt with utmost care, allowing my face to dip just beneath the frame.

There was nothing there but piles of dirty clothes.

Still...

I couldn't shake the feeling.

Tiptoeing to the window, I peeked through the curtains.

The glass was cold, covered in beads of precipitation that ran down its flimsy pane. Outside, I could make out the rough trunk of the oak tree and the moon, hanging on the horizon like a broken china plate.

I pulled the curtains fully open, chiding myself for being silly.

It was then that I noticed it: the large, black shape hunkering on one of the branches. It leaned forward when it saw me and spread its massive wings. The bird screeched, a sound so terrible it should have shattered the glass.

I fumbled backwards, tripping over a shoe on the floor.

"Aunt Dora!" I called out in panic. "Paul! Eve!"

The bird flew to the window, beating his wings and tearing its talons across the glass. It was trying to get in.

"Someone. Please! Help!"

"I don't see what all the fuss is about," Eve said as Paul scooped up the dead raven with a dustpan and the side of his shoe. "It's just a bird. We live in the woods, Maggie. You should be used to them by now."

"Not this one," I said shivering. Though I could see my breath in the cold, morning air, I wasn't shivering because it was cold. "This one wanted to get to me."

"Want me to bury it here?" Paul asked, presenting me with the carcass.

I shook my head.

If it were up to me, I'd have thrown the thing in the river, but Paul insisted that every living creature needed a proper burial, even the horrible ones.

"In that cluster of trees," I said, pointing to a spot near the side yard where I rarely ventured.

He took the raven and a small spade to the designated site.

"It was horrible," I said to Eve, recalling how the bird had beat itself to death on the window. "I've never seen anything like it."

"You need to get a hold of yourself." Eve's eyes followed Paul. "You're so jittery lately. And with all our other problems, a bird should be the least of your worries."

We watched as Paul dug the grave and buried the creature. When he returned he said, "Maggie's fear isn't irrational. It's part of the collective unconscious."

"The what?" Eve and I asked together.

"An information system passed down from generation to generation, almost like instinct. In many cultures ravens symbolize impending doom or even death."

Eve puckered her lips. "That doesn't bode well for us. Dark Root's full of the damned things."

"Ravens are also considered tricksters, masters of deceit and illusion." Paul's cobalt eyes flashed and he raised a finger. "Some say they are keepers of secrets, and not all of them good. So, in a word, Maggie should be worried, if she were the type to look for signs...which I think she is."

"Or," Eve said, handing Paul a small bottle of Purel from her purse. "He was a stupid bird who ate a bad worm."

"I don't know what to think," I said. "The last few days I've been seeing them everywhere. This one was just more aggressive. Maybe Paul is right."

"Ravens don't fly south for the winter," Eve pointed out. "Of course you're going to see them. I see them, too."

I pressed my palms together, wishing I could make Eve understand, but there was no getting through to her unless she experienced something for herself. "How do you know so much about ravens?" I asked Paul as he escorted us inside. "You a closet bird watcher?"

"Nope. Just always had a fascination with Poe after I saw a few old movies with Vincent Price."

"Poe? What's Poe?" Eve asked.

"Only the greatest horror writer, ever," he answered as he handed Eve her cashmere gloves.

They were heading to work and I was tempted to ride along so that I wouldn't have to be here alone. Aunt Dora was visiting Miss Rosa in the nursing home and I had no idea when she'd return.

"We weren't allowed to read Poe," I said, smiling at the irony. "Mother thought he was too scary."

"Well, you missed out. He was the Stephen King of his day."

"And he wrote about ravens? Sounds kind of dull, if you ask me." Eve brushed through her hair with her gloved fingers then checked her reflection in the living room mirror.

Paul nodded. "Listen to this...

"And the Raven, never flitting, still is sitting, still is sitting
On the pallid bust of Pallas just above my chamber door;
And his eyes have all the seeming of a demon that is dreaming,
And the lamp light o'er him streaming throws his shadow on the floor;
And my soul from out that shadow that lies floating on the floor
Shall be lifted-nevermore!"

He stopped his recitation and looked at his girlfriend, waiting for her to be as overcome by the poetry as he was.

"That doesn't sound spooky at all," she said.

"What? Are you kidding me? Maybe you didn't understand. The raven *says* Nevermore." When Eve still didn't respond he said, "It's scarier when you hear the whole thing."

"Is it long?" she asked.

"Yes."

"Then I don't need to hear it."

"I'm not sure I can love a woman who doesn't appreciate Edgar Allen Poe." Paul opened the front door and escorted her out. "That could be a deal breaker."

"I have other talents," she cooed.

"Yes. Lucky for you."

I suppressed a gag as I shut the door behind them. At least with Eve around, I didn't feel like the stupidest person in Dark Root. Unlike Ruth Anne and Merry, neither Eve nor myself had excelled in school. But at least Eve was comfortable with it. I grew increasingly uneasy at discovering all the things I didn't know.

I settled into Aunt Dora's recliner and flipped on the TV.

This house was as familiar and comfortable to me as my own house, maybe more so. This was the place where The Council conducted their meetings while we played hide and seek or made forts in the attic.

I noticed an open envelope on the end table beside me.

In dark red letters was the word *Urgent.*

I withdrew the letter. It was from tax office. The house was going up for sale, it said, unless past due property taxes of $13,589.00 were paid by the end of January.

I reread the letter, to be certain it was this house in question. It was. Miss Rosa, the home's owner, was in hospice care, and I knew she didn't have any money. Aunt Dora was also without income. That amount of money may as well be a million. This was huge news. Why had they kept this from us?

The TV sparked and died.

"Great," I said, trying unsuccessfully to turn it back on with the remote. Why couldn't I have useful powers, like turning things into gold? I covered myself with the crocheted afghan on the armrest, and closed my eyes, willing myself to sleep.

As I began to dream, the image of a raven filled my brain. It tilted its head, studying me, whispering...

"Nevermore."

"Maggie! Come quick girl!"

Aunt Dora's voice jolted me awake. I looked around, surprised to still find myself on the recliner.

"Maggie!"

I sprang from the chair and ran into the kitchen. Aunt Dora stood at the sink, standing on tiptoes as she pointed to a slender woman in a white dress, wandering our yard like a spirit.

"Who is she?" I asked, joining my aunt. There was an air of familiarity about her. A memory tugged at my brain as I took in her nest of dark, spiral curls, her pointed chin and nose, and her thin eyebrows that peaked over lash-less blue eyes.

My aunt placed her hand over mine. "A ghost."

The woman raised her eyes, a knowing smile on her ruby lips. She strode towards us, feet hardly seeming to touch the ground, and emerged at the kitchen door.

"How did ya get in?" Aunt Dora demanded, pulling open the kitchen door and talking to the woman through the screen. The woman stood a good foot taller, but my aunt was undaunted. "The spell should have kept ya out."

"Dora," the woman licked her lips. "What dark magick keeps you alive?"

"I could ask the same o' ya. Yer supposed ta be dead."

I moved protectively in front of my aunt, ready to act if needed.

The woman's pale eyes glimmered. "So this is the promising young witch. Maggie, we finally meet."

Aunt Dora raised her index fingers into the sign of a cross. "Get out, witch! We want nothing o' ya here."

"You are amusing, Dora." The woman threw her head back and laughed. "Finger crosses? Really? I suppose next you'll be telling me that you've sprinkled sea salt in the doorway to prevent me from coming in."

The woman pulled open the screen door.

Aunt Dora took a step back, pulling me with her, as the woman advanced inside.

"See," she purred, her right foot hitting the linoleum. "I think you're getting a bit rust...Arrrrrrr!"

The woman screamed, retreating backwards.

"I've still got plenty left in me," Aunt Dora said, shaking a fist. "An' don't ya forget it."

The woman balled her hands up into fists at her side. "You can't keep me out forever, Dora, no matter what magic you employ. When you lose this house I intend to make it mine."

"Who are you?" I demanded. "And what do you want?"

"Who am I?" Her eyes widened with incredulity. "Who am I? Leah said you were a simpleton but I hadn't thought you this hopeless."

"Larinda," I said as the memory came to me. I was six or seven, riding atop a float at the Haunted Dark Root Festival. Larinda appeared in the crowd. She had frightened me then. She didn't frighten me now.

"Maggie, don't talk ta her," my aunt warned. "She's darkness and lies."

"Now, now Dora," the woman puckered her lips thoughtfully. "I know we've had our differences, but the veil grows thin. Perhaps it's time to put our differences aside and ally."

"I'll never ally with the likes of ya. I'm getting my broom!" Aunt Dora bounded for the living room, opening and closing closets and drawers.

"You don't really want to buy this house," I said. Though she was taller than my aunt I stood eye to eye with her. I raised my chin to give me the illusion of extra height. "You're here for the Circle."

At the word *circle* one of Larinda's eyebrows shot up into an even more pronounced arch. She quickly composed herself. "That old thing? I'm betting it's been lost for years." Her eyes met mine, searching for affirmation.

I ignored the urge to look at the crystal bracelet I had taken from Mother in her hospital room. At that time, I had thought the Circle to be a metaphor rather than an actual artifact. The bracelet throbbed against my wrist, emitting a soft vibration I desperately hoped Larinda didn't detect. I blinked but held my face expressionless.

"If you must know," she said, her lips shiny with spittle. "I'm after a much bigger prize than the Circle or the house."

"What's that?"

Aunt Dora burst into the kitchen wielding a straw broom half her height. "By dark o' night an' light o' day, take this stranger far away!" She brandished the broom at the door. "Get, witch!"

Larinda backed away, her eyes hateful. "My cousin can't save you forever, Dora. There's only so much protection left in the world, and day by day, it's dying." Then she turned to me. "Maggie. Find me."

She slipped back into the mists, disappearing into the woods behind her.

"Should we go after her?" I asked. Beads of perspiration dotted my aunt's forehead and I helped her to a chair. She handed me the broom and I could still feel her energy coursing through it. "No. She's gone fer now. We swept out the riff-raff, Maggie."

"You did." I stared in wonder at my aunt. "What was it that kept her from entering the house?"

Aunt Dora wiped her brow with the back of her fleshy arm. "That was just something I put out ta keep the slugs away."

I chuckled, trying to return my heart rate to normal. "She told me she wasn't after this house or the Circle. What do you think she wanted?"

Aunt Dora lifted her round face and lowered her eyes. "It's best ya stay away from that woman. The devil can't get in unless ya invite her."

With that, I knew the conversation was closed.

A large black bird appeared in the yard scratching and pecking at the ground.

I shuddered, remembering my encounter with the raven early that morning. It flew away, and I was about to shut the door when I noticed something else in the dirt where the bird had been standing: long marks that, at this distance, resembled words etched in the earth.

I stepped outside, moving towards the spot.

Sure enough, in the dirt someone had carved out the words: 123 Old Raven Rd.

SEVEN

FULL MOON, EMPTY HEART

The Woods Outside of Dark Root
November, 2013

THE MOON WAS NEARLY FULL AS MY SISTERS AND I SHIVERED BENEATH THE carcass of an old, bare tree. The air smelled moldy and rotten, like meat that had been left out on the counter overnight. An owl hooted in the distance and I clenched my teeth, determined not to prove correct Eve's theory that I was scared of everything.

Ruth Anne aimed her flashlight at the earth, scouring the ground beneath the tree. Merry glanced up from time to time, searching the skies for birds or bats. And Eve complained about the chill and how she would have worn a thicker jacket, had someone warned her that we would be out grave-digging this evening.

"We aren't grave-digging," I informed her. "We are searching for mandrake. And I can't help that Aunt Dora made us find it tonight."

Ruth Anne discovered a clump of grass and dirt near the north side of the tree and we followed the beam of her light. She kicked at the spot and shook her head. "Negative."

"No offense, Ruth Anne," Merry said gingerly. "But have you ever actually *seen* mandrake?"

"Only in books."

"Then allow me." Without asking, Merry took the flashlight and crouched, checking the ground more deliberately. After several cold minutes she squealed, "I found something!" Then, looking to Ruth Anne she asked, "What do you think?"

It was an innocuous-looking leafy, green plant centered by purple flowers. Ruth Anne pulled out a folded piece of paper from her front jeans pocket and checked it against Merry's discovery. "Looks like the picture."

Eve took out her cell phone and began pressing buttons. "I'll bet there's an app for that, something that lets you take a picture of a plant and then confirm it against a database."

"Highly doubtful," Merry said. "But that would be a good idea. Would make my job so much easier. Maybe you could invent it, Eve." Merry looked at me over her shoulder. "Maggie, are you ready?"

I nodded, peeling off the leather gloves Aunt Dora had forced upon me. My fingers tingled with blue goo in the moonlight. "I hope this works."

"Don't worry," Merry stood, holding the flashlight steady while giving me a comforting smile. "If anyone knows her protection spells, it's Aunt Dora."

It was dangerous for a human––especially a witch––to come into contact with mandrake with their bare skin. Before we left the house, Aunt Dora had rubbed some ointment on my hands as she cast her protection spell, instructing me to keep the gloves on until right before I yanked the root from the ground.

"In the old days, witches had dogs do this," Ruth Anne said as she drew a small circle around the plant with the tip of her still unfinished wand. "They'd starve them for days, then throw some meat on the plant, letting the dogs fetch it out. If the root didn't kill the dogs, the owners would afterward."

"That's horrible!" Merry said. "I could never..."

"Me either," I agreed. "No wonder witches were considered evil in the old days."

Ruth Anne drew a second circle around the first as she continued to educate us. "That wasn't all witches, of course. But the ones who did shit like that certainly lent credence to the 'witches as evil' idea. Nice women, they say, never make the history books."

The temperature dropped rapidly and Eve and I hopped in place, trying to get warm. Steam rose up from the ground, like ghosts in a graveyard.

"I just want to get this done and get out of here," Eve said.

Ruth Anne's lips turned up at one corner. "But Eve, you need to do the dance."

"Dance?" Eve blew into her cupped hands. "What dance?"

"The dance of love," Merry teased, her eyes sparkling. "Put that new wand to use."

Merry and Eve had been out collecting branches for their wands earlier that day. Merry had found an ash wand to aid in protection and healing, and Eve had settled on a hawthorn wand to assist her in divination, glamour, and love spells. "But I haven't prepared it yet," Eve objected. "Right now, it's just a stick."

"The *love* stick," I teased, enjoying the chance to torment her a little. "Besides, I don't think it matters if it's prepared or not. Magick is all about belief. Do you believe in your wand, Eve?" I tried to keep the smile off my face.

"I believe we need to finish this before I turn into a popsicle," she answered.

Ruth Anne traced the third and final circle around the mandrake plant. "At least Aunt Dora didn't expect us to find the mandrake underneath a body or a hanging tree. Another tradition that luckily didn't carry over from the dark days. Like Tupperware parties."

We all laughed, except for Eve, who continued to complain about her impending dance.

Then, when Ruth Anne's circle had been drawn, a moment of somberness fell on us all. We had heard the horror stories associated with the plant, that while it was used for exorcisms and the prevention of evil, it could also absorb the evil of the energy around it, which was why it was feared, and why it had to be cultivated so carefully.

Merry waved her wand above the plant, banishing all negative energies from the root.

"I wish it was me picking this," Ruth Anne said, taking a deep breath and a step back.

"Yeah, me too," I said.

Aunt Dora had been in such a hurry to get the herb after our earlier encounter with Larinda that she slathered my hands in oils and then called my sisters before we could object.

"Now how do I dance?" Eve asked, a hand on her hip.

"Aunt Dora says to move around the outer circle, feeling the wind, whatever that means," I answered. "Just pretend you're doing interpretive dance in one of those artsy theater's you used to perform at."

"Funny," she said, lifting her stick in a threatening manner. "I've got a wand, and I know how to use it."

"Hey, if you want to trade," I said, raising my glowing blue hands. "I'm more than happy to let you take over the Chernobyl portion of this adventure."

"It's okay," Eve responded as she looked at my hands.

I inhaled, letting it out slowly. Billows of steam rolled from my mouth. "Everyone got their earplugs?"

We had been instructed that everyone except me needed to cover their ears to ward against the sounds the mandrake would emit once plucked from his spot.

"It's terrible," Aunt Dora explained, "like a dozen children screaming for their mothers."

I wished that I had ear plugs, too, but Aunt Dora said I needed to hear its cries in order for it to work. "Real magic comes with sacrifice, and there is no greater sacrifice than a small piece of your soul."

My sisters inserted their plugs as I made my way towards the center of the innermost circle. With each ring I passed, the air grew damper, stiller, and colder. I nodded to Eve and she took her wand, waved it overhead, and flitted about the outer rings. She dipped and swayed, asking the moon to look down on us with love.

I watched, transfixed as the moon kissed the tips of Eve's blue-black hair, sending star shards to the ground. Her delicate features were more pronounced in the night, her round chin and small nose lifted to the sky. She cast her wand into the Heavens, asking the Universe to pour down its love. If Merry was an angel, Eve was an elf. Eternal, ethereal, yet of this earth.

Ruth Anne coughed, breaking me from my sister's spell.

I stooped to the ground, plunging a spade into the compact dirt around the mandrake.

"I'm sorry to take you from your home," I said, as I chipped away the dirt. When the top of the root was fully uncovered I held my breath, my hands wrapping around the thick round clump.

"Pull, Maggie, pull," Merry's whispered, as she and Ruth Anne watched from the safety outside the circles. Eve continued her dance, lost in her salute to the moon.

I tugged, my hands slippery from the ointments, fighting the plant that desperately wanted to stay. I was about to give up when I felt it release its tethers.

It screamed its unearthly sorrows into the night.

I almost let it go as it let out the horrendous yowl, but I tightened my grip and continued to pull, toppling backwards with my trophy. As I stood up, I felt it squirm in my hands. Aunt Dora had warned me not to gaze upon it once it had been pulled, but something with a cry so horrible and human could not be ignored.

The root divided itself, growing in five directions in the shape of a starfish. The top was rounded like an oblong head and the remaining four divisions were long and twisted, like the broken arms and legs of a person. I looked closer. The node at the top seemed to wriggle, a small gape intermittently screaming then opening and shutting like the mouth of a newborn looking to suckle.

Dear God, what is this?

I clamped my hand around it, squeezing the breath from the root until the screaming ceased.

When it was quiet, I dropped to my knees.

Ruth Anne and Merry removed their earplugs and rushed towards me while Eve continued her dance. I opened my hand and gazed again at the mandrake.

"No, Maggie!" Merry called, putting out an arm to stop me.

But it was too late. The thing that had been screaming with pain moments before lay lifeless in my palms. I studied it, remembering where I had seen the face before.

The morning I had my vision on the front porch of Harvest Home. I handed it over to Ruth Anne who waited with an open box.

"My baby," I said, crying.

I sat in the backseat of Merry's sedan, wiping the blue goo off of my hands on one of Eve's scarves when she wasn't looking, trying to erase not only the blue ointment, but the memory of the event as well.

Merry peered over the steering wheel, trying to make out the road ahead of us while Eve hung her head out the window, navigating from the back seat next to me.

"Squirrel!" Eve called out. Merry twisted the wheel, avoiding the animal. "Deer!"

"Darn it, Eve. That wasn't a deer. It was a tree. And it wasn't in the middle of the road."

"Well, it's dark. What do you expect?"

Ruth Anne lounged in the front passenger seat, her bare feet resting on the dashboard.

She wore her ever-amused smile as she watched the scene but said nothing.

In the trunk, entombed in an old shoebox, the mandrake root slept.

I strained my ears to hear if it still cried, but all was silent except for the constant chatter of my sisters.

"It really didn't move," Merry said, trying once again to reassure me once we reached an area where the forest opened up and the moon could guide us. "It was a figment of your imagination. The madness of the root must have gotten through all the protection we had on you. That's good. It means the root is potent."

I cracked my window, not wanting to argue. I had felt it wriggle in my hands, floundering as it took its last breath, and no amount of rationale would change that.

"It occurs to me," Ruth Anne said, twisting her head to see us all. "That I've never had a beer with my sisters. What do you think?"

"I'm down," Eve said, as we hit the outskirts of Dark Root proper.

"You are?" I asked. "You mean you aren't going to see Paul now?"

All Eve's free time was spent with him lately. But now that I thought about it, she hadn't mentioned him all evening.

"Yes. I'd really like a beer. Or two."

"Want to call Paul?" I asked. "Let him know where you are?"

"Not really."

"Oh?"

Merry's eyes flickered in the rear view mirror. Ruth Anne removed a small notebook from her T-shirt pocket and gave Eve her full attention.

"Details," said Ruth Anne. "I need some conflict for my next book."

"Fine," Eve said, putting lotion on her hands. "I found several texts from a woman on his phone today. A woman he used to date."

"Ooh, that's good." Ruth Anne scribbled in her pad.

"I'm glad it's helpful. Maybe you could follow us around with a video camera and capture all the details."

"Sorry. Just have the pen and paper. Continue."

"I think you're worked up over nothing," I said. "So what if Paul texted his ex? He's smitten with *you*."

"Maggie," Eve said, turning her dark eyes on me. "What would you do if you found Shane texting a woman?"

"She'd lose her frickin mind," Merry said and Ruth Anne laughed.

"Maybe," I admitted, feeling a stab of jealousy at just the thought.

"You'd probably burn down his restaurant." Eve lowered her lashes, her face pensive. "I'm just trying to play it cool for now."

"Good luck with that," I said. With the exception of our mother, Eve was the most dramatic person I'd ever known. Playing it cool was not her style.

"So," Ruth Anne broke in. "That's two of us for a beer. Merry?"

Merry shrugged. "I suppose I can leave June Bug with Mama for awhile longer. They're probably both asleep, anyways. God knows I could use a bit of me time right now." She looked at me in the mirror. "Maybe I can ask Shane to look in on them in a bit. If that's okay with you?"

"Why would I care?" I asked, trying to play it cool myself.

"Well, maybe you'd want him to join us, instead."

"Let's make it a girl's night," I said, so that I wouldn't have to explain once again why I was avoiding Shane––especially when Ruth Anne was taking notes. "Even if I can't drink, it will be fun."

"Then it's unanimous," Ruth Anne put on her Birkenstocks as the sedan rumbled into the rocky parking lot of the only bar in Dark Root. "Ladies, let's have ourselves a little fun."

The bar sat on the far edge of town, out past the row of boarded-up, one-room shacks where lumberjacks and trappers had kept house in Dark Root's pioneering days. The bar itself had once served as an old saloon, and it was rumored that a shootout had even taken place there, when two drunken miners, acting on a hunch that they might find gold in this part of the world––and subsequently being disappointed–– drew pistols at each other and fired several rounds.

Luckily, both missed, but it helped fuel the bar's reputation as a *historical site* and it was never torn down thereafter.

In the 1950s, a man from Los Angeles purchased it, and while he kept the original frame of the building, he had redone the interior, adding in a jukebox and a secret casino in the back room. The place had been revamped several times since by several different owners, who all learned there wasn't a ton of money to be made in this neck of the woods, even in alcohol. It stood like a time machine now, incorporating every generation it had devoured in its decor.

Ruth Anne told us the bar's history as Merry parked the car.

"Do you know everything?" Eve asked, yawning.

"I make it a point to know where my beer comes from," Ruth Anne said, running her fingers through her chin-length brown hair.

"The Watering Hole?" Merry read the sign, scratching her head.

In our teenage years it was called *The Screaming Sasquatch,* a ploy to draw in tourists when it was rumored that Big Foot had been spotted several miles outside of town.

"When did the name change, Miss Smarty Pants?" Merry asked.

"Beats me, but I like it." Ruth Anne pushed open the bar door and we followed her inside.

"I wonder if Mother hung out here in her glory days," I mused, spying a picture of Stevie Nicks right next to an old photo of Elvis serenading a love-struck teenager.

My eyes darted quickly to Eve. Paul adored Elvis.

She gritted her teeth and stormed towards the counter.

"Three light beers." She looked at me. "And a diet ginger ale for the redhead."

"Hey, don't order for me. I don't like ginger ale." I turned to the bartender, a weathered man who had as many lines on his face as he had years. "I'll take a root beer."

"Way to show her, Maggie." Ruth Anne sniggered and took her drink.

I sipped my root beer and found a seat. "It's the principle."

We sat in a line of reupholstered bar stools, quietly taking in our surroundings.

There were a few others inside, a couple arguing in a corner near the bathroom, two men playing a game of pool, and an older woman with long gray hair dancing alone by the jukebox. It was a depressing scene, made even sadder by the fact that my sisters were getting drunk while I remained miserably sober. With each sip they became more talkative, revealing details about the condition of their lives.

"June Bug's been calling Frank, filling him in on what's going on in *our* family," Merry said, sloshing beer from her mug. "Then he calls me, screaming that he wants custody. Claims there's not a court in the world who would side with a mother who's a *practicing witch.*"

"I'd like to practice on him," Eve said.

"We'll testify in court on your behalf," I said. "Don't worry."

"Um, thanks." Merry's face went a shade paler.

"Don't worry." I winked. "We'll leave the black hats and brooms at home."

"I think Paul is bored with me," Eve said, after another drink and an appropriate pause.

"What makes you say that?" Ruth Anne asked, once again going for her notebook.

Eve gave her a threatening glare that Ruth Anne ignored. "He looks at magazines with women in bikinis."

"So do you," I pointed out.

"Maybe I'm bored with me." Eve slapped her hand on the counter. "Nope. Couldn't be. I mean, look at me." She jutted her chest out and the bartender gave her an approving, toothless smile.

"Wanna see something cool?" Ruth Anne put down her notebook and dug into the pocket of her baggy jeans, producing a little metal gadget, slightly larger than a cell phone. "This may be annoying," she explained. "But stay with me a minute."

Ruth Anne hopped down from her stool and tapped a button on the top of the device. A series of beeps and whistles sounded as she waved it around. The beeps ranged from barely audible to ear splittingly loud, but they never stopped.

"What is that thing?" I asked, covering my ears.

"An electromagnetic field reader, or EMF for short. Ghost hunters use them to detect areas where there may be paranormal activity. The theory goes that spirits omit a higher level of electrical frequency, so this little baby can help you find yourself a ghost."

She ran the device over me and it beeped so loudly and rapidly she had to shut it off. Merry and Eve pounded their fists on the bar, laughing so hard they spit out their drinks.

"Maybe Maggie's a ghost," Merry said, dabbing her eyes with a napkin.

"That would explain her love of wearing sacks," Eve agreed.

"Ghosts wear sheets, not sacks," I corrected her. "Hey..."

"It hasn't stopped bleeping since I came to Dark Root," Ruth Anne said, giving the device one last look before returning it to her pocket. "I keep it mostly shut off now." She returned to her stool and summoned the bartender. After ordering another round she said, "I've never seen anything like it, not even in New Orleans. And that place is filled with ghoulies."

Ruth Anne talked about some of the places she had been to and how the EMF reader reacted to each location. Merry and Eve grew bored with the conversation and began discussing a steamy book they had both read that was being made into a movie.

"Will you write about Dark Root? In your next book?" I asked Ruth Anne, nursing what was left of my soda.

She shrugged. "Dunno. But if I do, I will call it by a different name. I kind of like keeping this place our little secret. It's funny. I spent my early years trying to get out of here, and now I'm in no hurry to leave."

"I understand," I said, having had a similar revelation.

Dark Root was a part of us, whether we liked it or not.

Merry and Eve toppled from their barstools and stumbled to the nearest vacant pool table. Ruth Anne and I swiveled our stools to watch them.

"You know," I admitted, as Ruth Anne leaned back, her arms

stretched out across the counter. "I never expected to see you again." I felt myself choke at the words so I took another sip. "I thought you were gone forever."

"Me too," she said, the left corner of her mouth turning up. "I shouldn't have left you girls like that. Not when Miss Sasha was well on the road to crazy town. But I just couldn't take it. And when I found out who my dad was, some normal guy named Burt who sold cars in the South, I had to take that chance." She removed her glasses and wiped them on the hem of her shirt. "And until I got that call from Shane, I didn't think I was wanted back."

She tilted her head to me. There was no smirk on her face or any sign of her usual sarcasm.

"He's a good guy, Maggie. The kind of guy people love to read about. Don't screw it up."

Too late.

Eve and Merry racked up the pool balls, debating who the better player was.

"Just because you lived in New York, doesn't mean you have game," Merry said, grabbing a stick from a rack on the wall.

Eve measured her own stick against her height, frowned, and then tried another. "I'm warning you, I spent my weekends at the best nightclubs." She pulled her long hair into a ponytail as she sized up the table. "How do you think I paid my rent half the time?"

"Oh, is that how?" Merry's eyes rested on Eve's chest.

"Were all the pool tables in Kansas made of straw?" Eve retorted.

"Yes, and hay."

"Peas in a pod," Ruth Anne said.

I nodded, feeling that familiar wave of jealousy I had whenever Merry and Eve seemed too cozy.

It was a fairly even match, until Eve decided to show off. "Seven ball in the far left corner," she declared, sending the ball zooming across the table and into its called pocket.

Merry returned to us, ordered another beer, then stumbled back to the table, all the while muttering that she never should have taken up a game with a *ball expert* like Eve.

"You hold your liquor well," I said to Ruth Anne, who matched my sisters, drink for drink, but hadn't shown any signs of inebriation.

"I started drinking early."

"Before we picked you up?"

"No. In life."

"Oh."

There was a lot I didn't about Ruth Anne's lost years, a lot I might never know. I put my head on her shoulder, content to just sit in her presence, both of us watching the game that Eve was about to win.

"Too bad Eve can't let Merry have this one," I said.

Merry didn't have much, and asked for even less. But Eve was not the type who would back down from a win.

"Five bucks says you can't make her miss," Ruth Anne whispered as Eve lined up her next shot.

It was an easy shot that even I could make, but, with a little nudge to the left the ball would miss the hole completely and Merry might have a chance at a comeback.

"I'm not sure I can," I said, as Eve bent over the table.

"Well, if you want Eve to win and gloat all the way home..."

I took a deep breath and straightened my back, focusing my attention on the stick in Eve's hand as she slid it between her nimble fingers. As she aimed it towards the cue ball, I closed my eyes, imagining Eve hitting the side of the ball instead of the center.

"What the...?" Eve asked incredulously, and I opened my eyes. The cue ball spiraled towards one of Merry's balls, knocking it in instead. Eve scratched her head as Merry did a victory whoop.

"Nice." Ruth Anne said, slipping me the five.

"They teach you that in New York?" Merry taunted Eve, bouncing her way around the table, nailing her next shot. She followed it up by running two more, before finally missing the fourth.

"Right corner pocket," Eve said confidently as she leaned across the table, causing a group of men who had just walked in behind her to stop and stare.

Ruth Anne grinned at me.

Eve's ball rolled towards its destination, stopping shy of the pocket. It teetered on the edge of the hole, half in, half out. A strong breath could have sunk it. It wobbled for a moment, before pulling back, just a hair, but enough to keep it anchored on the table.

"Subtle," Ruth Anne said. We laughed as Eve's face reddened. She ran her hands over the table to check for "bumps" and "abnormalities."

Merry squealed, looking so much like her younger self that I half expected to see her pirouette in a tutu. She skipped around the table, ready to take her final shot, a look of determination in her sky blue eyes.

She made it. I didn't even help with that one.

"I won?" Merry raised her stick and threw her head back, her long, cottony hair grazing her waist. "Roar!" The men who'd been watching Eve switched their attention and clapped for Merry instead.

Eve, still looking confused, dumped her stick on the table and escorted Merry back to the bar.

"Did you see that?" Merry asked, her cheeks flushed and pretty.

"Yes, we did," I answered.

"I have no idea how I did it!"

I felt a little sorry for Eve and I gave her an apologetic look. Her eyes widened with understanding.

"Yep, you won fair and square," Eve said, putting an arm around Merry, more generous now that she realized it wasn't her own lack of skill that had cost her the game. "And, winner buys the next round."

"Ah, I wish. You're the one with the job." Merry plopped herself onto her stool, her legs not quite reaching the floor. "I'm just Mama's caretaker. I get paid in canned goods and copies of old *National Geographics*."

"That's more than I make," Eve said. "Every cent that comes in, goes right out as soon as I get it. How we'll get through this year is beyond me."

94

They looked at me. "Maggie?"

"I have exactly three hundred and twelve dollars left to my name." I had counted it out that very morning. "I don't know the price of baby food and diapers, but something tells me it won't last long. Plus..."

I didn't finish the sentence.

But *plus* the fact that Eve, Aunt Dora, the baby, and myself would be forced to move in with them at Sister House if we couldn't pay the property taxes on Harvest Home.

We stared at the empty glasses in our hands.

"You guys are bumming me out," Ruth Anne said, pulling out a wallet. "Barkeep, another round."

I marveled at the wad of money in her hand. "It's good to know that someone in our family is doing well," I said, as I was handed my fourth root beer of the evening.

"Novel writing doesn't pay much, especially when you have writer's block. But it keeps me in beer."

We raised our drinks in a toast to poverty, then giggled ourselves silly as we brainstormed ways to make money––selling Merry's hair, renting Eve out as a parade balloon, ebaying Ruth Anne's eggs that she swore she'd never use anyways––when a sight on the other side of the bar caught my eye.

Two men finished up their game of pool. The shorter man peeled five bills from a money clip and handed them to his acquaintance.

My heart raced with excitement. I reached for Eve and squeezed her hand.

"Ouch," she said, pulling away from me. "What was that for?"

I nudged my chin at the scene. She nodded slowly.

Maybe there was a way to make money in a small town like Dark Root, after all.

EIGHT

BULDING A MYSTERY

G ATHER CLOSE GIRLS. HURRY!"

Aunt Dora stood on the back porch wearing nothing but her nightdress and house slippers to guard against the cruel November winds. Her cotton dress flapped about her like a broken-winged bird but she paid it no heed as she wrestled with a mason jar, working the lid like an expert safe cracker.

She sniffed the air and with flaring nostrils announced, "I can smell Larinda on the wind. Like sour milk."

"But the moon isn't right," I said.

The protection spell Aunt Dora intended to invoke, a spell meant to keep Larinda off of our property, was meant to be cast during a waxing moon, which was still days away.

"Fer someone who doesn't work the craft, ya sure seem ta know a lot." She looked up, watching the twilight sun disappear behind the western tree line. "The spell won't be as strong, but it will put a dent in her powers, that's fer sure."

Merry wiped her hands on her teal wool sweater, and pushed her hair out of her face. Her lips were full and red, the result of wind and dirt that lashed at our faces. Her eyes were intent as she took mental notes, her head cocked as she strained to listen to Aunt Dora's directions muddled by the howling gales.

"Show us how to do it, Aunt Dora, and we will take care of Sister House next."

"Aye," Aunt Dora pulled a bitter smelling powder from the mason jar. "Put this on yer wands."

My sisters slathered their wands.

June Bug held up a pretend wand she had crafted herself and Aunt Dora added a bit of salve to it, as well. Seeing me empty-handed, Eve tried to kick a stick in my direction, but not before being caught by my all-seeing aunt.

"Still haven't chosen yers, I see."

"No," I said, looking down.

"Magic flows through ya more easily than the rest. But, if someone were ta ask me who the most promising o' the bunch was now, I wouldn't say ya. I'd say Merry. Ya could take a lesson from her." Merry's face flushed and she lowered her eyes, pretending not to hear.

Aunt Dora grabbed both my hands and wiped the powder across my palms. "One o' the reasons we have wands is so we don't have to put this on our bodies. Smells awful and takes hours ta wash off."

"Great," I said, as June Bug held her nose. "What's in this stuff?"

"Mandrake root, o' course, an' garlic, sage, beetle antenna..."

"What?" June Bug's mouth opened with disgust.

"Sorry love. That's the recipe."

Merry patted the top of June Bug's pink beanie with her gloved hand.

"Follow me."

We filed into a line behind my aunt, marching around the house in a giant, crooked circle. Aunt Dora chanted as she went.

"What's she saying?" June Bug asked.

"I think it's Hopi," Ruth Anne said. "She's asking for protection for the house and its inhabitants.

"I didn't know you spoke Hopi," I said, trying to match Aunt Dora's foot patterns as we completed our second revolution.

As we chanted and danced about our house I was reminded of the image of Max in *Where the Wild Things Are* as he participated in the wild rumpus.

"I *don't* speak Hopi." Ruth Anne held up her wand and gazed at it with knitted brows.

"'Tis done," Aunt Dora announced, coming to a stop in front of the back door as we completed the third circle. "We'll do the full ritual during the Solstice. This should hopefully keep her out till then." She leaned forward on her cane. "Doesn't mean we are safe yet. Watch yerselves. She's tricky."

Aunt Dora returned to the house, the wind slamming the back door behind her.

"Well, that was fun," Eve said. She pulled bits of leaves out of her hair. "Why does witchcraft have to be so dirty? And take so long?"

"When I take over," I said. "The first order of business will be to banish the three R's: Rituals, Rules, and Red Tape."

"Leave it to Maggie to half-ass witchcraft," Ruth Anne said, holding out her wand like a sword. The rising moon cast a mischievous glint in her eye.

Merry responded by holding out her own branch and the two engaged in a mock duel. I joined them, using my smudged finger. Only Eve held back.

"Afraid Eve?" I asked, clucking at her like a chicken.

She rolled her eyes. "I just don't want to get too close to you. You stink."

With my attention diverted, Merry went in for a killing blow. I crumbled to the ground in mock death.

June Bug ran to my rescue on the ground. "She's right, Aunt Maggie. You do stink. Is it your hands or the sweater? I can't tell."

Ruth Anne helped me up as Eve stepped forward.

"Let's see if this thing works," Eve said, tapping me on the shoulder with her wand. Flecks of green silver dust sparked out of the wand, like fireflies searching for home.

"Ooh!" June Bug said clapping.

Even in the dim evening light, I could see that my ivory, alpaca sweater appeared brighter.

June Bug sniffed me again. "You smell better!"

"Guess it works," Eve said. I inspected my hands. The powder had been erased too. Ruth Anne and Merry's mouths fell open and we followed Eve, up the back porch steps and into the kitchen, who seemed to take the whole thing in stride.

"What do you think Larinda wants?" I asked, as we gathered in the kitchen with Aunt Dora and prepared for dinner.

"Many things," Aunt Dora responded, stirring a pot as Eve and Merry added chopped vegetables and herbs to a boiling cauldron. Ruth Anne sat at the table with June Bug, helping her sound out the words to a book she was reading.

"What sorts of things?" Merry asked. She had unloosened her hair from its earlier pony tail and it hung down around her shoulders, like strands of fine, ivory ribbon.

"This house, maybe. It still holds residual magick from the days when the coven used it ta gather. And residual magick is still powerful, if ya know how to use it." Aunt Dora gave the soup a final stir and tapped the spoon on the side of the pot.

She closed her eyes and thought on the subject some more. "Or yer Circle, Maggie, even though she claims she doesn't. Or yer mother's spell book." Aunt Dora opened her eyes and wiped her hands on her apron. "Or even one of ya girls."

"Well, she can't have me," June Bug said, looking up from her book. "I'm staying with Mommy."

"Don't worry, hon," Merry said. "We took care of her and she won't be back."

"Don't go tellin' her that!" Aunt Dora said "It's good fer her ta be scared. It's good fer all of us ta be scared. Fear keeps ya on yer toes.

"Ya teach yer kids not ta talk to strangers, ta look before crossin' the street. It's the same thing. And Larinda, in particular, is someone we need ta be afraid of. The only witch capable of matchin' her was yer mother, and since she went an' got old..."

Aunt Dora shook her head, returned to her pot, stirring it unnecessarily fast.

"You said Larinda's specialty is illusion," I said. "What's Mother's?"

Aunt Dora's eyes narrowed. "Yer mother had the gift of healin'."

"Like Mommy!" June Bug said, beaming at Merry.

"Yes, like yer mother, but––pardon me, Merry, fer this––much bigger. An' it wore her out. She had ta stop or she would have ended up like poor Cayce."

"Cayce?" I asked.

Ruth Anne looked up and adjusted her glasses. "Edgar Cayce. A reported psychic in the early- to mid-part of the twentieth century. He predicted lots of things, some of which have come to pass, although there has been no conclusive proof..."

I halted my sister before she spewed out an entire encyclopedia of worthless knowledge. "What does that have to do with Mother?"

Ruth Anne raised an eyebrow. "Like Sasha, he was also a great healer. Could diagnose people's illness in his sleep. As a result, people came from miles away to get 'treated.' Uncle Joe had lots of books on him." She gave me a smug look then returned to her work with June Bug.

"Aye," Aunt Dora said. "An' his compassion took its toll, especially during the war. Drained him of his own life force." She allowed a heavy, sorrow-filled sigh to escape as she slumped her shoulders forward. "Same thing happened with yer mother, even with the wand. Ya can't spare one life and not another. Eventually it tapped her out. Power comes at a price."

It was strange, picturing my mother as compassionate healer and not the flamboyant show-woman of my youth. I tucked my hair behind my ears as I contemplated this.

101

"Maybe Larinda wants Grandma's wand," June Bug said.

Aunt Dora shook her head. "A witch only gets one wand and Larinda has hers. Besides, a wand has limited uses, and yer grandma's was about used up. A good reason not to squander it on useless things."

"Too bad they don't have on and off switches," Eve said, tapping hers into her palm. The ruby gem embedded at the end flickered and glowed with each flip of the wrist. "Or run on batteries."

"Yeah, you'd never have to do laundry again," Merry said.

Aunt Dora yanked the wand from Eve. "Stop that! Yer going to use it up before ya even figure it out."

NINE

KARMA POLICE

Sister House
April, 1994
Dark Root, Oregon

"WHAT'S WRONG WITH HER?" EVE ASKED, POKING A FINGER INTO HER mother's fleshy arm.

Miss Sasha lay draped over the ornate red sofa, not stirring an inch as the girls prodded her and poked her. The clock by the front door announced that it was four in the afternoon. A full twenty-four hours had passed since they had found her in this situation.

"Well, she's not dead or drunk," Ruth Anne answered, checking her mother's pulse and breath. "She smells like salami and coffee, but not wine. And she has a heartbeat."

Merry laid her head on her mother's chest. "She's been sleeping so long. I keep giving her my energy but it's not working."

"Stop wasting it on her, Merry!" Maggie scolded, marching to the phone in the dining room wall. "You'll only make yourself sick, too."

As her sisters continued to hold vigil, Maggie dialed her Aunt Dora's number. It wasn't just this episode that worried them. Miss Sasha had been losing weight, called the girls by their wrong names, and kept forgetting important events. And yesterday, while watching a sitcom—another strange thing for her to do—she had fallen over sideways on the couch and went to sleep.

Maggie explained this all to her aunt who said, "I'm comin' over!"

Within minutes, Aunt Dora's heavy footsteps were heard outside. She burst through the door like a no-nonsense angel of mercy.

"She's sick," Merry said. "We've tried everything."

Aunt Dora felt Sasha's hands and cheeks. "She'll be okay. She isn't as young as she used ta be. Time's takin' its toll."

Maggie had seen old people before, the sick and infirm who sat in wheelchairs outside of the Happy Days Nursing Home in Linsburg where Miss Rosa lived. They spent their days watching the sun and the squirrels, lost in a world no one could see. Surely, Mother wasn't that old. Though her hair was more gray than brown now, and the lines on her face connected like puzzle pieces, she was no older than Aunt Dora, who was doing fine.

Aunt Dora trundled to the kitchen and pulled a tea kettle down from a cupboard above the sink. "This will make her feel like her old self again, yeah?"

She rubbed her hands together, blowing into them before she began her work. She had Eve measure out pinches of this and dashes of that while Merry took notes.

Maggie thought about her aunt's words. She didn't want her mother to feel like her "old self" again, plagued by pains and forgetfulness. She wanted her mother to feel like her young self again, with soft brown hair and a sharp mind.

She explained this to her aunt.

"Maggie, there's a season fer everything. When a season's up, we make way for a new season. Tis the way it's always been and the way it will always be."

"That's not fair." Maggie crossed her arms and set her chin.

"Life isn't about fairness. It's about making the most of what ya have while yer here. Time gives everything its value. Remember that."

Aunt Dora handed Maggie a cup and she and Merry took turns

forcing the tea down their mother's throat while Ruth Anne and Eve opened curtains, letting in what was left of the hazy, late-afternoon light.

After several long minutes Miss Sasha opened her eyes, a soft smile on her lips.

"I'm thinking we should have a spring recital," Mother said, sitting up and smiling at each of her daughters. "We can present The History of Dark Root. Ruth Anne can write it and Eve can play Juliana. Merry, you can play me. You'd look fabulous in a boa and a flapper dress. Maggie...maybe you can work the lights."

"Yes, Mother," Maggie said.

Her mother was still crazy, but it was the same old crazy she'd always been, and not the semi-lucid type of crazy she'd slipped into lately.

She'd be okay. For now, anyways.

The Garden at Sister House
Dark Root, Oregon
November, 2013

"There are rules that must be followed," Mother said, raising a crooked finger as I pushed her wheelchair down the rocky path that led to our garden.

It was the second week of our lessons and Mother had begun calling for us separately.

I came most every afternoon, had lunch with my sisters, then spent the next hour or so with Miss Sasha, as she liked to be called, when she played the role of teacher.

"Rules, Maggie, rules," Mother repeated. "The world operates on a set of rules."

I wrestled with the iron gates to the garden, an ill-tended area of weeds, pet headstones, and forgotten relics like old barrettes and Ruth Anne's pocket watch.

As children, we'd spent many hours playing in the garden as Mother and Aunt Dora watched from the porch or the kitchen window. It was the closest thing we had to a park and provided a distraction from the forest that constantly beckoned us.

Mother had never joined us here and my heart pounded as I realized that today—after all these years—I would be sharing our private sanctuary with her.

"No grownups allowed," we had avowed back then, but we were all grownups now and those rules no longer applied.

Mother coughed into the crook of her arm, her chest rattling like a baby's toy. I stopped the wheelchair long enough for her to collect herself before pushing it towards the stone bench where Ruth Anne used to read as the rest of us played tag. I sat on the bench, facing my mother now.

She looked around, regarding the garden, as she beheld it from this perspective for the first time. She sighed heavily and exhaled into the wind, her breath floating off to join with the collective breaths of others that swept across the Universe. I felt a connection with her here, and I placed my hands on her knees, encouraging her to continue.

"Rules are especially important in witchcraft," she explained, her forehead wrinkling like tissue paper. Her once strong eyebrows were now sparse, white lines that stuttered above her pale, blue eyes.

She lifted a finger, twirling it inches from my nose.

"Rule number one. Never use your abilities to cause harm to another, or to yourself."

She leaned back, a knowing smile on her face. Though Mother was not an evil woman, she was also not one to shy away from a good curse or a well-worded incantation, when she thought the occasion warranted it.

When she saw the confusion on my face she clapped her hands and said, "Unless they deserve it! And even then, you should be careful."

"But, how do you know when someone deserves it?"

"That leads us to the next rule." A gust of wind lifted the fine wisps of her white hair, bringing them down to rest around her shoulders like a shawl. "Number two. Everything you do comes back to you."

"Karma," I said, to show her that I knew something.

Michael had taught me about karma, claiming that what we put out in the world came back to us, if not in this lifetime, then in the next.

"Karma, yes, but more." Her eyes narrowed, meeting mine. "As a witch, you're given gifts. And a gift should be treasured, taken care of. Karma says that what you put out into the world comes back to you. But for a witch, it comes back three-fold!"

"So," I said, the wheels turning in my head as I did the math. "If I do good things, like give money to charity, then I will get three times as much back in return?"

Mother's lifted her chin, her eyelashes fluttering as fast as butterfly wings. "Magdalene, this is what I'm talking about. You can't do something good for the purpose of getting something good back. That negates the act. Do you understand?"

"No," I sighed as the iron gate flew open and crashed shut, sending a flock of black birds who'd settled between the metal spokes off into the sky. They cawed in protest, but did not return. "If I knowingly do something bad, bad things come back to me, but if I knowingly do something good, I get nothing. It doesn't seem fair."

"Who ever said life was fair? I don't ever recall telling you once that life was fair."

"I know, it's just, well, shouldn't it be?"

"It's all about balance." She placed her wrinkled hand on my knee. Her words were strong, but her touch was soft. "The world exists in a constant pendulum of dark and light. Every good deed is a light in the dark, and as long as there is always one light burning, the dark cannot win. This is our cross, and it's not always fair."

"Suppose every light burns out. Then what?"

Mother shook her head, sadly. "Then we fall, Maggie. There are many other worlds fighting this same fight. Many more that have already fought and lost. No one knows why this is so, only that it is. A cosmic chess game and we are one of the few pieces left on the board."

"Don't you ever get tired of the fight?" I asked, standing up as both the sun and the temperature began to drop.

"Yes. I get tired of it. But the torch is being passed, and as long as Dark Root and the other strongholds on this plane fight the good fight, there is hope."

She pointed to a stick and I retrieved it for her.

Plunging it into the dirt and withdrawing a clump of mud she said, "Most witches draw their power from the earth, and you are no exception. The energy of Dark Root feeds you, Maggie, and your sisters. The closer you are to this place, the stronger your powers. Never forget it."

She took the mud and pressed it into my palm. It tingled as I mashed it between my fingers.

There *was* something special about the land here. Maybe that was why my powers hadn't always worked when I was away.

Mother's eyes snapped shut, then opened like a camera lens. She looked past me, violently shaking her head. Pointing to the woods she shrieked, "We will not forego the Solstice Ritual, Larinda! You will not extort me!"

I looked behind me, to see if Larinda had returned, but there were only shadows.

"Leave then!" Mother screeched, trying to pull herself from her wheelchair. "There is enough dark magick in the world."

"Mother," I said anxiously, passing my hand before her vacant eyes.

She moaned, whipping her head from side to side.

I tried another approach. "Miss Sasha, are you there?"

Her eyes flickered as recognition set in. "Maggie," she said, patting my face. "Where have you been? I've missed you."

Merry appeared on the porch, the wind whipping her dress around her. She called to us. "Hurry! The wind is picking up!"

I turned to Mother, my heart beating wildly as I grabbed the handles of her wheelchair.

"Let's get you inside the house."

We rolled across the cracked pavement and through the stony lot, the wind fighting us all the way. When we reached the porch steps, Merry raced down to help us. We lifted Mother from the chair and escorted her to the door.

"Now, darlings," Mother said, as we took her arms and entered the house. "Do be lambs and get me my fancy hat. I'm having dinner with the Duchess of Bedford."

A strange agitation swept through Sister House that afternoon.

Merry fought with Frank on the phone about custody rights, Ruth Anne complained that it was too noisy to write, and Paul wandered around, nodding at the right moments and saying the right things, but seemed so distracted by his phone I thought Eve was going to snatch it from him and flush it down the toilet.

Even June Bug had a bad day, claiming she'd forgotten to cap the lids on the jars that housed her collection of critters. She dashed through the house yelling, "Here, buggy buggy!" with a jar in one hand and a piece of fruit in the other, as the rest of us scratched our arms on the sofa watching *It's a Wonderful Life*.

Eve finally came up with an excuse to get us out of there.

"I'm taking Maggie to a baby sign language class in Linsburg," she announced in her usual fabulous intonation.

Everyone must have thought it sounded as abysmal as I did because no one asked to come along.

"Is it my imagination or is Mother acting particularly weird?" I asked her, as we sped towards Linsburg in Paul's black Explorer.

"Nope. She's really off her rocker now," my sister replied, not bothering to slow down for the squirrel that darted across the road.

I thought about Mother's rules of karma and wondered what fate Eve would have suffered had she had hit the animal.

"Sometimes when I'm with her, she is lucid and present," I said, remembering some of the more pleasurable talks I'd had with Mother in the last few weeks. I'd grown closer to her in those moments, and had even begun to understand what she might be like as a person, sans the Sasha Shantay mask. "...And then she flips like a light switch, talking to people who aren't even there."

"At least she remembers your name. She calls me Natalie and asks me to turn down her bed or *fetch* her some tea."

"Do you do it?"

She sighed. "Yes."

I watched the scenery whiz by the open window. Eve drove so fast I could hardly read the exit signs.

"She talks to Larinda a lot," I said. "It's unsettling."

The sun was beginning to set, casting waves of pink and orange swirls into the sky. Eve slowed as we rolled into the parking lot of a bar right outside of Linsburg. The lot was full of cars and the sounds of classic rock reverberated from the walls.

"She doesn't just talk to Larinda," I continued, trying to hammer in my point as Eve turned off the ignition. "She talks someone named Robbie, too. It's like when June Bug has tea parties with her stuffed animals, but there's no tea and there's no stuffed animals."

Eve's nostrils flared as she faced me. "Maggie, there's something you should know."

Eve never led off with the words *there's something you should know*. Those were words for people who took things seriously.

I clutched the door handle, bracing myself for the news.

"Mom's still sick, Mags. Very, very sick." A tear slid down her cheek. She swallowed. I watched the lump in her throat slide down. "We didn't want to tell you because..." Her eyes fell to my belly. "But the doctors don't give her long. Six months if we are lucky. Probably less."

Eve buried her face in her hands, weeping.

I shook my head in disbelief. "We cured her, Evie. We cured her, remember? She's okay, now. I know it."

I spoke to reassure myself as much as I did her. Everything we'd done: coming home, reopening Mother's store, cutting Leah's hair, and embracing Mother in our circle at the hospital. We'd saved her; we'd broken the curse.

"Maggie," she sobbed. "Mom has dementia and she's in the final stages. It was more than a curse. The dementia weakened her, making her susceptible to it, but..."

"But? But!?" I pulled at the door handle, trying to get out, but it wouldn't open. "Shut up!"

"...Merry's trying to buy her more time, but she doesn't know how much longer she can help her."

"Stop it, Eve!"

"...Merry thinks Mom's trying to hold on long enough to train us ...

"Is Merry a motherfucking doctor, all of a sudden?"

Why wouldn't the door handle budge? I yanked at it, my face hot and beaded with sweat. Eve didn't know what she was talking about. Merry didn't either. Even the doctors had their heads up their asses. Mother was going to be okay. That's what all of this was about. This whole Goddamned thing.

"Maggie please..." Eve looked at me, her eyes pleading. She put a hand on my shoulder and I felt her energy seep into me. It was surprisingly warm. "They made me promise not to tell you because..."

"Because I'm a pregnant basket case. I get it." The door finally broke free and swung open.

Six months.

They were giving Mother six months. Or less. The sounds from inside the bar were happy, jovial. How could anyone be happy when the world was falling apart?

Eve spoke again. I could see her mouth moving, but I only heard the beating of my own heart. She put both arms around my neck, pulling me to her.

111

Her tears washed over my face, but I didn't join her in crying. Mother hadn't been taken yet.

"We are going to beat it. Again." My heart thumped with new resolve. "With the money we make, we can afford better doctors. These Dark Root quacks don't know what they are talking about. Besides, we are witches, Eve. There has to be a spell, or potion, or amulet, or something..."

"Maggie," Eve said. "Witchcraft doesn't solve everything."

TEN

THE KIDS AREN'T ALRIGHT

WELL, THAT WAS A COMPLETE WASTE OF TIME." EVE STORMED OUT OF the bar, almost hitting me in the face with the door as she left.

"Yeah, yeah," I said, catching up to her.

We climbed into the Explorer and slammed our doors simultaneously. Eve turned over the ignition but didn't pull out of the lot.

"What gets me," she said, turning on the windshield wipers just as it started to rain. "...Is that you were able to rig the game against *me* that night at The Watering Hole, and yet here, you couldn't drop a pool ball into a sinkhole."

"I did the best I could," I said, refusing to look at her. "I never said I was a good player."

She snorted.

"That's an understatement. June Bug would have made a better partner than you."

"Well, maybe next time, you'll take her."

"Trust me. If she were two feet taller and had an ID, I would."

"I suggest you drive us home," I said, cracking the window to release some of the hot air that had accumulated inside. "It's not like we are out anything, just a few hours."

"Hours I'll never get back," she glowered, clenching the wheel at 11 and 1 o'clock.

"What would you be doing right now, anyway? Organizing your closet? Or combing through Paul's texts to make sure he's not talking to a woman?"

"I already organized my closet," she said, punching the gas.

"Goodbye, ladies," one of the guys we'd been playing called to us with a grin and a wave.

I flipped him off.

"Oh, great," Eve said, "for all we know he might be crazy. He could get in his car, chase us down, and rape us. Or worse." We squealed out of the lot, kicking up enough mud to paint the back window brown.

"What's worse than rape?" I asked, rolling up my window and locking the door.

"Maggie, I lived in the *city*," she said, emphasizing the word as if I had spent my entire existence in the hollers.

"So?"

Her chin trembled and her face paled. "There are lots of bad things that can happen to you. Take it from me."

I stared at her, wondering what she meant. But she quickly drew a smile back onto her face. "We just need to get better," she said, her words Southern-sweet.

"I think you need Prozac," I said.

"Have you been practicing like you were supposed to?" Eve flipped her hair back, her eyes focused on the road.

"Of course, I've been practicing. You were there."

We'd been up in the attic apartment over Miss Sasha's Magick Shoppe every morning before the store opened, working on our plan to get rich playing pool. Eve placed tennis balls and balloons strategically around the room and ordered me to perform "tricks."

"Put that one under the chair," she'd say, directing my attention to a blue balloon. "Roll that ball off the shelf..."

It was hard work, and I failed more often than I succeeded, but every once in a while a ball rolled or a balloon bounced and Eve and I would stand up, whoop around the room, and high five. I wasn't sure what made the difference, but I seemed to do better when I was calm and centered.

"I think I was too upset today," I said. "Maybe you shouldn't deliver bad news like that before we play a game."

Eve pressed her still-glossed lips together. "I just couldn't hold it in anymore. I'm not good at keeping most secrets."

I blinked rapidly at the word "most" as I realized there was a well of information inside her I didn't have access to.

"I'm glad you told me," I said. "I'm tired of everyone thinking I'm a delicate flower."

"More like a weed." She tossed me a smile as she turned onto a side road, a shortcut of hers. We fell into a deep thatch of woods where the rain never made it to the ground. The thick canopy of leaves collected water, funneling it down to the branches below, creating a series of intricate and beautiful waterfalls. Our own little rain forest.

I patted my purse, glad that we had only played a practice game. I couldn't risk losing even one dollar. I had somehow missed all of my shots, even the easier ones, and when Eve hit the eight ball just shy of the corner pocket, I couldn't nudge it the half-inch needed to sink it and win the game. My powers were on the fritz.

"Mother says our magic is tied to Dark root," I said. "Maybe we need to play in town."

"Sounds right," she said, as we cruised into town.

She took the road down Main Street. Most of the shops were closed for the evening, but the lights in Dip Stix Café still burned. We could see Paul and Shane through the window. They were laughing easily with a young woman who sat twirling her hair as she ordered. Eve's energy bristled and she put her foot on the gas.

"You're prettier than she is," I said.

"I know."

"And Paul's crazy about you."

115

"I know that, too."

"Then what?"

She tapped the steering wheel. "I've always known how to get men. I bat my lashes, ooh and ah over their skills, and pretend to act interested in their hobbies."

"Not to mention your magic," I said.

Eve was born with the gift of seduction. Most men couldn't be within several feet of her without falling victim to her powers. It was one of the reasons I had been so envious of her when we were teenagers.

"Yes, my magic." She bit her bottom lip. "I've just never learned how to keep one. Normally, I get bored before they do. I'm the one who gets text messages from exes and finds excuses not to come around"

"Is Paul avoiding you?"

"No, he isn't. That's the worst part. But he's on that damned phone, texting at all hours. I'm not used to feeling this...this insecure." She looked at me, lifting her palm. "How do you do it, Maggie?"

I gave her my best sardonic smile. "On the job training, I guess."

"Hmmm. Yes. I suppose."

I strained my neck, hoping to catch one last glimpse of Shane. He had not called, or stopped by since the morning he dropped me off at Sister House and I was surprised by how much I missed him. He had said he loved me, but now he avoided me as much as I avoided him.

"When did life get so crazy?" I asked, slumping back into my seat, wondering if Shane texted ex-girlfriends.

"I don't know," Eve sighed. "But I want to go back."

"Back?"

"To when I had some control over things."

"I don't think I've ever had that feeling."

"Pity."

Eve talked about slipping on a pair of warm pajamas and eating raw cookie dough as Harvest Home came into view. In the living room window, we could see Aunt Dora, her hands covering her face, her shoulders heaving.

"She's crying," I said. I'd never seen Aunt Dora so much as sniffle, and the sight broke my heart.

"What's wrong with her?" Eve asked. We remained in the vehicle, unsure of what to do next.

"She's scared. Scared of losing her sister, scared of losing her home, scared of a future that feels ominous...like we are."

Aunt Dora spotted us in the driveway and dabbed the tears from her eyes. She opened the door, speaking cheerfully. "My girls are home! I made cookies. Come inside!"

We gave her quick hugs on our way in.

"What are those fer?" she asked.

"Just because we love you."

After dessert I pulled Eve into the bedroom and locked the door. "Let's try again, Eve. I think we can do this. We can practice a little more and then play a few games at The Watering Hole."

Eve looked tired. "Maggie, let it go."

"Please, Evie. Think of what we could do with the money! Help Aunt Dora and Mother and Merry and us." I batted my eyelashes the way she had done in the car when showing me her man-catching moves.

"Fine," she laughed, her voice fairy light. "When did you become so persuasive?"

"I learned from the best."

"So it seems."

I tossed and turned in bed, watching the shadows. I had been lying here for nearly four hours and I still couldn't sleep.

I tried to get comfortable, pushing a pillow between my legs before flipping onto my stomach and then returning to my back.

All the while my digital clock counted down the time until the witching hour was over––that window between the hours of midnight and three a.m., when the veil between this world and the spirit world was at its thinnest. I had seen things in my life——ghosts and demons——and though I no longer feared them as I had before, on this night I wanted to be left alone.

At last, three o'clock came and I relaxed.

I thought about calling Shane, waking him from his dreams, telling him that I was falling in love with him, too.

"Really?" he'd ask.

"Yes." Then I remembered. "But..."

"But?"

"I'm pregnant with Michael's baby."

I imagined the heavy silence on the other end of the line.

I'd laugh, apologize, and say, "Ha-ha. Just kidding. You know what a prankster I am." Then, in my neurotic imagination, I'd hang up and he'd wonder what happened as soap opera music played in the background.

Even my fantasies were screwed up.

Though my pregnancy wasn't obvious to anyone but those who knew about it, I couldn't hide it forever. But until I got my act together——had a place I could call home and some money in my pocket——I wasn't ready to face him. My pride wouldn't let me. When I finally told him, I wanted to be strong enough to withstand his rejection, if that's what it came to.

In my peripheral vision, I saw something scurry across the floor, a dark shape the size of a toy car. It settled into the corner behind my chair. Was it a rat, or a ghost? I sat up on my elbows, searching the blackness. The shape dissolved into the floor, leaving a trace of its aura behind, like oil from a leaky engine.

Probably just a small spirit passing through.

"Well, you're no help," I said, sliding back into my bed. If the damned things were going to visit me in the middle of the night, the least they could do would be to listen to my problems.

A knock on the door startled me more than any spirit could.

I yanked the blankets up to my chin. "Yes?"

"Maggie, sorry to wake you," Paul said, his voice thick with worry.

"Come in."

Paul stepped lightly inside, flooding the room with illumination from the hall. He held the cordless house phone, his hand covering the mouthpiece. "It's that guy you used to date. The one Eve sent away."

The news both annoyed and amused me.

That guy was Michael, and he had driven all the way from Northern California a month ago to ask me to marry him. Eve had given him one of her special teas and immediately after drinking it, he took off in his van to pursue a woman he had never met in New York, instead.

"Is everything okay?" I asked Paul.

"I don't know. Sorry. He demanded to talk to you and said he was going to come see you in person if I didn't put you on the phone right away."

I took the phone and smiled to let Paul know it was okay.

"I can stick around if you want," he added.

"I'm fine. Thanks. I'll holler if I need you."

Before he left he said, "Okay, good luck." He left the door open a crack.

"Michael?" I said into the mouthpiece, bracing myself for the strange power he had over me. The first day I met him, I'd followed him out of Dark Root to help form his new religion. I would have stayed with him forever, had I not caught him and Leah together.

"Maggie! I'm so glad to hear your voice. I'm not sure what happened, but I've been to New York, following a woman I didn't know. They put a stalking order on me! What did you do?"

"Sorry, that's not my brand of magick," I said, stifling a chuckle.

"Anyway, that's not why I'm calling. I woke up from this dream. You were having a baby. My baby. Is it true?"

Michael had abilities of his own, though he insisted they all came from God and he was nothing more than a prophet.

To be honest, I wasn't sure where any of this came from, so I couldn't argue.

But if he really *was* God's prophet, I reasoned, the world would no longer be here, as he had predicted.

"Tell me I'm crazy." Michael almost begged. "I couldn't go back to sleep until I knew for sure."

I didn't want him in my life, not when I was almost emotionally free of him. But I couldn't bring myself to lie to him either.

With hesitation, I said, "Yes, Michael. I'm pregnant."

"I'm the father?"

"God, yes! Why the hell would you ask that?"

"Oh, Maggie. That's wonderful news. I'll go there, or you can come here and we can raise this baby." He made plans for us, rattling off a list of things we could do and places we could go. South America, where there was a religious revival, or maybe Africa, where the natives were hungry for "The Word"

"No, Michael." I stopped him. "Absolutely not. I'm staying here and I'm raising the baby alone."

"I have rights, too." His voice shook. "I will take you to court, if I have to."

I laughed. "I'm sure the courts will entrust a baby into the care of a certified stalker."

"That's not fair, Maggie! You probably did that to me."

"Yeah? Prove it." I could have taken it easier on him. He was under Eve's spell at the time. He was also under a spell when he had succumbed to Leah's *charms*.

Still, I couldn't forgive him, spell or no spell.

"Maggie, be reasonable. We can work this out."

I felt my face flush. Who was he to tell me to be reasonable? He couldn't step back into my life and start demanding things.

"All I want from you," I said, my throat tight and my voice short. "... Is money. Lots and lots of money. If your kid is anything like you, he'll be eating me out of house and home. Send me money and you may get a picture on Christmas."

"You can't call the shots. There are laws."

"Not in Dark Root."

There was a pause on the other end. "I'm not sending you anything if you don't let me see the baby, and that's final."

"I never expected anything from you, Michael, so it's a moot point." I was so angry I expected every light bulb up and down the hall outside to burst. I rubbed the crystal band on my wrist, soothing myself. The Circle hummed beneath my touch, sending tiny flecks of amber light into the dark, and calming me.

"Michael," I said, once my heart rate returned to normal. "I have enough problems right now. Please leave me alone."

"I can't, Maggie." His voice was soft but resolute. "I just can't." And he hung up the phone.

I relaxed in the bath, letting the warm water and Mr. Bubble wash over my body. Three Yankee candles flickered on a shelf, a soothing mixture of lavender, rose, and vanilla cupcake.

Between my adventure with Eve and arguing with Michael, I was fairly certain I would not get any sleep.

I'd been in this bathroom many times, mostly looking at pregnancy sticks or puking my brains out. This was my first bath here, my first time taking in the room's ambiance.

It was as old and outdated as the rest of the house, with fading floral wallpaper––a violent conglomeration of pink carnations and red roses––that lined all four walls. The once-lovely pedestal sink was tinged with rust, and the ornate, brass frame that encased the mirror had been crudely duct taped together at its corners.

In the days when this house served as a bed and breakfast this must have been a beautiful room. I could almost envision the barrage of guests wandering in and out of it to wash their faces or brush their teeth at the beginning and ending of each day. Those days were long gone and the only remaining evidence of its former beauty was the claw-footed tub in which I lounged, an original fixture of the house, still white after almost a century's worth of use.

I sunk deeper into the water, letting the bubbles cover my chin.

They didn't make tubs this big anymore, I thought, stretching out my legs before me. I breathed in the steam, letting it clear my sinuses and my mind. As much as I hated to admit it, Eve was right. I hadn't done very well at the pool game. I needed to get a better handle on my powers if I wanted to make this work.

I focused my attention on the top of the wallpaper straight in front of me, blocking all other thoughts from my mind.

"Peel," I whispered, tugging mentally at the corner of the sheet. "Peel," I said again, less a request and more of a command.

Nothing happened. I pressed my palms together in frustration. I might as well have tried to move a boulder.

Michael's crystal pendant pulsed around my neck, a rhythmic thump like the beat of a heart. I grasped it with one hand and rubbed my bracelet with the thumb of my other hand. The pendant was sharp, but the bracelet smooth. The pendant shouted for attention while the bracelet purred beneath my touch.

"Let's try this again," I said, embarrassed to be talking to my own jewelry. I closed my eyes, imagining the wallpaper sliding off in one smooth piece, neatly bundling at the floor.

I concentrated, seeing it play out in my mind's eye.

I heard a wispy sound. I opened one eye, and then the other. The paper began to move, not in a smooth fall but in waves, crinkling up like an earthworm on a walk. I gritted my teeth, willing the paper to fall. Finally, it loosened at the top edge and peeled away from the wall completely, dragging the rest of the strip to the floor with it.

For a century, this paper had held, and I had caused it to fall.

I was giddy with victory when the doorknob jiggled. I scooped the remaining bubbles over my body in case it was Paul.

"Occupied," I called out.

The knob turned fully and the door creaked open.

"I'm in the tub," I said louder. "If Michael called again, tell him I'm asleep."

The door continued to push open, slowly, as if it were made of lead. "Hello?" I said, searching for a towel. "Eve?"

I heard a noise, like someone squeegeeing a car window on an icy morning. Words began to materialize in the steam-covered mirror: 123 Old Raven Rd.

"Go away!" I ordered, suddenly panicked. "Go away, now!"

The door slammed shut, knocking a candle from its perch. The sound of a woman's laughter reverberated through the room. Every light in the bathroom went out and the remaining candles were doused.

An icy hand gripped my shoulder, pushing me down into the tub. I struggled as the water grew arctic cold.

"Help!" I managed to scream before my nose and mouth were submerged. I swallowed mouthfuls of soapy water as I sloshed around, fighting an invisible force.

The door flew open. Aunt Dora burst inside, brandishing her broom and tossing dust into the air. "I warned ya once, and that's all ya get. Leave now or face me alone!"

The small window above the toilet opened and a long, formless gale marked by Aunt Dora's glitter dust passed over me. The gale swirled momentarily, then rushed out the open window.

Aunt Dora was quick to close it and lock the latch.

"Ya okay?" she asked, handing me a towel.

"I-I think so."

"Larinda's bypassed the protection spell around the house. I don't know how, but she's grown in power." Aunt Dora stared out the window, scratching her head. "Her magick is illusion and she feeds on fear. If she can't make ya afraid, she has no power over ya."

With shaking knees, I dried myself, aware of how truly afraid I'd been. But the fear wasn't for myself. It was for my unborn child.

ELEVEN

CRIMINAL

AUNT DORA ADDED EXTRA LAYERS TO HER PROTECTION SPELL, THEN TRIED to reassure me. "Ya have yer mother's bracelet. That should keep ya safe."

"Why does she want me?"

"She enjoys her mind games. Have a brave heart. That's the key ta foilin' her."

Despite her words, I was worried.

Although I'd been raised in a coven, I'd never seen much magick. And here Larinda was, able to do things I never dreamed possible, and with ease. I only hoped Aunt Dora's protection spells could match Larinda's determination.

"Are you ready?" Eve asked, tapping her foot in my bedroom doorway as I tried to rake a comb through my wild mane. My hair was naturally curly but the pregnancy had made it frizzy, coarse, and completely unmanageable.

"You could be more understanding," I said, pulling my hair into a ponytail at the nape of my neck. "I'm still traumatized."

"Not as traumatized as I am by that outfit. No pregnant woman should ever put on a pair of jeggings."

"Oh? Is that what these are?"

We had taken a trip to Linsburg earlier so Eve could grab a few supplies for the shop.

While she was out witch-doctoring, I had wandered into a Rite Aid.

I found a display that said: As Seen on TV. Beneath it were boxes of stretchy, one-size-fits-all jeans with elastic waists and tapered ankles. I thought Eve would think them fashionable, especially since they cost thirty bucks, but I guess I was wrong.

I didn't need to dress to impress anyway.

That was Eve's job. She would lure them in and I would count the money.

The Watering Hole looked much the same as it did on our previous visit: peanut shells on the floor, torn vinyl booths, dim lighting, and a juke box that lumbered through one Nirvana song after another. There were only a handful of patrons inside.

Good. The less witnesses, the better.

"I'll get quarters and rack up," Eve said. "You get us something to drink."

I headed to the bar, realizing Eve got the better end of the deal. She'd be out a dollar and I'd be out seven bucks.

But hopefully, if all went well, money wouldn't be an issue for us soon.

"Light beer and a..."

"Root beer," the bartender said, his smile revealing a gold tooth in the right side of his mouth.

"Um, yeah. Good memory." I slid a ten across the counter. A tan hand appeared out of nowhere, grabbed the bill, and handed it back to me.

I looked up to see that the hand attached to Shane Doler.

"It's on me," he said, taking a barstool and motioning to the free one next to his.

I glanced in Eve's direction. She was busy talking to a man in the corner, tossing her hair and batting her lashes.

"I didn't know you came here," I said, wondering what the odds were I would run into him here of all places, doing this.

"Only when my mind's on a pretty girl," he grinned, the dimples in his cheeks deepening.

I tried not to notice the way he looked: the way his brown curls had grown a fraction of an inch since last we'd talked, or how his eyes twinkled every time he spoke. And I tried to ignore the way he smelled, an intoxicating mix of Irish Spring, drugstore cologne, and beer. His presence always did strange things to me and I tried to ignore those feelings as I played with the buttons on my blouse.

He laughed, raised his mug, and took a drink.

"Ah," he said, wiping his lips with his hand. "That's what I needed."

"I didn't peg you as a drinker."

"I wasn't. Until tonight." He inspected me over the top of his beer, his eyes half-closed and dreamy.

"So what's new?" I asked, glancing at Eve again, who now had two men in her court. She was laughing at their wit, touching their shoulders. They were smitten, as most men were under her charms—both manufactured and magical.

Shane warmed his hands by rubbing them, then cupped them over mine. I sat up, arrow straight, on my stool. "Just counting down the hours until I get that kiss." He leaned in, his lips mere inches from my own. He massaged my hands and my body grew suddenly warm. "How about now?" he asked, moving one hand to my knee.

I ached for him. I tried to reason it out, to find one good reason why I shouldn't. But his energy, his smell, it was too much. Almost against my will, I leaned in closer.

My heart beat rapidly. His scent was intoxicating.

"C'mon," he said, squeezing my knee. "Give Papa some sugar."

"You're drunk!" I removed his hand from my leg.

"Only a little."

He beckoned for the bartender to bring him another round. "A cowboy's got a right to drink once in a while."

"You've had enough, I think."

I tried to wrestle the beer away, but he won the battle as half of it sloshed across the counter.

"I could take you to court for that," he joked as he mopped up the spilt beer with a stack of napkins.

"There are no courts in Dark Root. And," I continued, dabbing at the beer stain on my shirt. "Just because you grew up in Montana and wear that silly hat, you are not a cowboy. A cowboy has a horse."

Shane raised his arms in a stretch, kicking out his long legs. His T-shirt rose up, allowing me to glimpse his lightly muscled abs. "That, my dear, is a technicality. Someday I'm gonna have that horse and a pretty little cowgirl to ride off into the sunset with." He lowered his arms and wrapped them around my waist. "Will you be that cowgirl? Pretty please?"

I pushed one of his arms down as the other found its way back around me. "You're like a human octopus," I said. "You need to go home and get some sleep. Let me call you a cab."

"What? It's still early." He checked his wrist and chuckled when he noticed he wasn't wearing a watch. "I like this place. I have music, fine company, and love." He clamped both my hands in his and put them to his chest.

"Seriously, Shane. Do you have a designated driver? Did Paul come with you?"

"Maybe you can give me a ride. Will you give me a ride, Maggie?"

The double entendre made me blush, partly from embarrassment at seeing him like this, and partly for what he was implying. "Shane, come on." I turned to the bartender. "Can you call him a taxi please? He needs to go home."

"Home? Home to what? I live in an apartment above a fondue bar. I'm a cowboy with a fondue bar! That's not home, Maggie. That's not a place I can hang my hat." He pulled my fingers to his lips. "I got a great idea. We can move in together. I can build us a little house. A ranch house!" His eyes lit up. "Wouldn't that be swell?"

"Swell?" I took his grabby hands and planted them on the bar counter. "That's it. You're no longer allowed to watch The Andy Griffith Show."

Out of the corner of my eye I saw Eve motioning for me to join her. One of the guys placed his hands on her bottom and her eyes told me that I'd better hurry.

"Mag-gie," Shane slurred, gazing at me from beneath his lush, dark lashes. "We could get married. Start a family...wouldn't that be n-ice?"

"The cab will be here in five minutes," the bartender said.

"Shane, go home, okay? We'll talk tomorrow."

"Is that your way of saying you don't want to live with me?" He grabbed his hat on the counter and pushed it onto his head. "You won't hold my hand. You won't kiss me. And now you don't even want to live with me. That's just great."

Eve practically hopped as she tried to wave me over.

I stood, torn between staying with Shane—who was clearly drunk off his ass—and Eve, who might be in trouble. The headlights of a cab appeared outside the window and I knew he'd be okay.

"Shane, I have to go." I reached into his front jeans pocket and he smiled, pushing his hips against my hand. I could feel the beginning of his arousal. "Don't get too excited. I'm just getting your keys."

His expression turned sulky.

I found his keys and dropped them in my bag. "I'll bring these by tomorrow. Your ride's outside. Go home and get some sleep, okay?"

Reluctantly, I joined my sister and her two companions. They were older than her by at least twenty years. She smiled at me gratefully as I approached.

"Maggie, meet Bob and Larry. I told them we might be up for a quick game or two."

Larry, a balding man with a mustache that covered his entire upper lip, sidled over to me and slipped an arm around my neck. I gracefully stepped out of his clutch, but not before Shane approached, scowling.

"It all makes sense now," Shane said. "Why you don't call me. Why you don't want to live with me. Take good care of her, man," he said to Larry as he passed.

Shane stomped away, trying unsuccessfully to slam the door on his way out.

I should have run after him, explained the situation to him, but it was pointless. In Shane's liquored up head, he wouldn't understand.

I hardly understood, and I was sober.

I watched through the window as Shane climbed into the cab. I could only hope that he had gotten so drunk he'd forget this whole evening come tomorrow when I dropped off his car.

"Gentlemen," I said, staring resolutely at the pool table, my fingers tingling with electricity. "Let's play."

Twelve

SEX AND CANDY

Dark Root, Oregon
The Woods
Time: Unknown

*H*E PUSHED HIS WAY THROUGH FOG, THICK AS COTTON CANDY, IGNORING *the dense undergrowth that grabbed for his feet. He smiled confidently as his eyes met mine.*

"You came for me," I said.

"You knew I would."

"Yes."

I thought for a moment, my mind muddled. "But how did you find me, Shane? Here, I mean."

"I can always find you, Maggie. Even in your dreams."

He closed the distance between us, his body so close to mine I could feel the heat rising off of him. Our breath and the fog became one. He rested one arm on the tree behind me. His body was damp and sticky, evidence of his restless sleep.

The trees closed in around us like a curtain. We were alone here, unchained by the burdens of reality. We could do...anything.

"Miss me?" I teased, resisting the urge to pull him closer. He had come for me. It was his quest to finish. "I mean, really Shane, I've had

admirers before, but never ones who stalked me in my dreams."

"Well, then," he said, his face so close I could still smell the alcohol on his breath. "Maybe they didn't admire you as much as I do."

I swallowed hard, trying to think of something else to say, something light and coy.

"You should have at least given me some warning." I adjusted the collar of his T-shirt. "Then I could have put on something sexier."

He lifted a playful eyebrow. "Your wish is my command."

In the twinkling of an eye, my shirt was replaced by a long billowy skirt and no blouse. I dropped my hands from his collar to cover up my exposed breasts. He pulled them away and studied me.

I dropped the schoolgirl smile as my breathing deepened. I ran my hand along his square jaw, then to the soft curve of his chin, down his round shoulders, stopping at the hollow of his neck. I let my hands roam across his shirt, feeling the soft swell of muscles beneath cotton.

He watched as his warm breath fell across my face.

"I want you," I said, pushing my hand up through the bottom of his shirt, feeling the smoothness of his abdomen and the soft hairs around his navel.

"You can have me," he said, pushing me back against the tree behind us, the tree where he had carved our initials. "We're meant to be together, Maggie. Not just now, but forever."

"I know." I tilted my head back, offering him my neck. I burned so hot I thought I might set the whole forest on fire.

"No, Maggie, you don't know." He took my chin firmly in his hands, forcing me to look into his eyes. "You keep running from me. You keep hiding from me. But you can't hide here. I can always find you here."

"I'm not running now, Shane."

He released my face and clasped my hands in his. He lifted them over my head, pinning me to the tree. "That's because I won't let you."

The left corner of his mouth turned up into a crooked smile and he narrowed his eyes.

Still pinning me, he pushed my legs open with his knee and drew his lips towards mine. I jerked my head from side to side, letting him wrestle me back each time. He was larger than me, able to overpower me. I grew wet thinking he could take me anytime and there was nothing I could do about it.

With his full weight, he pressed into me, releasing my hands.

I could push him back now, if I wanted. If I wanted.

"I'm going to take you now," he said, his hand moving up my skirt until he found my thigh. "I'm going to do what I should have done to you years ago. I'm going to claim you, Maggie."

"Will it hurt?" I asked, pulling on his hair in a desperate attempt to get as close to him as I could.

He flashed me a wicked grin. "Only if you want it to."

I woke drenched in perspiration, my mind and heart still racing from the dream.

I had never had a dream that real or personal before and I couldn't get the image of Shane Doler, pinning me against the tree, out of my head. I busied myself throughout the morning, trying to hold back the blush from my cheeks.

At last, Eve and Paul went to work and I slipped into Eve's bedroom, undetected.

The dream did something to me, charged me. As I rummaged through Eve's dresser, I realized how silly I had been. If the reality of what it would be like to be with Shane was even one tenth as good as the dream, I was going for it. Screw my pride. Screw saving him. Screw saving myself. I threw a fantasy life out the window in favor of real.

It didn't take me long to put together an entire outfit from Eve's extensive wardrobe: a drape-y, hunter-green blouse with a low-cut neck, a long, charcoal-colored skirt with a slit up the side, black ankle boots a size too small, and a pair of real gold, hoop earrings.

Once dressed, I studied myself in her full length mirror. The loose fabric of the blouse hid my belly and accentuated my neckline and chest, both of which were quickly becoming my best features.

"I'm a gypsy," I said, snaking my hands above my head and thrusting out my left hip. "And I've come to steal your heart, Shane Doler."

I practiced an enticing look in the mirror, lowering my lashes as I tried to pull a dimple out of my cheek. I'd need more practice on my alluring stance. For now, I hoped the clothes were enough.

My face was flushed red so I dabbed on a bit of Eve's powder, which hid my freckles as well as the blush. Two stones. I'd have to play it as low-key as possible, if I were going to get past Aunt Dora without notice.

"Ya look nice," she said suspiciously as I zipped through the living room towards the front door. "Ya should wear yer hair down more. Brings out yer emerald eyes."

"Thank you. I'm off for the day. Be back by dinner." I gave her a quick kiss on the cheek and rushed out before she could ask any questions.

The morning was especially beautiful. The sun shone brightly, multi-colored leaves painted the ground, and the sweet smell of the forest filled me with energy.

"I can't believe I ever hated this place," I said, floating towards Shane's pickup. I jingled his keys. They sounded like church bells.

"We belong together," I said, practicing my speech. "Yes, I'm having Michael's baby, but he's not in my life anymore. You're the only man for me and we can work this out together."

I nodded satisfactorily as I turned over the engine. Together. Nothing could stop me now.

I parked in front of Dip Stix Café and surveyed the town. The book store and the candy shop were already open, drawing in customers with pre-holiday advertisements: *Get your sugarplums here!* Across the street I could see Evie through the window of Miss Sasha's Magick Shoppe, happily applying a henna tattoo to a middle-aged woman. All was right with Dark Root; all was right with the world.

"Get ready Shane," I said, fluffing my hair in the rear view mirror and giving wink. "I'm coming to get you."

By night, Dip Stix Café was an upscale, fondue restaurant that drew in locals as well as hipsters from neighboring towns; by day it was an old-fashioned diner, specializing in biscuits and gravy and club sandwiches. As the only eatery in Dark Root, it did pretty well, and kept both Shane and Paul busy.

As I entered the café I was reminded once again how much it had changed since the days when Uncle Joe owned it. The Elvis plaques and checkered tablecloths of yesteryear had been replaced by modern paintings and twinkling lights strewn across ivy-filled planter boxes.

Even so, it still felt like home.

I sat at my normal station, a small, round table near the window where I could take in the sunshine and do some people watching. Though the foot traffic in Dark Root had lessened since Halloween, there were still plenty of shoppers, carrying bags and totes as they wandered from shop to shop.

Paul came to my table, a weary smile on his face.

"I still can't believe we did this," I said, swelling with pride as counted the occupied tables in the diner. "Two months ago this place was dead."

"Yeah," Paul said, his jaw quivering as he suppressed a yawn. He closed his eyes briefly, did a quick shake of his head, then opened them wide.

"Rough morning?"

"You could say that." I noticed that his hair hadn't been combed. "The breakfast rush is about over, so I think I'll be okay."

"You guys need an extra hand," I said, looking around for Shane, who was most likely manning the grill in the kitchen.

Paul's face grew pensive at my suggestion.

I didn't want him to think I meant he wasn't capable of doing his job.

"Any biscuits left?" I asked, quickly changing the subject as I perused the menu.

Muffins, scones, omelets, and biscuits. Simple fare, but very good.

"Of course." Paul's shoulders relaxed and he leaned in conspiratorially. "Want a cappuccino? Not to brag, but I added in an extra pinch of nutmeg and pumpkin. It's so good it should be outlawed."

Paul did make the best coffee and I nodded eagerly, sneaking a glance out the window. If Eve or Merry caught me with a cappuccino I'd get a stern lecture on the "dangers of coffee." Only Paul and Ruth Anne seemed to care about what *I* wanted.

He turned to place my order and then, as if forgetting something, turned back me and knelt down. "Mags?"

"Yes?"

"Do you know what's going on with Eve? She's acting weird lately."

"Oh?" I said, trying to suppress an ironic smile. She'd been saying the same of him.

"She leaves for work before I'm even out of the shower, saying she 'prefers to walk' even when it's raining. When I go to meet her for lunch, she's suddenly busy with a million things she needs to do 'for the store.' And at night...well, let's just say there's not much happening then, either. She sleeps in her room and I'm up in the attic, haunting it like a lonely ghost." He scratched the back of his neck. "I don't get it."

I could have told him the truth, that Eve knew he was in contact with a former girlfriend, but I kept my mouth shut. The last thing I wanted was to be involved in their problems.

Plus, I was certain they'd get through it on their own in a day or two.

"The store is keeping her busy," I said, squeezing his hand. "She's trying to keep it afloat until next year. Then things will get better."

"I can't help but feel you're keeping something from me," he said, licking his lips. "I wish someone would tell me what's going on."

He sighed heavily and we both glanced across the street to where Eve stood behind the counter reading a magazine. There was not a customer in sight.

"Research," I said.

He laughed and then excused himself to take care of my order.

Twenty minutes later, Paul brought my food and I ate in silence. Between each bite, I mentally practiced what I would say when I finally saw Shane. It was almost ten and with each passing minute, I grew more anxious and more frustrated. He should be out here, mingling with customers, wiping down tables and assisting Paul. A knot formed in my stomach when Paul returned to take my now-empty plate.

"Where's Shane?" I asked.

"Haven't seen him this morning," Paul said, excusing himself to tend to something in the oven.

Hadn't seen him this morning?

I'd sent him home in a taxi last night. What if he hadn't made it home?

What if Shane, being so drunk, had forgotten where he lived and never made it back? Or what if the cabbie didn't understand English and took him to an entirely different town? Or what if––the thought made my stomach sick––what if the taxi had gotten into a wreck and Shane lay dying in a trench somewhere?

I checked my phone. No voice mail messages or texts.

I jumped from my table and searched the dining room for a newspaper. I found one in the corner booth, spread out to the edge of the table. It was a Linsburg paper, but it would still have important news from here.

I tore through it, scanning each headline to see if there were any accidents reported. The only news at all was that "record fall colors had been reported by the foliage department."

Nothing about a car wreck or a kidnapping.

I sighed in relief, then wondered if I should call the hospital? I took a deep breath, trying to reason it out. A noise from above caught my attention. Shane's bedroom. Of course. The poor guy was probably just getting out of bed, nursing a hangover. I was so relieved I raced upstairs, vowing to help him and Paul out for the day, if needed.

"Shane?" I asked, knocking on his door. "Are you okay?"

I thought I heard shuffling in the room, but there was no answer.

I knocked again, stiffer this time. "Shane? It's Maggie. "

There was a definite thump inside, followed by a stern silence.

"I'm coming in."

I turned the knob and fell through the door, my mouth opening in surprise. There, standing before me, was Shane and a pretty blond woman. Her hair was mussed and she wore nothing but a black silk robe.

"What's going on?" I asked, my mind reeling.

Then it dawned on me that she was the same woman I'd seen Shane talking to the other day. She looked as surprised as I did and took a giant step back, tightening the belt on her robe.

"Maggie," Shane said, reaching for me. He was dressed in shorts and a T-shirt, the same T-shirt he wore in my dreams last night. I glared at him, then turned, racing back down the staircase, not bothering to grab the handrail.

"I thought you were different!" I shouted over my shoulder. "But you're all the same!"

Tears stung my eyes and I missed a few stairs, twisting my ankle. Still, I didn't slow down.

"Maggie!" Shane called again. "Please wait!"

"Go to hell, Shane." I rushed past Paul, purposely knocking the cell phone from his hands. I ran through the dining room and pushed open the door. Every light bulb in the restaurant shattered, spraying miniscule fragments of glass across the café. Even the twinkling Christmas lights.

THIRTEEN

ONE HEADLIGHT

MOTHER AND I NESTLED ON THE SWING, MY FEET GRAZING THE WORN, wooden planks of the porch.

Years ago, my sisters and I had piled on this very swing, rolling across Mother's lap, jockeying for a position near her. Her feet had touched the ground then; now, they floated like two thin branches in house shoes. I half-listened as she phased in and out of lucidity, her conversation a mixture of the present and the past.

"You had your hair done," I said, trying to bring the conversation back around.

She patted her hair and smiled. "Merry washed it for me. She's such a good girl. Want to smell it? It smells like apples." She tucked her head beneath my nose.

I took an obliging sniff and agreed.

Then, looking up at me with a sudden youthful glimmer in her eyes, she whispered, "Want to see a trick?"

"Sure," I said, patting her leg.

She checked to see if we were alone, then squared the knobs that were her shoulders as she took in a long, raspy breath. She raised an unsteady hand and pointed it at a scattering of leaves that had collected near our feet.

As we watched, the leaves drew together, forming a stiff pile like ball bearings around a magnet. Leaves from all across the porch swept into the pile, clearing the entire deck.

"I can't believe it!"

Mother was known for her spells, enchantments, and talismans, but never for her raw magick. Yet, here she was, calling the leaves.

"Why didn't you ever show--"

"Shh!" she silenced me, lifting her chin and spreading her fingers. "I'm not done."

She raised her arm higher and the leaves followed suit, forming a long, thin tower before us.

"Make a wish," she said, then blew on the column like it were a candle on a birthday cake. Wisps of orange, red, and gold danced before us, twisting and turning in the air, unwilling performers in her magical circus.

At last, they spun into a tight funnel. I reached out, plucking a yellow leaf from the spiral as the other leaves continued to swirl.

Mother clenched her hand, leaving only her index finger exposed. Gritting her teeth and leaning forward, she said, "Leaves of yellow, gold, and brown, dance for me upon the ground."

The funnel broke apart, creating individual cyclones that intertwined across the porch, weaving in and out of one another in patterns of circles and stars.

"That's amazing," I said, spellbound.

I could move balls and balloons, nudge them, push them, alter their course a little, but I didn't have this kind of control. I was suddenly humbled in Mother's presence, embarrassed by all my insignificant shows of superiority throughout my life.

"I never knew," I said.

"It's nothing," she said, her arm collapsing to her side. The leaves didn't drop, as I'd expected them to, but flittered out into the world like dandelions. "You should have seen me when I was young, Maggie. I could move mountains."

"I believe you." I poked at the floating leaves like June Bug poked at bubbles. "How come we never got to see this side of you?"

She cleared her throat and loosened the top button on her nightdress. "It's not a good idea to squander magic, especially on cheap tricks. It's exhausting and it leaves a hole in the world. I think I need a nap, now."

I assisted Mother off the swing and to the front door.

Before entering the house, she looked over her shoulder at me and said, "There are better ways to spend your powers than on dancing leaves. If you use it all up on that sort of nonsense, you won't have any left for the important stuff."

Her eyes flickered a moment, but she said no more.

"Mama, you look tired," Merry said gently as she took Mother's arm and escorted her to her bedroom. Still dazed from the show, I watched them ascend the staircase together, my mind full of wonder.

"Hola," Ruth Anne said, hardly looking up from the TV show she was watching. "Want to go turkey hunting? I'll get my shotgun."

"I heard that!" Merry called from the staircase. "No hunting! Just bring me back an organic, free-ranged turkey. From a *store*. I don't like putting anything toxic inside my body."

"Except for Frank," I said, causing Ruth Anne to spit out the soda she was drinking.

Merry came down the steps and put her hand on her hips. "I heard that, too."

"Just kidding," I said. "Geez."

"Now get. And try to get one that's already defrosted, okay? We are behind on preparations as it is."

"Yes, dear," said Ruth Anne, grabbing Merry's keys from the coffee table and a bulky jacket from the coat rack.

A fire crackled enticingly in the fireplace and I wanted to stay inside with it, drink hot cocoa, and watch the lights twinkle on the gaudy, silver Christmas tree. I still hadn't gotten over my encounter with Shane the day before and I could use a little holiday cheer and mindless television.

"Some other time," I sighed longingly as I opened the door and caught a cruel gust of wind to the face.

"Yes," Ruth Anne said, turning her head up towards the sky. "Let's hurry. A storm is coming."

The storm had come, as Ruth Anne predicted.

Five minutes outside of Dark Root, on the road to Linsburg, we were caught in it. Heavy rains slashed at the windshield and tore at the tires. It pelted the hood of the car like bullets in a war zone, making it near-impossible to see, even with the wipers going full speed.

"Maybe we should pull over?" I asked.

But Ruth Anne was on a mission, both hands gripping the steering wheel as she pushed on the gas, using only memory to guide us towards the highway.

"Or at least slow down," I added, buckling my seat belt and pulling it taut across my chest.

The road narrowed––a small stint of loneliness flanked by thin trees and deep ravines.

"This doesn't look familiar," I said, rolling down the window to try to see through the rain.

Ruth Anne shot me a sideways look but kept driving.

"Times like this, I miss Florida," she said, taking off her glasses to clean them.

"Want me to drive?"

"No."

Ruth Anne was headstrong and stubborn, a trait we shared, passed down from our mother. But while my stubbornness was usually the result of not wanting to do something, Ruth Anne's stemmed from her need to complete a task, no matter the consequences.

I remembered her bragging to Aunt Dora as a kid that she could read *Gone With The Wind* in four days, and she stayed up late nights and missed meals to accomplish the undertaking. Ninety-six hours later, she emerged from her bedroom victorious and raccoon-eyed, waving the novel triumphantly in the air. Aunt Dora quizzed her and Ruth Anne answered every question correctly.

She might be a junk food eating cynic now, but she still had the same willfulness and fortitude she'd always had.

I took short, deep breaths, trying to calm myself.

With every pothole in the road she hit, I laid my hands across my belly protectively.

Maybe the child didn't need to worry about my deathtouch. Maybe he'd need to worry about his Aunt Ruth Anne's driving, instead.

"Music?" I asked, hoping the steady beat of something besides the rain would take my mind off the situation.

Ruth Anne popped in a CD, sending Metallica blasting through the car. As the chorus kicked in––*enter night, exit light*––she tightened her grip on the wheel, narrowed her eyes, and pressed the gas pedal down to the floorboard, plowing through the rain and fog.

I shut my eyes, one hand still on my belly and the other on the pendant around my neck.

After several minutes she flicked my knee and said, "You can open your eyes now, chicken."

Sure enough, the road had opened up and the fog had lifted. Even the rain had lessened here.

"Easy peasy." She grinned.

"Yeah, for crazy people."

"I come by it naturally." She paused, licking her lips. "If memory serves me, you were a bit reckless in your youth too. Motherhood is changing you, Mags."

"Someone's gotta keep the family name going."

Worry swelled up inside me, as it always did when I thought about the tremendous responsibility I was taking on. If I couldn't keep a plant alive, how in the hell did I expect to keep a kid alive?

"You'll do great," Ruth Anne said, sensing my distress. "It's like having a pet. You feed it. You change its litter box when it stinks. Easy Peasy."

I scrunched up my lips.

"I've never had a pet. Not even a Chia Pet."

"Well, then," Ruth Anne slapped her right hand on the wheel. "The poor thing is screwed." She looked at me, punching my right arm when she saw I wasn't laughing. "Don't take life so seriously. Things will be fine. I mean, with an auntie like me, what could go wrong?"

"Indeed."

"You know," she said, staring out at the road before us. "We probably could have gotten the turkey from Dark Root Grocery. I doubt Merry would have known it wasn't organic, especially if we took off the wrapper and put it in a pan in the fridge."

"Oh, she'd know, all right. She can smell preservatives a mile away. And if she didn't figure it out, June Bug would have."

"June Bug's a neat kid, isn't she?" Ruth Anne said, her eyes softening.

"Yeah," I agreed. "You ever think of having kids?"

"Me? I'm afraid that ship has sailed, my dear." I was about to ask her what she meant, when she changed the subject. "Speaking of having kids, you talk to Shane yet?"

"No." I admitted. "Why?"

"Because I need to know how this shit resolves itself for my book."

"I thought you wrote romances. My life is as far from a romance as the sinking of the Titanic."

"Bad analogy. Titanic was a great romance."

"I disagree. It was doomed. The movie made it seem romantic, but for Rose it was heartbreak followed by years of living alone afterwards. Not to mention hypothermia."

"And people think *I'm* a cynic." Ruth Anne scratched her head. "The reason Titanic was so romantic was because it was a perfect love that could never be. No reality to screw it up. And, Jack and Rose got to be together in the afterlife. That's pretty cool."

"Maybe that will be me, then." I stared out the window. "Hurray for the afterlife."

"I write paranormal romances. The afterlife plays heavily in those kinds of stories."

"Goody." I lowered my eyes, a knot forming in my chest. "At least don't use my name in your book, okay?"

Ruth Anne gave me a sideways smile. "That, I promise you."

"Watch out!" I yelled, pointing at a deer darting across the road.

Ruth Anne wrenched the wheel hard to the right. We narrowly missed the deer, but our car slipped off the side of the road, losing traction as it rolled down a muddy slope.

I pressed my back to the seat, clutching the belt across my chest as the sedan slid into the forest, gliding along the wet earth beneath its tires.

"Brakes!" I ordered.

"I'm trying!" Ruth Anne wrestled with the steering wheel, trying to navigate the vehicle as it slipped further down the embankment. A rushing river came into view and Ruth Anne frantically punched the brakes.

I fingered the crystal bracelet on my wrist. "Make it stop, make it stop, make it stop," I repeated.

Ruth Anne pushed herself back against her seat. "Hold on! We're going in!"

"Stop!" I commanded the car.

At once, we came to a sudden and abrupt halt, just feet from the river. With sweat-drenched faces we stared at one another, then whooped and high-fived in relief.

Ruth Anne got out of the car as I wrestled with my own stuck door. "Now, that's a near-death experience!" She threw her head back and howled. "What a rush!"

"When I was talking about happiness in the afterlife, I didn't mean now."

"No time like the present."

"Where are we?" I asked, still fighting to open my door, which was blocked by a heavy branch.

Ruth Anne pulled out her phone. "I have no idea," she said, shaking it. "GPS isn't working." She tapped several buttons and held it to her ear. "Phone either."

"Of course not."

"We're stuck in about two feet of mud. Got a spell to fix that?"

"I think I'm out of magick for the day." I shivered, wrapping my arms around my chest.

Ruth Anne popped the trunk and handed me a small blanket that Merry must have kept for picnics or emergencies.

"Gotta give it to Merry for always being prepared," she called from the back of the car. "There's a box of organic granola bars in here, two flashlights, several gallons of water, another blanket, and some flares. There's even a neck pillow and some romance novels. We won't die out here, at least tonight."

Ruth Anne tossed me one of the romance novels. A handsome young cowboy on the cover kissed the neck of a pretty, young blond. I threw it back at her, remembering my encounter with Shane and the young woman in his apartment

"We can send up the flares," I suggested.

"Negative. Too many trees. We'd have to get to the main road, or a clearing."

I looked up the embankment. It was steep, muddy, and littered with branches and fallen trees. It would be a feat to climb, but I could do it. "Let's go," I said, finally getting my door open.

"Hold on there, Jill. I won't be responsible for my pregnant sister tumbling down a mountain. You stay with the car. I'll find a place where my cell phone works or I can send up the flares. One way or another, we are getting out of here."

"Why are you more qualified than me?" I asked, crossing my arms.

"I lived in the Everglades for three years. Plenty of alligators, swamps, and moonshine. I think I'll be okay."

146

"Well, I lived with a group of people who were always preparing for the end times. I think I know how to take care of myself."

"Point taken. And if we end up having to live out here, I will let you take the lead. But right now, I'm walking."

Ruth Anne took the flares, two granola bars and a flashlight, and stuffed them into her pockets. "Stay in the car, okay? And don't run the engine unless you have to. We need to save the battery." She grabbed several large branches and piled them in front of the tires. "That should brace the car, in case it starts to slide again. I hope."

I swallowed, imagining me sleeping in the car as it slipped quietly into the river. After being dunked by an invisible hand in the bathtub, I wasn't keen on being submerged.

Maybe I'd add more branches after she left, just to be safe.

"Good luck," I said, suddenly worried. I ran to give her a hug.

"Quit that, or I'll tell everyone how mushy you've gone."

"I think they already know."

"If I don't make it back, tell the old woman I love her." Ruth Anne winked, and then picked up a long stick. She inspected it and nodded. "Stay put," she instructed, pointing the stick at the car.

I nodded obediently and watched my sister disappear into the thick blackness of the ancient woods.

I checked the time on my phone repeatedly, waiting impatiently inside Merry's sedan as minutes, then hours, rolled by. It was an old flip-top phone, functional but not fun, and I wished for one like Ruth Anne's, with games to play to pass the time. With nothing else to do, I decided to entertain myself with a silent game of I Spy: Forest Edition.

I spy, something slithering in the leaves.

I spy, something crawling from out from under a rock.

I spy, something watching me from a tree branch.

Admittedly, it wasn't a comforting game, and each new discovery caused my skin to ripple and my legs to draw closer to my chest. But it kept me alert. It also lessened the dread that threatened to overtake me as I thought about Ruth Anne out in the forest all alone. I dug into my memories, trying to recall if she'd been the outdoorsy type as a kid. Truth was, though we were all children of the forest, I was probably the only one who ever ventured out into the woods. I took long morning runs, trying to find myself among the trees because I didn't seem to fit in at our house.

It should be me out there, lighting flares and looking for help.

But as Ruth Anne pointed out, I was pregnant––a convenient excuse that I allowed.

I spy, a big, pregnant coward.

And then the darkness came.

Like a slide show presentation, one moment I watched the silver currents of the river rush before me, the next moment it became an oil slide, oozing across the landscape, devouring the light around it.

"C'mon Ruth Anne," I said, hopping up and down on my seat. The inside of the vehicle had fogged up and I cracked the window, braving the cold in favor of visibility. With every leaf that crunched or branch that cracked, I jumped, hopeful that Ruth Anne had come back, yet knowing it was not her who created those sounds.

I had to pee so badly it hurt and I ventured over to a little stump I had *spied* earlier.

Huddled in my blanket, I pushed up my skirt and squatted, wondering if Merry also had toilet paper in the trunk of her car? As the stream hit the ground, it rolled down the slope towards the river. It stopped, not quite making its destination. But where the trail stopped, I noticed something sparkle beneath the glint of the rising moon, something I wouldn't have seen in the light of day.

I took five giant steps forward and hovered over the glimmering object: an old road sign half-buried in the mud. I kicked away the dirt and lifted it with one hand, shining my cell phone light on it with the other.

It was one of those crazy old signs in the shape of an arrow.

"What the...?"

I swiped at the remaining dirt trying to read it, as the night around me grew deathly quiet.

123 Old Raven Road.

"Holy hell!"

I dropped the sign and dashed back to the car, retrieving the spare flashlight. Then I scrambled back to where I had found the old sign.

"You've got to be kidding me." I shone the beam across the arrow shape. Sure enough, the words matched those written in our backyard and on my bathroom mirror.

I waved the light across the ground, a small beacon in an ocean of black, looking for...something.

There it was. A path wide enough for just one person to transverse, carved through the woods.

I spy an old dirt road.

I stepped forward, casting my light into the trees. Without the moon it was pitch inside, a blackness that could swallow me whole.

I knew that I should wait for Ruth Anne to come back. We could investigate together.

But Ruth Anne might not come back.

And I had lived with Mother and Michael long enough to understand that there were no coincidences in life.

In the pit of my stomach, I knew that I had been led here, and it was a path I needed to walk alone.

I said a quick prayer of protection and cast my flashlight beam forward.

FOURTEEN

LOSING MY RELIGION

I ENTERED THE WOODS, MY FLASHLIGHT A SMALL CONSOLATION IN THE LABYRINTH of darkness.

The trees pulled back, allowing me to inch forward, and then clamped shut behind me, sealing me within. I fought my panic, trying to keep a clear head as I followed the path. I'd been called here for a reason.

It was a long trail, curving and turning, purposely constructed for confusion. Fear kept me warm, at least, and I dropped the blanket on the ground.

At last, I came to a small dale. The moon and stars flickered overhead, no longer obscured by the woods, and I could make out an old shack in the middle of the clearing, an abandoned dwelling with a smoke-blackened front wall and boarded up windows. The door was ajar, allowing an orange glow to escape. Three brass numbers, darkened with soot, hung clumsily over the door.

"123," I said. I had found my destination.

"*Maggie.*"

Someone whispered behind me. Then a dozen little whispers echoed all around me, like children telling secrets in a schoolyard.

"*Maggie. Maggie. Maggie.*"

The trees behind me had shut. I could only go forward.

I waved my free hand around me, reciting a spell remembered from childhood.

In this sphere, I cannot be
Harmed by witch, or magic being
As long as I walk in the light
This bubble keeps me through the night

For good measure, I rubbed the crystal bracelet on my arm and kissed the pendant that dangled from my neck. Superstitious, I knew. But superstition and magick went hand in hand.

The door flew open. A fire crackled within.

"Hello?" I stepped forward, casting my flashlight into the house. The walls and floor were covered in layers of soot and sawdust. A small bed, a nightstand, a rickety table with two chairs, a heap of blankets, and a faded painting of a sunset comprised the rest of the furnishings. In the center of the room sat a large, black, steaming cauldron, fueled by a fire pit beneath.

"Hello, Maggie," said a deep, female voice. The pile of blankets on the floor rose up, taking form.

"Hello, Larinda," I answered, watching the blankets transform themselves into the shape of a woman. "We meet again."

Larinda threw back the cowl of her cape and laughed. "Really, Maggie? I expected something less cliché from you."

I shone my light across her body, starting at her pointy black slippers, up her gray wool dress and black cloak, across her face. She was not beautiful. The lines and angles of her shape were unsoftened by feminine curves: her nose too sharp, her lips too thin and long, her eyes too narrow. But she was a commanding presence, and her dark hair hung in stark contrast to her alabaster skin and blood red lips. She had a handsomeness that suited her age.

"As you can see," she said, raising a pointed eyebrow. "I'm no great beauty. Never have been, really. That was all your mother. She was beautiful, charming, strong, and willful. All the men ignored me when she was in the room. As her cousin, I grew up in her shadow. Something you and I have in common, right Maggie?"

I pressed my lips together but didn't speak.

"But we were family, and you don't turn your back on family. Am I right?" Larinda's eyes flickered, burning like the embers beneath the cauldron. She softened her eyes, a slight smile touching her lips.

"It was impressive how you handled my daughter." She snapped her fingers and Leah appeared on the bed, looking tired and confused. "Cutting off her hair. Brilliant. You see, *that's* the sort of thing I expect from the great Maggie Maddock."

A witch's power was directly related to the length of her hair and I had shorn Leah's, rendering her magically impotent, at least until it grew back.

Leah turned to me, her face expressionless.

"But I'm not the fool my daughter is," Larinda said, stepping so close I could smell her breath, a mixture of soil and soot.

I stepped back. "What do you want?" I asked, shining the light into her eyes.

She didn't so much as blink. Placing a finger into the cleft of her chin like she hadn't given the question much thought until now she said, " I need something from you." She took a lock of my hair, coiling a red strand around her finger. I grabbed her wrist firmly until she let go.

"You're as fiery as your hair. Just like your father."

"I'm leaving," I said. "I'm done playing your games."

"You can try." She cocked her. "But the forest here is outside of your mother's jurisdiction. It obeys me."

I swallowed hard, knowing she was right. "If you don't want the Circle, what do you want? Stop with the games!" The cauldron hissed at my words.

Leah rose from the bed and added kindling to the fire pit. Then she sat back down and continued to stare vacantly ahead.

"On the Winter's Solstice, you and your sisters will perform a ceremony meant to keep certain *things* out of Dark Root. More specifically, me and my kind."

"Your kind?"

"Witches. Those whose interests don't align with your mother's."

"So? Why should you care if we do?"

"I have my reasons."

"She doesn't want your kind of magick in Dark Root."

"And what kind of magic is that?" she asked, fluttering her lashes innocently.

"Dark magick. Summoning. Banishment." I tried to think of what else Aunt Dora had told me. "Demonology. Necromancy."

She licked her lips, as if she had tasted something delicious. "Don't let your mother and aunt fool you, young Maggie. We've all dabbled in *dark* magick from time to time. I've known your mother for years. She wasn't always the *good* witch. You will test your powers, too. It's in your blood."

I stood taller, meeting her eye to eye. "Then you don't know me."

"Oh, I know enough." She lowered her lashes. "How's the pool-playing coming along? Making any money yet?"

I glared, clenching and unclenching my fists. From the corner of my eye I noticed that Leah had managed a smile.

"If you need money, I have plenty of it. More than enough for you to buy your Dora's precious Harvest Home."

Larinda opened her palm and produced a gold coin, then closed her hand and it was gone.

"On the solstice, you will not perform that ceremony," she said flatly. "In return, I will give you enough money to last you a lifetime, and leave you and your family alone. Forever."

My fingers trembled at Larinda's promise. But one gold coin didn't mean anything.

"I don't need your money," I said. "And you already seem to be able to come and go in Dark Root as you please."

"When your mother transferred the Circle to you...and I know she did by the way...the dome slipped. Parts of me *are* able to get in. My essence, so to speak. But my tribe and I need to be able to enter completely, without restriction. That's where you come in. Only she who wields the Circle can ensure the spell takes shape. All I ask is that you forgo it for a year."

"Assuming everything you've said is true, why would I do that?"

Larinda paused, appraising me.

She passed one of her hands over the other and produced a crystal ball, the size of a snow globe. Pictures moved within the glass.

"In Dark Root grows a unique tree, the Lightning Willow, which has fed itself for the last century on the magick of the land." Larinda waved her hand and the image of a golden willow tree appeared in the ball, a metallic river rushing behind it.

"When your mother dies, and she will, very soon I think, the tree will die too."

"Don't talk about my mother dying." My fist clenched again.

"It's a fact of life, Maggie. All things die. Your mother may be a witch but she won't live forever. Her fault, really."

I wondered what would happen if I hit her? Would Larinda take the blow, or turn to ash? Or perhaps seal me inside this cabin forever? I dug my fingernails into my palms to keep from striking her.

"Leah, the dunce that she is, has not chosen her wand," Larinda continued. "I simply want her to have access to the tree. She will cut her wand before the sun sets on your mother's life. That's all I ask. Then we all go our separate ways."

"Why would I allow that?" I reiterated.

With another wave of her hand the image of the willow was replaced by one of Mother, sleeping in her bed. "The Lightning Willow has special healing properties. You can take a wand from the tree, too. We take ours, you take yours. Save your mother..."

"Stop it!" I shouted. The ball in Larinda's hand disappeared.

"Very good, Maggie. What you just did was a mild form of banishment. See? We all walk the line."

155

"I'm done listening to your propaganda. Aunt Dora told me what a liar you are. You probably want to get into Dark Root so that you can cause harm to us all. Just like you sent Leah to do before."

Larinda's face went a shade whiter. "I never sent her to cause harm. She had one simple order, retrieve the Circle, and she bungled it. I'm sorry your family suffered because of it. That was never my intent." She glided towards the cauldron, stirring the pot. "Stay in denial if you will, but we both know your mother is sick. She doesn't have long left. Months maybe." She looked up from the pot, her eyes twinkling. "The willow can not only heal people, but extend their lives. Indefinitely, perhaps."

"That's impossible."

"Long ago, your mother cut a branch from the tree. She used the wand to keep herself young. All of us, really. That was one of the allures of joining The Council. No matter how what our differences, we all wanted eternal youth.

"But then she began to use it on outsiders. Soldiers, the sick, even a common prostitute once." Larinda spat in disgust. "She squandered its power. The more she used it on others, the less she used it on us.

"Sasha developed these ideologies. Said she didn't want to live forever, that no one should. Eventually, she stopped using it on herself altogether. As for us, we had to beg for it. Crawl around like dogs at her feet for a fix."

Larinda's face morphed from disgust to rage.

"Who the hell was she to decide for us what was best? The power got to her head. When your mother locked the wand away, it only had one charge left. And to this day I don't know if she used that last charge or not.

"I only want what I deserve. What we all deserve. We are witches. We shouldn't be bound by normal laws." She floated towards Leah, lifting her daughter's cheek. "The end is coming, Maggie. We've held it back for too long now. But it *is* coming. And when that day comes, mankind will suffer. Greatly. I suggest you prepare yourself now."

"People are always saying the world will end," I said. "But it never does."

"That day is shielded from us," Larinda said. "Even us. But when that day comes, think what would happen if you had a wand that would heal those you love the most: your sisters, your aunt, your friends, your mother." Her eyes fell to my stomach. "Your child."

My lips trembled and my heart thumped in my ears. "And if that day never comes?"

"You can use it now. To save your mother. Or others you love."

Larinda placed a hand on Leah's shoulder. "Someday, I will be a grandmother. I want my grandchild to live in a world without disease and fear. I want this for his generation. Not mine."

"You don't mean a world. You mean a select few."

Larinda's eyes brightened. "I shielded the location of the Lightning Willow many years ago. Do not perform the ritual and I will show you where it is. We will both get our wands and life will go on. Forever."

Shouts outside the cabin startled us both.

"Maggie! Maggie!" It was Shane. A beam of light shone through the boards in the window.

Larinda hissed, drawing her cloak around herself and Leah. A thunderous clap sounded beneath the cloak.

In an instant, the women vanished, replaced by two ravens.

Shane and Ruth Anne burst inside. The black birds screeched as they flew out the door, whisking past my rescuers.

"Thank God for Shane!" Ruth Anne covered me in my discarded blanket. "Or I never would have found you."

"What the hell were you doing all the way out here?" Shane asked, looking around the room. The fire was gone and the cauldron was bone cold. Only smoke and soot remained.

"Keeping warm," I said, my eyes following the birds who became one with the night.

FIFTEEN

SPIDERWEBS

WE CALLED A TOWING SERVICE IN LINSBURG. SINCE TOMORROW'S Thanksgiving, they won't be able to get here until Friday."

Shane's eyes did not move from the road as he drove us home.

I sat quietly beside him while Ruth Anne occupied herself in the back seat with a bag of Tootsie Rolls left over from Halloween.

"Merry will be so upset." I chewed on the ends of my hair, imagining her face when she heard the news. "Not only did we not get her turkey, we ruined her car."

"She'll be alright," Ruth Anne said, chomping on a mouthful of candy. "I already talked to her on the phone. Her insurance should cover most of it, after we meet the deductible."

"Deductible? How much?"

"Five hundred."

"Ugh." I slunk down in my seat as I added the cost to my ever-growing expense list.

"I'm glad you're okay," Shane said, placing a hand on my knee. I left it there a second before removing it.

"Maggie, I wanted to talk to you the other day when you saw me and…"

I glared at him, my eyes unblinking.

"...it really wasn't what it looked like," he said.

"Okay, then what was it?" I glanced over my shoulder to see if Ruth Anne was paying attention. She wasn't. Now that we were within cell range, she was busy with her phone, playing games or surfing the net.

"I can't tell you that, but you have to trust me."

"Oh, I've heard that before," I said. "Men always tell you to trust them while they're sneaking around behind your back."

"One guy breaks your heart and you think we're all like that!" He slammed his palms against the steering wheel as he pulled into the driveway of Sister House.

Merry stood in the window, talking on the phone. Eve sat on the porch swing, staring intently at something on her lap.

"If you want to believe that all men are bad, far be it from me to try and convince you otherwise," he added. "I'm just the guy that's went out of his way to rescue you...let's see, at least four times that I'm aware of."

"Rescue me?" I turned on him, my mouth dropping incredulously as Ruth Anne slipped out the back door. "For your information, I didn't need rescuing tonight. I had things perfectly under control."

"Oh, did you?" He pushed his cowboy hat further onto his head. "Well, maybe I shouldn't have come, then."

"Maybe you shouldn't have." I bumbled out the door, slamming it behind me.

"From now on, you can save your own neck," he said, peeling out of the driveway.

He turned on the radio, blasting an obnoxious country song as he rode away.

"Fine!" I yelled back, but he was gone. I didn't need him, anyway. He could go rescue someone else. The image of the blond woman filled my mind.

As I stomped up the porch steps, the patio lights went off.

"Do you have to do that every time?" Eve sighed.

"Sorry. Didn't mean to. What are you doing out here?"

"Oh, nothing."

I gave her a suspicious once-over as I stepped into the light that emanated from the living room window. She had something on her lap. A book. "The complete works of Edgar Allen Poe? Since when do you read?"

"I read."

"Yeah? What?"

"Magazines and stuff."

"Hmmm." I sat next to her on the swing. "You're really worried about Paul."

She snorted. "Hardly. I just wanted to see what all the fuss about Poe was about. Frankly," she said, putting the book in her gigantic purse. "I don't get that poem. So the raven says 'nevermore.' Is that supposed to mean something?"

I shrugged.

"If the raven actually said something useful, I could see it, but nevermore? What kind of word is that?"

The light in the window flipped off and we sat in darkness. Soon a soft, flickering glow emanated from the glass. We turned to see Merry setting a white candle down on the floor of the living room.

She sat in front of it, with legs crossed and eyes closed, and planted her hands on the floor beside her. She chanted and a golden orb of energy surrounded her as silver sparkles shone from her fingertips. We were witnessing a private moment, and though I felt like a peeping Tom, I couldn't take my eyes off my sister.

She looked so calm, so serene. In spite of the fact that she took care of Mother, day in and day out, warred with her ex-husband, and got news that her car had been in a wreck, she still managed to exude an energy of peace.

"She's beautiful," Eve said.

"Yes."

"I wish that I could be more like her." Eve cast her eyes downward.

I squeezed her hand. "Me, too."

161

The candle went out. The doorknob turned and Merry stepped onto the porch.

"I thought I sensed you two out here," she said, the light still clinging to her, lighting up her face like a halo. Her arms were bare but she didn't seem to notice the cold as she joined us on the swing.

Eve and I moved apart, making room for Merry in the middle.

She placed a hand on each of our laps, allowing her warm energy to course through us. Eve and I peeled off our sweaters, tossing them onto the porch, then rested our heads on Merry's shoulders, bookends to the woman who was more like a mother to us than a sister.

We swung, our feet leveraged against the ground, pushing and releasing in unison. Merry sang to us, a sweet tune about the stars and a little girl who traveled among them, a song she used to sing when we were children, though I couldn't remember all the words.

It didn't matter. All I wanted was to bask in her glow, to feel her energy, to sit on the porch swing of my mother's house for all eternity with Merry and Eve, where I felt safe.

"Are you mad about the car?" I asked, folding my hands into my lap.

"No. I'm not mad about the car. It was an accident."

"How about the turkey?"

She laughed. A lyrical laugh.

"Of course not." She paused for a moment, her full lips puckering, her long lashes fluttering. "I do think," she said, measuring her words. "That you are keeping something from me. That is what really bothers me."

I almost told her everything. About our pool games, the taxes on Harvest Home, Larinda, and how she had engineered the entire event tonight.

But either shame or fear of upsetting her stopped me.

"I know what you two have been up to," Merry said, gently. Eve and I raised our heads but didn't speak. "Not going to confess then? Doesn't matter. I was shown it in my visions."

Merry never lied and we knew we had been caught.

"Oh," was all I could reply.

"Remember the creed? What you put out comes back to you..."

"...three times," Eve finished.

"We are trying to help," I said.

"There are other ways, Maggie. Have faith."

I pondered this as I listened to the sounds of the night: insects, small animals thrashing through the leaves, a raven calling out from the woods. If there were other ways to help, I didn't know of any. Merry might have faith, but mine was depleted.

In my opinion, faith only worked when you did.

"Now," Merry said, tapping us each on the leg. "Tomorrow is Thanksgiving, a perfect time to express our gratitude for what we *do* have. Love and family. And that is how we'll carry on."

"Yes," Eve and I agreed.

"Now, ladies, I need to get some sleep. You can stay here, if you don't want to walk home."

"We'll be okay, Merry," I assured her. Eve and I had made the walk between Sister House and Harvest Home so many times, we knew the route by heart.

On our walk home, I thought about what Merry said, about being grateful and carrying on. I wanted to be good like her, I really did. And I planned to be. Just as soon as our problems were fixed.

"After the holidays we stop this," I said as Harvest Home came into view.

"That should be long enough, if we keep winning like we have been. I think if we can keep the shop going until February, my perfume should sell well enough to get us through the spring. And I know a banker...I'm sure if he sees how well we are doing, we could use the shop as collateral and get a loan for the taxes."

"Yes. So just a few more games then. Agreed?"

"Maybe one tonight? Bar's closed tomorrow."

"What about things coming back to us three times? Merry made me feel a bit guilty, taking money from people like that."

"I thought about that, too. We have to be extra good in the future. Volunteer at schools..."

My eyes lit up as I understood. "Man a soup kitchen. No, wait... bring soup to a soup kitchen."

"Yes."

It sounded reasonable. Enough good acts could negate the bad. Besides, we were doing it all for a noble purpose anyway. I placed a hand on my belly as we opened the front door of the house. By the time by the baby came, everything would be settled and I could devote myself to being a good mother like Merry.

"Okay, so it's settled," I said. "As of the New Year, we call it quits. Pinkie promise."

Eve and I put our little fingers out, interlocking them.

A pinkie promise: the highest form of magic.

"I'll grab Paul's keys," Eve whispered, as we snuck past Aunt Dora to get cleaned up.

"You'd think he'd get smart and start hiding them."

"You'd think," Eve said, her eyebrows arching. "But hiding things is not a man's strong suit."

"The usual," I said to the bartender, who I had come to know as Sam.

He waved a two-fingered hello, and commenced pouring our drinks. I think he knew we were hustling, but he had a mild crush on Eve, and looked the other way.

"You smell," I said to Eve as we scoped out the place.

It was empty except for a handful of people: two couples and a man wearing a yellow polo shirt and khaki slacks, who sat alone in the far corner, playing with his cell phone.

I nudged Eve and she smoothed her dress into place, a tight, black, knit number that sat low in the cleavage and high on the thigh.

"I do not smell," Eve said, running her hands through her sleek pony tail. "I smell clean. You're just too used to smelling like a barn animal."

I covered my sweater defensively. "Alpacas are not barn animals. They live outdoors."

She rolled her eyes and seated herself at the bar, crossing her legs so that an ample amount of skin was on display. I sat next to her, kerplunking myself unglamorously onto a stool.

Tonight was her show. I would assist from the sidelines.

"Think we can stop by Dip Stix after?" she asked innocently over her wine glass.

"I doubt they'll be open, but okay. Why?"

"They'll be open. Paul said they are pulling an all-nighter. Cleaning and whatnot for the holidays."

I spun my stool to face her. "Oh, I see. You want Paul to see you looking like...this."

Eve made a sour face. "I do not."

"Maybe make him a little jealous? Wondering where you've been all night?"

"Shut up."

I laughed and returned to my root beer, wishing it was whiskey. "Sorry," I said, giving her a comforting smile. "You look beautiful."

"Thank you," she said.

Her self-esteem had taken a hit lately. The least I could do was to tell her the truth.

We waited thirty minutes, keeping one eye on the man in the corner and the other eye on the door. One of the couples left, but no one else came in.

"I guess he's our mark," I said, using a term I'd heard on an old movie.

Eve nodded, slammed down her second drink and sauntered over to the man in her three-inch heels.

"Ever see him before?" I asked Sam as he wiped down the bar. I had been here so many times lately, I felt like I was a part of the inner circle.

Sam leaned forward. "He comes in from time to time. Always alone. Always in the corner talking on the phone. Has the personality of a used car salesman. Tips horrible. I'd never trust him alone with my sister."

In spite of Sam's ominous words, I was glad to hear it. I felt less guilty when I imagined the men we hustled were bad guys of sorts and that Eve and I were modern day Robin Hoods.

Eve settled herself in the chair across from the man.

I could tell he was shocked by his good fortune. She was young, while he bordered on middle age. She was fit, while his midsection spilt over the top of his pants. She had a full head of dark hair, while his was so blond and thin you could see his scalp. He looked at her the same way Ruth Anne looked at a cookie—like he'd devour her, the second they were alone.

The man walked to the bar, gave me a disinterested look, and returned to Eve with two fresh drinks.

She batted her eyes gratefully and pulled on her most demure smile. As the evening progressed, her innocence would turn to seduction, turning her charms and her magic up a notch. She'd ask him if he wanted to play a game, teasing him about knowing how to use his stick. The man would smile wickedly at the challenge. They'd bet five bucks and she'd lose the first game, put out her bottom lip, and pout. And pout.

The man would tell her how pretty she was and offer to give her the money back.

"No." She'd shake her head. "I want to win it back, fair and square."

"Okay."

She'd win the next game. This sometimes required a little help from me.

"I can't believe this!" she'd say, almost breathless.

The man would be a little flustered, a little embarrassed, scratching

166

on the back of his neck, wondering what had happened. It was only five bucks, he knew, but it was more than that. He was looking to make time with my sister, and to do that, he had to impress her. He had to win.

They'd keep playing, upping the stakes. She'd win most games, but let him win once in a while to keep him in.

"Tell you what," she'd whisper, when he'd had several more beers. "Last game. Winner takes all."

"All?"

"All." She'd bite her bottom lip as she looked up at him with her doe eyes. He'd swallow, uncertainly, but end up agreeing to anything to secure the evening.

"Another soda?" Sam asked, breaking me from the scene.

"Sure," I answered. "Got anything stronger?"

"Diet coke?"

"That works."

A group of college kids filed in, and Sam left to check their IDs.

I returned my attention to Eve and the stranger. Eve was having a hard time making her shots because the man kept leaning in too close behind her whenever she leaned over the pool table.

"Give me some room?" she asked, trying to keep the flirt in her voice.

The man took a step back, his hands inches from her backside, poised like he wanted to grab her. I was so focused on watching him watch my sister, that I forgot to assist her and she missed her shot.

She shot me a questioning look. I shrugged apologetically.

The man licked his lips. His striped ball rolled smoothly across the green felt and landed in its hole. Eve's eyes widened at me.

"Sorry," I mouthed.

This time I hadn't forgotten, but his will to sink the shot had been stronger than my desire to stop it. I focused harder on the next one, managing to halt it just before it fell into the corner pocket.

Eve moved to the other side of the table.

The man followed closely behind, his hands tracing the shape around her body, his hips thrusting near hers as she bent over. He was drunk. Drunk on alcohol, drunk on desire.

The energy around him warped. It was perverted, unclean. It made me ill.

He reached around her and grabbed her breast. Eve turned angrily, the sweetness gone from her face. He stepped back, then tried to repeat it. It was at that moment that I realized I was not a modern day Robin Hood. I was a pimp.

The man moved to grab her again.

I slammed my mug and twenty bucks on the bar and stormed towards them.

"Time to go," I said, yanking Eve by the arm and pulling her to the door.

"Who are you?" he asked, following.

"I'm taking her home," I said, ushering her outside.

"Maggie, what the hell is wrong with you?" Eve demanded, trying to pull away.

"You gals lesbians?" he asked, clapping his hands together. "Because I'm okay with that."

"No." I glared. "Sisters."

"Whoo-ey! Even better."

Up close, the man had a plastic face, doughy and jowly, with a sharp nose and thin lips. His only attractive feature was his large, hazel eyes––simple eyes that betrayed every thought he had, and none of them were good.

"You can't leave," he said, grabbing Eve's free arm as he followed us out. "We had a bet. And I was winning. You can't welch on a bet."

"Take this," I said, tossing him every dollar I had in my pocket as I scanned the dark parking lot for Paul's black blazer. I found it parked near a silver Cadillac.

"Hey!" Eve objected. "I could have beaten this clown."

"Clown? A few minutes ago I was your sexy teddy bear. Did you forget that already?"

"Come on, Eve," I said, pulling her along the wall. I wanted to stay in the light of the bar as long as possible. "Let him keep it."

"But Maggie..."

"I don't want the money," the man said, his face reddening. "You know damned well what I want."

He grabbed Eve's arm, yanking her away from me.

"Leave me alone!" she screamed, trying to pull away, but his grip was too tight. "Leave me alone!" she repeated, trying to hit him with her purse, but he had her arms firmly secured.

He spun her around, pinning her in front of him so that they both faced me. "Don't think I didn't recognize you," he said to Eve as he kissed her neck. "I know who you are." One hand traveled down the length of her torso, stopping near her hips. "And I know what you like."

"Leave her alone!"

He smiled. "Make me."

Anger rose up inside me as I remembered a similar incident in a bar parking lot. Two men had thrown me into their car, then tried to assault me as I begged them to stop.

Shane had come then, ripping them off me.

But I didn't need Shane now. I didn't need anyone.

I charged at the man, full force.

I felt an electricity course through me, an energy gathered from the air and the ground around me: the magick of Dark Root. A blue spark shot from my hands as I slammed into his beefy arm. He fell backwards, his eyes half-closed as he hit the brick wall. He slid down the wall, blood trickling from his mouth. When he landed on the ground, his entire body fell over.

"Maggie!" Eve gasped, running to him and holding up his limp wrist. "What have you done?"

I opened my hands, stretching out my fingers. Blue currents buzzed around my fingertips.

"I think he's dead," she said, looking helplessly up at me.

"No," I said, joining her on the ground. We listened for his heartbeat, his breathing, his pulse, any indication that he was still alive. None came.

Yer father had the deathtouch.

Eve's face was drained of color. "Maggie! I think we killed him!"

Sixteen

Baby Did A Bad, Bad Thing

Halfway between Dark Root and Linsburg
May, 1994

MAGGIE AND HER SISTERS GATHERED IN THE OLD CHURCH THAT SAT exactly halfway between Dark Root and Linsburg. Built in the early nineteen hundreds, it did its best to mend the fences of these rival towns, towns separated by economical as well as ideological differences: mining, God, ecology, and witchcraft.

That rivalry existed to this day, though it was friendlier now, good-natured exchanges between old friends through jokes and jabs at the local bars.

But some folks, mostly country people, held on to the deep-seated feud that had lasted almost a century, a feud kept alive by well-meaning parents and grandparents––hushed talk about the days before "the witches came," and "this whole Goddamned part of the world turned into a Goddamned tourist trap."

The old church was typical of its generation. Chipped white paint with blue trim and stained glass windows. It even had its original steeple. Newer and fresher churches had sprung up in the last fifty years, mostly in Linsburg, but this church still held service every Sunday to a handful of people. Carrying on. Carrying on.

"I don't want to go in," Maggie said, clutching the doorway with both hands as her sisters marched in dutifully beneath her arms. Her mother gave her a firm push on the back, dislodging her.

"If I have to go in, so do you," she said.

It wasn't the presence of God that frightened Maggie, the omnipotent being who knew her every deed and thought, more powerful than her mother or even Santa Claus.

It was something stronger and even more persistent. Death.

One of Miss Sasha's friends had passed three days before, a Linsburg woman who'd come to Mother searching for answers on love and health.

"If you dab this oil on the inside of your wrist, Bob will turn his head back towards you," Mother directed the woman. "If you put this in your tea every morning, you will keep your heart strong."

But Miss Sasha's magick was not enough to turn Bob's head away from his lover––a beautiful woman half his age––or to keep the woman's heart beating.

On the third day after Mother's visit, she had collapsed into her still-warm tea.

And now they all convened, waiting for the service to begin so that they could say their goodbyes.

Miss Sasha and the girls were ushered into seats at the front of the church, where a long, black coffin sprawled out before them. Maggie drew her feet under the pew, trying to put as much distance between hers and the coffin as possible.

"Don't be silly." Mother scolded her. "Death's not catchy."

But Maggie wasn't so sure.

The women in Mother's circle had been falling like dominoes lately, one right after the other.

Bad heart. Diabetes. Lung cancer. They came, asking Mother for help, pleading. "We know you have the ability. Share it with us, please!"

Maggie'd never forget the urgency in their eyes, or the brief *sadness in her mother's, when all she could offer them was salve for their chests and teas for their hearts.*

Eventually, they were all overtaken.

The service went on, as a man in a long, black robe talked about eternal salvation and going to a better place, a place where there were flowers in the winter and no one got sick. Maggie thought it sounded nice. She just wasn't sure she wanted to die to get there.

At last, the robed man called up several people to speak about the deceased.

Through tears, they talked about the woman's devotion as a mother and her services to the community. When they finished, the pastor prompted the entire audience to come and view the coffin.

"I don't want to," Maggie said to her mother. "Please don't make me."

"She looks the same as always. Pretend she's sleeping."

But she did look different. Her olive-toned skin had grown pallid, her limbs seemed bonier, and her hair looked like strands of frazzled yarn. The woman had never been lovely, but now she looked spectral.

Maggie noted another difference as she stared into the coffin, an indefinable element that separated the living from the dead. She stared at the body, trying to figure it out.

Then it dawned on her. There was no life force, no energy. Just emptiness.

The thought saddened her, to an extent that she felt it all the way down into her stomach.

It wasn't fair.

None of this was fair. Why should someone be given a life, then have it taken away? What was the point? She looked at the line of people behind her, listening to them whisper about what they should eat for lunch or where they should spend their next weekend.

Why should they continue on, Maggie wondered, while this woman lay here cold? "It isn't fair," Maggie declared out loud, turning her glare onto the crowd.

"It is the natural order of things," her mother said, placing a hand on her shoulder.

"But why? Why do we live only to die? Who decided that was a good idea?"

Mother gave Maggie a sad, weary smile and Maggie noticed how old she looked. She would die too, Maggie realized, leaving her and her sisters alone.

In that moment Maggie vowed never to have a child. It would die, or she would.

Either way, someone would be left behind.

Maggie took one final glance at the woman, etching her image into her brain. Life might go on for the others, but Maggie would honor the woman's memory by spending the day alone in her bedroom, with every light off.

She reached inside her skirt pocket for the wildflower she had picked while playing in the woods that morning. It was crumbled now, and a few of its purple leaves had fallen away, but it was still lovely and the only offering she had. As she placed the flower on the woman's chest, the woman's eyes popped open.

They stared at her, with wide, bulbous, empty lenses.

Maggie screamed and pushed her way through the crowd and out the door.

When her mother caught up, she scolded her fiercely for making a spectacle of the family.

"She woke up!" Maggie insisted. "I swear it!"

"For Heaven's sake, Maggie," Miss Sasha said. "Get ahold of yourself. If you are going to take my place someday, you can't be afraid of something as trivial as death."

Dark Root, Oregon
November, 2013

"This can't be happening," Eve buried her face in her hands, her shoulders rising and falling as she tried to catch her breath.

There was no doubt about it. The man was dead and we had killed him.

Correction. I had killed him.

"Eve, snap out of it," I said, pulling her hands from her face. "We need to figure out what to do."

"What to do? What to do?" Eve bordered on hysteria, the cool demeanor she normally wore replaced by one of sheer terror. "What *can* we do? He's dead!"

I kicked at him, trying to nudge him onto his side. He wouldn't move. His mouth popped open and blood ran down the sides of his cheeks. His hazel eyes stared up at us accusingly.

"How can you be so calm?" Eve asked, as I studied the corpse. "You, of all people, should be freaking the fuck out."

I should be. I was practically phobic when it came to death.

Yet here, when confronted with the corpse of a man I had just killed, a macabre sort of calm washed over me. It was almost dreamlike in its irrationality. People couldn't be alive one moment and then gone the next. That wasn't the way the universe worked. We had warning. We had time to drink our tea before we fell in, face first.

"Maggie," Eve said, covering me with something. "Are you okay?"

"No. I'm not okay. I don't think I'll ever be okay again."

A car pulled into the parking lot and a handful of college students tumbled out. They walked past us, one of them almost stepping on the man. "Old people can't handle their booze."

"We need to call the police," I said.

Eve grabbed me by the shoulders. "We can't. We...I might go to jail."

"It was *self-defense*, Evie. That man assaulted you. I *pushed* him

175

off." I enunciated the word, so that we got our stories straight. Move along, no *deathtouch* to see here. Just a good, firm pushing. "He hit his head because he was drunk."

I opened my purse and Eve clamped it shut.

"Maggie. Wait. It...it might have been my fault. The reason he assaulted me."

"We were trying to hustle him, I know. But we didn't take his money. And that still didn't give that asshole any right to attack you. No man has that––"

Eve cut me off. "No, Maggie. That perfume we made a few weeks ago, the one I was experimenting with. Remember? I put some on, to try it out. I put a lot of it on, in fact." She pressed her lips together, wringing her hands. "I thought we'd be going to see Paul afterwards. He's been so distant lately. I heard him tell Shane that he would be going to Seattle soon. I thought...Oh, God, I thought..."

"You thought you'd use your perfume to make sure that didn't happen."

Eve buried her face in her hands again and sobbed. "Oh, God, Maggie. I'm so embarrassed."

"And sorry," I said, looking at the guy by our feet. "I hope to hell you're sorry."

"Yes."

She wiped away her tears, streaking mascara across her cheeks.

"You could have told me," I said, shock replaced by a bolt of anger. "You could have fucking *told* me that you had Man Attack all over you, before we went out. What the hell, Eve?"

"I forgot, okay? I just wanted us to get the money and go see Paul. That was all that was on my mind. And how can I tell you anything? You make fun of everything I do. You think you would have let that one slide? That I'm so insecure about losing my boyfriend that I have to resort to magick? Could you have held your tongue for that?"

I stared at Eve. She stared back.

The corpse lay quietly between us. It was madness, every bit of it.

"Okay," I said, wiping my forehead. "We are in this together, right?" I held up the finger that I had lanced during Mother's ritual. We were bound together as sisters and as witches. We had each other's backs.

"Let's get him in his car. I'll drive and you follow. We'll head back to Sister House and wake Merry and Ruth Anne. They're smart. One of them will know what to do."

Eve pressed her lips together, bobbing her head in agreement.

I reached into his jeans pockets, trying not to look at him as I remembered the corpse in the church whose eyes snapped open. But his were already open. I resisted every instinct I had to run through the parking lot, screaming. Finally, I found a set of keys. I clicked the little button on the keychain and the lights on a silver Cadillac went off and on. I drove it to where Eve waited, leaving the passenger door open and the engine running.

"You shouldn't be lifting," Eve said.

"I shouldn't be doing a lot of things," I said. "You take his legs. I'll get his shoulders."

He didn't move the entire drive to Sister House.

Not that he should have. He was, after all, dead.

Still, I kept one eye on the road, and the other on my passenger's stiffening body buckled in beside me, half expecting him to pop up at any time and say, "Hey, that was a great nap! Can you drive me back to my hotel?"

But he didn't.

He sat still as a mannequin, his eyes staring straight ahead, his mouth slightly open, the rivulet of blood drying on his cheek.

There was absolutely no sign that he was alive, or had ever been alive. His absence of life was even more obvious as I exhaled the cold night air, steam coming from my mouth like a locomotive, while my passenger sat breathless.

All my life, I'd feared death, been paralyzed by the thought that someday I, and everyone I knew, would wind up six feet underground, as if we had never existed at all. Yet, here I was, driving calmly down the deserted back roads of Dark Root like it was any other night, with the man I killed beside me.

I still couldn't wrap my brain around all that had happened, but on one thing I was clear: I was going to do something about it. For every spell there was an anti-spell. For every power, an opposing power. If I had the *deathtouch,* then someone out there had the *lifetouch.*

And if anyone possessed such a power, it was my sister Merry.

I pulled into the driveway, surprised to see the light in the nursery still on. Ruth Anne must be awake, pecking away at her keyboard or reading a book.

The thought comforted me. If Merry did have the *lifetouch*, Ruth Anne might know how to activate it.

Eve pulled in behind me. Without saying a word she scrambled out of the car, her face glistening under the pale moon.

"Here," she said, sheepishly handing over Mother's spell book. It had been in my room and she must have pilfered it. "I've been studying spells."

Love spells, no doubt.

I took the book and texted Ruth and Merry. "Come outside. Now. Don't wake June Bug or Mother."

The curtains flickered in the nursery and the light went off. A minute later Ruth Anne and Merry joined us on the porch steps, their faces heavy with worry.

"What's wrong?" Merry asked, putting a hand to her chest. "Is it Aunt Dora?"

"No." I shook my head, trying to figure out how to tell them what had happened. The horror of the event began to creep up again, and I pushed it down.

There'd be plenty of time to process it all. I had to keep my head, at least for now.

Luckily, I didn't have to be the one to tell the story. Eve told them, in fits of hysteria intermixed with woeful sobs, about how we had ignored Merry's warning and were out hustling pool, and about the man who had come on too strongly.

"It was my fault," she said, gasping for breath. "I wore my perfume. Maggie was trying to save me."

"What do you mean your fault?" Merry asked.

I pointed to the car, and the passenger inside that neither Ruth Anne nor Merry had noticed.

"I have father's *deathtouch*," I said simply, showing them my offending hands. "I killed him."

"What?" Merry bounded down the steps towards the vehicle with Ruth Anne following. "Maggie, what did you do?"

"I didn't mean to," I said.

Seeing the man through Merry's eyes, I envisioned him—not as the creepy stranger who wouldn't leave Eve alone—but as a person with family and friends who were probably waiting for him somewhere.

"I didn't mean to," I repeated, as Merry cradled the man's head in her arms.

We wept. We all wept.

Except for Ruth Anne, who stared curiously at the moon.

"Can you do anything Merry? Anything at all?"

Merry had been working over the man for the last twenty minutes, the color draining from her small frame as she tried to pump her energy into his.

At last, worn and tired, she withdrew from the car.

"It's not enough," she said, falling back against the side of his Cadillac. "If you had gotten him here when he was almost dead, maybe. But he's dead, and there's nothing we can do about it."

She held out something to show us. "I got his driver's license. His name was Leo. Leonard actually, but I think he went by Leo. He was forty-three years old and an organ donor."

"We're going to jail," Eve cried. "And then to hell."

"Did you try your wand?" I asked, desperately. "Maybe if you use your wand..."

Merry shook her head. "I tried everything."

Eve snatched the license away from Merry, reading his stats aloud repeatedly.

"We're not going to jail *or* hell, and this man is not staying dead!" I turned to my sisters, fixing them with a resolved stare. "If I have to violate every law in The Universe, we are fixing this. We were given powers for a reason. There has to be something we can do."

My voice cracked as I spoke, panic settling over me. I had counted on Merry being able to fix this. I hadn't allowed myself to think about what would happen if she couldn't.

"You heard Merry," Eve said. "There's nothing we can do."

"No." Ruth Anne startled us. She had been quiet until now. "If you're really willing to violate every law of The Universe, there may be something we can do. But I'm not sure it will work, and I'm not sure we are up for it."

Ruth Anne regarded me blankly, academically, sending a chill down my spine.

"Anything," I said. "I will do anything."

"You might have to."

SEVENTEEN

BACK TO GOOD

IN THE DAYS WHEN IT WAS THE COUNCIL OF THIRTEEN, I OVERHEARD A discussion––an argument really. Dark Magick, Miss Sasha called it, though some didn't agree."

Ruth Anne took a deep breath, sending soft plumes of smoke into the night as we gathered around her.

"There were certain spells our mother didn't believe anyone should have access to. Claimed they were unnatural, and went against everything Dark Root stood for. Banishment. Summoning..."

"Necromancy," I said, remembering my conversation with Aunt Dora.

"You mean?" Eve asked.

"Yes. Bringing back the dead," Merry confirmed solemnly.

Ruth Anne's eyes took on a faraway look. "Miss Sasha sealed those spells off. Forbade their use. Of course, some of the others, especially Armand, were furious about her decision. 'Who are you to determine what we should have access to and what should be sealed?' he demanded. But Miss Sasha was firm and stubborn, as usual. Too much power in the wrong hands, she insisted, could be dangerous."

I regarded my sister. Ruth Anne was older than us and remembered things from the old days. "So, you think the spell...the necromancy spell...exists?"

She shrugged. "Your guess is as good as mine, but it sure caused problems in The Council once she made the decree. If it didn't exist, why did it cause so much turmoil?"

Eve opened Mother's spell book and flipped through pages. "I'm not seeing it," she said.

"She may have gotten rid of those spells altogether," I said.

"Doubtful," Ruth Anne said. "Our mother may not have been a fan of such magick, but she hated ignorance more. She'd never destroy arcane information like that."

"Look! The last page is thicker than the rest!" Eve showed us a page four times as thick as the others in the book. "And it's blank!"

I ran my fingers over the last page, looking for bumps or incriminating marks, something that would indicate a spell.

"Some spells can only be read by the light of the moon," Ruth Anne said.

Eve lifted the book. We squinted at the blank page, trying to squeeze out words where there were none.

"Maybe it needs to be a certain phase of the moon? Like a full moon?" Eve suggested.

Merry put a finger to her chin, her wide eyes darting around. "If Mama was serious about hiding these spells, she'd put them where no one could look."

A thought clawed at my mind. "Her room! C'mon."

"Quiet now," I said, holding my fingers to my lips as we crept across the floorboards of the living room and up the stairs.

The staircase protested our combined weight with creaks and moans. As I went to turn the doorknob, Eve clamped her hand over mine.

"Let me," she said.

Eve had always been the sneakiest and the stealthiest among us, as quiet as a cat when she wanted to be. We watched, not daring to move, as she twisted the brass knob to the right, soundlessly opening the door.

The bedroom was dark, save for the sliver of a moon that shone through the window, casting its crescent beam directly onto Mother's face. Her eyes were half-opened, in the same manner as Leo's, staring into the canopy above her. She looked doll-like in her large bed.

I kept an eye on her as Eve tiptoed across the floor, rolled up the carpet, and revealed the chalky outline of the pentagram.

We then scoured the room, pulling open drawers, looking under knick knacks and behind frames, searching for hidden alcoves, quietly and desperately seeking out the lost spells. I tripped over the furled carpet and fell headlong into Mother's bed. We all froze in place but Mother kept sleeping, her eyes not even blinking.

After several minutes we all shrugged at one another.

We'd searched every spot, and had come up empty. Perhaps we'd been wrong to think the missing spells were in here. I sighed, motioning for the others to follow me out. As I stepped forward I heard a creaking in the floorboards where the carpet had been. I touched my foot to the spot again, and once again the floorboard groaned.

I removed my phone from my pocket and aimed the light at the wooden plank. It looked exactly like the rest of the floorboards, except newer. My sisters gathered near me and we lowered ourselves to our hands and knees to for closer inspection.

"A knot!" I pressed my fingers into the pine knoll, expecting it to move. Nothing.

"Try again," Ruth Anne whispered, the room so cold I could see her breath. I pushed my entire palm into the knot and the side of the board suddenly gave way, dropping into a small, open pit.

We turned towards the bed, but Mother slept.

I reached inside, feeling around inside the small, dark hole. I crawled my fingers along the insides, looking for...

"Scrolls!" I said in a booming voice, then quieted myself as I removed a dozen or so from the chamber.

183

One by one, I handed them all to Merry.

Ruth Anne glanced out the window. The moon was high, illuminating her thoughtful face. "How long has it been since the, um, incident?"

"About an hour, I think. Maybe a little more."

"I hate to be the bearer of bad news, but I don't think we have much time. According to some legends, the soul completely leaves the body within three hours. If you can't bring him back before then, you never will."

"Oh." I opened one of the scrolls. It was blank. "Invisible ink?" I asked, reaching for the nearest candle.

Ruth Anne stopped me. "Most likely. But if our mother went to such lengths to hide these, she wouldn't use ordinary candle magick to read them."

"We have to try." I lit a red candle and ran the flame across the parchment. No words appeared.

"Now what?" Merry asked, worry all over her face.

"Moon magick?" I asked.

Ruth Anne took the scrolls and crossed the bedroom, positioning herself in front of the window. She squinted through her glasses as she attempted to read one, then another. "No dice," she said. "But these could require the light of a full moon. If so, we're screwed."

"Mirror magick?" I asked tentatively, checking Mother's book.

"It's worth a shot," Ruth Anne said. "Eve, I know you have a mirror somewhere in that purse of yours."

Eve rummaged through her handbag and produced a large compact. Ruth Anne held a scroll to the mirror as Merry and I crowded behind her, but the parchment wasn't giving up its secrets.

"Maybe there's nothing on these scrolls," I said, slumping against one of the bedposts.

Merry waved her hands over them.

"Oh, there's something on them, alright. Dark things. Spells that should have been destroyed a long time ago."

"I think we should just turn ourselves in," I said.

Merry raised her chin. "No, Maggie. It's not just about you and Eve. It's about that man in the car out there. We have to try and fix this." She passed her hands over the scrolls again, stopping at each one as she sensed its energy.

"This one," she said, removing one and handing it to me. Her hands trembled, a sign that she had depleted too much of her energy with the task.

"But how?" I asked. "We still don't know how to read it."

Merry closed her eyes and a soft glow enveloped her. "We try it all."

"Of course!" Ruth Anne said, as Eve relit the candle.

I unfurled the scroll and stood before the window, facing away. Ruth Anne held up the mirror so that the moon cast its glow onto it and it bounced back onto the parchment. Eve ran the flame of the candle along it.

"Holy Hell," Ruth Anne said, shaking her head. "It worked."

Sure enough, black letters in archaic script began to appear.

At the top of the scroll were the words: *Recipe for Raising the Dead.*

We scoured the house, collecting the list of ingredients imbedded on the scroll: the wax from three black candles, an assortment of herbs, a lock of hair from an innocent.

The last was achieved by snipping a strand of June Bug's hair while she slept, all the while trying to keep Merry calm as she watched a golden lock from her daughter's head fall into a silver bowl. We even managed to find a box large enough to "entomb the subject"––the box from Paul's metallic tree.

All that was left was *a wand of life.*

"Mama said she lost it," Merry sighed as we stood in the living room. "This may be the end of the line."

A memory trickled into my brain.

I raced towards the door that guarded Mother's sitting room,––a room filled with treasures hoarded across the decades and the one room in the house we had never gotten around to cleaning out because the job seemed insurmountable.

My sisters caught on and were by my side.

"Door of steel, door that's locked, let us in with just a knock."

I was surprised that I remembered the spell. Eve gave the door a quick rap. A click on the lock let us know the incantation had worked.

"Impressive," Ruth Anne said. "Good work, Maggie."

I flipped on the light. The space was the size of a small bedroom, and packed from wall to wall with an assortment of boxes, bins, knick-knacks and, no doubt, secrets.

"Where shall we start?" Eve kicked at a box as she headed in.

"Help me clear a path," I said, wading through a waist-deep collection of Mother's belongings towards the far back corner of the room.

Around me, my sisters pushed and piled crates to the side, allowing me squeeze through. The musty smell was suffocating, and I had to cover my nose with the back of my arm to keep from retching.

At last, I found my way to the spot where I had seen the shining object the last time I was here. Ruth Anne and Merry joined me while Eve guarded the door, worried perhaps that it would shut and lock us in.

We sifted through pictures, newspaper clippings, and small pieces of furniture, tossing them all aside even as nostalgia did its best to lure us in.

"Merry, you sense anything?" I asked, sifting through a bin of costume jewelry.

She put her hands to her temples. "This room has too much energy from too many people. It's actually making me sick."

"I guess I was wrong," I said. Maybe the wand really was lost.

"I'm sorry, Maggie." Merry stumbled over a trunk to stand beside me. "We'll figure something out."

"Well, lookie here," Ruth Anne said, pulling on a stick half-buried beneath a carton of photo albums. She bent over, tugging at it, as if she was trying to pull a stubborn weed from a garden.

At last, it gave, sending her tripping over the box behind her.

She lifted the stick as our mouths dropped open. It was thin and sleek, pale yellow in color, with an emerald gem attached at the end. Ruth Anne waved it and a soft, green glow illuminated the room.

"It looks just like the wand in the book," Merry said.

"Only more beautiful," I added.

"Let's get this done," Eve said, holding the door open as we stumbled to the entrance. "Before it's too late."

EIGHTEEN

MAN IN THE BOX

THERE ARE NIGHTS WHEN YOU QUESTION JUST ABOUT EVERYTHING: WHO you are, where you've come from, what your purpose is, how you got to your current place in life.

And then there are nights when you just accept things.

Nights when you stand beneath a silver moon, digging a shallow grave for a man you murdered. A man who probably had a wife and children, a mother and a job. A man who probably wouldn't have tried to molest your kid sister, if she hadn't been wearing a perfume enchanted to entice men in the first place.

These are the nights you try not to think.

Because if you think––about the corpse sitting in the car a dozen feet away, about your inability to determine wrong from right, about the fact that your mother was right about you after all, that you walk the line, just like your father––you just might go mad.

And I couldn't go mad.

Anyway, it was Thanksgiving, officially, and I wasn't going to let this little *incident* ruin the holidays.

"No!" I said aloud as I plunged my shovel into the earth and tossed out another spade full of dirt. "I'm going to keep it together!"

"Maggie, you okay?" Merry stopped digging and faced me, her eyes concerned. In this lighting, as her gold hair framed her sweet face, she looked more angelic than ever. "You can take a break, if you need to. We'll be okay."

"Me? I'm fine, Merry. Thanks for asking."

I caught my sisters shooting each other knowing looks, looks that said I wasn't *all right*, that in fact I had lost my marbles.

"I'm fine," I repeated emphatically, tossing out an extra-large helping of dirt and wondering how much deeper we would need to dig.

The spell said to encase the subject in a box, then bury him under the light of a waning moon, but it didn't specify how *deep* the grave needed to be. An unhelpful omission. Since the "subject" would eventually dig his way out of that grave, clawing his way through the box and layers of muck, I conjectured we shouldn't dig it too deeply.

The experience would be traumatic enough for the poor guy as it was.

Fortunately for us, however, the timing of his death couldn't have been better, being a waning moon and all. If I've learned anything from this ordeal, it's that if you are going to commit murder, and have any intention of bringing the deceased back to life, always plan it around the correct moon cycle.

Lucky break for Maggie!

"I think," I said, continuing to dig. "That this might be a lucrative business. Bringing people back from the dead. If it works out, we might start charging for it. Gotta bring in more money than that stupid magick store does."

"Maggie, stop," Eve said, wiping her forehead with cashmere gloves she would never wear again.

"I'm just saying...why not? We can call it Bodies R Us. They're not dead unless we say they're dead." I grinned at Ruth Anne, sure she'd appreciate my joke.

She shook her head and continued digging.

"What?" I asked, throwing my shovel onto the ground. "Are we too good for death jokes now?"

Merry pressed her lips together. "Honey, you've had a terrible shock and now it's finally setting in. Go sit on the porch steps and we'll finish this. We'll call you when it's done."

"No!" I screamed, surprising myself with the shrillness of my voice. I tore at the air with both hands, as if being assaulted by an invisible man, tears stinging my eyes. "I won't sit by while my sisters bury the man I..."

I choked, unable to finish the sentence. I lifted my trembling chin. "Neither hell nor jail is good enough for me."

Someone's arms wrap around me. I recognized the vanilla and lavender scent as Merry's. I hyperventilated in her arms as she held me, cooing me to quiet.

"It's okay, honey. It will be okay."

How could I explain to her that it wouldn't be okay? Nothing might ever be *okay* again. Even if we did manage to raise him, I had the *deathtouch*, just like my father. And there was no coming back from that.

"What if we can't do it, Merry?" I sniffed, wiping my nose on her shoulder as I stared at the Christmas tree in the front yard, the box that would soon be a coffin.

"We will," she said, brushing the hair from my face. "You'll see."

"I think this is deep enough," Ruth Anne announced, tossing her shovel onto the ground. "We'd better hurry."

I let out one final sob of self-pity and nodded.

Merry grabbed my hand and we converged on the car.

"I'm sorry," I said to the man in the passenger seat.

He sat buckled in, staring straight ahead. I removed his seat belt, noticing the stiffness of his body we hefted him from the car. You hear that the dead are cold, but you can never imagine how cold. It's not a freezer type of cold or a snow type of cold. It's an empty chill, like floating in deep space. A coldness without hope.

"We don't have much time," I said as we lowered him into the box.

He didn't quite fit and we pushed on arms and legs, stuffing him inside like an unwilling Jack-in-the box.

Merry wiped the salve she had concocted across his face and neck. It smelled horrible, like ashes and mold. Next, she reached into her pocket and produced Mother's wand.

"Once he's completely buried, we use this," she said.

"Paul says that in the old days, people were often buried alive," Eve said, fighting back a shiver. "He said gravediggers found coffins with scratch marks on the inside."

"Maybe they weren't buried alive," I suggested. "Maybe they were guinea pigs in spells like this one."

"Maggie, you're not funny."

"I know."

At last, it was done. The man who'd been buying us drinks and pawing at my sister only a few hours ago was now four feet underground in my front yard. I wanted to stick a cross in the earth, or a stone, something to mark this place.

But I couldn't think like that. I had to believe he was just sleeping and would wake up shortly, and we'd all go back to our normal lives.

Merry lifted the wand. The emerald-colored gem shone so dim, it faded into the night. The wand was dying, too.

"We could use this on Mama," Merry said, her voice almost a whisper.

There was a cold silence that passed between us. If the wand had one charge left, did we waste it on a stranger? Or did we try and save the woman we loved, who hovered very near death herself in the bedroom upstairs? It could buy her time.

Our heads turned in unison towards her window.

"No," I said, resolutely. "There's still hope for Mother, but there's no hope for this guy. We have to use it on him."

Merry nodded and we gathered around the grave. She lifted her wrist, ready to cast the wand, but I stopped her.

"Give it to me, Merry. I have to be the one."

"But Maggie," Merry protested. I knew what she was thinking. She had the gift of healing, while I had the curse of...

She handed it over.

My hand shook as I took it. Merry might have the right kind of magick, but my powers were greater, and I had Mother's Circle.

My sisters held hands, chanting words from Mother's scroll, indecipherable gibberish that produced an ethereal sound when spoken together, like angels falling from heaven.

I raised the wand, catching site of a raven that roosted between the spokes of the old garden gate, intently watching me.

It was now or never.

The price of the *deathtouch* had to be paid.

PART II

NINETEEN

EVERLONG

Dark Root, Oregon
Sister House: The Front Yard
Time: The Witching Hour

"YOU'RE A DREAM WALKER."

"Yes."

Shane stood before me, dressed in a pair of jeans and a white t-shirt. Downy brown curls cut across his forehead, framing his storm-gray eyes and his strong brow. He noticed my appraisal and waved his hand. His shirt was suddenly gone.

"This better?" He smiled crookedly, inching closer to me.

I held my breath as he stepped through the fog, stopping so close I could feel his breath on my neck. He leaned in, tilting my chin back with his fingers, grazing my neck with his lips.

"Why are you here?" I asked, confused. He wasn't supposed to be here. "It's not safe."

I pulled away from him and looked around. We stood in the front yard of Sister House.

The ground was moist beneath my feet, the sky starless and without light. We were all alone.

"Why not?"

"I...I'm not sure." I had secrets, many secrets. I closed my eyes trying to bring them up. Pictures of a baby, a pool table and a Cadillac danced in my head.

Then my brain settled on an image: a blond woman in a black robe. My face reddened. A thin string of lightning lit up the sky, followed by a clap of thunder.

"That woman..."

Shane shook my shoulders. "Do you really take me for that kind of man, Maggie?"

"Then what was it?"

He looked to the side, finding the raven that still perched between the spokes of the iron gate.

"I can't say. But you need to trust me."

"I don't trust in anything anymore," I said, even as I tilted my head back, giving him access to my neck and shoulders. His lips grazed my skin, nibbling and kissing their way down to the hollow between my breasts.

"You have secrets of your own," he whispered, his nails digging into my shoulders. "Tell me your secrets, Maggie."

Secrets. Yes. So many secrets.

"Tell me," he said, pushing me against something solid. We were back in our grove, at our tree. I reached back, searching for the carved heart. I found it and pushed my fingers inside its rough grooves.

"Tell me," he repeated, pressing his full weight against me. He raised my chin, forcing me to meet his eyes. "Tell me your secrets, Maggie."

"I...I can't. Not yet."

Shane pressed his mouth over mine, pinning me to the tree while his hands roamed my body freely.

"God, Shane," I said, as he nibbled my lips and my chin between rough, hot kisses. He rolled down the elastic waist of my skirt, exposing my hip.

"I could find out if I wanted to," he said. "I could watch you during the daytime, and I could come to you at night. I could follow your every move, Maggie. Is that what you want?"

"Yes," I said, lifting one leg and wrapping it around the top of his thighs, folding him into me. "No. I mean, no."

He pulled back, his eyes resting on the pendant around my neck. He reached for it, clamping the crystal in his fist.

"It's him, isn't it?" he said, lowering his brow as he tightened his grip on the pendant. "I could rip this from you, if I thought it would make you forget all about your precious Michael."

"Shane...stop."

"But that's not your only link to him, is it? I sense him all over you."

He released the necklace and it thudded heavily against my chest.

"I'm jealous, Maggie. So very, very jealous. Jealous that he has you in a way I never will." He pulled me by the waist, his tongue plunging into my mouth. I could taste the salt on his lips, the hunger on his breath. "I'll stop if you want me to," he said, running his hands up the small of my back. "Say the word and I stop."

But I didn't want him to stop. In our dreams he could do anything. And in our dreams, I would let him.

"Maggie." One hand moved to my breast, squeezing it gently. The other hand moved to the side of my face, lifting my lips to his. "Oh, Maggie..."

Dark Root, Oregon
Sister House,
6:22 AM
Thanksgiving Day, 2013

"Ma-geeee?"

"Yes, that's good. You're doing great."

"Magggg-eee."

"Yes! Try one more time."

"Mag-ee!"

"Perfect!"

"Yeah, he's a regular boy genius."

"Don't listen to Eve. You're doing wonderful!"

"A zombie savant."

"Now, Eve. Don't call him that. He has feelings."

"Are you sure?"

"Owweee."

"Stop poking him! Don't worry, Leo. Merry will protect you."

"Shut up, you two. I think she's waking up."

"Maggie? Maggie?"

I blinked against the light that was being shone in my face, trying to force my eyelids fully open. Four faces stared down at me. My sisters and...

I sat upright, screaming.

"Shh." A hand cupped my mouth and I recognized Merry's voice. "You'll scare him."

I struggled against Merry's hand, taking deep breaths through my nose. When Merry was sure I wasn't going to scream again, she released me and helped me stand. Two heavy blankets dropped to the ground. We were still outside Sister House, but it was morning, so early that the sun was only half-visible on the horizon.

Eve retrieved one of the blankets and wrapped it around my shoulders. My sisters smiled at me, seemingly in good spirits. Leo lifted a pudgy finger, pushing it into my shoulder so hard I almost fell backwards.

I recoiled in horror.

"Mag-gee!" he said, a slack-jawed grin on his simple face.

"We did it?" I asked in disbelief as I avoided his next thrust.

The back of my head throbbed where I had hit the ground.

"Apparently." Ruth Anne removed her glasses and wiped them with her grimy X-Files T-shirt that read *I Want to Believe*. "You know, I've never actually heard of a successful resurrection, biblical references aside."

"If you can call this successful," Eve said.

Leo had scooped up a handful of rocks and was shoving them in his mouth.

"How long was I out?" I asked. "It felt like days."

Ruth Anne checked her phone. "About four hours. You hit the ground pretty hard. Had us scared for awhile, but when you started talking about Shane we knew you were going to be okay." She smirked. "I hope it was a good dream?"

I blushed at the memory, feeling very exposed.

"Hey," Ruth Anne said. "Don't sweat it. There are more important things to worry about right now."

"I still can't believe..." I said, unable to finish the sentence.

I looked Leo fully over for the first time.

He was still dressed in his slacks and polo shirt, but they were so covered in filth that you'd be hard pressed to say what color they were anymore. His thinning, blond hair was now a muddy gray, plastered against the side of his face. And though he could walk––and even run––his back rounded in a perpetual arch as he raced through the yard, kicking up leaves.

The entire scene was surreal.

"I'm tired and hungry," I said, giving in to my baser needs, the only things that made sense anymore.

"You and me both," said Ruth Anne.

"Stop that!" Merry ran after Leo as he tried to catch a bird.

He wasn't sly about it, but ran after it with his arms flared wide and with all the zest and enthusiasm of a preschooler. He didn't catch any of the birds, but this didn't dampen his spirits as he took off soaring towards the next group of starlings he saw.

"Maybe he never really died?" I suggested to Ruth Anne.

He was twice the size of Merry, but easily out-dodged her.

"...Maybe he suffered brain damage when his head hit the wall?" I said.

"Two hours without a pulse? That's not just dead, Maggie, that's dead-dead."

"So..." I asked hesitantly, tugging at the side of my skirt. "What happened?"

"Let's just say you should be glad you weren't awake for it."

"Tell me, please."

I needed to hear it, for my own absolution. If I had killed him, I needed to hear all the grim details on how he had come back.

"There was dirt...lots and lots of dirt spewing up from the ground, like a volcano shooting magma. And the screams. You can't imagine such horrible screams. A banshee's screams would have sounded better. Merry tried to help, but I stopped her. It had to be all him for it to take." Ruth Anne shook her head. "That's all I will say. I can't even write anything that horrible."

Ruth Anne pulled her lips inside her mouth, taking a long pause, then cracked a smile.

"Luckily, Leo here took a shine to Merry as soon as he was free. She made it all better. Classic case of imprinting. He thinks Merry is his mommy."

We watched Merry guide him back to our group, holding his grubby hand without a trace of disgust on her face.

"You think he will get...better?" I asked, as Merry wiped drool from Leo's bottom lip with a Kleenex she almost magically produced.

Ruth Anne shrugged. "In every culture, they talk of bringing people back from the dead, but you never hear what happens afterwards. Your guess is as good as mine. He seems to be advancing fast, though. When he first broke free, he could hardly stand up or put two syllables together."

"Yeah," Eve said, peeling her filthy, leather gloves from her hand.

"Our little boy is growing up." Merry sat Leo down on a tree stump and gave him one of June Bug's picture books from the car.

"Fun-nee!" he said, pointing to an illustration.

"Yes, yes. Funny. That's right. Now you be good boy and look at the pictures, okay?"

"Oh-kay."

"This is unreal," I said as Merry joined us. "Someone pinch me, please?"

"I'm too tired to pinch anyone," Merry moaned, her words heavy with exhaustion.

There were bags under her eyes and her clothes were the color of the earth she stood on. Only her golden hair still shone, as if immune to whatever darkness the world threw at it.

"I'm sorry I wasn't awake for this," I apologized to her. "You shouldn't have had to tend to him yourself."

"You did what you were supposed to do. You brought him back." Merry glanced towards Leo and sighed. "I can't keep him, though. Not with June Bug and having to care for Mother. What are we going to do?"

"I'll find out where he's from," Eve said. "Maybe we can drop him back off?"

"We can't take him back like this!" Merry put a hand to her hip. "We need to care for him until he can care for himself. It's our duty."

"Don't look at me," Ruth Anne said, taking a step back and lifting her hands, palms out. "I can barely remember to feed myself, let alone someone else. The poor guy wouldn't last long in my room."

"I've never seen you miss a meal," Eve said. "Though, I still can't figure out how you stay so skinny."

"We are not going to pick fights now!" Merry intervened. "What about you, Eve? You could keep him in the apartment above Mother's store."

"Oh, no. He'd destroy the place."

She was right. All that work getting the store back in order would be wasted with Leo around. I dug the toe of my shoe into the dirt, waiting for the others to ask me, but not one of them looked in my direction. Indignant, I spoke up.

"What about me? I'm responsible for this, after all."

Merry bit her bottom lip, Eve bit on her nails, and Ruth Anne scratched her head.

"What choice do we have?" I asked.

Merry looked at me, her eyes wide and compassionate. "Honey, he's going to be a lot of work. You'll have to feed him and bathe him and even help him use the bathroom. It's too much."

"You do all that with Mother," I protested.

"But you don't."

"The worst I could do is kill him again." I let out a nervous laugh. When no one said anything I squared my jaw and straightened my shoulders. "I'm taking him. I took care of June Bug while Merry was in the hospital. Maybe I didn't do a great job, but I did it."

Merry's eyes crinkled at the edges. "You're right, honey. And you did a great job with June Bug." She cast a final glance at Leo, fighting through her instinct to take him herself. "We'll all help. Hopefully, he'll be back to his old self soon and we can take him home."

Home. When all was said and done, we all just wanted to go home.

Merry ran her fingers through her hair, encountering a tangle. "It's set, then. Maggie, you take Leo and the rest of us will help." She yawned, stretching her arms into the morning sky and revealing a midriff that was far too thin. "Now, ladies, if you'll excuse me, I have to make my daughter breakfast, soak in a hot bath, and a take very long nap. Call me if you need me. I'll keep my phone close. See you at six?"

"Six? Why? What happens at six?" I asked.

"It's Thanksgiving."

"Are we really still doing that?"

My sister's face became stone. "Yes, we are still doing that. We need to have some sense of normalcy in this family. I won't have June Bug reporting to her father that we missed a holiday." She yawned again, her face softening. "Besides, this is the first time in fifteen years that we will all be together for the holidays. We can't miss it, no matter what the world throws at us."

"I suppose," I said, wondering how we could pretend that anything was normal again as Leo flittered around the front yard, flapping his arms like he were trying to take flight.

Maybe for us, this was as normal as it got.

Eve seated herself in the backseat of Leo's Cadillac as Merry and Ruth Anne headed inside, waving sleepy goodbyes. I caught up to Leo and grasped his dirty hand, resisting the primal urge to drop it and run screaming into the woods.

He was dead. I was holding a dead man's hand.

Panic rose up inside me.

It was the yellow collar of his polo shirt, hardly visible beneath the layers of mud, that brought me back.

"It's gonna be okay," I said, to both of us.

"Merr-Eee!" he wailed, clenching and unclenching his free hand in my sister's direction as she disappeared inside the house.

"You'll see her later today," I said, leading him to his car. He climbed into the passenger seat obediently, sniffling as I buckled him in. As I walked around the car to the driver's side, I saw something on the ground.

Mother's wand, charred and broken in two. The gem lay next to it, devoid of color.

The wand of eternal life was dead.

TWENTY

JEREMY

A
T LEAST I GET A CAR FOR A WHILE," I SAID TO LEO, WHO SAT BESIDE ME playing with the automatic window button as he called out for Merry every time the window rolled down.

Behind us, Eve had curled into a fetal position, snoring so loudly I was surprised she didn't wake herself. The whole scene would have been comical on any other day, but this morning, with my head still throbbing and weariness threatening to consume my entire being, it didn't even warrant a snarky comment.

"Sit down!" I ordered Leo, who stuck his head out the window like a dog.

Flecks of dried on dirt were being picked off by the wind. When he didn't comply I pulled him sharply by the arm and pushed him back into his seat. He fought me a little, wrenching my hand away, but I slammed on the breaks and tightened my grip.

Eventually, he gave up and sulked all the way to Harvest Home.

"It's for your own good," I said, as he rubbed his wrist. If Merry were here she'd be giving me "that look"––the look that said I could have handled the situation better. I took a deep breath and pulled into our driveway.

"Eve, we're here," I said, thumping her on the shoulder. She sat up and rubbed her eyes, giving a little start at the sight of Leo's face.

"Didn't mean to drift off," she apologized, smoothing her long, blue-black hair into place. "I guess I'm more tired than I thought."

"You had a long night. Help me get him inside?"

"Yeah."

We escorted Leo to the house, each of us taking an arm.

He could probably walk on his own, but I didn't trust that he wouldn't run off into the woods. He stepped in a puddle and quickly withdrew his foot, shaking off the mud as an expression of hysteria overcame his face.

"It's just mud," I said, pulling him along. "Suck it up."

Leo looked at his leg and nodded as we continued the trek up the porch steps. The scents of pumpkin and nutmeg drifted out the windows, causing my stomach to growl.

"Mmm." Leo lifted his nose, sniffing at the air.

"Well, he's hungry. That's a good sign, right?" I asked Eve.

"I suppose. But good luck getting any of that food."

Aunt Dora had always been a stickler on not letting us get so much as a taste before dinner was ready, especially a holiday dinner. Between Leo and my rumbling stomach, it was going to be a long, long day.

Eve hesitated when we got to the front door. "How do we get him past Aunt Dora? She's not going to let a man she doesn't know stay in her house."

"Leave that to me."

She bobbed her head in a nod, too tired to object.

As we stepped inside, Aunt Dora popped her head into the living room. "I hear ya didn't get the turkey," she said, frowning. "Thank goodness fer Shane. Wonderful boy." Her eyes took in Leo. "Who's this?"

"This is Leo. A friend of mine from Woodhaven. He has no family so I said he could spend the holidays with us. Hope that's okay?" I gave her my most innocent smile.

Aunt Dora appraised him suspiciously but didn't press on.

Before she could speak again, I asked, "What's this about Shane?"

"He got the turkey. Said he will cook it an' take care o' the dressin'."

"Shane's coming here?" I looked down at my filthy clothes and then to the grinning, finger-sucking man beside me. "Why didn't anyone tell me?"

Aunt Dora placed a flour-whitened hand on her hip. "Because he ain't comin' here. We're all goin' ta his. Now go help yer friend clean up. There's linens in the cabinet."

"You're going too?" I said.

Aunt Dora didn't go anywhere lately, claiming the pain in her hip made it almost unbearable.

"Aye. We all are. Could be yer mother's last..." She shook her head, not finishing the sentence. "Well, enough o' that. Back ta bakin' pies fer me."

She limped back into the kitchen without the aid of her cane.

Mother's last Thanksgiving.

I looked at Leo, remembering the broken wand. He had taken the last bit of magic from it, leaving it dead.

"I hope you're worth it," I said.

He titled his head to the left, hearing my words, but not understanding.

But there was still a tree somewhere within the boundaries of Dark Root; a magical willow.

I hadn't taken a wand yet. I could get my own.

I wasn't sure where it was, but I knew someone who did.

Larinda.

The phone rang.

I fumbled inside my pocket, trying to pull it out, while testing the bath water with my other hand.

"Hello?" I answered, expecting it to be Merry or Ruth Anne, checking to see how I was "coming along."

The masculine voice on the other end surprised me and I almost dropped the phone into the bathtub.

"Maggie? Happy Thanksgiving!"

"Michael? What do you want? And since when do you care about Thanksgiving?"

I turned off the water, tucked the phone between my shoulder and ear, and sat Leo down on the edge of the tub. "Arms up," I said.

"What?" Michael asked.

"Sorry, not you."

Leo lifted his arms and I pulled off his polo shirt, and then his undershirt. His chest was a bit hairy and his belly had a slight bulge, but he didn't look unhealthy. There was even a color to his skin that made it hard to believe only a few hours ago he had been...

"Maggie? You still there?"

"Sorry, I'm kinda busy," I said, hearing the agitation in my voice as I helped Leo take off his shoes.

"Well, did you hear what I just asked you?"

"What? No, say again?"

"Maybe I could see the baby during the holidays? Under your supervision, of course. We could do family Christmases and Thanksgivings, that kind of thing."

His words stopped me mid-shoe-pull and I dropped Leo's feet, grabbing the phone with both hands "Michael, you don't celebrate holidays. And we aren't a family!"

"I know I didn't in the past, but I've changed Maggie. I've grown."

"No one grows that fast in two months!"

Another long silence on his end, followed by the words, "You did."

I gritted my teeth, trying to hold back the barrage of curse words that came to mind. My growth, in part, had been because of him. Him and his deceit. I took a deep breath and exhaled, relaxing my grip on the phone. I had other things to worry about now.

"Sorry Michael, this isn't the best time. Can you call back later?"

Not waiting for an answer, I hung up.

"Merr-eee." Leo tilted his head back and wailed the words, as if he just realized that his future was entirely in my incapable hands.

"Shut up," I said, yanking at his zipper. "Merry's not here." He dropped his hands to his side but didn't help as I wrestled with his pants. At last, they loosened and I pulled them to his knees, then had him stand to step out of them.

I tried not to look at his exposed body. "Now, get in," I said, my head half turned away. Leo didn't move. "Get in!" I repeated, pointing at the bathtub.

His eyes bore into me but he continued to stand there.

I gave him a good shove. He outweighed me by at least fifty pounds and I could hardly budge him. "Please, Leo, please," I begged, feeling the tiredness overwhelm me. Where the fuck was Eve right now? Probably sound asleep when she should be helping me.

I kicked off my shoes, hoisted my skirt, and stepped inside the bathtub. "See? Not that hard. Now you do."

He continued to stare at me, blank-eyed and slack-jawed. I was tired. So tired. And the back of my head throbbed where I had fallen. All I could think about was finishing his bath and getting into bed.

I bent down and splashed my arms so that he could see the water wasn't dangerous. Then I scooped up a handful and splashed him in the face.

"Ow-ee!" he yowled, stepping back and stumbling into the sink like I had doused him in acid. "Merr-ee!" He swiped at the droplets of water.

I worried that Aunt Dora would barge in, but part of me wished she would. She'd know what to do.

Leo wept near the sink, his bottom lip trembling. The sight of him, a naked, forty-something-year-old man weeping in my bathroom, coupled with the exhaustion that swept over me like a tidal wave, was too much. I dropped into the tub, still fully clothed, and buried my face in my hands.

"I can't do this," I said, unable to stop the tears. "I can't do any of this." The ends of my hair swirled around me in red, psychedelic swirls.

I watched them curiously as I continued my cry. A soft hand on my shoulder startled me.

I looked up to see Leo, staring down. There was something in his eyes. Some glimmer of the humanity he must have had before life had turned him into a woman-grabbing prick, as if he were trying to reach across that chasm of death and remember.

His words were slurred, but understandable. "I-I'm...s-s-sor-rry."

I raised my eyebrows, feeling the weight on my soul fall away. "Oh, fuck, Leo. I'm sorry, too. I'm so fucking sorry."

I reached out my hand, guiding him into the bathtub, one foot, then another. He sat down, facing me, him naked, me in my clothes. Dirt washed from our bodies and joined my hair in the mad swirl as we scrubbed each other clean.

"Magg-ee," he said, touching my chin with the tip of his fingers.

"Yes, I'm Maggie. You'll be all better soon," I said, stepping out of the tub and offering him a towel. "And then you can go home."

"Home?" His eyes widened as he spoke the word.

"Soon." I took his hand and led him down the hall, his body still clothed in only a towel. We had rooms to spare but for now he would be sleeping in my room. I dragged a twin mattress down the hall from the Huntsman Room and into my own, setting it next to my bed.

"You tired?" I asked. He ignored the mattress on the floor and plopped down onto my bed, moving his arms and legs around like a child making snow angels. "Okay, you take that one, I'll be here on this one. Stay put, okay?"

I collapsed face-first onto the mattress, not bothering to slide out of my wet clothes. "Stay put," I repeated as my eyelids clamped shut.

As I drifted off, I heard the rustling of Leo on the sheets, the sounds of Aunt Dora bustling around the kitchen, and the ringing of my cell phone in my skirt pocket. But all I cared about was sleep. I could sleep a thousand years, and that still wouldn't be enough.

TWENTY-ONE

TWO PRINCES

A LOUD KNOCK ON THE DOOR ROUSED ME AND I FOUGHT THROUGH THE heaviness to open my eyes. I almost screamed as a broad, dull face hovered inches above mine.

"Good grief, Leo!" I said, sitting upright. "I hope you weren't that creepy when you were..."

Alive?

"Dooooor." He pointed, drool seeping from the corner of his mouth as Eve burst in.

"It's about time you showed up," I said, tripping over the mattress on the floor as I got to my feet. "Lock the door behind you."

Eve thrust a sheet of paper at me.

"I was trying to find out more about our mystery man." Her skin was pale and there were dark circles beneath her eyes.

I took the paper and read as she narrated along.

"Forty-three. Never married. No kids. Works as a traveling salesman for a tech company. Only known family member is a mother in Linsburg."

"Linsburg! Oh, Eve, that's awesome." I gave her a grateful hug. A few days of rehabilitation and we could pawn him off on his mother.

"Thanks," she said. "How soon do you think he'll be, um, better?"

Leo sat on my bed, picking at his bare toes. Eve grimaced.

"Maybe that was something he did before the accident?" I suggested.

"Yeah, not likely. Unless he had a foot fetish." Eve rubbed her hands together. "I will spend the next few days trying to gather more information about him. When I was an actress in New York, I played an amnesia victim. The only thing that brought me back was a picture of my dog. Maybe it's the same sort of thing."

"Maybe," I said, dubious. "But what else can we do?"

"By the way," Eve lowered her voice. "Aunt Dora wants us dressed and ready to go in an hour. I tried to let you sleep as long as possible, but she was starting to ask questions." She leaned in to me. "I also told her Leo would be bunking in one of the spare rooms. She seemed okay with that."

"Good thinking." My hair was still wet and I pulled it into a messy bun on the top of my head. I waited for Eve to say something about my hairstyle, but she didn't, evidence that tiredness had taken over her fashion sensibilities for the time being.

"What shall we wear?" I asked. I hadn't done any laundry in a week.

"I'll find you something of mine to wear. You attend to him. I got a duffel bag out of his trunk and he had some spare clothes in it."

"We are taking him?"

"I think we have to. Unless we want to chain him up in the backyard?"

We looked at Leo and he shot us a toothy smile, then continued playing with his feet.

"He's our chain now, Maggie. For better or worse."

I wasn't crazy about seeing Shane, but it hardly seemed to matter anymore, in light of the newest developments. Murder has a way of putting things in perspective and I had more important things to worry about at the moment.

I drove Leo's Cadillac as he played with the dials on the radio, howling along to various songs, his mind trying to latch on to lyrics and melodies he remembered. When he'd hit a certain line or key I found myself saying, "Yes, that's right. Good, good."

Eve rolled her eyes in the rearview mirror, not thinking the horrendous sounds coming out of Leo were good at all.

"Later," I whispered and he smiled, putting a finger to his lips to show me that he was in on the secret.

Leo looked around when we arrived at Dip Stix. I had had to bribe him with candy to get him into the car. When he saw that there was no candy waiting for us, he gave me a look that said I was a big, fat liar.

"Don't worry," I said, taking his hand and following Eve into Dip Stix. "There are mints inside."

"Swank," Eve said as we entered the café.

I stopped in the entryway, my mouth dropping as I took in the room's holiday cheer.

The white lights I had "popped" had all been replaced by newer, stouter models that were intertwined with strands of red and green, neatly outlining the windows and the arch that separated the dining room from the kitchen. Near the bandstand, a small tree with a silver garland twinkled at us. The pictures on the wall had been wrapped in foil and ribbon to make them look like presents, and instrumental Christmas music played softly in the background.

But the most beautiful addition of all was the oak harvest table that sat in the center of the room, surrounded by a dozen, hard-backed chairs. The table abounded with candles, crystal glasses, white china plates, place cards, and an assortment of trays and covered dishes. Smells of turkey, hot rolls, and pumpkin pie permeated the room.

I tightened my grip on Leo to keep him from darting to the table without me.

"It's beautiful," I said as Aunt Dora emerged from the kitchen. Paul had picked her up hours before, so she could help them finish up dinner.

"Aye," she said, plunking a pie onto the table. "An' without a woman's touch. I never would have guessed it possible."

"Can-dee?" Leo asked again, looking forlornly around.

Aunt Dora narrowed her sharp eyes, but returned to the kitchen without a further word.

"She's on to us," Eve said, removing her coat and seating herself at the table.

"I know."

I pulled out a chair for Leo and sat him between myself and Eve. Leo cocked his head, listening as Paul and Shane argued about spices from the kitchen. Aunt Dora emerged once again, throwing her hands into the air.

"I give up," she said, easing into the chair next to Eve. "If the boys want ta run the whole show, who am I ta stop them? I tell ya, I'll never get used to these modern times."

The door chimed and June Bug pushed through, her cheeks the color of apples and her eyes flashing with holiday enthusiasm. Bits of dried leaves clung to her pink beanie and pearl gray sweater. She picked them off as she made her way towards us.

Merry and Ruth Anne followed through the door, holding Mother's arms as she hobbled forward.

"Who's he?" June Bug asked, seating herself across from Leo, who studied his reflection in a spoon.

"A friend," I said, as Mother settled into her chair at the head of the table.

Ruth Anne sat by Mother and Merry fell in next to June Bug.

"June Bug, that's the special visitor I told you about," Merry said, tilting her chin to the side. "Remember, he doesn't have any family to be with for the holidays, so we are going to make him feel like he's a part of our family. Right?"

"He's weird," June Bug said, removing her gloves and placing them in her mother's purse.

Leo opened and closed his mouth repeatedly, like a puffer fish.

Merry frowned. "That's not the way we treat our guests, young lady. Now mind your manners, or no pie for dessert."

216

"Well, he is," June Bug shrugged, as Leo licked a fork.

I snatched the utensil from his hands. He seemed about to object when he noticed Merry.

A dopey grin overtook his face. Merry leaned across the table, and patted his hand.

"Hi, Leo," she said. "Good to see you again." Taking a sip from her water glass, she asked casually, "You enjoying your Thanksgiving so far?"

"Thanks-givvv-ing?" he asked, trying out the word.

"Why do you talk like that?" June Bug asked.

Leo stared at her a moment, before turning his attention back to Merry.

"Leo doesn't hear very well," Merry answered. "And sometimes it's hard for him to talk."

June Bug's eyes lit up. "Oh? Like he's deaf?"

"Yes, yes. So we have to speak slowly, okay?"

June Bug accepted the explanation and proceeded to tell Leo about the earth worms she had seen that morning, in loud, drawn-out words. Merry sighed, obviously relieved. Mother studied the china as Ruth Anne and Aunt Dora talked about the impending cold weather to come.

"I can feel it in my hips," Aunt Dora said, as Ruth Anne confessed to not knowing a "real winter" in years.

Eve reached behind Leo and tapped my shoulder, drawing attention to Paul who stood near the kitchen, a cell phone in his hand. "He's still texting her," she whispered, her face tightening. "I don't know why I bothered to come."

"Really?" I whispered back. "That's what you're upset about? It was your petty insecurities that got us into this mess in the first place."

"They're not petty," she said, her cheeks flushing to the color of the cranberries on the table.

Paul put the phone to his ear and disappeared around a corner.

"I'm sorry," I said, sensing the helplessness inside her. "I know it's hard."

"It is. And thank you."

"What's a lady gotta do ta get some wine around here?" Aunt Dora bellowed, clanking a crystal glass with her spoon as if she were going to make a toast.

Mother snickered, then coughed so loudly she clutched her chest. We sat silently, waiting for the cough to subside.

"Hurt?" Leo asked me, pointing at Mother.

"Yes."

"Sad." He started to rise, perhaps to comfort her, but I pulled him gently back into his seat.

At last, Mother became aware of our new companion. "And who's this?" she asked, one brow arching slyly over her cloudy, blue eyes. "I don't believe we've met."

"Miss Sasha, meet Leo. A friend of Maggie's," Ruth Anne said quickly.

"The baby's father?"

I turned quickly to see if Shane was nearby. Fortunately, he hadn't left the kitchen.

"No, just a friend," I said, hoping she'd drop it.

There was a spark in her eyes that told me she knew something was amiss, but a coughing fit interrupted her thoughts and she lost interest in Leo as she tried to regain her breath.

"I'll help you, Mother," I avowed under my breath, squeezing the cloth napkin in my fists.

I had raised a man from the dead; surely, I could stop my mother's illness from progressing.

"Sorry to keep you ladies waiting." Shane emerged, carrying two bottles of wine and a corkscrew. "We wanted this day to be special for you."

He stopped, mid-step, as he noticed Leo. Shane regained his composure and proceeded around the table, pouring wine into everyone's glasses but June Bug's and Merry's.

"Cider for you two," he said, winking.

"Maggie needs cider, too," Eve said and I shot her a furious look. She shrunk down in her chair as she realized she had said too much.

"Oh?" Shane asked.

"No. Wine's fine," I lied.

"I'm Shane, by the way," he said, extending a hand to Leo.

Leo looked at him strangely and didn't respond.

"A friend of Maggie's," Mother said, smiling.

"Yes," I agreed, feeling Shane's eyes burn into me. "Shane, this is Leo. And he'll be drinking water, if that's okay?"

Shane gave me a curious look but left his cup empty. "So sport, you in Dark Root for business or pleasure?"

"Plea-sure," Leo grinned, latching on to the word. "Magg-ee."

I caught Ruth Anne's lips twitching, resisting the urge to break into laughter.

"I see," said Shane, scratching his head. "Maggie's full of surprises. Well, let me know if there's anything I can do to make your stay more comfortable." With that he returned to the kitchen

"Pleasure, Maggie?" Eve whispered from my right. "Maybe the dufus has some use after all."

"You're a sick woman," I said. "Keep laughing and I'll send him your way."

Eve's eyes drifted to Paul, standing under the archway, pecking buttons on his phone. "Maybe that's not a bad idea."

In spite of everything, Thanksgiving turned out better than expected. The turkey was moist, the wine flowed freely, and Mother, quite lucid, regaled us all with stories from her youth.

"Did you really use your magick to give a woman warts, Grandma?" June Bug asked, picking at the massive drumstick on her plate.

"Not just any warts," Mother said, her eyes taking on a wicked glee. "Warts the size of jelly beans!"

"That doesn't sound very nice," Merry said.

Aunt Dora stamped her fists on the table, causing some of the wine in the glasses to spill over. "The woman had it comin'! Trying ta steal yer mother's beau. Warts was the least she deserved!"

Beau?

That word caught our attention and we all turned our heads. Mother had never spoken of romance or *beaus* before.

"Which beau was that?" I asked, smiling over a glass of wine I pretended to sip for Shane's benefit. Leo had fallen asleep after his third piece of pumpkin pie, and rested his head on my shoulder. Shane bristled as he walked by, carrying away empty plates.

Mother examined me for a long time, then pursed her lips and said, "Maggie, is it so hard to believe I once had a beau?"

"Armand?" I asked, taking a stab by naming the only straight male I'd ever heard her speak of.

She shook her head, then blew her nose into a tissue. "No, not Armand. This was way before him." Her eyes glassed over as she picked through the seeds of her memory.

"Were you in love?" I asked, noticing Shane, who had found a seat alone at the end of the table.

"Oh, Maggie." She sighed.

"Were you?" June Bug asked as we all leaned in.

"I was young." Mother's lips were taut but drawn up at the corners, creating a dimple in her left cheek I'd never known she had. "His name was Robert."

Robbie?

"We met at a dance. He was in the service and I spotted him in his uniform. With one smile he swept me off my feet."

She shook her head, her eyes moistening.

"Now, the country was opposed to war, and me, too. What was going on in the rest of the world shouldn't concern us. But he got me caught up in his convictions, his enthusiasm that the whole world needed to be free and that even though we were geographically disconnected, a connection existed between all of us. He changed my ideas on... everything."

Aunt Dora nodded solemnly in agreement.

"Did he, um...did he...?" I couldn't bring myself to ask the question, but I didn't need to.

Mother dabbed her eyes with the Kleenex.

"Yes, Maggie, he did. Bravely, I hear." She caught her breath, a haunting, gasping sound from her soul. Aunt Dora placed her hand on her sister's shoulder.

"We lost a lot of young men that year," Mother continued. "War's dirty work, but often necessary. Like our work here, it can fight back the encroaching dark."

Merry looked at Mother. "It's okay, Mama. You don't have to talk about it anymore."

Mother recovered herself and stared hard at Merry. "But I want to talk about it! If I don't talk about it, it's like he never existed. Dora and I might be the only ones who still remember. I've been wishing him away too long."

"There's nothing you could have done," I said, trying to console her. "But at least you have the memory."

"Oh, Maggie. If only I'd been near him, I could have used my wand..." She swallowed. "But I could only save so many."

Aunt Dora took her cane and rose, lumbering up behind her. "Death takes us all eventually, Sasha. Ya couldn't have helped fer ever."

Leo stirred beside me. I patted his head, lulling him back into his dreams.

"What was his last name?" Ruth Anne asked, pulling out her notepad. "Maybe we could get in touch with some of his relatives?"

Mother fixed her steely eyes upon Ruth Anne, lifting her chin defiantly. "Maddock."

My heart beat wildly in my chest at her announcement. I exchanged wide-eyed glances with the others. *Maddock.*

Our last name.

Mother rose, more with strength that comes from determination than from muscle.

"Shane, thank you for a lovely evening," she said. "That's the best food I've had in quite a while." And then to Merry. "I'm tired. Please take me home now."

I was still stunned by Mother's announcement when Shane tapped me on the shoulder. "Maggie, can I have a word with you before you go?"

The room had mostly emptied out.

Ruth Anne and Merry had taken Aunt Dora, Mother, and June Bug home, leaving Eve and myself to assist with the cleanup. Leo still slept in his chair, snoring loudly enough to rouse himself from time to time, before drifting back off to sleep.

I nodded and followed Shane to the plush booth in the rear of the dining room. A rush of nostalgia swept over me as I remembered the last time I sat in this booth, the night Shane had debuted his remodeled café. A month ago, but it seemed like a lifetime.

"Firstly," Shane said, sliding in beside me. "I want to apologize for last night."

"Last night?"

His face turned red. "Um, yes. Last night?"

"Oh." The dream came back to me. Shane pressing against me, clenching my pendant in his hands. My eyes widened. "So, you really can...?"

"Yes, since I was little. It's not something I do often. And I'd like to think I have no control over it, but I do. A little anyway."

"But how?"

"Well..." he ran his fingers through his hair, squeezing his eyes shut. "If I fall asleep thinking of someone, sometimes I can enter their dreams."

"I see." My heart beat rapidly as I realized he really had come to me.

"I apologize if I wasn't a gentleman. I may have been caught up by your charms."

"Oh, you don't need to apologize," I said, blushing at the memory.

"Yes, yes, I do." He bent his head, revealing the soft hairs on the back of his neck. "I'm not like that, really, I promise."

"Oh." I tried to hide my disappointment. I liked the real Shane, but the dream Shane...

My knees weakened at the thought.

"Secondly," he continued, meeting my eyes once again. "I'm still sorry for what you saw the other day. It wasn't what it looked like."

The lights around us flickered off and on as I thought about *Dream Shane* doing those things to that other woman. I gazed at him coldly. "You're a grown man, Shane Doler. You can do whatever you like."

"Yes, that's true and thank you for that, but——"

"We are both adults," I continued, jealousy rising inside me. "We can both do whatever we like."

Shane pressed his palms together. "Maggie, if you weren't so hard-headed and you listened for a change, you'd see there was nothing going on with me and that woman."

"Like I said, do what you want."

"Goddammit, Maggie. Why do you have such a thick skull? I don't want to do anything with her!"

"Then why did you?"

"I didn't. You know, talking to you is like talking to a brick wall."

"Hey, I wasn't the one with a strange woman in my room."

"No, you're the one with the strange man in my diner."

"So?"

"So? So? Who is he anyways? And where is he staying?"

"He's staying at Harvest Home. And he's an old friend, like Eve said."

Shane focused on Leo across the room. "He doesn't look that old."

His eyes shifted as a thought ran through his brain. "Is this the secret you've been keeping from me? This new man?"

"No! And anyways, it's none of your business. Is this why you called me over? To interrogate me about Leo?" I crossed my arms and stared defiantly back.

"No, I called you over to tell you that I was sorry for the dream and for what you saw that morning, neither of which I had much control over."

"So, you're not sorry you did it, just that I saw it?"

"I didn't *do* anything."

"Like I said, do what you want."

"Fine, Maggie. I'm done trying to explain. But if you had an ounce of faith in someone, things might get easier for you."

"Who says my life's not easy?" I demanded, scooting out of the booth. "My life is fine, thank you. And stay out of my dreams!"

"That's our Maggie," Shane hollered as he stomped into the kitchen. "The lone wolf." I felt his eyes traveling back to Leo. "Or maybe you've found your pack-mate."

"C'mon, Leo," I said, waking him. He rubbed his eyes and looked around the empty diner. "Merr-ee?" he asked.

"No. Merry went home. But Maggie's got you. Maggie won't let anything happen to you."

He reached up and looped an arm around my neck.

"Magg-eee," he crooned, planting a kiss on my cheek.

A glass broke somewhere in the kitchen.

Sometimes all you can do is wait.

Wait for a friend. Wait for a lover. Wait for winter to turn into spring. Wait for the man sleeping in your bed––who by all rights should be dead and buried right now––to get better and live again.

But three days after his resurrection and, besides adding a few new words to his vocabulary--Pixie Sticks, Twizzlers, and gummies--there was little indication that Leo was ever going to get better.

"I can't do this," I said, as much to him as to myself. "I'm not cut out to take care of anything."

Leo sat on my bed, watching ravens from the window. "Pretty birdies," he said, tapping the glass with his finger.

"Yes, yes, pretty birdies," I agreed, looking around the room for something to do. We had hidden out for the last three days, away from the questioning eyes of Aunt Dora and the accusing looks of Shane. In that time I had done my best to educate Leo about the world. He showed no interest in any of it except for the Cookie Monster and "birdies."

And candy.

Leo's sweet tooth exceeded both mine and Ruth Anne's put together. If he wasn't fed constant sugar, he'd bang his fists on the walls and bump around the room, knocking things over until we gave in.

Eve went on candy runs at least three times a day but it was never enough.

"You can't have anymore," I'd tell him, then he'd ball up his fists and cry so loudly I was afraid it would alert Aunt Dora.

"I'm done," I said to Eve when she made her afternoon delivery. She dumped a bag of Tootsie Rolls onto the bed and Leo covered them with his arms to show he wouldn't share.

I stuck my tongue out at him.

"What else can we do?" Eve asked. "We can't take him to his mom's yet. Not like this."

We stared at the slobbering, shirtless man with a mouthful of chocolate. Except for underpants, I had given up putting clothes on him because it was impossible to keep them clean.

"You take him," I said. "I've done my part."

"Oh, no! If you think you're bad at it, I'd be worse. Even the thought of taking care of someone gives me the hives." She scratched at her arms and the sides of her waist.

"I'm calling Jillian," I announced.

"Whatever," Eve said, still scratching as she left the room.

"Don't you walk out on me," I said, tripping over the floor mattress and yelling at her down the hall. She didn't look back as she descended the staircase. "Fine! Go back to work and leave me alone with him. That's all you ever do!"

I slammed the door and faced my ward. He held up the empty Tootsie Roll bag, flashing me a chocolate smile.

"How did you eat them so fast?" I said in both awe and disgust. "Did you eat the wrappers too?"

He shook the bag at me.

"I'm not giving you anymore! You are going to get sick if you keep eating candy. Have some of that asparagus Merry sent over."

Leo looked at the plate on my dresser. "Yuck-ee."

"I know. But good for you. Look." I took a bite, forcing myself to smile, even though it tasted like shoe. I handed him the plate and he shoved it away.

"If you never get better, you're never leaving!" I said, grinding my teeth together. "Now eat your damned vegetables."

Leo crawled backwards on my bed, bracing his back to the wall. His eyes widened with what I assumed to be terror at the plate in my hands.

"Geez. I'm sorry." I scraped the asparagus into the wastebasket. It smelled like urine. "Look, all gone."

Leo smiled sleepily. I tugged on the ends of his feet, pulling him prone. I gave him his favorite pillow and covered him up with a blanket. "Take a little nap, okay? Maybe we'll take a walk later, if the weather's nice."

He yawned. His eyelids fluttered shut and he fell asleep.

I grabbed my cell phone and went into the hall. I hadn't talked to Jillian in almost a month. I dialed her old number, hoping it still worked.

"Hello?" An airy voice picked up the phone. I immediately felt Jillian's energy, as crisp as a spring morning.

"Hi," I said, shyly. "This is Maggie."

"Maggie! I was expecting you to call."

"You were?" Relief flooded me and I realized how much I missed the woman. Though I'd only known her a short time, we had shared a strong and immediate connection.

"How are things?" she said, her voice light yet prodding. "You didn't call just to shoot the breeze."

I took a deep breath, trying to figure out what to say. Finally, I blubbered out, "Everything's wrong, Jillian. Everything."

"Maggie," she said, her voice calm and motherly. "I'm here. Now start from the beginning."

And so I did.

I told her what had happened since our last conversation: how we had rallied to save Dark Root, how I'd cut off Leah's hair, how Ruth Anne had returned, how my mother had recovered, and the discovery that I was pregnant.

"Honey, I already knew all that."

"You did?" Bolstered by the confessions, I then told her how Mother was sick again and that she told us about her wand, and how Larinda wanted into Dark Root to gain access to the Lightning Willow so her daughter Leah could select a wand from it.

I also told her how I could get my wand, too, and heal Mother.

There was a tense, palpable pause on the other end.

"Those things, I didn't know. Larinda must be desperate. Maggie, listen to me, okay? She is a powerful witch. She is clearly not being fully forthcoming with you. Don't bargain with her, no matter how enticing the offer."

This was all so confusing. I didn't know what to think any more.

"Maybe Larinda would hold up her end of the bargain?" I ventured.

Again, another long pause.

"Maggie, there is an important rule that you should know. Each tree only bestows one wand. Miss Sasha already selected a wand from that tree, so it is impossible for Leah, or anyone else for that matter, to get one from it. Unless..."

"Unless what?"

"Unless your mother dies. Only then will the Lightning Willow be released from the pact it forged with her years ago."

My shoulders slumped.

I cried into the phone. Low, unyielding sobs until I couldn't cry anymore. I had thought I had this all worked out. I had no idea where to go from here.

When I finally stopped, she said, "There's more to this story, isn't there?"

"Yes. But please don't hate me."

"I could never hate you."

Shame swept over me as I confessed to using my powers to hustle men out of their money, and how one of those men had attacked Eve, and I used my *deathtouch* on him.

"We killed him," I said.

A tense pause at the other end. "I see."

"Am I going to hell?"

Jillian was a psychic-medium, able to predict the future and communicate with the dead. If anyone knew who was headed for hell, she did.

"Oh, honey, no," she said, a smile returning to her voice. "No one goes to hell for trying to help someone they love."

"But he only attacked Eve because of her enchanted perfume."

"Honey, that's not the way spells work. In order for a spell to take effect on someone, they must already have the tendency in their nature. Kind of like alcohol."

"Oh." I cracked open the door and peeked at Leo, still sleeping on my bed.

It was hard to believe that this naked man-child had that sort of degeneracy in him. I dredged up the memory of him grabbing at Eve, the lustful look in his eyes. The Leo of that night was not the same Leo I knew now.

"That's not to say that Eve should be creating perfumes like that."

Jillian's voice tightened. "When you mess with the laws of nature, you have to expect there will be consequences."

"Yes."

"I sense there's even more. Spill it."

"We found Mother's wand. It was buried in her locked room. We used it on Leo, and brought him back to life."

There. It was out in the open now. I had shared my secret and I felt immediately lighter.

"That's not possible!" Jillian gasped. "Even with your mother's wand!"

"It is. And we did it."

"Oh, Maggie! Does anyone know?"

"Just me and my sisters."

"Hasn't anyone told you that you should never summon what you can't unsummon?"

"I-I..."

"Talk about messing with the laws of nature! Even Sasha wouldn't have attempted that!"

After another long, aching pause she spoke again, her voice had softer.

"I'm sorry. I blame myself, really, for not helping with your rearing. Sasha and Dora could only do so much for a woman with your *abilities*. Maggie, you must keep this secret, even from your mother and aunt. Their minds are old, and though they mean well, there are those who will take advantage of their fragile state. If Larinda knows the full extent of the Lightning Willow's abilities, or yours for that matter...well, let's keep this to ourselves for now until I figure out what to do."

"But what do I do with Leo?"

"Leo?"

"Yes, the man I, uh, well, he's here with me now. I keep thinking he'll get better but he's not."

"Is he dangerous?"

"Not at all. He's sweet, actually. Nothing like he was that night."

I heard pages being flipped in the background. "He's not really alive, Maggie. Not like me and you. You know that right?"

I nodded into the phone, a sob catching in my throat. I was beginning to see that.

"You must escort him back to the realm of the dead. There may be a spell for that in your mother's book. And we'd need the right wand, one made for that purpose." She sighed at the enormity of the task as she slammed her book shut.

"A death wand?"

"A Wand of the Underworld."

"But I only get one wand. I can't choose that one!"

"Time is short. If you don't act soon, Leo may be trapped between the two worlds forever. He will grow weaker and sicker, slowing deteriorating away. That's not fair. Not to him, and not to you."

"Why did I save him if I have to send him back?"

She sighed. "Everything happens for a reason. Maybe you'll find your reason."

"I don't think I can send him back, Jillian. Isn't there another way?"

"Maggie, it's the compassionate thing to do."

"I can't. I just can't."

"You don't have a choice. I'm sorry, darling."

I finally convinced Eve to sit with Leo for a few hours so that I could *get my head together*. I ventured out into the woods, like I had when I was a kid, thinking things over in the solitude that only the trees could provide.

Jillian was wrong.

I did have a choice.

She had warned me against Larinda, but I wasn't afraid. Larinda's magic was fed by fear and I'd stared death in the face, quite literally, and there was nothing Larinda could do that could scare me more than killing a man and bringing him back to life. I'd get Larinda to tell me the location of the tree. Trick her if I had to.

Then, when Mother died, I would take my wand from it before Leah could. With it, I'd resurrect Mother just like I had done with Leo. My powers were stronger than anyone realized. With the aid of the Lightning Willow, I could bring them both back to full health.

I could even charge people for healings and save this damned house in the process!

It was a solid plan, except that it relied on Mother passing and keeping Leo healthy until then. The circle in all its glory. I also had to find Larinda, and my instincts told me that the shack in the woods was no longer there. But I was sure she'd make an appearance.

Until then, I'd look for the tree myself.

I returned to my bedroom, ready to share the news with Eve. When I opened the door, I almost fell over laughing at the sight. Leo sat on a chair, his hair twisted up in bows , wearing a face full of makeup.

"What are you doing to him?" I asked, spitting into a Kleenex and swiping at the red on his lips. "He isn't a doll."

"I know." Eve removed a bow from his hair. "But he saw me putting on my makeup and wanted me to fix him up, too. What could I say?"

"No?"

"Easy for you to say. You weren't the recipient of his puppy dog eyes. Leo, make your doggy eyes."

He widened his hazel eyes and turned his mouth down in a pout. It was comical––and horrible.

"I suppose you taught him that, too?"

Eve spread her hand. "We ran out of candy and he sucks at Scrabble. What were we supposed to do? I do have something to show you, though." She reached into her handbag and removed her tablet. "Check this out."

Leo and I gathered behind her as she pulled up Facebook. A photo of Leo with slicked-back hair on a golf course smiled smugly back at us.

"He looks like a real douchebag, doesn't he?" she asked.

"You cracked his password?"

"I wish I was that smart," Eve said, her eyes flashing. "It was all Leo." She scrolled through pictures and instant messages, stopping on a picture of Leo with his arm around a woman half his age. "I guess it's like muscle memory. I handed him the tablet and he typed in his password. He's a good boy." She scruffed his hair.

"Well, at least he's a good boy now," Eve continued. "Maybe not before. Has about twelve girlfriends in four different states. None of them know about each other. Hasn't seen his mother in two years. And, he admitted to a friend that he's been scamming money from his work. Nope. Leo wasn't a very nice boy at all."

"Wow," I said, as Leo pointed to pictures of him parasailing over sky-blue waters. What Jillian said, about spells only working on people who had that in their nature already must be true. Still, it was tough to reconcile this innocent with the pompous, scamming, womanizer on the Facebook page.

"I don't feel so bad about killing him now," Eve said, putting her tablet back in her bag.

"Eve! Don't say that!" I covered Leo's ears, but he shook my hands loose.

"It's true. You should see what he wrote in some of those messages. Told three different women he was going to marry them. And he was practically stalking a fifteen-year-old in Washington. He was scum, Maggie. Consider it a public service."

I opened my mouth to defend him, but she stopped me.

"Before you get on your pulpit, which you conveniently drag out only when it suits you, check this out. I got into Leo's bank account. The guy is loaded. Nearly 14,000 dollars in his savings account and half that amount in his checking. And we have his password, debit card, and checkbook."

"Are you serious?"

"Aren't I always?"

I sat on the bed, imagining everything we could do with that much money: Pay the taxes on Harvest Home, take Mother to a real doctor, buy diapers and formula for my kiddo. "We can't take that. Can we?"

"Well, we gotta feed him now. And clothe him. He eats his weight in gummy bears. He won't be cheap."

"Yeah, but..."

"But what, Maggie? What's he going do with the money, especially if he stays like this?"

"We should at least *try* and make him better first, don't you think?"

"How? How is he going to get better? I think we are saddled with him for awhile now, and if that's true, twenty grand isn't going to get us very far. But it will at least buy us some time."

A lump caught in my throat. Eve was right. Leo was in our care, indefinitely.

I fell back onto the bed, covering my face with my hands as I rolled across the sheets. Even if we were responsible for him now, it didn't seem right, taking his money.

"Give me some time," I said. "If we find that tree..."

"We aren't going to find that tree. Wise up."

"Let's at least wait until the holidays are over before we make any decisions. Deal?"

Eve's eyes became calculating slants. "Deal."

"I still have hope," I said, sitting up and patting Leo's arm.

"That makes one of us. We can't keep the wolves at bay forever. If we don't do something, we will lose this house. And we may lose Mom."

"I know."

Twenty thousand dollars was enough to pay the back taxes, but it would also seal our fates. We couldn't spend Leo's money and then release him. I wasn't ready to go down that road without trying to fix things myself first.

Twenty-Two

Everything to Everyone

L EO FOLLOWED ME THROUGH THE DENSER PARTS OF THE FOREST, LIFTING UP branches and carrying me over boulders as we trekked our way through the back woods of Dark Root.

We set off from Harvest Home at dawn each morning, me driving Leo's car, then traveled by foot through the woods, our faces turned upwards towards the sun as our boots sloshed through knee deep mud.

We were on a quest to find the Lightning Willow, the tree Mother had cut her wand from, the tree that would save us all.

There wasn't much time.

Mother grew paler and thinner every day. Her ramblings were almost incoherent and Merry reported that she was frequently wetting the bed. The doctor that came to check on her said that, aside from a few drugs for pain, there was nothing that could be done for her.

Leo, too, had changed. Though his comprehension of the world around him increased, he slept more, up to sixteen hours a day, roused occasionally by nightmares of a *bad man* waiting for him in a dark hole. He may have been a slime ball in his former life, but there was an innocence to him now, and my resolve to "fix" him grew stronger by the day.

A few waves from a life-giving wand, I reasoned, and he'd be healthy and whole again.

We only needed to find the tree.

Larinda knew where it was. She had admitted to putting a spell on it, ensuring that it remained hidden until she was allowed inside Dark Root. I had tried to call her using every summoning spell in Mother's book, but to no avail.

So we went out on our own, knowing the futility in trying to find an invisible tree, but hoping that we'd stumble upon it anyway. All I had to go on was the image that had appeared in her crystal ball. The willow stood before a flowing current of water, though I couldn't tell if it was a stream or a river. There were so many channels of water in and around Dark Root that it seemed an impossible task and I wasn't sure where to start.

"Think we should call it a day?" I asked Leo as the sun dipped behind the trees.

He enjoyed these outings, listening to birds, digging for bugs with sticks in the mud, and collecting pine cones and leaves. He thrust his bottom lip out at my question.

"Oh, all right. Five minutes more," I said.

He smiled and immediately set to tossing leaves into the air and running beneath his autumn parachute.

"...And if you don't fight me when it's time to go, I've got some gummy bears in my bag." I had learned that bribery was the fastest way to get him into the car.

"Oh-kay." He blew on a handful of dandelions, watching the tiny white hairs swirl into the wind. "Pretty!"

When every wisp had floated away, we turned back towards where we had parked. Just then, a flurry of black movement caught our eye.

"Birdies!"

Leo pointed to a flock of black birds that rose up from the ground, cawing and flapping wildly as they followed the curve of the river deeper into the woods. Leo sprang forward, giving chase. "Birdies!" he repeated, arms opened wide as he chased after them.

"Leo! Wait!"

I ran after him but he was quicker. He leapt over branches and tangles of plants as I tripped behind him, my own breath labored by my pregnancy.

"Please, wait for me!"

The birds flew to the other side of the river and disappeared.

Leo continued after them, stumbling through the water as he tried to keep his balance. The birds reappeared, shooting up from the trees. Leo hobbled on, his hands clawing for the sky as if he could pluck a bird out of mid-air.

"Leo!" I hollered, falling further behind.

He was waist deep now, his lips trembling and body shivering. I pushed on, breathing heavier with each step. The current caught him, careening him against rocks as he was pulled downstream. He let out squeals of pain as he tumbled along.

He went under, then emerged, his blond hair plastered to his face. I caught up and ran alongside him, begging him to grab on to one of the many branches extending from the riverbank.

The currents grew stronger. Leo struggled to stay afloat, bobbing up and down as he flailed his arms and called out, "Magg-eee!"

He couldn't swim. Perhaps he could in his former life, but he couldn't now. I watched helplessly as he was tossed along like a rag doll. He lengthened his arms towards me.

"Help Leo. Please."

"I'm coming, Leo." I pumped my arms with new resolve. "Grab that tree!" I yelled, pointing to a low branch in front of him. "I'm almost there."

He caught the branch with one hand, as the rest of his body jounced over the water. The river was stronger than his grip, ripping him from the tree. He launched forward, crashing into another large rock. He wrapped his arms around the rock and met my eyes.

"That's it," I said. "Hang on."

I dipped my finger into the river and felt its chill; It was cold enough to stop a heart.

"Magg-eee," Leo whimpered, his eyelids fluttering close. "It hurts."

I checked the ground. There were a thousand sticks but none of them were long enough to use. I pulled on tree limbs, but the rain had made them too soft and pliable to be broken off with my bare hands.

Without thinking, these words tumbled from my lips.

Rushing river, icy winds
Release my friend, I do implore
Who lay broken, beaten, crying
Hovering near death's dark door

Guide me towards the item true
That will help me save this man
I invoke the powers through
The Magick of Dark Root.
Amen.

I aimed my hands in the direction of a large branch that hung over Leo's head. Using every ounce of energy I could gather, I mentally pushed it down towards him. It was a slow lumbering journey, the branching fighting against me, but eventually it dipped within reaching distance.

"Get it, Leo!"

Leo hooked it with one hand, then the other. When he was anchored, I slowly reeled the branch back. Leo's feet skimmed the river until he was safely lifted up and back onto the bank.

He released the branch and I released the spell, sending it shooting back into place.

Leo lunged at me, his arms outstretched and a goofy grin on his face, practically knocking me over as he hugged me.

"Leo, you scared me so much! I thought something bad was going to happen to you." I swallowed the lump in my throat as his wet arms enfolded me. "Don't ever scare me like that again, okay?"

He squeezed me tighter. "Okay." Then he let go of me and took a step back, his almond eyes widening. "I love you, Magg-eee."

My eyebrows softened. I brushed a lock of his wet hair from his face. There was a truth in his eyes, a truth that told me he wasn't as simple as he appeared. I took a deep breath.

"I love you too, Leo."

From the other side of the river, the flock of birds ascended once again into the skies, then plunged into the water like an arrow.

What emerged was not a bird.

Leo's eyes widened. "Who?" he asked, pointing.

"Larinda."

"Maggie," the woman said, rolling over the water towards us. Her thin red lips twisted into a knowing smile. "You called?"

Twenty-Three
Heart Shaped Box

O NE MOMENT LEO AND I WERE STANDING BY THE RIVER, SHUDDERING
against the cold.

The next we were transported inside a cabin, where a warm
fire greeted us. It was all illusion, but it was a damned good illusion.

Leo's teeth stopped chattering and his clothes even began to dry.

"You're braver than Leah gave you credit for," Larinda said, the
corners of her mouth twitching. Her eyes slid to the right, taking in her
daughter who sat like a lifeless doll once again on a cot in the corner of
the room.

"This isn't the same cabin," I said, ignoring her and taking in the
surroundings. For all intents and purposes it looked the same, but
lacked certain details. Leo sat beside me, playing with a bug that ran
across the table.

"And you're smarter, too." Larinda nodded approvingly. "Have you
ever considered switching teams?"

"Teams?"

"It's a figure of speech, of course. We're all on the same team." She
sat her mug on the wooden table between us and leaned in, proceeding
in a near whisper. "What I meant to say is that I've always wanted a
daughter. A daughter that doesn't disappoint me. Sasha was right to
have children the way she did."

241

Behind her, Leah flinched.

Larinda sat back, reclaiming her mug. "We are related in many ways."

"Even if Leah and I share a father, that doesn't mean we are related." I nearly spat. "I've got enough sisters already. Ones that aren't rats."

I shot a glare at Leah but she continued to stare straight ahead. It was not the smug-faced weasel I knew from Woodhaven.

"Of course you do, darling. But that's not what I meant. Your mother and I are cousins. That makes us family. And I can offer you things your mother never could." She ran her finger in a slow circle around the rim of the mug, her lips slightly puckered and her eyes cast down into the liquid. With both hands, she slid the mug my way, an acidic odor wafting up my nose.

"Is this what you want?"

I peered into the cup, almost against my will. The liquid was clear but the foam on the top had taken shape, an outline of a willow tree. I lifted my eyes to see her smiling.

I pushed the mug back, rippling the surface and destroying the image.

"I'm the only one who knows the location of the tree. I offered you a deal once, which you weren't inclined to accept."

"Your deal was garbage." My anger flared and the embers in the fireplace popped.

"Is that the best you can do? Flaring fires and popping light bulbs? Her eyes shifted to Leo and narrowed. "No, Maggie. I think you are far more capable than you pretend. I have a feeling you are very capable."

"You weren't going to admit that Mother needs to die before Leah could have her wand," I said. "Everyone says you're a liar and they were right. But why?"

"You wouldn't remove the dome, had I been honest. Like you, I find that honesty is not always the best policy. Another thing we have in common."

"Why didn't you just tell Leah where the tree was? The spell doesn't stop her from coming into Dark Root. She could have waited around for Mother's death, like the vulture she is. A situation that will soon be fixed."

"Leah is far too stupid. She's a piece of clay that can't be molded into anything usable."

Once again my eyes drifted unwillingly to Leah, who shifted her position and stared into her lap.

"I offer you another deal," Larinda continued. "You forgo the ritual on the solstice and on the morning after, I will put your mother into a state of suspended animation. It will feign her death and void her deal with the tree. Leah cuts her own wand from the tree and we use it on your mother, and anyone else you choose."

Her eyes flickered once again to Leo, sparkling knowingly.

"I'm sure you can find a few uses for a life-extending wand, don't you agree?"

"Counter offer. We don't perform the ritual, you still put the suspended animation spell on my mother, and then you show me where the tree is. I cut *my* wand from the tree and use it on whoever *you* need. In return, you gain access to Dark Root for the year." I cringed at these last words, thinking of Leah and Larinda moving freely about my town, but I could endure their presence if it meant helping Mother and Leo.

And, I could probably keep a better eye on them.

"Really, Maggie? I recant what I said about you being smart. What could I possibly want from Dark Root?"

"The magick in the soil. It will increase your powers."

Larinda's smile disappeared and her eyes widened in anger. She waved her hand and Leah disappeared, leaving only an empty cot. Standing, she snapped her fingers and the fire behind her died.

"I don't know what you've heard, but someone has been filling your head with nonsense. I don't need any of Dark Root's precious magick. I have enough of my own." She stormed towards the far window, her dark gown grazing the floor. "It's not the soil that has power, Maggie, it's the bloodline that runs through it. Generations of witches whose collective magic has made it all the more potent." She fixed her pale eyes on me.

"But that can happen anywhere. And it is. You can stay and try to salvage something here, or you can join me. When the end comes, I will be the one prepared. Can you say the same for Sasha and Dora?"

"The end will only come if we give in to the Dark," I said, flustered, trying to remember what I'd been taught. "We are the lights of the world."

"Mumbo Jumbo. The end is coming, whether we prepare for it or not. It can only be delayed for a while. And, it's coming sooner than you think. I suggest you take my offer so that when the Darkness does descend, you'll have some assistance in keeping what you love alive." She lifted her chin and softened her face.

"This is your last chance, Maggie. Take my offer. Everyone wins."

"I will find the tree on my own," I said, more confidently than I felt.

"Will you now? It seems to me you haven't had much luck in that endeavor so far." She put a finger to her lips.

"Take my deal, Maggie. It's your only chance. Let Leah collect her wand and use it on your mother. It will buy her another ten years, at least. You have my word. As a witch."

Mother had always said that when someone gave their oath as a witch, it was binding.

To break that oath would be to sever the powers of the bloodline.

Larinda pressed. "At dawn on December 22nd, we will meet. I will place the spell on your mother, and then I will take Leah to the tree. We're all winners this way, Maggie. Just like it should be with family."

I explained Larinda's proposal to my sisters over dinner at Sister House, while Leo and June Bug patrolled the front porch looking for *roly-poly* bugs.

Mother slept upstairs, not even rousing to eat.

"You can't trust Larinda," Eve said, slamming her empty wine glass onto the table as I concluded my story.

"She gave her oath as a witch," Merry said, trying to squeeze the flaws out of the argument. "As far as I know, an oath like that can't be broken. Not if she wants to keep her powers anyway. What do you think, Ruth Anne?"

We turned towards our eldest sister, who had been listening intently as she piled seconds of mashed potatoes on her plate.

"I've never heard of a loophole as far as the oath is concerned, but I'm still doubtful."

I furrowed my brow. "Why?"

"Even if she upholds her oath, if we don't perform the solstice ritual, she'll still have the run of Dark Root for a year. With that wand and her power, she could create all manner of chaos. Maybe even negate all of the work that's already been done here. I'm with Eve on this."

Merry's eyes widened. "Maybe she wants access to Dark Root to do something even more terrible to Mama while she's under the sleeping spell! We can't let that happen!"

I swallowed. They were right, of course. Larinda couldn't be trusted, no matter what oath she took. "Okay, no deals with Larinda. We perform the solstice ritual to ensure they stay out."

"You know," Merry said thoughtfully, staring out the window at June Bug and Leo. "The wand was destroyed during the resurrection. Perhaps that voided the contract with the tree already?"

"Merry! You're a genius!" I said, reaching over to hug her.

"I am?"

"We can probably take a wand from the Lightning Willow now. And if not, well...there's always Plan B."

Ruth Anne removed her glasses and squinted at me. "Not trying to be a Debbie Downer here, Mags, but have you considered that keeping Miss Sasha alive is cruel? The wand doesn't turn back time, it just immobilizes it. She gets a few more years living in pain and confusion, then what?"

"Well, we don't lose her." I said.

The chandelier over our heads flickered at my words.

"I could use that time to get better at healing," Merry offered. "And keep training June Bug. Maybe in a few years and we could erase the dementia and the pain."

"Maybe." Ruth Anne returned the glasses to her face. "Or maybe she continues to sleep up there like Rapunzel for the next ten-to-twenty years."

"Sleeping Beauty," Eve corrected, then shrugged. "Sorry, wrong fairy tale."

"We've got to try," I said. "June Bug needs her grandmother and so does my baby."

Three sets of sad eyes turned on me. I had said the "b" word––an admittance of a future I didn't like to think about. But I couldn't deny it any longer.

I was having a baby and I wanted my mother to be a part of its life.

Ruth Anne patted my hand. "I know this is hard, Mags. Losing someone you love is always hard."

"I'm going to find the Lightning Willow," I said. "And if the tree won't let me take the wand, we put the feign death spell on Mother ourselves and get it that way. Mother is going to live, with or without your support, Ruth Anne."

Ruth Anne looked at me solemnly. "Maggie, you have my support. I'm just pointing out the facts. And here's another. When the wand was destroyed, it may have weakened Miss Sasha, since she had absorbed some of its essence during its creation."

"Do you think that's why she's gotten worse?" I asked, my voice cracking.

"I dunno. Maybe."

"Then we have to find the tree now!"

"But how?" Eve asked. "Illusion magick is so powerful. She could have made the Lightning Willow completely invisible or made it look like something else altogether."

Maybe Ruth Anne was right. Maybe things had run their natural course and we should just enjoy the last few weeks we had with our mother. That was the most logical thing to do, and the most honest.

Leo and June Bug burst through the door.

"This way, Leo," June Bug said, leading him into the powder room.

"What's wrong?" Merry asked.

"Ouchies." Leo pointed to a large blue bruise near his wrist. Around the bruise, his skin seemed to peel away.

"I don't know how he got it," June Bug said. "It just started."

But I knew. Mother's time was short, but so was Leo's.

And I wasn't prepared to lose either one of them.

"Go to sleep," I ordered Leo, who sat on my bed, beating his head against the wall. "It's late."

"Not tired," he said, folding his arms across his chest.

I climbed into bed and pulled him onto his back. He fought me but he wasn't strong enough to resist. Not anymore. Eventually he settled into a deep sleep. I fluffed my pillow, ready to try for some sleep myself, when my phone rang. It was a California area code and I hit decline. It rang again. Decline. Again.

"Geez, Michael, what do you want?" I asked, not bothering to say hello.

"Maggie, I've been thinking of you and the baby. Please? I really need to be there for my son."

"Who says it's going to be a boy?" I asked. "Or that it's even yours?"

"You did."

"Oh." I stifled a yawn. "Well, maybe I lied."

"Stop punishing me, Maggie. I know what I did was wrong. I'd do anything to take it back, but I can't."

Michael had been under Leah's spell when he had been unfaithful to me.

I wrestled with this bit of trivia on my continuum of whether or not I should forgive him. I was leaning towards compassion at the moment as I watched Leo sleep. Then I remembered Jillian's words: that a spell will only work on a person who has it in their nature already.

I tightened my grip on the phone, ready to hang up.

"I'm not asking to be a part of your life," he continued. "Just our child's. I want to help."

"If you want to help," I said, drawing up the image of his arms around Leah. "You'll stop calling me."

"You can't keep him from me, Maggie."

"Yes, Michael. I can." If there was a spell that could keep Larinda out, there was probably one to ward off adulterous ex-boyfriends as well.

He exhaled into the phone. "A kid needs to know his father."

"I never knew mine, and I'm fine."

"Are you, Maggie? Are you?"

That time, he hung up the phone.

"Maggie, wake up. We've got trouble."

I opened my eyes to see Ruth Anne and Eve hovering over my bed.

"Don't wake Leo," I said, pulling hair out of my mouth. He was sprawled across the mattress on the floor, snoring peacefully.

"The fuzz is here," Ruth Anne said, pulling the blankets from me.

"The cops?" I asked, rubbing my eyes.

"One cop. And he's asking a lot of questions." Eve opened my drawers and tossed me a pair of sweat pants and a T-shirt.

"What? Why?"

"Someone has reported our friend, Leo here, missing. And the bartender identified you and Eve as the last people to be seen with him."

I jumped into my clothes, running through scenarios. "We can take Leo downstairs? Show the cop that he's okay? Then he'll leave us alone."

"And what if he starts talking about birdies or screaming for candy?" Eve asked.

"You're right. Fuck."

"Cut the potty mouth and get your ass downstairs," Eve ordered. "You're going to act innocent and charming and say whatever you need to say to make Mr. Policeman go away."

"And what if he doesn't go away?"

"We might make a potion."

"That's what got us into this mess."

"What are we going to do with the monkey, here?" Ruth Anne asked, nodding to Leo. "I don't think it's a good idea to leave him in this room alone. The walls are paper-thin and the cop will be able to hear him thumping around up here if he wakes up."

"He won't wake up," I said, checking Leo's breathing. It was steady and deep. He was out for at least a few more hours. "Give me five minutes and I'll be down."

"Be quick," Eve said, pushing out her chest. "I can only hold him off with these for so long."

"Hang in there, Leo," I said, kissing him on the cheek. "I'll be back again soon."

The officer was young, probably right out of the academy, with golden hair and trusting blue eyes.

He reminded me of some of the recruits we had back at Woodhaven, young men not yet jaded by life, who still believed they could do some good in the world.

In about five years, he'd be hardened by the same old sob stories and endless red tape, but for now he believed in the justice of the system and probably of the world.

"Miss Maddock," he said, extending a ring-less left hand to shake. "Sorry to bother you. My name is Officer Braden and I'm investigating the disappearance of a man named Leonard Winston. His mother reported him missing a couple of days ago."

"Leonard?" I asked. "Is that his full name?"

Eve shot me a look.

"You know him, then?"

I bit my lip. I had no idea what Eve and Ruth Anne had already said and I didn't want to contradict their stories. Fortunately, Ruth Anne chimed in.

"We already told the officer that you only saw him briefly. That you were at the bar for a girl's night out with Eve and that you met him playing pool."

"And then Ruth Anne came and picked us up. That was the last we saw of him," Eve concluded, wiping her hands together.

Officer Braden took out his pen and nodded. "The bartender on duty that night said about the same thing, but I thought I'd see if you could provide any additional details on that night."

Ruth Anne's eyes slid to the window when Officer Braden wasn't watching. Leo's car was parked outside.

Oh, fuck. He knows.

"Well," I said, as sweetly as I could. "I'm sorry it has to come out this way, Eve, but that's not entirely true."

Eve blinked several times as I turned back to the cop.

"You see, I knew my sister really liked Leo. She'd been playing him pool all night, flirting like she does. But every time Leo came to the bar to order drinks, he looked at me. And there was chemistry there." I looked at Eve once again. "I'm sorry, Evie, but I slipped him my number when you weren't looking."

I twirled my hair around my finger and looked away.

Eve glowered at me. She didn't like to be cast in the role as second-best. I hoped Officer Braden interpreted it as a sign of her jealousy.

"So he came and picked you up later that night?" she asked, folding her arms. "That's so typical of you."

The officer shifted uncomfortably.

"I didn't mean to start any family trouble."

Ruth Anne bridged her fingers together, cracking her knuckles. "These two fight over men like two birds fighting over a worm."

The officer scratched his head with the end of his pen. "So, Leonard's been staying here then?"

"He was here that night. Then I took him to the airport in Eugene. He had to go to Seattle for a business meeting. Asked me to take care of his car until he got back."

"Seattle, huh? Did he say what hotel he was staying at?"

"The Marriot?" I took a shot in the dark.

"And what day did he leave?" The officer scribbled in his notepad.

"Um, Thanksgiving Day."

"Have you heard anything from him since?"

"Not a word. I'm kinda worried, too. I've had men disappear on me before but never one who left me their car." I bit on my nails and glanced out the window.

"Ma'am, I don't mean to get into your personal affairs, but I wouldn't hang out with someone like Leonard Winston if I were you. He has a record."

"A record?"

He paused, wondering how much he should tell us. "Aggravated sexual assault in two counties. Swindling. Embezzlement. He served nine months in Washington for identity theft. He's been clean for the last two years, as far as I can tell, but with repeat offenders you can never be too careful."

"If he's so awful, why are you looking for him?" Eve asked as Officer Braden put away his notebook.

"His mother is concerned. Says he sends her a check on the first of the month like clockwork. When she heard he was last seen in Dark Root, she got quite upset. This may sound crazy, but his mother is concerned that witchcraft is involved. Your family's reputation around here is pretty well-known."

"That is crazy," Eve said.

251

"So you aren't witches then?" Officer Braden asked, raising an eyebrow.

Ruth Anne shrugged. "It's a show for the tourists. Keeps the town alive. Do we look like witches to you?".

The officer laughed uneasily. "Ma'am, I've never seen a witch before, so I couldn't say. But some folks can get real superstitious. I grew up near Linsburg. A lot of people believe this town was founded on witchcraft. The real kind."

"And what do you believe?" I asked.

He laughed nervously. "I like to think I'm a bit more enlightened than that. But with the older generations, superstitions die hard. I'm telling you this more for your own protection than as an accusation."

"Sorry to disappoint, Officer," I said. "But we're just ordinary people."

"No disappointment here. You all seem like pretty nice folks. I'm just doing my job. The Marriot in Seattle, you say?"

"Uh-huh."

The officer nodded uncertainly. I could tell he wasn't buying our story. He handed me a card. "I'm going to check out his car on the way out, if that's alright? If you hear anything more, please give me a call."

"Witches honor," I said, winking.

Officer Braden scratched the back of his neck. "And if we don't hear anything from him soon, I will be back." He nodded goodbye to each of us and left the house.

We stood in place, watching through the window as he checked Leo's car inside and out, making a few notes in his pad. Then he drove away.

Aunt Dora flew in from the kitchen. "I don't know who this Leonard is, or why ya girls are hidin' him, but ya have to take him back to his mother's. Right away!" She fixed us with a steely gaze. "Our family's got enough trouble right now."

"Yes, ma'am," we all said, staring at our feet.

"Maggie!"

Leo called down to me, a tint of fear in his voice. He had woken up and I wasn't there.

"He needs ta go!" Aunt Dora repeated, then stormed off to the kitchen.

I had hoped to keep Leo with me until the solstice, to see what we could do to "heal" him, but with the cops and Aunt Dora on my back, we decided he needed to go home as soon as possible.

"When you do get the wand, you can go back and fix him right up," Ruth Anne explained pragmatically, to lessen my guilt.

Being our last day together, I promised Leo a trip to town that morning for Minties, his favorite thing. His eyes lit up and he hurriedly dressed himself in slacks and a short-sleeved, polo shirt with an emblem of a soccer ball on it. I added a sweater to cover up the bruising that was developing on his arms.

It was a quiet ride into town. Leo didn't speak, as if he knew this was his last day.

Even the trees seemed more solemn, hanging their leafless heads along the road, lined up like soldiers coming back from war. I reached over and patted his leg from time to time.

On one such pat, he startled me by saying, "Sorry, Maggie."

We found an open space in front of Dip Stix and I parked, both of us sitting in the seat for a long time before he unbuckled and opened his car door, a feat he had just learned to do.

We were unofficially saying goodbye.

We entered Dip Stix and Leo's mood brightened as he saw the Minties by the cash register.

"We need to eat first," I said, steering him towards the far corner booth in the back of the café.

"Hey, rock star." Paul called to me from the kitchen when he heard my voice. "You here for pancakes?"

"Pancakes? Sure. Is Shane around?"

"He's upstairs. Want me to get him?"

"No, don't. We're here because, well, Leo is leaving and he wanted one last trip into town."

"I'm sorry to see him go," Paul said, more to me than Leo. If he had ever guessed Leo's true condition, he hadn't let on. "A short stack and two forks coming right up." A few minutes later, Paul emerged with a plate and a bottle of syrup.

Leo gobbled half the stack down before Paul even made it back to the kitchen

"Sorry, we didn't eat dinner last night," I said when Paul saw our near-empty plate.

"No problem." Paul hesitated a moment and finally said, "Mags, do you have a moment?"

"Okay."

I whispered to Leo that I would be right back then followed into the kitchen.

"It's about Eve," he said, pouring more batter onto the hot griddle. It sizzled and popped as the edges turned a golden brown.

"I figured."

"She's still not talking to me."

"Paul, you're texting your ex-girlfriend. What do you expect?"

Paul's face turned green. "Oh. She knows, then?"

"Everyone knows. Welcome to small town life." I leaned against the opposite cabinet, one eye still on Leo as he dumped syrup onto his plate and proceeded to lick it clean. Luckily, there were no other customers in the café at the moment.

Paul wiped his brow with the back of his forearm, then returned to cooking.

"You are only *talking* to your ex, right?"

"No. Yes. It's complicated."

"Complicated?" I pushed my hair behind my ears. "What does that mean?"

"It means sometimes people come back into your life and everything changes."

"Why are you telling me this? I'm Eve's sister, remember?"

"I know that. I was hoping you'd understand, since you went through something similar with Shane and Michael."

"Eve overheard you say you were going back to Seattle. Are you in love with this other woman?"

"I was, a long time ago." He turned off the stove and fixed me with his steel-blue eyes, eyes so blue they were almost black. I'd been taken in by those eyes once. It was amazing what power eyes had over the soul. "We were together seven years, Maggie. I've only been with Eve a couple of months now."

"You've only been sleeping with Eve a couple of months. You two have been friends for a few years. And, you *love* Eve now."

"Yes."

"So, why would you give up your job here, my sister, and your friends to be with some ex-girlfriend?"

His eyes fell to my belly.

"Oh, I see," I said. Paul had a kid. And though he loved my sister, his heart was being pulled elsewhere. "When will you tell Eve?"

"Soon. As soon as I figure everything out. I promise."

"She deserves to know, Paul."

"Yes. I just need to get things straight in my head first."

Shane came in, his white shirt starched and his khaki slacks ironed. "Hello, Maggie," he said tersely. We hadn't spoken since Thanksgiving.

"Hello, Shane," I said, just as formally. "Sorry I can't stay but Leo and I have to go by Sister House today. We're heading out tomorrow."

"Heading out? Where to?"

"I'm taking Leo home," I said.

"I assume you mean to his home?"

"Yes, in Linsburg."

Shane laced his fingers behind his head, leaning back in a stretch. "That's too bad. I'm going to be hiring soon and I was hoping your friend would apply for the job. I could use someone who knows his way around a syrup bottle." His eyes twinkled with amusement.

"You're unreal."

"I've got applications in the back room. Let me know."

I marched back to Leo, handing him a pocketful of wet wipes. "Let's go."

He stumbled after me, dizzy with sugar and covered in syrup, not even stopping for Minties on the way out.

Twenty-Four

Good Riddance (Time of Your Life)

ERRY'S FACE WAS COVERED WITH A WET TOWEL, IN THE SAME SALMON color as her skin.

"She's hurt," June Bug said, pointing to the couch where her mother rested.

"I'm fine, honey." Merry smiled, dropping the washcloth into a bucket on the floor and revealing a shiner.

"What happened?" I asked, helping her to sit. Merry pursed her lips and I knew she wasn't going to explain in front of June Bug.

"I'll take care of your mommy," I assured my niece. "Can you go play with Leo for a while?"

June Bug regarded me for a moment, then nodded, taking Leo's hand and skipping off.

"So?" I asked, when they were out of hearing range. "What happened?"

Ruth Anne joined us, carrying a tray of tea and store-bought cookies.

"I was in the room with Mama," Merry began. "She'd been sleeping all morning and I was trying to wake her up, to get her to eat a little something. Oh, Maggie, she's getting so thin. I can hardly get broth down her anymore.

"Anyway, I finally got her to sit up and eat. She was so tired that

257

after every bite, she'd fall asleep and I'd have to wake her up again. Then, after she woke up about the fifth time or so, she starts talking about wanting to go to the garden with Robbie."

"Robbie?!"

"I told her she had to eat, but she kept saying Robbie was waiting for her and that she wanted to be with him." Merry burrowed her face in her hands and I noticed that she no longer wore her diamond wedding ring.

Ruth Anne poured us tea. "I'm not trying to sound foreboding, but in most every culture around the world, people who are about to die report end of life experiences just like this one."

"What are you talking about?" I asked.

"An end of life experience is a vision that's said to herald the transition between this life and the next. Mainly in the form of visitations from deceased family and friends. It happens just before the person..."

Ruth Anne ran her finger along her neck.

"What do you mean you aren't trying to sound foreboding? That's the most foreboding thing I've ever heard. No one wants to hear that Ruth Anne!"

"Don't hate the messenger."

"Stop it, you two," Merry said, lifting her face. "There's more."

"More?"

"Yes. After I fed her and changed her sheet––we've been going through a couple of sheets a day now––I tucked Mama in. As I was about to leave she pointed to something behind me. 'Robbie,' she said with a huge smile on her face."

Merry leaned forward. Her eyes were wide. "There was an energy in the room, I swear it. I felt a presence behind me. I turned, and, and..."

"You saw him?"

"Yes. He was there, as clear and as solid as the two of you. And he was so young. Twenty-two, tops. He wore an army uniform, but not the kind they wear today. Old-fashioned ballooned pants that tucked into his boots and a wide-brimmed hat with a chin strap."

258

Ruth Anne pulled out her notepad and drew a picture of a man in the outfit Merry described. It was a crude but effective rendering. "Did the uniform look like this?"

"That's it. Like something in an old movie."

"That's no Vietnam or Korean War getup," Ruth Anne said. "That looks much older."

"What are you suggesting?" I demanded.

Ruth Anne tapped buttons on her smartphone. "Look at these," she said. She slid her finger across the phone, revealing one old photo after another. Stone-faced boys in uniforms and chin-strapped hats stared back at us. The captions read: *Soldiers of The First Great War.*

"World War One?" I asked, my jaw going slack. Mother said he'd died in a war, but it couldn't have been *that* war. "That would mean Mother's much older than we thought."

"Much, much older," Ruth Anne agreed.

"When I saw this man, actually more like a boy, standing there in Mama's room, I tried to shield her from him. All I could think of was that he was a stranger trying to hurt her."

"Or hurt you," I said.

"I never thought about that." She shook her head. "I told the man to leave. All the while Mama kept saying 'Robbie, Robbie' and she was reaching her hand out to him and he was reaching his hand out to hers, right through me, like I wasn't even there. Feeling his hand inside me was such a shock, I think I might have screamed. As their fingers were about to touch, a woman appeared."

"Larinda?"

"Yes. She was standing behind the man, smiling, but Mama didn't notice. All she cared about was reaching Robbie. I grabbed Mama's hand before he could touch her. That's when I lost my balance and fell, hitting my head on her nightstand." She pointed to her black eye.

"...It all happened so fast. When I looked again, Robbie and Larinda were gone and Mama was sleeping. When I checked on her she said she loved me and thanked me for taking care of her. Then she went back to sleep. Not another word about Robbie or Larinda. It was as if it never happened."

"Freaky," Ruth Anne said. "If Miss Sasha really did have an end of life experience, that doesn't explain why Larinda was there. In most every documented case, it's only friends and family who have already passed." Ruth Anne pulled at the tufts of her brown hair, scrunching her eyes in concentration.

"It's all just one of Larinda's illusions," I said. "She wanted to spook you."

"Well, it worked."

I looked at the crystal bracelet on my wrist: Mother's Circle. If I hadn't taken it from her at the hospital, the dome wouldn't have slipped and Larinda never would have gotten inside Dark Root.

"It's not your fault," Merry said, sensing my distress. "The Circle was meant to be yours. Now we need to fix what's been broken."

"I know." I filled my lungs with air then pushed it out. "We have to keep our wits until then."

Merry dabbed the washcloth to her eye again. "I was caught off guard. I'll try not to freak out if I have another encounter."

"You're exhausted, that's why."

"I'll try and be a bit more help," Ruth Anne said, taking the last cookie from the tray. "Then maybe Larinda will come to me. I'd love to have a chat with her."

"Good luck with that. She only comes when she isn't wanted."

I heard Leo laughing in the next room, a series of grunts and snorts.

I turned to Merry. "Ruth Anne probably told you already, but I'm taking Leo home tomorrow. That will be one less worry, anyway."

Merry nodded. "Yes. She told me about your visit from the cop this morning. June Bug and I are really going to miss Leo."

"Me, too."

"You did all you could," she said. "And maybe he's a better person now than he used to be?"

"Maybe I am, too."

I spent the evening saying goodbye to Leo. Though he'd been with me less than a month, I couldn't imagine life without him.

"Now Leo, remember not to talk too much, at least at first," I instructed him, folding up his shirts and packing them into his duffel bag. He had what he had come with and a few extra items I had purchased for him with the cash he had in his wallet: a pair of jeans, two new shirts, a package of socks and a package of underwear.

"You might miss me," I said, folding his pants and tucking them into his bag. "But I'll be thinking about you. Got that?"

"Can-dee," he whined, staring out the window.

"Oh, will you quit whining about candy? This is important, Leo! You are...you are leaving." The last word caught in my throat.

He lowered his head. I felt bad for scolding him.

"Want a Pixie Stick?"

He nodded, holding out his hand for the treat.

Before I packed his wallet I looked at his driver's license. "I didn't know your middle name was Geoffrey." There was so much I didn't know about him. So much I'd never know.

"Where we going?" he asked, placing his candy-coated hands in his lap.

I regarded him curiously. He had spoken a nearly full sentence, one that required thought and perception. "We are going to see your mother. Do you remember your mother?"

He blinked twice but didn't respond.

"I'm sure she's really nice. And she will take good care of you."

He took my hand and held it, interlocking our fingers. "Magg-ee my mother."

I yanked my hand away. "No, Leo! No! Maggie's not your mother"

I tossed his duffel bag into the hall while he stared at me. "Stop looking at me," I ordered. "Help me pack. Find the rest of your things."

But he didn't move. He continued to sit in silence, watching as I removed every trace of him from my bedroom.

How much did he really understand? I wondered. Perhaps there was a whole world going on inside of him he wasn't able to articulate. Or maybe he was starting to remember his old life.

Panic slammed me in the chest. If he *was* starting to remember...

"Leo, do you remember when we found you?" I asked, hurrying back to the bed. "Do you remember that night?"

He nodded, fiddling with his thumbs.

"What do you remember?"

"Dark. Scary. Dirty." He pedaled his feet up and down on the hardwood floor, shaking his hands by his side.

"Anything else?" I asked, biting my lip.

"Worms."

"Worms?" Oh, God. Poor Leo. Alone and scared in the dark, fighting his way through dirt and worms to come back. And it was my fault.

I wanted to tell him not to worry because I would take care of him. But it was his real mother's job now.

"It's bedtime," I said. "Want me to tuck you in?"

"Uh-huh." He crawled under the covers. I shut off the light and pulled the blanket over, kissing his cheek. He smelled like crayons and baby powder.

"I'm sorry," I whispered, stroking his hair. "For everything."

He was asleep before I spoke the words.

"Have sweet dreams," I said, waving my hands over him, casting a spell of peace upon him as his slumber deepened.

The next morning Eve printed me out a map. "His mother lives just outside of Linsburg. Easy drive. It will take you less than thirty minutes to get there."

I folded it in two, and put it in my purse.

"So you're not taking any of his money?" she asked, as she poured herself another cup of black coffee. Unlike me, her exhaustion didn't show on her face, only in her mannerisms––the way she tapped her foot on the ground, paced around the room, and slurped down one cup of coffee after another.

"No. I'm not taking any of the money."

"Not even a little?"

I hesitated.

It was tempting. There was so much we could do with it.

But it wasn't ours.

"Not even a little. We've already screwed with karma enough, don't you think?"

"You keeping the car, at least?"

"I don't know. I shouldn't."

"If you had a car, you could visit him. It's not like he's going to be driving for a while."

"Poor Leo," I said, watching him color in one of June Bug's books at the far end of the table. "He probably isn't going to be doing much of anything for a while." The guilt returned and my chest tightened. "Do you think it's fair dumping him on his mother like this?"

"She's the one looking for him. Besides, when you're a parent, you're a parent for life."

For life.

I wondered how anyone could do it. The anxiety, the frustrations. It was hard enough taking care of myself, without constantly worrying about someone else.

Leo held up his artwork, a smile extending across his simple face. He had worked hard to stay in the lines and to use every color in the box. "For Maggie," he said, sliding the picture across the table to me.

My heart fluttered as I took it.

"Thank you, Leo. I'll treasure it, always."

I was beginning to understand.

His real mother deserved to have him back.

263

This was her son and she'd love him no matter what.

"Leo, it's time. Ready to go home?" I came up behind him, squeezing his shoulders.

They felt small and knobby. Despite my efforts, he had lost more weight.

He looked around the dining room. "Leo home."

"Yeah," I said, swallowing hard. "This will always be Leo's home, too."

Leo's mother lived in a district dubbed "Shrub Town" by the locals, a string of ramshackle houses settled willy-nilly around a large hole that may have once held water. I'd visited there with my own mother once, when I was a kid. We had gone to cure a woman who suffered from a particularly bad broken heart.

The woman had been a wreck, greeting us in a half-open robe that revealed one sagging breast as she uttered incoherent noises that only Mother seemed to understand. Her house was equally awful, with dishes swimming in stagnant sink water, a floor so covered in grime I couldn't make out its original color, and piles of dirty clothes strewn over the sofa.

I had stayed outside most of that visit, peeking in the windows from time to time as Mother counseled the woman. After an hour, Mother was out, leaving the woman with an amber locket in the shape of a heart, an incantation to read beneath the light of a new moon, and instructions to burn her philandering husband's picture in the flames of a purple candle.

"What happens when she casts the spell?" I had asked Mother on our drive home.

"He disappears."

"Disappears? Where to?"

"I don't know."

I looked into my lap, fiddling with the friendship bracelet Merry had made for me.

"Don't worry, Magdalene. She won't do it."

"Why not?"

"As much as people want to get over a broken heart, they still cling to love. Even hopeless love. If she casts the spell, she gives up any chance that her husband will come back. It takes a particularly cold heart to put on the locket and recite the incantation. In all my years, I'm not sure anyone has ever done it."

"Why would a person want love from someone who doesn't love them back?" I asked. "I don't get it."

"That's one of the great mysteries of life," Mother answered, staring out her window as if it were the abyss the offending husband disappeared into. "But it keeps me in business."

"Maggie," Leo tapped my on my thigh, jolting me from my memory. "Music?"

"Sure."

He turned on the radio, blasting *Living La Vida Loca*. He danced in short, jerky motions as he tried to sing along, pulling some of the lyrics from his memory and forgetting others.

I wondered if he would ever fully recover, if he had enough time. Had he suffered temporary brain damage in the *accident* or a complete flushing of the mind and soul? It was as if someone had tried to put a puzzle together by jamming the pieces together, getting only a few in just the right spots.

"Want a cheese stick?" I asked.

"Candy."

"Eat the cheese, first. It will make you big and strong."

Leo proudly showed me his muscles, unaware that much of his mass had been lost and his arms hung like bat wings. I smiled sadly and turned away.

"And some fruit," I added, handing him a baggie full of apple slices. He frowned and pushed it back.

"I cut those myself and you're gonna eat them. Got it?"

"Got it," he said, taking the bag and forcing an apple into his mouth. "Yucky."

"You'll thank me for it later."

But there would be no later. Once I dropped Leo off, I knew I might never see him again. The thought left me profoundly sad. I adjusted the rear view mirror and gunned it.

"Three miles till our exit," I said, feigning cheerfulness.

Leo munched on his apple but didn't look at me.

We had reached the end of our road together and Leo was alive enough to realize it.

Twenty-Five

WHO WILL SAVE YOUR SOUL

THE HOUSE WAS SMALL——A SQUAT BUILDING WITH ONE DOOR AND THREE windows. The lawn was dirt with a few weeds shooting up near the walkway. The neighboring houses that had sprouted up around it were larger and newer, encroaching on it like they were waiting to gobble it up.

But the small house held, an unpleasant reminder of the shadows of the past.

When Leo saw the house, he shook. I had to drag him out of the car.

"No, Magg-ee, no," he said, digging his heels into the ground as I pulled him along.

"It's gonna be okay," I assured him, even as a prickly sensation crept down my spine.

I knocked and the curtains in the front window fluttered. After a moment of seeming deliberation, the front door opened.

"Mrs. Winston?" I asked, peering at the small, wrinkled face with squinting eyes that hovered in the crack of the door. "I'm Maggie and I'm with your son."

I stepped aside, revealing Leo. The door opened wider, the room beyond it devoid of light.

"My son! Where have you been?"

We sat in Mrs. Winston's living room, an area with one loveseat and a TV. Aside from the single, mosaic crucifix that hung on the wall, there was no color to the room. I tried not to stare at the cockroach that burrowed itself in the crack of a floorboard.

"I'll make you some tea," Mrs. Winston said. Her tone was formal but not friendly.

Leo sat next to me, pressing his shoulder into mine.

"Scoot over," I said when his mother left the room. If she saw us like this, she might assume we were lovers.

"I've missed you, Leonard." She returned with two cups and a package of saltines. She sat the tray down on a crate that served as a coffee table. "I'd offer you more but this is all I have, right now. I was saving the tea for a special occasion."

"This is fine," I said, forcing myself to nibble on one of the crackers. "You have a lovely home."

"Don't lie to me," she said, still standing. "I know this place is not lovely. All the beauty of this place disappeared when Leo's father left." She smoothed her sparse gray hair into place and straightened her equally-gray skirt. Then she turned her attention to Leo.

"When you didn't send a check this month, I got worried. That's not like you. Figured something must have happened." Her eyes flittered to me. "He doesn't call. Never has. But at least he always sends me grocery money. Let's me know he cares and that he's still alive. Two hundred and twenty dollars a month. That's more than his father ever sent."

"Mrs. Winston..." I began.

"That's *Miss* Winston," she said, extending a left hand without a ring.

"Miss Winston..."

"I thought maybe Leo had left me for some floozy, too." she interrupted. "The men in this family never could take care of their

268

responsibilities. It's like the good book says: the sins of the father are passed down to the son."

I was caught off guard by her statement but continued on. "Yes, well, you see, Leo has had an accident."

"An accident?" Her hand went to her chest. "What kind of accident?"

"He hit his head on a rock just outside of Dark Root."

"You're from Dark Root?" Her eyes narrowed and she leaned forward to get a better look at me. "The witch town?"

"Um, yes." I glanced around the room, feeling the walls closing in on me.

"And how did he *hit* his head?" she asked, a strange new look in her eyes. I'd seen that look from strangers' eyes a few times in my life—and it frightened me.

I rubbed my hands together.

"Uh, he got back from Seattle last night. When he came for his car, we went for a walk before supper. He slipped near a river. I helped him back and he spent the night in our guest room. He woke up still not feeling great, so I drove him here."

She arched an eyebrow. "Your mother was Miss Sasha, correct?"

"Yes. Is, actually."

She blinked slowly, her lips puckered in contemplation. "Well, it's lucky for my son that you were there to help him. I guess I owe you a thank you."

Leo fidgeted beside me and I hoped he wouldn't jump in and start talking about candy or worms, or any of that.

"How are you doing, son?" she asked.

In response, Leo tucked his face into his hands and hid behind my shoulder.

I nudged him out.

"He may have a concussion," I said, as calmly as I could. "My sister's a nurse and said he should be watched for a day or two."

"Maybe I should take him to the doctor, then?"

"I'd give it a few days," I said, taking a sip from my cup to hide my nervousness. "I think him being here, with you, is going to heal him right up. Isn't that right, Leo?"

He nodded dumbly. I held back a sigh of relief.

"I have his stuff out in the car. I will bring it in," I said, setting my cup down on the crate and standing.

"Thank you. Perhaps you'll stay for Bible study? Would you like Maggie to stay for Bible study, Leo?"

He nodded.

I had no problem with Bible study, but I wanted to be out of this place as soon as possible.

"Um, I had better not. My mother's expecting me home. I have to take her shopping." I opened the door, setting one foot outside. "I'll be right back with his things."

Miss Winston followed me out. As I neared the car, she caught me by the shoulder. "I'm not sure what you did to my Leonard, but that is not my son."

"Pardon?" I asked, spinning around and unloosening her grip on me.

"That *thing* you brought me is not Leo! Leo would never agree to Bible Study, even with a concussion and even for a pretty girl."

My knees shook. "I don't know what you mean," I said, struggling to keep my voice steady.

"I know who you are and *what* you are. The sins of the father are passed down, as are the sins of the mother. Witches, all of you. You've put a spell on him, haven't you? It's blasphemous."

"I better go," I said, backing up. "I'll bring his car around tomorrow when I have a ride."

"Yes, you do that. I'll be calling the police as soon as you're gone. In the meantime, I'm going to do my best to get the devil out of that boy. He was a worthless heathen before, just like his father, but now he's an abomination."

How dare she?

Leo was not an abomination!

The Circle hummed against my wrist as anger welled up inside me. Miss Winston noticed.

"Who or what did your family bargain with for their powers?" she asked advancing.

I reached my hands forward to stop her. My fingers tingled. I remembered...

The *deathtouch.*

My hands still shaking, I sidestepped as she lunged forward, retreating to the Cadillac.

Leo's face appeared in the doorway. "Maggie!'

"C'mon Leo, we're going!"

He bolted outside, charging past his mother and into the car.

"You're not taking my son!"

"Stay away!" I yelled.

The front window of her house cracked, then shattered to the ground.

She looked at it, then looked at me. "You'll pay for this. All of this!"

"I'm sorry," I said, jumping into the car. I spun out of her driveway with the gas pedal pushed all the way to the floor.

But not before I noticed the amber locket in the shape of a heart hanging from her neck; a locket given to her by my own mother, years ago, to cure her broken heart.

Twenty-Six

Champagne Supernova

Y OU'RE LUCKY I LIKE YOU," I SAID, DRIVING THE SPEED LIMIT AND CHECKING
my rear view mirror for cop cars. "Well, do you miss your
mother?" I asked as we took our exit and headed into Dark Root.
"No," he said. It came out almost out as a sigh.

I squeezed his hand. "I'm sorry, Leo. I'm sorry you had such a
crappy mother. It wasn't fair to you and it kinda explains some things."

"Minties!" Leo squealed as we drove past Dip Stix Café. I ignored
him and headed for Sister House.

"Hurts," he said, as we bumped along the dirt road.

"It's just gravel," I said. "You'll be fine."

"Leg hurts," he informed me as we pulled into the driveway. He
pulled up the leg of his pants. Another bruise had developed near his
ankle.

"Do they all hurt?" I asked, noticing a small, blue-black mark
behind his ear.

"Yes."

I pressed my lips together "Don't worry. June Bug has lots of Band-
Aids." He took my hand and followed me in. "I think Eve's been baking,"
I said, sniffing the air. It smelled like bananas and vanilla. "Maybe she'll
share."

"Yay!" he said, but his voice was weak.

"I knew I should have gone with you. When did you develop a heart?" Eve turned to me, crossing her arms as if she expected an answer.

"Women often become more compassionate during pregnancy," Ruth Anne said. "Especially to things that are in need."

"Leo is not a thing!" Merry snapped. "I wish you'd both would stop referring to him like he's a piece of furniture."

"You're just defending him because he has a crush on you." Eve rummaged through her purse and produced a pink lip gloss, which she applied perfectly without a mirror. She slammed it back into her bag and sat down.

"Now what? That cop will be looking for Leo. Here."

Merry paced across the living room, fanning her face with her hands. "Eve's right. We can't have the police crawling around here. One mistake and I lose June Bug."

"Wait till Frank finds out Leo's a sex offender," Eve said. "Then things will get really ugly."

"He's not a sex offender," Merry said, wringing her hands and glancing at June Bug as she raced past. "Not anymore, anyway."

Ruth Anne sat back in the dining room chair and stretched her legs. "It might not come to that. If Maggie took him to see his mother, he's not technically missing anymore."

"That's right," Merry said, her shoulders softening.

"I still don't think it's a good idea to keep him," Eve said. "We've got our own problems."

"Eve, he is our problem!" I said. "He's like this because of us. And if you could have heard the way she talked about him...she called him an abomination. An abomination! What was I supposed to do? Leave him there with her?"

"That was the plan. It's not like he can understand her anyways."

"He understands more than you know."

"Does he understand why he's weak and covered in bruises?" Merry asked.

I had no answer for that question.

"Maggie, can you come here for a minute? Ruth Anne, you too." Merry called to us from halfway up the staircase.

Eve stood ashen-faced behind her. I glanced around the living room. June Bug and Leo were playing Operation on the floor. Mother sat on the sofa, watching them. There were no police cars in the driveway.

Merry's eyes widened, beckoning.

"What now?" I asked.

We gathered in Mother's room with the door shut and locked.

"We found this in Mama's drawer," Merry said, handing me a photo.

It was a picture of a good-looking man, about twenty years old. He was dressed in a uniform, like the one Ruth Anne had pulled up on her phone.

I turned it over. On the back, in Mother's script, were the words: Robbie Maddock, April, 1915.

"Mother's beau," I said.

Merry handed me another photo. "Now, look at this one. It's the same man, and he's with Mama."

There was no mistaking that the shockingly young woman in the photo was our mother. She knelt on a blanket, her long, wavy-brown hair cascading down over her shoulders, framing her round face. Beside her, with his knees tucked into his chest, was the same young man from the previous photo. He wore civilian clothes: a white shirt, gray slacks, polished shoes, a floppy hat, and suspenders. She smiled into the camera while he smiled at her.

Behind them I could make out a river. And a willow tree.

"The Lightning Willow!" I said, feeling both exhilarated and disappointed at once. The tree was nothing special to look at, but I knew in my gut this was the one.

Merry handed me a box. "We found dozens of pictures of Mama and this man. The years on the back all read 1914 and 1915. That can't be right, can it?"

"They all look authentic," Ruth Anne said, flipping through the pictures in the box.

"That would make Mother almost a hundred years old," I added.

"Correction." Ruth Anne held up a photo and wiped it with the sleeve of her shirt. "That would make these pictures almost a hundred years old. It would make Miss Sasha around one hundred and twenty."

"Good, God. How old was she when she had us, then?" Eve tried to do the math on her fingers when Ruth Anne answered.

"At least eighty, if not ninety."

"So when I saw him in Mama's room, it wasn't just an illusion," Merry said. "He was really there."

"Now we have this photo of the Lightning Willow," Ruth Anne said, clenching the picture of Robbie and Mother in her hand. "We can blow it up and use it to look for landmarks." She turned to me. "We ride at dawn."

Leo and I stayed the night at Sister House.

I slept on the couch, tossing and turning. I kept an uneasy eye on Leo as Eve's words about him being an ex sex offender played in my head. He slept in a sheet fort across the living room, surrounded by an army of stuffed animals and Pillow Pets. June Bug had stroked his hand to sleep, reassuring him that we would all be there in the morning for him. Merry had done the same for me when I was a kid.

Like mother, like daughter, I thought, wondering what kind of child I would bring into the world?

The next morning Ruth Anne woke me up.

"Time to get up, kiddo," she said, grinning down at me. She was dressed head to toe in camouflage. "The day looks clear. Let's head out." I yawned then panicked when I didn't see Leo. "Relax, he's having breakfast with June Bug and Miss Sasha"

Sure enough, Leo was seated at the table between the two as Merry poured syrup over his waffle.

"I feel like someone hit me over the head," I said. "What time is it?"

"It's only six. We get up early at *Chez* Shantay." Ruth Anne tossed me my jacket and a pair of her hiking boots.

I put them on and stumbled after Ruth Anne, grimacing as I remembered the last trip I'd taken with her. We had ended up in a ditch.

"Don't worry," Ruth Anne said, handing me over the keys. "Merry grounded me from the car. You're driving."

Ruth Anne carried two maps, one from the turn of the last century when Dark Root was first founded and one from about two decades ago, when a surveyor had reestablished the area boundaries. When we'd blown up the photo of Mother and Robbie, we saw that the Lightning Willow stood in front of a river. According to the maps, there were three substantial waterways near Dark Root. We were going to systematically inspect them all.

"If it's meant to be, it's meant to be," Ruth Anne said, marking our first stop on the more recent map.

"I wish I were as Zen as you. What changed you?" I asked, steering off the main road and heading to a spot I had already checked out with Leo.

"Changed me?" She rolled her neck in a circle and it cracked several times. "Life, I guess. If you don't get the bear, the bear gets you."

She rolled down her window, letting the wind catch her shaggy, self-cut hair. Her glasses whipped off her face but she caught them before they were flung to the wilds. She saw me staring. "Just because I'm a four-eyes doesn't mean I lack coordination."

We parked and hiked to a river that was so clear I could see the rocks at the bottom. Ruth Anne pulled out a pair of binoculars and surveyed the surroundings. "See anything?" I asked.

She shook her head. "No, the tree is hidden, remember?"

"Then how do you suggest we look for it?"

"We *feel* for it." She pulled out two extendable walking sticks and handed one to me. "Use it to feel the area around you. Especially empty areas. She might have been able to make it visually disappear, but not physically. No one can do that, not even David Copperfield."

We spent the day playing Blind Man's Bluff, looking for an invisible tree up and down the waterways of Dark Root, feeling with our sticks along the way. I told her about Michael and Woodhaven. She told me about her father, the man who had taken her from us.

He died her freshman year of college, prompting her to drop out and become a writer.

"What did you write about?" I asked, poking my way through a series of sharp objects along the waterway.

"A girl from a large family who feels all alone."

"Based on a true story?"

"Only part of it."

"Did it have a happily ever after?"

"There are no happily ever afters, Maggie. But sometimes we get lucky and have a few happy minutes."

Night was coming and we hadn't made any progress, except for a series of X's we marked on Ruth Anne's maps. I was tired, hungry and, after hearing Ruth Anne's story, a little sad.

"If we don't find it," she said, as I drove us home. "Know that you gave Leo a few minutes of happiness he may not have otherwise had. Seems to me, his existence was pretty miserable before you came along."

"Thank you," I said, brushing a strand of hair out of my eyes. "But we'll find it."

"Are you sure about that, Mags?"

"Yes." Although I had my reservations, it was time to call in the big guns.

We returned to find Mother and Leo on the swing, huddled up close and whispering secrets. They didn't notice our appearance.

"What was it like, Leo?" Mother asked, with eyes half shut. Her hair flew like dandelions seeds behind her. "Was it beautiful?"

He shook his head. "Scary. Dark."

She patted his knee. "It will be better next time. Robbie tells me there's a beautiful garden you can wander in for days. And music. Oh, the music. I heard it once. It still calls to me."

"Mother!?" I said, storming up the steps. "What are you telling him?"

She only smiled.

"I'm sorry," I said. "I just don't want him to be scared."

She regarded me, an ancient wisdom in those crystal blue eyes. "I think you're the one who's scared, Magdalene."

TWENTY-SEVEN

BENT

YOU DON'T HAVE TO GIVE ME THE SILENT TREATMENT," I SAID, STUDYING Shane.

His face remained stoic as he gripped the steering wheel so tightly his knuckles were drained of color. He didn't stop or even slow down when we came to forks in the road or stop signs. His focus was straight ahead, and he hadn't spoken a word to me since we got into the truck.

"If you didn't want to help me, you could have told me," I said, rolling up my window, which he immediately rolled down with a button next to his left arm. "And you don't have to freeze me, either, literally or metaphorically."

I had hoped to illicit a smile with this clever line, but his eyes never moved from the road.

At last, we arrived at Sister House.

Shane pulled to a stop and got out of the truck without saying a word. I jogged behind him, trying to keep up. He stopped at the door, his manners getting the best of him, and knocked politely.

"Howdy Merry," he removed his hat and tossed it on the nearest chair. "Is your ma up?"

"Uncle Shane!" June Bug dropped her crayons and ran to give him a hug.

"Mama's upstairs sleeping," Merry answered. "You should have let me know you were coming. I could have made you some lunch."

"Thanks, Merry, but I just ate. I'm here to see your ma."

"I can wake her."

"No, don't. Maggie, will you escort me to her room?"

Mother slept in her bed, naked and uncovered.

I hadn't seen Mother unclothed, ever.

I looked away, knowing how embarrassed she would be when she found out. But not before I noticed how loose her flesh was, hanging off her bones like chicken skin.

Merry blushed and covered Mother with a sheet. "I should have checked her first," she said.

"What do you need?" I asked Shane.

He looked around the room and pointed to an upholstered chair near the window.

"Can you girls drag that over? Put it next to the bed."

While we got the chair, Shane removed his jacket and rolled up the sleeves of his white work shirt. "How deeply does she sleep?" he asked.

Merry answered. "Very. I can vacuum in here and it won't wake her up. She's always been a heavy sleeper, but lately it's just scary."

"Well, that's good for us. Can you light a candle and some incense if you have it? I don't *need* these things, but it helps me get where I need to go quicker."

I wrinkled my brow, watching as he settled himself into the chair while Merry attended to the candle and the incense. It occurred to me that he had done this before. Probably many times.

"Turn off the lights, please. Then I need total silence. You ladies can stay in here but don't make a sound, okay? It may take some time for me to go under and when I'm there, I may or may not speak. I'll wake up on my own. Got all that?"

We nodded.

Shane slid deeper back into the chair. His right hand held the photo of Mother and Robbie, while his left reached out to Mother's.

She snored loudly, but did not wake up.

"Here goes nothing," I whispered to Merry.

She looked at me strangely, still not understanding what we were doing.

But she trusted us enough——or at least, she trusted Shane enough——to let it happen.

"So you know where the tree is?"

Shane still refused to speak to me directly.

In response to my question, he flipped on the windshield wipers, even though it wasn't raining.

We left Sister House, drove down Main Street, then took a sudden right down a narrow road I hadn't really noticed before. "Road" wasn't exactly the right word; it was more of a path, forged through a grove of tightly knit trees.

Leo slept in the backseat. Shane occasionally looked at him in the rearview mirror, sliding his jaw from side to side.

"Damn it, Shane. Talk to me!" I stamped my foot on the floorboard. "After everything you've put me through, you could at least talk to me."

His head snapped in my direction. "After everything *I've* put you through? Unbelievable."

He turned back to the road. The trees were packed tightly around us and his truck took a beating as branches keyed their way along the side of the pickup.

"Yes. You're the one who had that woman in your room. How do you think that made me feel?"

"Don't get me started on strange sleeping partners," he said, his eyes shooting to Leo once again.

"Leo is not strange." I lowered my voice. "He's my friend."

"A very close friend. He's been staying in your bedroom, if I'm not mistaken."

"Have you been spying on me?"

"In case you've forgotten, I can spy on you whenever I want."

"Oh, you would use your *remote viewing* abilities to spy on me, wouldn't you? Not very chivalrous, Mr. Cowboy."

"I never said I did that. I just said I could. I saw Leo in your window one night when I was dropping Paul off after work."

"Oh," I said, slightly embarrassed and wondering what he saw. "Still, I told you, he's just a friend."

"And so was the woman in my room." He steered right, avoiding a large branch in the road, then proceeded forward. There was a clearing ahead.

"Who was she?" I finally asked. "You said I got it wrong, so tell me. Is she your long-lost sister?" I twisted the last word to let him know I wouldn't buy a story like that.

Shane slammed on the brakes, put the truck in park.

"You're not the only one with secrets, Maggie Mae. I've got a whole closet full of skeletons ready to fall out. Be careful what you wish for."

"What are you talking about, Shane?"

"We all have secrets." He looked back to make sure that Leo was still sleeping, then returned to me, his voice hushed. "Do you really want to know who that woman was?"

"Yes! I need to know."

"Alright." His eyes rolled back into his head and he let out a heavy breath. "When I was a young man, right after high school, I was handpicked by a group who found my talents very interesting."

"Your tracking ability?"

He nodded. "The government had already been working with people like me. The ultimate spies, you know?" He stopped and coughed into his hand.

"They offered me the chance to see the world. My grandmother had

284

just died and, well, you know my parents weren't in the picture. This seemed like a good opportunity for me."

"Go on," I unbuckled my seat belt.

"So I enlisted. I was grouped with other 'gifted' individuals. We were taught to locate anyone or anything, with just a picture of that person. We were tracking down terrorists and spies. It was pretty exciting, especially to a twenty-year-old farm boy from Montana." He raised an eyebrow. "The training produced an interesting side effect: I became adept at lucid dreaming. Eventually, I could enter people's dreams."

I felt the familiar blush hit my cheeks as I remembered his visitations.

"After a couple of years, I had to get out. My views and The Program's––as we referred to them––didn't always line up. I took a leave of absence and told them I'd return, but I never did. I came to Dark Root instead, where it's nearly impossible to be traced by the outside world."

I blinked several times, trying to understand what he was telling me. "You're AWOL, then?"

"I was never officially in the military, so no. But I think The Program would love to have me back. I know things..."

Shane took off his hat and scratched the back of his head.

"So, who's the woman?" I asked, ashamed that I was still focused on her after his confession.

"Her name is Irene. She was one of my teammates. She got out, too, a couple of years ago, and when the dome went down, she was able to track me. Came to warn me that *they* are still looking for us. That's all there is to her showing up here. Scout's honor."

"Oh, Shane."

I reached over to hug him.

I was relieved about the woman but frightened that he had people after him. He'd kept this to himself far too long.

"Why didn't you tell me?"

"The less anyone knew, the better. These people...they're not all nice guys. I didn't want you or your family involved."

"Oh, my God," I said, the finality of it sinking in. "I'm so dumb. God, I'm so dumb. I'm sorry. Are you sure Irene won't tell anyone where you are?"

I could taste the iron in my words as I said her name.

He paused, rubbing his chin. "I doubt that. Irene and I had a special relationship."

Jealousy stabbed at me once again.

I liked to pretend that Shane didn't have a life before Dark Root, but there was so much about him I didn't know.

"So, now you know some of my history." He lifted his hands, spreading them across his lap. "Hope you don't hate me."

"And nothing happened between you and Irene that night?"

"Absolutely nothing."

"I believe you."

"Good. Someday you'll tell me your secrets, too" he said, pulling me in and stroking my hair.

"Yes. Someday soon. I promise."

"Does it have something to do with this tree we are looking for?"

"Partly, yes." I resisted the urge to look back at Leo.

"Be strong, Maggie Mae. I'm here for you, okay?" He put the truck back in gear and we continued down the road.

I kept my head was on his chest as he drove and I listened to his heartbeat. I had a million questions: about his time with the government, his training, and Irene, but they could all wait.

This was all that mattered now.

He startled me from my thoughts as he parked the truck once again. "There's the river from the photo and your ma's dream, up ahead."

I squinted.

Sure enough, I could see the faint outline of a silver channel of water off to our right.

"We can't get there in the truck," I said.

The trees before us were too cloistered together.

I gave one final glance to Leo before crawling out of the truck. Shane took my hand. We walked into the woods, moving through the darkness as one, strolling towards the light.

TWENTY-EIGHT
ONE OF US

W̲E PASSED THROUGH THE FOREST, FIGHTING THE UNDERGROWTH ALONG the way.

Suddenly, it opened up. We entered a clearing the size of a football field, a welcome relief after the constricting woods. It was bright here, even on this, the first day of winter.

We blinked, blinded by the light of the sun as it reflected off the roiling river, casting rippling beams across a still-green meadow.

I scanned the bank, looking for the Lightning Willow.

"Are you sure this is the spot?" I asked Shane.

"Don't you feel it?"

"Yes." My fingertips tingled and hummed. The magic was so powerful here I half-expected to see a gathering of fairies.

"Straight ahead," he said, pointing to a knoll overlooking the river.

I shook my head. "There's nothing there."

"Trust me."

"The illusion spell," I said, understanding.

Shane grabbed my wrist. "We've got company."

Two lithe figures emerged from the trees behind us, approaching within a dozen steps. Leah looked plain and minuscule next to her statuesque mother. The only resemblance between the two was the menacing look in both sets of eyes.

"Yes!" Larinda looked around satisfactorily as she stepped further into the glade. "I remember this place. It's been too many years. Thank you, young man."

I held out my hands in warning. "We didn't have a deal, Larinda. You and your rat-daughter need to leave."

"She doesn't need your permission," Leah said.

"You're not illusion this time," I said to her. "Your momma finally let you out to play?"

I returned my attention to Larinda. "This is our forest. You have no power here."

"That may be true," Larinda answered. "But until the winter solstice, Leah still has free reign of this land."

"That will be remedied tonight."

"Precisely why we move today." Larinda stroked the back of Leah's short hair, kneading it like a cat's paws.

"Maggie, don't speak to her," Shane said, stepping between myself and the others. "She wants you to play her games."

"You may have gotten the Circle but the wand is mine," Leah spat, jutting her long chin out.

Her beady eyes flickered from myself to Shane. She removed a knife from the back pocket of her jeans, and raised it in a threatening manner. "When I'm done taking the wand, I'll show you what it's like to be cut."

"Make mommy proud," Larinda said, waving her hand over the top of her daughter's head. With that, Leah ran forward, racing towards the river where Shane had proclaimed the tree to be.

I pulled a vial from my bag and sprayed white powder in Larinda's direction––salts taken from Aunt Dora's cupboards that morning. She hissed and retreated back a long step.

"Watch her," I instructed Shane, pushing the vial of remaining salt into his hand. "If she tries to cross into the glen, douse her with this."

I pulled the knife I had carried with me since looking for the tree from my bag as well, and raced after Leah.

"Maggie!" Shane called, as I charged forward. "Wait! It's not what you..."

His words were lost to the wind as I sped forward.

Leah was light and nimble and had gotten a good head start, but I was stronger and had been a runner in my youth. I pumped my arms and lengthened my stride, panting as I worked to overtake her. Soon, we were neck and neck. I rammed into her side, hoping to knock her down.

She stumbled but did not fall.

"Let me cut my wand," I said, gasping for breath. "Then I will help you."

"You've made a fool of me once, it won't happen again."

She sped up and I matched her, though my lungs burned and my stomach cramped.

"I need this to save my mother," I said. "Leah, please!"

"What do I care of the old witch? You've had your chance, now you'll come begging to me."

I wheezed, feeling like my lungs were going to explode. The pregnancy had weakened me, but I couldn't let her win. If she were to swipe so much as a twig from The Lightning Willow, there was no hope that I would get my wand.

My mind filled with the image of my mother, holding her grandchild––my baby.

I lowered my head and plowed forward, passing Leah. I lifted my knife, ready to slice into the air. The tree had many branches; I just needed one.

From my left, Leo appeared, charging out of the woods a dozen yards away. I jerked my head back. Larinda was still caged behind Shane but her arm was lifted, a finger pointed in the air, directing the flight of a large, black bird that sailed over the water.

"Leo! Stop!" I yelled, as the sound of Leah's footsteps grew closer.

"Birdie!" he said, racing towards the icy river ahead.

"No, Leo, no!" I changed direction.

Leah let out a triumphant "whoop!" as she motored forward.

Leo outstretched his arms, ready to plow into the waters to get the bird. I lunged at him, grabbing the back of his shirt, pulling us both to the ground. He rolled backwards, landing on my leg. A searing pain shot through my body and I cried out in agony.

Helplessly, we watched as Leah reached the spot where the Lightning Willow must be.

She spun left, then right, swinging her knife wildly in the air.

"Yes! Yes! Yes!" Leah chanted like a madwoman, flailing her weapon at the empty space. In her single-minded delirium, she lost track of her precarious position and stumbled, one leg twisting over the other as she slid down the muddy slope and into the river.

"Leah!?" I raised myself to hands and knees, watching her head bob up and down as she was carried downstream, disappearing around the bend.

Behind me, Larinda screamed. I turned in time to see her dissolve into the mist.

As suddenly as they had come, they were gone.

Shane crouched down on the knoll and scooped up a handful of dirt.

He sifted it through his fingers, then wiped his hands on his jeans.

Behind him, Leo sat cross-legged in the field, looking for bugs.

"There's no tree here, is there?" I asked, my heart sinking.

He stood and shook his head. "There hasn't been a tree here in twenty years, Mags."

"What? Of course there is. Larinda put a spell on it to keep it hidden. Mother's dream must have been convoluted. She didn't remember the exact location."

Shane looked at me with a mixture of compassion and pity.

"Larinda never put a spell on it. That was a lie. Your ma kept the tree hidden from her, then cut it down herself after Eve was born. Well, her and what was left of The Council."

"But why?" I asked, furrowing my brow. "It doesn't make sense."

"She was so old, Maggie. She'd lived a long time and had lost the love of her life. Her body hadn't aged much, but her soul was stretched across time like taffy." His eyes took in the earth where he stood. "She stopped using the wand on herself to preserve some of its potency. Once she had her daughters, she didn't need to live forever. Her legacy continues through you girls."

"You got all that from her dream?"

"Yes. And you'll be happy to know that in her dreams, her mind isn't convoluted at all. In fact, it's beautiful in there."

"But if she destroyed the tree then we can never..." I wanted to cry. All this work, for nothing.

Shane thrust his hands into his pockets and looked towards the sun. The stubble on his face was just beginning to show and his hair was still mussed from wearing his hat. He took a deep breath, as if deciding how much to share with me.

"You brought me out here for a reason. Tell me what you know, please?" I stepped close enough to smell the coffee on his breath. I inched even closer, removing the distance between us. "Tell me, Shane."

He touched his lips to mine. It was so quick that it hardly even qualified as a kiss, yet I felt my entire body jolted alive.

He pulled away and took my hands. "When Sasha cut down the tree, she began to age rapidly. All those years were catching up to her at once. But your mother's a smart woman. She saved a cutting from the Lightning Willow and planted it, not telling anyone. A guarantee that a part of that tree would live on."

"She did? Why?"

"Just in case she needed it. To make sure that she was around long enough to see you all grow up and continue the work she'd began."

"A cutting," I said in wonderment. "But where?"

Shane pointed. A few dozen yards away and hidden in a clump of firs, was a beautiful golden willow. It stood twice my height, its boughs glowing like they'd been kissed by a wandering band of angels.

The circle of life continued.

I approached it, kneeling before it like an altar. "The Lightning Willow's daughter," I said, lost for words of any real meaning.

Shane put his hands on my shoulders. "Your tree of life, Maggie. You can take your wand now."

I stood and lifted my knife. The willow's limbs quivered delicately, anticipating the slice of my knife. The wind caught my hair, sending it spiraling around me like the rust-colored leaves on Mother's porch.

The flash of sun on steel was almost blinding.

It was the day of the winter solstice. I would have my wand this day, as my mother had, in some bygone era before.

Twenty-Nine

A Long December

I HAD STOOD BENEATH THE MOON ON THE NIGHT OF THE WINTER'S SOLSTICE many times in my life––as a child watching Mother and The Council perform their rituals, and as an adult at Woodhaven, missing my family and imagining that they, too, were standing beneath the same moon, missing me.

But on this cold December night I stood beneath the moon, not as a girl watching or a woman wondering, but as a witch, claiming my birthright as successor to Miss Sasha Shantay, my mother.

I wasn't alone.

My sisters gathered with me in the garden.

With flowing white robes and unbound hair, we joined hands, a representative from each of the four elements. Ruth Anne as Air: constantly floating and searching, never quite settling. Merry as Earth: solid and stable, nurturing yet firm. Eve as Water: smooth and transparent, yet deep and turbulent. And me as Fire: necessary *and* dangerous, with the ability to grant life *and* death, seeking to be tamed, even as my will ran rampant.

"Got your wands?" I asked.

My sisters produced sticks from the deep pockets of their gowns.

I glanced behind me at June Bug and Leo huddled on the bench. Mother sat next to them, parked in her wheelchair.

June Bug raised her pretend wand and Mother patted her knee approvingly.

Leo watched on, a mixture of confusion and anticipation on his broad face.

"Good job on the garden, Leo." I winked at him. He'd spent the afternoon clearing out the weeds and collecting the treasures he'd found there, which he presented to Merry with a bashful smile.

"Did you write the spell?" Eve asked.

I reached into my bra and produced a crumpled piece of paper.

"You do know that's why God invented purses, right?" she asked, as I un-crumpled the page.

I read the spell aloud, looking into the starless night sky.

Oh, Winter Moon
Of darkest night
We call to you
To aid our fight

Against those
With hearts like coal
Who wish to garner
Dark Root's soul

We call to you
Protect our home
Shield us with grace
In your Celestial Dome

When I had finished, my sisters clasped their hands around the base of their wands and lifted them to the heavens.

Their heads were thrown back. Eve and Merry's hair grazed their waists, while Ruth Anne's short hair barely hit her shoulders. I tilted my head back and aimed my empty, outstretched arms into the night.

The wind blew around us, stirring our dresses and hair. I was alive, connected to every living thing in the universe. The Magick of Dark Root trickled through me.

We held the stance. A light cracked above us, momentarily splitting the night in two. The light touched the tip of each of my sisters' wands, setting their colorful gems aglow. It coursed directly into my fingertips, pulsing through my body, down into my feet. The ground around us became a sea of electric eels, cerulean zig-zagging lines that sizzled, then died.

My body trembled but I remained firm in my pose.

"Look!" Leo said.

The gems of the wands and the tips of my fingers shot clear blue light back into the sky. The beams merged together at a central point far above us and then expanded, casting four wide rays of light out in a canopy around us. The beams widened as they bound for earth, disappearing behind the horizon of trees that surrounded us.

We were cloaked in a dome of pale blue light. The spell was done.

Still trembling, I lowered my hands.

Leo ran for me, squeezing me in a tight bear hug. "Love Magg-eee," he said.

"Love you too, Leo."

"You girls did good," Mother said, her eyes the same pale blue as fading dome. "I couldn't have done better myself."

I blushed at Mother's compliment. Though her feet were small, her shoes were going to be large ones to fill.

"Are we done here?" Eve asked, putting away her wand and pulling out her smartphone. "I need to check my...hey!" She shook her phone then tapped it against the palm of her hand. "I can't get online."

Ruth Anne checked her phone as well. "Seems we lost the internet again. I knew it was too good to be true." She shrugged, putting her phone away. "Maybe I'll get some writing done now without the distractions."

"I think we could all use a break from that," Merry said, her eyes

297

resting on June Bug. "Maybe just appreciate what we have here, instead of trying to look for it in the outside world."

"Easy for you to say," Eve said. "You don't have nine pairs of shoes in a virtual shopping cart waiting for check out."

"Its okay, Evie," I laughed. "We'll do it the old fashioned way. Go to Linsburg and buy them in a real store."

"What? Oh, Maggie, that's so 1997."

"I don't know about you, Eve. But I kinda miss the '90s."

"Things were simpler then," Ruth Anne agreed, as she and Merry helped Mother to the house. As we opened the front door, the smell of Aunt Dora's blueberry scones greeted us, causing my mouth to water and my stomach to rumble.

"I guess we took those times for granted," Merry said.

We gathered around the dining table. Aunt Dora appeared wearing an apron and carrying a tray of cider and candy canes. Behind her, the aluminum tree winked and blinked.

"You never know what you have when you are young," Merry continued. "All you can think about is that there is something bigger and greater out there in the world and you're missing out."

"Amen," I said.

"So, Maggie, I take it your wand is being prepared?" Mother looked at me from her spot at the end of the table, her hands folded and a white eyebrow raised. There was a twinkle in her eyes, an intelligence that said for tonight, at least, she was completely here with us.

"Yes. It will be done soon. I'm thinking it will be ready early next year. A new beginning, so to speak."

"A new beginning." Mother closed her eyes and rested her hands on her lap. "Yes. I'd very much like that."

PART III

THIRTY

RETURN TO INNOCENCE

January, 2014
Dark Root, Oregon

W E MADE IT THROUGH THE HOLIDAYS, MOSTLY INTACT.
Paul confessed his secret to Eve: He was the father of a three-year-old little girl named Nova who currently lived in Seattle with his ex-girlfriend. Paul told Eve that although he was no longer involved with his ex, nor had any intention of becoming involved with her, he was leaving to be closer to his daughter.

"What about me?" Eve screamed, throwing brushes and shoes at him, as Aunt Dora and I tried to make ourselves scarce.

Paul retreated into the attic, showing his face only at Christmas when he presented Eve with a photo album he had made, pictures of the two of them over the last year, first as friends, then as lovers. Eve said she didn't want it, but after he left the room she sat down on the sofa and looked at each photo, intermittently laughing and crying.

"He's the love of my life," she said, with her head in her hands as I joined her on the couch. "How will I live without him?"

I thought about Mother and Robbie.

If the dates on the pictures were right, Mother had lost him almost a century ago, and had lived a long, full life on just those memories.

"I don't know, Eve. But you have us. You *will* be okay."

Michael continued to call and I continued to ignore him, but on Christmas I finally answered the phone.

"Oh Maggie, I know I haven't been there for you like I should have, but please let me be there for the baby. I'll do anything."

I looked at my family in the living room as they gathered around the tree, telling stories of Christmas pasts. And I thought about Paul, who was leaving everything and everyone he loved to be a part of his child's life, and Leo, whose own father had disappeared, leaving him with a mother who held him in nothing but contempt...and June Bug, who eagerly awaited her father's call each night.

A child needed as much love as he could get in this world, and though I might never forgive Michael for what he did, my baby––our baby––deserved the chance to know him.

"Okay," I finally said.

"Okay?" There was crazy laughter on the other end of the phone. "You mean you'll let me see the baby?"

"Holidays, at first. You can come here and spend time with us. No taking the baby out of Dark Root. We'll figure it out from there. That's all I can give you at the moment."

"That's enough, Maggie. I just want to say thank you and apologize again. I am so..."

"Please don't, Michael. I've heard enough sorries to last me a lifetime. Just show up, okay? I'm due in late Spring. Maybe you could come for that."

"I'll be there. I know how to drive now."

I smiled. Michael the driver. What was the world coming to?

There were many changes in that month between the Winter Solstice and the first full moon of the New Year, but some things remained the same, like Mother's dementia and Leo's steady deterioration. Neither of them showed signs of getting better. With each passing day they looked weaker, sadder, and dimmer.

It wasn't just their bodies that were dying, it was the spark of life inside them.

On a bitterly cold January morning, I stared at the wand in my lap. It was shiny and sleek, and had been equipped with a ruby red gem at the end. Mother, in one of her rare lucid moments, confessed that it was the most beautiful wand she'd ever seen.

I lifted my wand, turning it over in my hands. It was indeed beautiful.

But I hadn't taken my wand from the Willow's Daughter. As I had lifted my hand to cut the branch, I stopped short. Mother and The Council had cut down the tree because they realized that without an end, time is meaningless. It is only because life is short, that it also important. Whoever, or whatever, had created this balance eons ago knew what they were doing.

It was now time to let things run their natural course. With a little help from me.

I walked out to the porch and dialed Jillian's number.

The unenlightened, as Mother referred to "non-witches," often believe that all spells are cast beneath the light of a full moon, in an open meadow, at precisely midnight. And while this may be true in some cases, those of us within the inner circle know that there are some spells that can only be cast behind closed bedroom doors.

These are the powerful spells, that give heartbeat to the craft.

"Okay," Merry said, opening the door to Mother's bedroom to let Jillian and I inside.

Merry dabbed a Kleenex at her eyes. June Bug, Ruth Anne, and Eve stood near the foot of the canopied bed. They had come early at my request. Once I began the incantation, there would be no further time for words.

Jillian lit a white candle.

I opened a bookmarked page in Mother's spell book and looked solemnly around the bedroom. Mother had not taken her duties lightly and neither would I. I was my mother's daughter, blessed, or cursed, with these *abilities*. The next generation of magick would fall to me.

"This spell looks different from the others," I said, reading the words for perhaps the tenth time that day.

"It's an old Celtic spell," Jillian said. "Translated, of course."

My sisters gathered in closer, holding hands.

"The spell will only take effect if they are willing." Jillian warned me, the candle dancing like a ghost before her face.

If they were willing.

I cleared my throat and looked to my mother, who was propped up in her bed against the wall. "Sasha Benbridge Shantay, do I have your full permission to perform the ritual?"

Mother closed her eyes then opened them again. "Yes, Magdalene. You have my full permission to perform the ritual."

"And do you do this with a glad heart?"

"I do."

I turned to Leo, who sat next to her on the bed. I filled my lungs with air as I pressed my lips together, then exhaled and asked him the question.

"Leonard Winston, do I have your full permission to perform the ritual?"

Leo's bottom lip trembled and his eyes began to run.

"Don't cry, Leo," I said, handing Eve the book and tossing back the hood of my cloak. I sat on the edge of the bed and took his hand. "You don't have to do this."

"Yes. My...my permission," he answered.

"Leo..."

"My permission!" he said, firmly.

"And do you...do you do this with a glad heart?" I swallowed, barely getting the words out.

"Yes, Mag-da-leen."

I kissed the tips of his fingers and put his hand to my heart. "I'll never leave you," I said.

"I-never-leave-you-either-Maggie."

My heart felt like a stone that had been hammered to bits. "I can't do this!" I looked helplessly at the others in the room. "He doesn't understand!"

"Maggie," Jillian said, her eyes unyielding. "We all have to do difficult things in life. Don't let your feelings get in the way of what needs to be done."

I cried. I couldn't help it. I wasn't my mother. My mother didn't shed tears like this. She was strong. I wasn't.

"I'm too emotional," I said to Jillian. "I care too much."

"That's why you were chosen."

My teeth chattered as I looked to Mother and Leo. I wasn't sure how much they would understand, but I needed them to hear this anyway.

"I wanted to tell you both how much I love you. You've given me so much. I just...I just..." I choked and had to stop.

It wasn't fair, loving people only to have them taken from you. I dug my fists into my eyes, willing the last of the tears away. It wasn't fair, but that's the way it worked. We came into this world, we lived, if we were lucky we loved, and then we said goodbye.

Hopefully, we left the place a little better for our time here.

"It's time," Jillian said, glancing out the window. The moon was high in the sky. There would not be another chance after this one.

I looked at my sisters. Their hands were linked in a chain.

"Okay, ladies," I said, lifting my chin. "Let's do this."

I crawled into the bed between Mother and Leo, feeling less than regal. I had lost all sense of nobility when I broke down in tears. Jillian handed me my wand and Eve offered back my book. I shook my head at Eve. I knew the spell by heart. I closed my eyes and began the incantation as my sisters fed me their energy.

May the silver cord

That binds you
To this plane
Be serenely severed
Releasing you
From grief
From pain
May you find the light
In the darkness
And flowers
In the garden
And Music
In your heart
May your soul
Be lightened
On the journey
As you start
May your memories
Grow stronger and longer
Mixing with those
Who have come before you
And those who come after
May your journey be filled with wonder
And laughter
Be brave, dear soul
As you transverse
The boundaries
Of this Universe

When the spell had been cast, I steadied my breath, focusing only on the blue flame of the candle in my mind's eye. I melded into it, feeling its heat, watching the flame grow bigger, until it filled my mind completely and I was nothing but an expansion of the light.

At last, I stood in a very bright room, a wondrous cavern filled with immense love. It was so overwhelming and beautiful I almost fell to my knees. I twirled once, trying to find the source of the love.

And then the light went out.

Though I stood in complete darkness, I wasn't afraid.

There was a comforting presence with me, or all around me. I didn't belong here, but I wasn't sent away. Two forms took shape beside me: Mother and Leo.

We joined hands and stepped forward, like Dorothy and her companions on the road to Oz. Only this road was in shadows and we weren't sure what awaited us at the end. After seemingly endless steps, there was a small pinprick of light that punctured the darkness, like a solitary star in the night sky.

"There," Mother pointed ahead.

I stopped and gripped her hand. "Are you scared?"

"Terrified," she said. "But I'm so ready. I've been ready for a long, long time, Magdalene."

With each step the light expanded.

"Maggie!" Mother gasped. She was transforming beside me, from a withered old lady with a stooped back, to a formidable, heavy-set woman of middle age. I looked to my left at Leo. His shoulders had broadened, his arms grew flesh, and the bruises on his body softened then disappeared.

Mother stopped and looked at her smooth hands.

"I'm beautiful," she said, pulling on a strand of her thick brown hair. She cocked an ear. "The music! Do you hear the music?" She stood on tiptoes like Alice looking through a keyhole. "I can see the garden Robbie told me about!"

I didn't hear the music or see the garden. "Mother..."

"Look again!" she said. The light flooded outward like someone had opened a stage curtain. Before us was a field of technicolor flowers. "We must hurry!" She dropped my hand and ran forward, her floral nightshirt replaced by a white, cotton dress. Her curls bounced behind her. Leo and I quickened our pace, to keep up.

"Robbie!"

A figure emerged, a young man dressed in an army uniform with a wide-brimmed hat that fastened around his chin. He reached from the light into the darkness, his fingers awash in a soft blue glow.

"Robbie!" Mother said again, her fingers reaching for his.

Robbie's uniform disappeared, replaced by suspenders, trousers, and a gray cap hat. A lock of blond hair fell into his kind blue eyes as their hands met.

She turned back to me and said, "I love you," before disappearing into the light. Leo ran after her.

"Leo, wait!" I said, grabbing his arm. There was no one waiting to greet him in the light. "I must have made a mistake. You can't go in there alone."

Leo straightened his shoulders and softened his face. "Don't be afraid, Maggie. I'll be okay, now."

"You're talking better," I said, noticing that the hair on his head was thicker than before, and his arms were muscular and firm. "Let's go back," I said. "I'll take care of you. Maybe if we go now you can keep this new body?"

Leo shook his head sadly and took my hands. "No, Maggie. I need to be here."

"But..."

He raised his eyes, searching for the words. "When this happened before, I went to a dark place. There, I really was alone."

I swallowed. "You mean when I..."

"It wasn't your fault." He ran his hand through my hair. "You saved me, Maggie. Now I get to go here." He waved his arm and the light before us shimmered.

"Oh, Leo! What will I do without you?"

"Take care of your baby, the way you took care of me. I'll be there with you, I promise."

I tried to cry, but I couldn't. There was only love here, even in the dark.

"Ready?" he asked.

"Yes."

Leo linked his arm in mine and we marched forward. "They won't let me in," I said.

"I know."

When we had reached the entrance to the light I saw figures move, dozens of people in clothing from all time periods, like a cast from a large, multi-verse play. They were laughing, talking, walking.

A man in jeans and a denim work shirt looked up from the book he was reading, saw Leo, and smiled.

"Dad," Leo said simply. The man reached his hand into the swirling vortex that separated our reality from his. "Dad, meet Maggie."

"Thank you for bringing my son to me," he said. "I'll take it from here."

I stood on tiptoe and gave Leo a hug, feeling the solidness of his shoulders. This was it. "Don't forget me," I said.

"Never." He kissed me on the top of my head. "I'll miss the smell of your hair the most, I think."

I smiled.

"Don't be sad. You gave me the chance to know what it was like to have a real mother. I can't thank you enough."

Leo pulled away, then entered the light, his body disappearing into stardust as he slid across the meridian.

"Goodbye, Leo," I said, closing my eyes. When I opened them again, I was once again alone.

At the far edge of the light, I heard the trickle of water and saw the outline of a silver-blue river. In front of the river stood a majestic willow, with branches that glowed like fireflies.

I didn't need to worry about Mother or Leo. They were in a place elevated beyond my loveliest dreams.

We buried them both, in the shade of the Willow's Daughter.

I remembered Leo's comments about dirt and worms but I knew this time would be different. They weren't stuck in limbo. They were where they needed to be.

"Maggie Maddock, Guardian of the Underworld," Jillian smiled, handing me back my wand after the service. "Not many people have the guts to create a wand that lets them travel between the planes of life and death. But, as you've seen, when you've lived a good life, death is nothing to fear. One question though: Where did you find the wood for it? This type of yew is rare, even in these parts."

When I couldn't bring myself to cut a wand from the Willow's Daughter, Shane took me to the tree where he had carved our initials many years ago.

"Where did I get the wood for my wand?" I repeated, feeling the weight of it in my hand. "Well, Jillian, that's my little secret."

"Fair enough. We're all entitled to a few of those."

I drove her back to Sister House. We sat in silence until we hit a bump and the radio turned itself on. *Living La Vida Loca* played. For an instant, Leo sat beside me, dancing in jerky motions as I told him to eat his apples.

"You never get over it, do you?" I asked Jillian, pulling up the drive.

"Over what, hon?"

"Being a parent."

She stroked my cheek. "No, my dear Maggie. You never really do. You're going to make one heck of a mama."

"How do you know?" I asked, still worried.

"Let's just say I have my ways."

My sisters, all dressed in black, came out to say goodbye to her. She hugged them all and whispered something into each of their ears. Eve's face softened at her words and she nodded in understanding. I wanted to know what Jillian had told her, but as had been pointed out to me, we were all entitled to a few secrets.

I loaded the last of Jillian's bags into the trunk of her rental car then turned to her, giving her one last hug. "Thank you so much for coming for me. I couldn't have done this without you."

Jillian looked at my sisters. "I think you would have been okay, but I'm glad you called."

I stammered, then asked her the question that was on my mind.

"Jillian, how am I going to raise this baby, if I have the *deathtouch* like my father?"

Jillian smiled. "You do know there's only been one documented case of Armand's *deathtouch*? And it occurred only when he, was, well... intimate with a woman."

"Intimate?" I asked, confused. Then it dawned on me and I blushed. "Oh...Who?"

"Larinda. But it seems she survived. So I wouldn't worry too much about it."

"But I...I killed Leo with these hands," I said, holding them up.

"You did that to save someone you loved. It was an accident, not the *deathtouch*."

"Okay. Thank you." I pressed my hand to my stomach and felt the flutter of life inside me.

Jillian took me by the shoulders and looked me squarely in the eye. "This isn't goodbye. I'll be back."

"Promise?"

"Yes. There's so much more you need to know. Secrets that have been kept from you, but the time is coming to change all of that."

"Good secrets?" I asked hopefully.

Jillian tilted her head back, her shoulder-length charcoal hair bouncing behind her. "Oh, Maggie, you do make me laugh. Yes, my dear, good secrets. Be strong, okay?"

"Yes."

She climbed in her car and drove away.

We stood in the dirt driveway, waving until she disappeared.

"Look!" June Bug pointed to a tight cluster of dandelion seeds that spun before us, before floating towards the maple tree on the perimeter of the yard. On the limb of the tree perched two birds: a raven and an owl. They watched us curiously before flying off in opposite directions.

In the air was the scent of roses, crayons, and baby powder.

I smiled and turned towards the house. All was as it was supposed to be.

THIRTY-ONE
CLOSING TIME

I WIPED MY WAND WITH A POLISHING CLOTH AND PLACED IT INTO A SEALED BOX in the back of Mother's magick shop. The wand would find a good home, once I had one of my own.

The taxes had come due on Harvest Home, and we were no closer to paying them than we were in the beginning. We could solve some of our problems with magick, but not all of them. And I was okay with that. I had seen what happened when you messed with the balance of things too much.

Even witches had to be selective.

For now, I'd have faith. I knew that Mother and even Leo were watching over us now. I'd ride the tide, letting whatever happened, happen.

"We still have Leo's money," Eve reminded me as we closed up the shop.

"Uh, Eve..." I wasn't sure how to break this to her. "We don't have Leo's money anymore. Except for a few hundred bucks I kept for emergencies."

"What do you mean?"

"I sent it to his mother."

"All of it?"

"Well, technically, Leo did, before he left us."

"She's a nut job, Maggie! What were you thinking?"

"I was thinking it was the right thing to do. Besides, its bad money, Eve. We both know Leo didn't come by it in the right way. It would have caused us nothing but trouble." I paused. "And all his mother really wanted from him was his monthly check. This will keep her from asking questions, at least for a while."

"I can handle trouble," Eve said. "But I can't handle being a pauper."

"If it's any consolation, I thought we'd keep the car. I had Leo sign over the title." I had struggled with this as well, but he and I had spent so much time driving around in it, I wanted to keep it for the memory.

"I guess that helps."

We stepped onto Main Street. Paul was parked right in front of the shop, his Explorer laden with luggage. He was leaving for Seattle today and had come to try, once again, to say goodbye to Eve and to explain why he needed to go.

She waved him away, saying nothing. With a hurt look on his face, he nodded a goodbye to me, then drove slowly on.

"You should at least tell him how you feel," I said, staring after him.

"He's leaving me, Maggie. What am I supposed to do? Beg for him to stay? Ask him to choose between his kid and me? It's easier for him this way."

"You big softie, Eve! Here I thought you were being your usual, bitchy self."

"Hey!"

"But you weren't. You don't want to force him to have to choose! So you're just letting him go. I'm not sure if I'm impressed or sad."

"Yeah, well, he's got enough on his plate." She crossed her arms as she stared after him. He had stopped to get out and say goodbye to a local man who had become a regular of his at Dip Stix.

"You could go with him," I said, carefully.

"What?"

"You could go to Seattle. Be with him. He's going for his daughter, not his ex."

"And leave the shop? And you?"

"I've got two more sisters to fill the void."

"You make me feel so warm and fuzzy."

"Seriously, though, you could go with him."

"Maggie, in case you haven't noticed, I'm not cut out to be a mother. I'd probably screw that kid up worse than I'm screwed up."

I put my arm around her neck. "I don't think you're all that screwed up. A little warped maybe, but definitely not screwed up. I'd trust you to babysit my kid."

"You would?"

"Yes. As long as you didn't try to braid his hair."

She paused, looking at me, then Mother's shop, then at Paul.

"Go to him," I said.

Paul returned to his car. Eve shouted to him, waving him down as she raced towards him in boots with two-inch heels. They spoke animatedly through the car window.

Ruth Anne emerged from the bookstore next door, carrying a stack of paperbacks, each depicting a bare-chested man on the front cover. "Research," she said when she caught me gaping. "I think I'm ready to write my next book. This place really is a great muse."

"That, it is."

"What do you think she'll do?" Ruth Anne asked, nodding to Eve who was still talking to Paul.

"I'm not sure." I felt sad thinking of a Dark Root without Eve. "But wherever she goes, this will always be her home."

"Very poetic," Ruth Anne said, the left side of her lips crooking up into a smile. "Maybe you should be a writer."

"Ha-ha. How about I feed you a good line every once in a while, and you can pay me royalties?"

"Sounds fair."

We continued to watch Eve, neither of us knowing what she would do. After a long pause, Ruth Anne said, "So, Maggie Mae. How's your own story coming?"

I smiled at my oldest sister, lifting my chin to catch the last ray of sunshine. "Let's just say it's in progress."

"Oh?" Ruth Anne rummaged into her back pocket and handed me an envelope. "Aunt Dora asked me to give this to you." It was postmarked from California.

"Michael," I said, taking a deep breath as I tore open the letter. "I already told him he could see the baby on holidays, what more does he want?"

Dear Maggie,

Thank you so much, for everything. As I've said, I know I haven't always been there for you, but I promise to be there for our child.

I sold Woodhaven. It was a place we had built together, and it's only fair that half of the proceeds belong to you. You shouldn't have many problems financially for a while.

With Love,
Michael

With trembling fingers, I dug at the bottom of the envelope. Sure enough, Michael had sent me a check. It was three times the amount we owed for taxes on Harvest Home.

Three fold.

I screamed so loud, people turned in my direction to see if I were okay. I passed Ruth Anne the check. "Look! We can pay the taxes on Harvest House, fix up Sister House, put some money into the shop. Everything's solved now! Everything!"

Ruth Anne handed it back to me. "An almost perfect ending," she agreed. "But I wouldn't say *everything's* solved. Every story needs a happily ever after."

"I thought you didn't believe in those."

"Maybe I'm coming around." She nodded to the café across the street. In the diner window, I saw Shane lighting candles, preparing for the evening crowd.

"It's time," she said.

She was right.

I removed the crystal pendant from around my neck that Michael had given me and cupped it in my hands. "Goodbye," I said, kissing it. I couldn't keep living in both the past and the present. I squeezed it, then dropped the pendant into the nearest trash bin.

I took a deep breath and stepped bravely into my future.

The doorbell chimed when I walked into Dip Stix.

Shane looked up from his table, clearly surprised to see me.

"You want dinner?" he asked as I approached.

"No." I raised my lips and pulled his face down to mine.

"Mmm," he moaned as our lips met, our mouths slightly opened. "I've been waiting for that a long, long time."

"Me too," I said, smelling the soap on his neck and the mint on his breath.

I drew back, taking his face in my hands. "But before we get too far there are a few things I need to tell you." I wasn't sure how he'd react, but as Ruth Anne had once wisely said, if it was meant to be, it would be.

Shane turned the neon sign to Closed and led me to our booth at the rear of the restaurant.

And in that still diner on that cold, January evening, with nothing but the glow of the candles and my faith in the man I had fallen in love with, I confessed everything to Shane Doler. Not just what had recently transpired with Mother, Leo, the pool hustling, and my baby, but everything I had ever done.

When I had finished he wrapped his hands around mine.

"None of that matters. I love you, Maggie Mae, and I'll love your child." He kissed the tips of my fingers, every one of them. "And now it's time for me to tell you my secrets."

I held my breath, waiting for his confessions. Until a few days ago I had thought I had known everything there was to know about Shane Doler.

317

But you never really know someone. We all carry our burdens quietly through life.

Whatever he revealed to me, we would deal with it together.

For secrets, once told, lose all their power.

And love, lived in the light, erases all the darkness of the soul.

About the Author

April Aasheim grew up with three sisters and two brothers. She has been fascinated by witch lore since she was assigned to write a paper on the Salem Witch Trials in the 7ᵗʰ grade.

April is a mother and a wife and the "owner" of her reluctant familiar: Boots the Cat.

When she isn't writing she enjoys Zumba, belly dancing, Hallmark Original Movies, reading, and board games.

The Magick of Dark Root is her third novel.

If you enjoyed the book please consider leaving a review on the vendor site where you purchased it. A short review is fine and greatly appreciated. Word of mouth is essential for any author to succeed.

Get in touch with April on Facebook or visit her website at:
http://aprilaasheim.blogspot.com

Want to read more in the Daughters of Dark Root series?
If so, check out book 3 here:
THE CURSE OF DARK ROOT (Part 1)

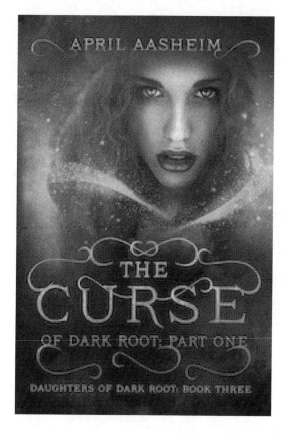

Made in the USA
San Bernardino, CA
19 August 2017